KONSTANTIN FEDIN served briefly in the Red Army as a young man, then turned to writing as a more congenial form of expression. Originally a romantic lyricist whose stories expressed regret for the passing of the pre-Revolutionary way of life, the author soon evolved into the psychological realist whose post-World War II novels *First Joys* and *An Unusual Summer* won for him the Stalin Prize.

Cities and Years represents one of the earliest attempts by a Russian writer to depict the impact of war and revolution on the Soviet intellectual. Far more than a mere exposition of dialectical difficulties, however, the novel probes incisively yet sympathetically the private lives of its protagonists, freely acknowledging the inevitable victory of emotion over intellect. *Cities and Years* is a major Russian contribution to a great and vital period in Western literature.

W

CITIES AND YEARS

9 5920

A novel by

KONSTANTIN FEDIN

Translated by

MICHAEL SCAMMELL

 A LAUREL EDITION

Published by
DELL PUBLISHING CO., INC.
750 Third Avenue
New York 17, N.Y.

First printing—May, 1962

Printed in U.S.A.

We had everything before us,
we had nothing before us.

CHARLES DICKENS

~~~~~~~~~~~~~~~~~~~~~~~~~~~~~~~~~~~~~

As far as wine was
concerned, he drank water.

VICTOR HUGO

CONTENTS

A CHAPTER ON THE YEAR
WHICH CONCLUDES THIS NOVEL

A SPEECH

"Dear neighbors, most excellent residents, honorable citizens! I leaned out of this window with a predetermined plan: I am bored, dear neighbors, I am gnawed by melancholy, honorable citizens, my heart has dried up and curled into a corkscrew, like lemon peel on a sun-scorched pavement.

"Honorable residents! It is true that the one thousand nineteen hundred and twenty-second year is already here.

"In front of me are eighty-five windows, not counting two attic windows, one basement window, one skilfully drawn on the wall by a pre-war painter; nor the one in which you can all distinguish the upper part of my figure.

"I could tell you a story about every one of these windows, but I know you won't listen to me. Therefore I beg you to cast your eyes only on that window there, down below, where this morning a striped feather bed was coming to pieces as it was desperately beaten by a red-armed housewife with a ramrod. And then on that window there, to the right, through which the tinkling of a *domra** pours from morning to night; and again on that one at the very top, beneath the attic, where a phonograph is perpetually grinding out popular songs; and again to one last window right opposite me, which is so freshly puttied; tomorrow it will be painted.

"Honorable citizens! The Republic is not a bad thing

*A stringed instrument similar to a banjo or mandolin.

after all. In a Republic one can beat feather beds and lay them out to air in the sun, with no fear of having to make up the family bed in the evening with only the feather bed cover. In a Republic it is possible to have an ear for music and to learn to play the *domra*. It is quite obvious that the method of government has had no effect upon the soundness of phonograph records. And finally, the Republic has learned comparatively easily that painted window frames are excellent for withstanding wind and bad weather.

"Dear neighbors! Is it worth mentioning that out of the eighty-five windows in our courtyard mine alone is not decorated with packets of cheese and sausage, pots of sour cream and sour milk, saucepans, milk jugs, butter dishes, bunches of spring onions and succulent red radishes? Even the farthest attic window, no bigger than a ventilator, outdoes my empty spiderwebbed windowsill, which preserves undisturbed the indelicate traces of my esteemed landlady's cat, Sailor.

"Now the white nights are here and summer rests in our courtyard after sweating it out all day. Eighty-five windows are open wide. I took advantage of this to deliver my speech to you—to you, mister phonograph lover, and you, neighbor, showing your feather bed, and to all you owners of saucepans, butter dishes, flower pots and radishes—to all of you who have thrust your heads out and are listening to my resilient voice.

"Oh don't be afraid: my speech won't drag on. I wanted to ask you one question, one only—and then I'll finish.

"Most excellent residents, honorable citizens! It is certain that the year twenty-two is already here. It is certain because we are eating sour cream and sour milk, we are learning to play the *domra* and we air our feather beds. It is certain because, however unrevolutionary they are, the Republic does not object to the activities I have enumerated. And, honorable citizens, does it not seem to you . . ."

At this point in the speech a shout cut into the hum of the voice which reeled around in the stone box of adjoining houses:

"Andrei!"

The man in the unbuttoned shirt ceased talking and

looked toward the shout. Then he started back inside his room, ran to the window again, leaned out as far as the waist, and asked in a flattened voice:

"What number apartment?"

"Let's meet on the street!" fell into the well.

Andrei, as he was—unbuttoned and disheveled—ran out of the room.

The landlady locked the door behind him, looked into the courtyard and, glancing at the eighty-five windows, jabbered with twitching lips:

"For a long time I've thought he was crazy! Oh, this is terrible!"

A LETTER

My dearest,

Here I am writing to you again, and again I don't know what I ought to say.

I'm most of all afraid that you will tear up the letter as soon as you recognize my handwriting.

No. Most of all I'm afraid that I'm writing to a dead person. That you are dead. I'm not expressing myself properly; that you are already dead and I'm writing to you.

Marie, my little one, one thing has become clear to me. You remember, many things seemed clear to me before. Now only one: I've got to sit down beside you and tell you everything in its proper order. Somehow I can't remember everything in its proper order. One thing is clear. If you hear me out then I'll understand everything and you won't shout any more, as you did then, two years ago. How you shouted then, Marie. . . .

I'm mixing something up.

Wait, I'll walk about the room and think a bit, about the simplest way of telling you what is most necessary, Marie. . . .

*Yes. It seems to me you will understand me if I tell.
. . . No, first here's what.*

*The whole muddle (I think I would have found the
strength to write a proper letter if it weren't for this),
the whole muddle is because I've decided. . . . Marie,
I don't know what's the matter with me! I'm coming to
you. I've decided. I can't go on any longer. I don't care.
I'll stop up my ears and run away. Let them howl, or
die, let them! I must come to you.*

*Kurt is a real man. I met him today here in Peters-
burg, wholly unexpectedly. He says he'll take me, that
is, help me. He knew me by my voice, although it was
in strange circumstances. Everything is wrong with me.
Kurt said immediately that I need a change of climate.
Of course I didn't say a word about wanting to see
you. I agreed about the climate. I find it rather funny,
Marie, when they talk about the climate, or nerves.
Although I'm very tired. But Kurt doesn't get tired.*

The point is that . . .

*I've read over the beginning. Here's my story. I have
remembered how in winter I came across a little dog
which was scratching at a closed door with its front
paws. The dog's master was asleep, probably, or
maybe he didn't want to open the door: there was a
snowstorm. I went up to the door and saw the red
marks of the dog's paws on the trampled snow. In
scratching at the door the little dog had bloodied its
paws.*

*It couldn't understand that it wasn't at all needed in
this world.*

I understand this. That is, about myself . . .

June 13th, morning

*Today Kurt came. We agreed finally. I'm coming to
you, Marie!*

*After his departure I calmed down. He has nice
hands, shoulders, mouth. In his presence the room
takes on some sense. The table, bed, windows immediately seemed pleasant and useful to me. Kurt is a well
organized person. I've read over what I wrote yester-*

day. I'm sending it to you; see what I'm like now. It's true about the little dog.

I am, of course, more to blame than you. But I don't reproach myself for what probably seems to you to be my worst offense against you, against us.

I really must establish some kind of order. Everything is mixed up inside me. I don't know exactly where and when I went wrong irrevocably, or lied, or made a mistake. Between the most recent events (that is until you came here and then disappeared—other than that in fact there have been no events) I find no connection. Perhaps there is one. It's some kind of tangle, all these years.

About the dog.

All my life I've tried to get into the circle. You understand, so that everything in the world went on around me. But I always got washed away, carried off to one side.

I bloodied myself for nothing.

This is how I understood it.

To begin with, however, a few more words. Recently I had to get some papers. They asked the question: "Your profession?" I couldn't answer. Suddenly I thought: What profession was I preparing for before? I got lost, it came out stupidly.

You understand, I'm afraid of forgetting my thoughts all the time, I'm afraid of getting lost.

I walked through the commercial quarter. I looked through some gates. Thick fortress walls went down into the ground. There were rusty locks on the doors of the warehouses. And all over the yard there was goose grass, stinging nettles, burdock, iron hoops, rubble. Just like a vacant lot.

I felt sick at heart. Against my will. It was so bleak and depressing. I thought of some universal end. My hands went cold.

But I was still . . . in a word, I didn't stop scratching. . . .

And now, only the other day, near Moscow, a friend pointed out a new radio station to me from the Pok-

lonnaya mountain. They built the tower during the revolution. At first it collapsed. They put it up again. With unsuitable tools, keeping their mouths shut. They put it up. Its waves reach America.

"You know," my friend said to me, "now we are going to build a station whose waves will girdle the entire globe. Moscow transmitting—Moscow receiving. Around the world."

I thought this was stupid then. But at that point I looked him in the face. . . .

In short, I gave up scratching.

It's futile, futile, to hell with it! Goodwill, love, desire—there's too little of this. And then, it's completely unnecessary. In order to eat and drink you need neither goodwill nor love. These people virtually are doing no more than nature forces them to do. They notice nothing under their feet, they are constantly going forward and upward. And with as much tension as if they were not people at all, but some kind of coils, Ruhmkorff coils. If you tell them about rusty locks, goose grass and rubble they don't understand a thing. They're in the circle; probably in the center of the circle.

I am pierced by the thought that I'm writing to a dead person. If it's so, I'll resurrect you so you can understand I wasn't lying.

My trouble is I'm not made of wire.

You've got to understand me, Marie.

Andrei

A TRANSITION FORMULA

The committee consisted of seven men. All were intently watching Kurt, who was speaking; even the secretary repeatedly tore himself from his notes and gathered a triangle of shallow wrinkles on his forehead, as if eavesdropping on what had to take place somewhere beyond the limits of the room. In the chairman's seat sat a man whose thick spectacles remained focused on the same spot while Kurt was talking.

Kurt stood directly opposite the chairman with his fists pressed upon the table and he tossed his head briefly at the end of each sentence. He spoke without pausing, as if reading from a book; and his speech was bookish. A rash of sweat particles had broken out over his upper lip.

"I summarize," he said.

"This man was in a state of moral decline when he confessed his crime to me. As far as I was able to observe, his power of reason was also impaired. I knew that all this was the result of a terrible shock in his private life. Therefore I treated his confession with extreme caution. But I have trained myself to think objectively and act according to the dictates of my reason. Consequently my memory renewed all my meetings with this man in Semidol, the facts of his personal life connected with the margrave and finally the circumstances of the margrave's disappearance from the German Soviet of Soldiers' Deputies in Moscow. The actual course of events coincided down to the minutest detail with what I heard from this man during his last walk. He confessed to me among other things that he was preparing to seek out the margrave, because he was the only man who might know something of the girl he loved. No doubt remained: from personal motives he had saved the life of our enemy and betrayed the cause which we all serve. As a man he became odious to me, as a friend—I had been his friend—loathsome. I killed him. The following day I made inquiries about the margrave. He is in fact living prosperously in his castle near Bischofsberg and, as befits an unsuccessful adventurer, is using his powers in the service of his native art, speculating in pictures by German masters. There had been no mistake. The police think the murder was committed with criminal intent. Until I had informed the committee of this affair, I did not consider it necessary to refute that version. I shall submit myself to your decision."

Kurt ended as if he had snapped shut a book he had just finished reading.

The chairman turned to each member in turn.

"No questions? . . . Comrade Wahn, be so kind as to leave the room."

Kurt went out. In the adjoining room he wiped his face with a handkerchief, lit a cigar and settled down comfortably in an armchair, preparing to wait. Blue ribbons of smoke, intertwined, started swaying in the middle of the room. Among them appeared someone's mouth, from below a doubled fist slowly opened out sideways into five fingers and to them was joined an arm, bent at the elbow, which stretched out towards Kurt.

"Nonsense!". he growled and blew violently on the smoke. The blue ribbons funneled down into a draught of air and disappeared.

"Comrade Wahn!"

The seven sat as before around the table. The chairman aimed his spectacles at the secretary. The latter raised a sheet of paper and proclaimed:

". . . having heard Comrade Kurt Wahn's communication, has unanimously decided: that the said comrade's course of action be considered correct, that the matter be not recorded in the minutes, that the shorthand record be destroyed, and that it return to the normal business of the day."

The secretary folded the paper in two and tore it up.

"Sit down, Comrade," said the chairman.

Kurt pulled up a chair. He was calm and relaxed, as if he had never doubted he would receive such an invitation.

CHAPTER THE FIRST
ON NINETEEN NINETEEN

PETERSBURG

A man must spend a large part of his life away from the sky, away from direct broad-chested winds, he must grow up in a closed order of iron pillars, spend his childhood on the cast iron of stairways and the asphalt of roadways in order to be at home in the city, like the woodman in his wood.

His leg knows when it stands on iron rails, when on rotten woodblocks, when on slippery ringing cement. And his ear recognizes where rooftop rainwater is falling and what has been pounced on by a sudden tearing gust of wind.

A man who knows the city as the woodman his wood has no need of light. He remembers every corner, knows any street and all the houses, old and new: the ones dismantled for fuel, the ones boarded up, the ones abandoned and unfinished.

Especially the unfinished ones. The fences of such houses have disappeared long ago. But somewhere inside the paralyzed brick skeleton, the remains of props stick out, a beam lies about half covered in rubble, or a pole with a wooden cross nailed to it has not yet been torn out.

It does not hurt to recall these props, beams and crosses in the third year of the new calendar.*

At the end of October, in the third year of the new calendar, darkness hung over Petersburg. With a whistle and

---

*With the advent of the Soviet regime there was a change from the Julian to the Gregorian Calendar.

roar the darkness was driven from the northwest by a damp
lop-shouldered wind.

Petersburg sloughed its iron husk, and the husk banged
clanging along the rooftops and fell, grinding its teeth, into
the stony bottoms of the streets.

Below, it was as dark as the insides of a tunnel.

Houses were deserted, houses collapsed, houses vanished. Wet eyeless tunnel walls stretched out and criss-
crossed in the darkness.

And along the wet eyeless walls and stony bottoms of
the tunnels swept the iron husk, screeching and clanging.
The wind flattened the stony city with its lop-shoulders,
stripped the worn-out skin off in bits, and hurled it into the
slimy darkness.

The white apish paws of an automobile snatched at the
benumbed cold-oozing tunnel walls, and passed away as
quickly as they had appeared. And the auto's siren howled
like a dying jackal.

A man, blown along by the wind, scarcely distinguishable from the stone facing of the tunnels, slipped lightly
and quickly through the pools of water, feeling his way
around corners and projections. For an instant he melted
into a black wall, as if entering a gate. Then he groped his
way up onto a slippery mound. He lowered himself into a
hole. He crawled into a corridor as narrow as a grave.
Over his head a cracked sheet of corrugated iron banged
steadily against a stone.

The man took a newspaper from his pocket, covered his
chest and shoulder with it, fumbled in the corner of the corridor for a bundle, hoisted it up and carefully crawled back.

Via the corridor, the hole, the mound, through the black
wall—into the slimy darkness of the tunnels, and farther—
via the slimy darkness, blown by the wind, sliding through
the pools of water.

A man who knows the city as the woodman his wood has
no need of light.

The man found a gate, a door, stairs, then another door.
There he shrugged the bundle from his shoulder, found one
key, then another and a third—French, very long with a

joint in the middle, patented by engineer Tubkis—and opened the locks, one after another.

In the kitchen he lit the "Economy" lamp (a quarter of a pint of kerosene per week) and took off his coat. He measured with his fingers: the log could be sawed into four pieces of twelve inches, and each piece into one, two, three —eight sticks. Two twelve-inch sticks equal one pot of coffee. Sixteen times. That was good.

"Who the devil knows how long this caper will last. Sixteen times . . ."

When he turned the log over—a notice. Stuck smoothly with red paste. Written in indelible pencil. The pencil had run:

Tutoring in French and Ger. for all Classes of
High School. Moderate prices.
17 PETROZAVODSKI STREET, APT. **3**
Also stockings darned and repaired.
We also keep rabbits.

He shook his head and said aloud:

"What have our intellectuals been brought to, eh?"

He took the log away and put it in a cubbyhole.

He opened a cupboard built into the wall. From a jar of millet he took a small rag. He poured millet from a paper bag into the jar and covered it with the rag. On the jar he placed a large stone, round as a bun.

"Mice. The bastards."

He lit the iron stove. He boiled the water and put some wheat in the frying pan to fry. With the boiling water he washed some soup from a saucepan and washed a plate. Then he cleaned the sink with bast and bath brick. He took off his tunic. Rolled up his shirt sleeves to the elbow. When there came a smell of burning he stopped washing the sink, grabbed a knife and, scraping the burnt grains from the frying pan, said about five times:

"Coffee. The bastards."

Then he looked in the cupboard. In jars there was wheat, barley, ground wheat, ground buckwheat and ground bar-

ley, and herrings. In bottles—linseed and sunflower seed oil.
In a canvas bag—Caspian roach. In paper bags—salt, bay
leaves, gelatin. There were three pounds of gelatin. He
said:

"Gelatin, eh?"

He took a book of Maupassant's—*Madame Husson's
May King*—and moved the lamp closer. He put on his tunic,
cleaned his nails with a pen-knife and sat down in a broad
armchair to read, perching his pince-nez on his round nose.

He came to the lines:

I hope you haven't lunched yet?

No.

*What luck! I'm just sitting down and I've got an excellent
trout.*

He threw his pince-nez on the book and remarked:

"Gelatin, a coupon a pound, three weeks running, eh?"

Suddenly he pricked up his ears.

Someone was knocking, but quietly, uncertainly. Better to
wait. He waited. A louder knocking. He jumped up, closed
the cupboard, locked it, looked at the table. Bread—under
the napkin, the box of saccharin—into his pocket.

"Who's there?"

"Does Sergei Lvovich Shchepov live here?"

"And who is asking?"

"Startsov."

"What do you want?"

"Startsov, from Semidol, Andrei Startsov."

"From Semidol?"

"I have a letter for you from your son, from Aleksei
Sergeyevich."

"A-a-ah! Well then, well then. Just a minute."

He commenced operations. A bolt at the top of the door,
a bolt at the bottom, engineer Tubkis's lock, a regular lock,
the French lock, a chain.

"You know you can't rely on anyone these days—not
even your own son. Thieves everywhere, just thieves, scoundrels and bandits. Very pleased to meet you. Yes. Now you
see—this is how I live. I wash pots, saw firewood, cook for
myself, do my own washing, sew, trim the lamps, polish my
shoes, clean out, pardon, the latrine. Welcome. Here, you

see—blisters on my hands, blistered hands. They stink of burning from the coffee, or kerosene from the lamp, and of castor-oil from the cutlets. I'm cooking potato cutlets in castor-oil. That's how it is. Please take a seat. There's coffee. I'll just sweep up, I forgot to sweep up. You here for long? On business?"

Startsov took the kitbag from his back. He stood there, tall, muddy gray, in a sopping army overcoat whose sleeves hid his fingers, with sloping shoulders and a collar without points.

"I don't know," he said, "I didn't find anything out today. I'll know tomorrow morning."

"A genuine councillor of state! Look, with these hands, everything myself. From eight in the morning till twelve at night. And what do I get for it? Yesterday they gave out half a pound of Caspian roach again and a pound of gelatin. And what do I want with gelatin? It came on the plan. Fine. And if fishing rods came on the plan? Say, two rods to each citizen? What do you want me to do? Rubbish. . . . A letter from Aleksei, you say? Well, how is he? Here's the coffee. I have some bread. . . ."

"I have bread," said Startsov.

While reading, Sergei Lvovich twitched his nose and the upper part of his pince-nez slowly inclined toward the paper. Sergei Lvovich tilted his head farther and farther back and his face narrowed and grew haughtier.

"He's married!" he exclaimed, slapping the letter with his fingers. "He's married, married an actress! I can just imagine!"

He straightened his pince-nez and his eyes sought the line where he had stopped. Then he placed the letter in a book, leaned on the table and looked his guest in the eyes.

"Well, of course. That's how it is now—just like kids. Once merchants used to write: *We have the honor to inform you that Ivan Ivanich Sidorov has entered our firm on an equal footing. We beg you to note his signature.* But here there's not even that: I inform you that your name will be borne by a singer. There's not even a name—Darya, Marya, Agrafena? God knows who she is!"

"Her name is Klavdia . . . her patronymic . . . I've forgotten," said Startsov.

"And her surname? Some Kultyapkina or other—stage name Razdor-Zapolskaya, dramatic ingénue in parts with no words or movements. . . . However, it's all the same, isn't it? I ask you, it's all the same, isn't it? Eh?"

"But why?"

"Because everything's gone to the devil's belly now. Everything! You and I are now porridge in the guts of some devil or other. Gastric juices are working on us; next we'll crawl along the intestines, through the duodenum, the small intestine, the large intestine and the rectum. That's what we are."

Sergei Lvovich took the little box of saccharin out of his pocket, stuck a small white tablet on his spoon, dropped it into his glass. For a moment he did not move. Then he held the little box out to Startsov.

"Thank you, I take it without."

Sergei Lvovich carefully closed the box and suddenly, swiftly as a child, broke into tears.

"You say, why is it all the same? Well, what am I to Aleksei? It's good enough that he informed me. Otherwise, one fine morning he could have sent me four snotty-nosed kids with a note: *Dear Papa, I'm sending your little grandchildren for you to take care of, I myself am going on a trip.* Do you think it was any different when he became a pilot? He came once and said: 'Good-by, I'm going to the front, maybe I'll get my block knocked off, we won't see each other again.' 'How can you get your block knocked off when you're a warrant officer in the Russian service?' 'Oh,' he answered, 'they've reconsidered. I've been flying a hydroplane for the last six months and now I'm assigned to the front as an instructor.' What's left for a father to do? I blessed him. And what do you want me to do now? Bless him and his Kultyapkina, Razdor-Zapolskaya! They don't give a damn either way, whether I bless them or not. But even that's fortunate, believe me, fortunate. I have another son, younger. . . ."

Sergei Lvovich suddenly stood up, raised his arm and shouted somewhere into the corner:

"I disown him! Before God and man I disown him! There is no second son! There was, but he died, turned to ashes, to dust; he's vanished, dead, dead. . . ."

He collapsed into the armchair, banged his head on the edge of the table, sobbed, banged his head again and began to twitch:

"Lyovochka is dead, he's dead! The unhappy wretch, the wretch! . . . Completely lost!"

Startsov stood up, moved his lips, sat down and got up again. But Sergei Lvovich shook his head and suddenly, quietly:

"He's not worth remembering, the good for nothing, let alone tears. That's why I say that everything's gone to the devil now. Children have become traitors and fathers have become hardened. Without regret, without tears, without heart, they are hardened and cold, just like this slab. Yes, I can talk to you, a stranger, with a quiet mind, like writing a commander's report, or a doctor taking off a gangrenous arm: my son Lev is a thief. Not metaphorically, but simply in point of fact—a thief. He robbed his father, robbed his aunt, robbed his friends. Yesterday the criminal investigation department came to look for the former nobleman's son Lev Shchepov, who was caught stealing. He's stolen a watch, three suits, linen, a coon-skin coat and silver spoons. I've put three locks on the door: every day there's a theft. I planted an ambush, a detective sat in my room while I went out to work. He sat there three days. Then he grins at me: Comrade Shchepov, excuse me, he says, but I'm at home here. Then I slapped Lev's face and threw him out. He went to spend the night at his aunt's and robbed her. I am telling this to you, an outsider. I have no son Lev. He has fallen from me like a scab. He has fallen together with everyone else, people for me now are thieves, traitors, scum!"

Behind the black window the broken iron of a drainpipe clinked hollowly. The thin damper of the iron stove tinkled absent-mindedly somewhere beneath the ceiling—the wind was alternately pushing and sucking it. Sergei Lvovich stirred the saccharin in his glass with a teaspoon.

"He had a Soviet wedding, I suppose?"

"I don't know. I think so—yes," replied Startsov.

"Then God help him."

Startsov laughed. Sergei Lvovich looked at him with his quick eyes, narrowed and elusive, as if he had only now remembered that it was necessary to examine his guest.

"Andrei, what is your father's name?"

"Gennady."

"Are you here on business, Andrei Gennadyevich?"

"I've been mobilized. I've come to join the army here."

Sergei Lvovich shifted his gaze to the half-open closet with its provisions.

"I would have invited you to stay the night. . . . Aleksei here asks in his letter. . . . Only it's two degrees in the room. . . . I heat only my kennel. . . ."

"Never mind, I'll wrap myself up. . . ."

"Well, if you're not afraid. . . ."

Startsov lay on the leather couch as he was, as he had lain all these nights—in wagons, on stations, in the Moscow barracks—in his overcoat and boots with his kitbag under his head.

Sergei Lvovich inspected the closet with the provisions, locked it with the key, added a small nickel-plated padlock, took *Madame Husson's May King* under his arm, the "Economy" lamp in his hand and went into the bedroom. There, at the head of the bed on a small table, went a watch, a lighter set in mother-of-pearl, a case for the pince-nez, *Madame Husson's May King,* a silver monogrammed cigarette case and a tiny piece—one square in all—of old pre-war chocolate. Having made an envelope of the blanket and crawled inside it, Sergei Lvovich sighed, stretched out his arms and closed his eyes for a minute. Then, revived, he slowly placed the piece of chocolate in his mouth. Again he closed his eyes. Then he lit up, inhaled the smoke deeply and turning on his side took the book from the table.

The regular clinking of the piece of iron behind the window was hardly audible here.

THE TRENCH PROFESSOR

"Listen, listen, someone's knocking!"

Startsov tried to raise his eyelids. They were as heavy as the lid of a galvanized trunk.

"Andrei Gennadyevich, someone's knocking!"

Without budging, Startsov said:

"Well so what."

"I think that if it's a search . . ."

And again Startsov said, without moving:

"Let them in, let . . ."

He heard slippers scuffing hastily over the floor. Farther, farther. They stopped. They scuffed again. Nearer, nearer.

"Andrei Gennadyevich, but you're not registered!"

"I have papers. I'll explain. . . ."

A loud groan rolled around the walls. The slippers hurried. But immediately, as if having completed a small circle, they flapped again under his very ear.

"But if it's a raid . . . you know . . . the raiders. . . ."

"I have a Mauser," said Startsov and opened his eyes.

Before him stood Sergei Lvovich, with a fur coat thrown over his shoulders, in a long nightshirt down to his knees and faded knitted underpants which clung tightly to his scrawny calves. A lamp trembled in his hand, throwing warm splashes of color over his chin and nose and Sergei Lvovich's face seemed fat at one moment and peculiarly thin at another.

"Do you have permission?" he asked quietly.

The walls began to groan louder. Sergei Lvovich rushed to unlock the door. Indistinct noises briefly merged and rumbled around the rooms. Then suddenly a thin voice began to complain:

"I work sixteen hours a day! Six at my job, six at home, I stand four hours in line, then there's guard duty and the labor conscription! I'm fifty-two years old. . . ."

Someone from a distance and hollowly, like an ax upon an empty barrel:

"Don't delay us, Citizen! . . ."

The fur coat slipped from Sergei Lvovich's shoulders and
he tried to catch it with one hand, twisting around like a
clumsy young mastiff trying to catch its tail.

"They drive us to the devil's mother to dig trenches in the
middle of the night! With a knife at our throats! It's not
enough for us to clean out cesspools, chop firewood, God
knows what, stand in lines. . . . Dig earth for gelatin?
And what the . . ."

"What time is it now?" asked Startsov.

"Three o'clock. Three in the morning. Surely . . ."

"Do you know what? I'll go in your place. I've slept
enough."

Sergei Lvovich brought the lamp up to Startsov's face.

"Go and say your place is being taken by another man,
somewhat younger and . . ."

"Stronger, of course, stronger! Just look at those shoulders," interrupted Sergei Lvovich.

He shot these words out on the move, wrapping his fur
coat about him and hurrying toward the door.

Accompanying his guest he exhorted him gratefully and
touchingly:

"I wish you, I wish. . . . Call in. . . . If you are de-
layed spend the night here, move in even: you know I'm
all alone. Very pleased . . ."

Just by the door he caught Startsov by the sleeve, stood
on tiptoe and whispered:

"Evidently it's bad there!"

"Where?"

"There . . ."

"I'll take a look," answered Andrei and ran down the
stairs in the dark.

Outside a roll-call was being taken beneath the dim spot
of a sooty street lamp.

"Apartment twenty-seven?"

"Here!" shouted Andrei.

And hollowly, like an ax upon an empty barrel, a voice
rapped:

"He bought himself off!"

Then a dark mass hid the lamp from Andrei and the same voice boomed above his head:

"Papers!"

They tumbled into a hollow wet tunnel, into a black channel of cold, in a dumb clustering herd. Somewhere overhead someone's footsteps pattered along the iron husk, like a flail on a threshing floor. Collars raised, hands in sleeves, backs hunched, faces to the ground, under their feet—forward, unfailingly forward, only forward, into the black channel of cold.

And suddenly into backs, backs of heads, necks, under feet—noses, stomachs, knees, one against the other—every single man, right down to the last. And in front:

"Halt, ha-alt, ha-a-aaa!"

Slowly, by touch, eyes screwed up, peering forward and to the sides, hands, fingers, elbows back—the crowd began to spread out to right and left. But in front:

"Damn it! We've run into something!"

"Where are you barging to, may the Lord forgive me?"

"But the comrade is leading; I thought he knew the way . . ."

"Roosters think. . . . Look, my damned coat tails have come off!"

"You yourself could've . . ."

"Ha-ha!"

"To the left, Citizens, here a match-length away!"

"There was no fighting but they got wounded!"

Like blind men—not in a herd—a human crowd with human laughter—they skirted a wooden stake and crosspiece tangled in barbed wire. They scraped matches and struck white sparks from their lighters for the wind to sport with.

In the open around the bend a clock dial gleamed unexpectedly, like a rising moon. It was smooth, clean, clearcut and surrounded by the illimitable blackness of the night; it shone without giving light and it showed a quarter to eight.

From this dial the men walked briskly and set up an unremitting hubbub.

"Associations can be very strange," Startsov heard a quiet little voice. He stared into the darkness. A small silhouette the height of his shoulder was hurrying along beside him.

"Very strange. I have an acquaintance, the curator of a museum. Owner of a unique collection of eighteenth-century miniatures and of a library on the history of the miniature. Now of course he's grown poor, sold off his furniture, his pots and pans and all sorts of trifles. He reached the end of his tether. What should he begin with—the miniatures or the library? For a while he tormented himself, tortured himself—then began with the library. And do you know, from that day he forgot everything, all that was in the books and chronology, periods, styles generally—everything. All he does is look at his medallions, porcelain and enamel, smiles, lights up—and that's all. And no matter what he tries to remember he gets mixed up."

"What association are you talking about?" asked Andrei.

The quiet little voice from the impenetrable darkness, above the hubbub of people and the whistling of the iron husk, laughed at itself as if apologizing:

"I was talking about the electric clock. Look, it's still shining, and it looks as if it were still a clock, yet the hands have already stopped, they are standing still, they aren't budging. It's shining but it will certainly go out. . . ."

"Nonsense!" suddenly escaped from Andrei and he realized immediately that this word was not his own and that Golosov pronounced it differently.

"It's on a direct cable, that's why it shines," came a voice from behind.

They stopped still in that same cold channel, without reason it seemed; it seemed they could have stopped much earlier, yet they could have gone farther. A red funnel of light from someone's cupped hand struck a broad face, pock-marked and striped with wrinkles. Then the light of a cigarette glowed in place of the face. A sleeve crept up to the light, the light flared and illuminated the strap of a watch.

"Ten to," boomed the mass.

Somewhere the darkness began to cluck, the road heaved

and trembled; about two hundred yards away a white bell-tower grew out of the ground and beside it ruins, deathly cold in the shudder of a searchlight. Then the clucking changed to a hum, to a knocking to a thunder, to a roar, and casting a shroud over the houses—from the church across the ruins, from house to house, the farther the swifter—a straight thrusting horn of light struck their faces and blinded them.

From a thundering mountainous truck someone yelled penetratingly, overcoming the crackle and vibration:

"How ma-ny pee-o-ple?"

"Thirty."

Shovels screeched and clanged as they were scattered, bouncing and standing on end in the roadway.

"Four-tee-een! Throw out some more!"

"Enough!"

And again the earth quaked under their feet, again the deathly cold searchlight snatched at the houses, ruins, fences; then immediately the black channel toppled over and clapped down on the people and all were blinded.

"Split up into two."

They walked to the ruins in small groups, holding hands. There they brought out matches and looked for rafters. It was impossible to see from where, from all sides, they dragged chips, boards, laths, frames, plywood, and rolled up a wet log. At its ends, covered with chips, they lit fires.

A stentorian voice boomed impatiently:

"Well what's up, Citizens, you've stopped?"

Then someone's large hand, shaking in the mild light of the fire, was lifted heavily to a forehead, lowered heavily onto a stomach, waved from shoulder to shoulder, and a calm voice called out:

"God be with you, Comrades!"

And then a dozen or two backs slowly bent toward the ground.

Iron banged and scraped by the fence, knocked together out of billboards, where the shift, turning up the roadway, had gone. Andrei threw his coat open, wiped his sweaty neck with his hand and squatted on the asphalt. A woman with a small strap drawn about her, clumsy, stout, panting, cleaning the sticky mud from her hands with a rusty scrap of tin, asked:

"Well, Professor, how d'you like turning stones?"

The man the height of Startsov's shoulder stretched as if waking up and laughed:

"Well, you know—it's fine! I can't convey to you exactly what I feel. Sometimes you're walking along the street, accidentally you lift your head, suddenly—the sky! You feel so wonderful inside you. For years you don't see it, don't notice it, as if there were nothing. And suddenly you make contact. It turns out to be—the sky! . . . It's something like that. . . ."

"It turns out to be—manure."

"Quite right, manure, dirt. But to make contact is marvelous."

"I could understand it if there were—fervor," came a voice jerkily and wheezing.

The stout clumsy woman suddenly recollected:

"That's it exactly! In February the barricades built themselves. But now it's barracks."

The wheeze added:

"The main thing is, what are we defending? The right to destroy."

"To destroy," sounded from behind.

"To destroy," fluttered from in front.

"Fervor," said the professor, staring at Andrei, "fervor is an hour, a day, a week. Fervor is a fever. It is impossible for people to toss in a fever for whole years."

"And why must it toss?"

"But, Professor, culture . . ." said someone.

"Culture," sounded from behind.

"Culture," fluttered from in front.

And again as if laughing at himself the professor apologized:

"You know, as a student of history, I was never able to discover an idea that disappeared without trace beneath the ruins of an academy, a city or a state. I couldn't. And I'm completely calm: at this moment neither biology, history, art, physics, nor the knowledge in general accumulated by mankind, is under any threat."

"Ideas can be conceived only by mankind. But mankind is doomed to self-extermination."

"Extermination," sounded from behind.

"Extermination," fluttered from in front.

"I don't see that," objected the professor.

"But what about the clock?" asked Startsov.

"What clock?"

"There at the crossroads. It's shining but it will go out, it will certainly go out. . . ."

"About the museum curator? Oh, but that was sentiment, human sentiment! Gentlemen!" (The professor exclaimed: "Gentlemen!" but turned to Andrei alone and spoke a friendly reproach.) "Who will deny that it is painful for us to regard our own death?"

"Death," caught up the wheeze.

The fence of billboards began to rumble and groan and drowned their quiet talking. The fires died down, then, for a moment, bathed the men in red flames before lowering the light steadily to the ground.

A bank rose up along the length of the whole trench, from sidewalk to sidewalk in a straight transversal line. When the next shift entered the trench the shovels were moving slackly and the earth was rolling back down the bank and into the hole. Then a precipitate hail of solid clods poured over the crest of the bank and down on the fires, spattering the upturned cobblestones. The scraped iron of the shovels tinkled against the soil, like scythes on a dewy meadow, the men warmed up and worked furiously.

At six in the morning the man whose voice boomed like an ax on an empty barrel jumped down into the trench, measured the bank with his eye, walked from end to end, climbed out onto the roadway and boomed:

"All right, Citizens! Thank you!"

"So the republic's thanking us?" said the wheeze.

Someone sighed with a moan:

"In vain, oh Lord!"

They shook themselves, cleaned themselves up, scratched themselves, divided up the remains of the chips, extinguished the charred logs in puddles, laughed and marched in a noisy crowd into the last hour of nocturnal darkness.

Startsov drew a long way ahead. The voices behind him melted away and the city replied to his footsteps with stern silence.

Suddenly in front of him he heard snatches of a lively ringing tune. He pricked up his ears and walked quicker, stepping only on the soles of his feet.

The small silhouette the height of his shoulder, its hands thrust deep into its pockets, all hunched up and disappearing inside its overcoat, was digging swift, short little steps into the pavement and resolutely humming:

Aux armes, citoyens!

Startsov took it up:

Formez vos bataillons!

The professor turned smartly on his heels, and somehow bird-like fixed the tiny coals of his eyes on Startsov, exclaiming cordially: "Oh, it's you?" and seizing him impetuously by the arm, tugging it in time with the song, as if urging him to join in, as if trying to move, to stir Startsov, continued almost loudly:

Marchons, marchons. . . .

And he dug his meticulously, jauntily, enthusiastically, short, ringing little steps into the wet pavement.

Thus in the desolate, dank city, which had sloughed its iron husk, during the last hour of nocturnal darkness, the two of them walked arm in arm with a song which has no equal. And when the song ended, one said:

"Oh, to be born again. Just once again, my God! A hundred years from now. To see people weep at the very mention of these years, to bow before a rotten fragment of a banner, to honor an operational communiqué from the staff of the worker-peasant Red Army! But here—look! look!—this newspaper, smeared with flour and coming unstuck from the fence; it's being torn by the wind and doused with rain. Yet in a hundred years a tiny piece, a fraction of this sheet will be sewn into an altar cloth, as a relic, as the holy of holies! . . . Oh to be born in a hundred years and to say suddenly: 'But I lived then, lived during those years! And once, on a raw cold night, in Petersburg, in Petrograd, in Peter, I dug trenches with these very hands. I walked along a deserted street, through the city which was dying and fighting, fighting and dying, walked arm in arm with a soldier of the Red Army, here with this, here—look!—with this arm I held a red soldier, like this!' Well, you are a red soldier?"

"I'm on my way . . . that is . . . I'm due to be assigned today. . . ."

"You, perhaps, will still see. . . . I, of course, won't last and I won't do. Life is hard now both on the spirit and on the flesh and on the beasts. If only you could imagine how vexing it is on occasion—one wants to cry, you know! Maybe it's old age. Yes, old age. And now . . . Permit me to . . ."

All of a sudden the professor appeared in front of Startsov, clasped the back of his head with one hand and pressed his trembling lips thrice to his cheek.

"I have to go left. Don't be offended. Good luck!"

And he whisked around the corner.

Andrei halted.

Burning air scorched his face—so clearly, distinctly, palpably that he shuddered. The recollection was unexpected and stunned him. Out of everything that had taken place on the station at Semidol, that had happened during that last day of farewell, only one feature, one elusively brief sensation had been stored in his memory. The rest had rolled up into a dense tangled ball:

Dusk, discordant voices, placards and banners rolled up for convenience, a crush on the narrow station platform. Under his feet a creaking box swaying from the shouts, then the hasty, business-like kisses of his friends, then faces seeming shy and guilty: then the scurrying about over the black tangled tracks and the trip to the town—a solitary, long trip. All this was a dense tangled ball, pushed into the background by his clear relentless will—yes, the will, the desire, the wish to experience once again the feeling of absolute freedom, that same feeling which had come to him in the fields at Sanshino—a feeling of disembodiment.

But here is what had shattered the constancy of his will, what had hurled that whole day aside like a cannonball, that last day in Semidol—and here is what had made it a day of farewell:

The night was cold. The sky was unusually high and the stars in it were dead. The square before the station did not lie as it usually did, like a vacant lot, but stretched away like a desert. The horse was moving its legs, the hired cab was lurching to right and left but there was no sensation of motion, no movement. All of a sudden a figure indistinguishable in the night jumped onto the step of the cab. The horse stopped.

"Rita!" cried Andrei.

"I wanted no one to see," she said breathlessly. Then she fell on his neck, pressed her icy lips to his mouth, brushed against his face, his neck, his hands with her cold hair, yet despite the autumn cold of the night, of her lips and her hair, she scorched him:

"Farewell!"

He should have cried out, because a cry had risen in his throat, because Rita had burst away from the cab and fled into the night, because suddenly it seemed as if he were leaving his mother, leaving forever—he should, he ought to have cried out, but instead of crying out he prodded the cabby in the back and with a tremendous effort forced from his throat:

"Drive on!"

And again everything was pushed aside by his lucid will to undergo, to experience, to feel again as soon as possible what had come to him in the fields at Sanshino.

"Drive on, drive on, drive on!"

And now, in the cold of the night, from the cold contact of a stranger's lips, a burning breath scorched his face, distinctly, palpably, and the recollection of that last day, which had become a day of farewell, was bitter. But just as quickly the bitterness was washed away by his persistent will to experience! And Andrei dashed into the darkness, crying to himself:

"Drive on!"

Oh, if only he were now in the seat of that driver who came spurring his roaring car around the corner, swept it within two fingers' width of a cast-iron column, plunged it into a puddle, hurled it into the air, righted it, straightened it, slammed it into the endless straightaway of the avenue and urged it on in a cloud of spray, in a screech of wheels, in the crackle of the motor, roaring, crashing, thundering! Every second—death, in every dent—death, in every pot hole—death, at every post—death, on the turn—death, on the straightaway—death! And it was wonderful, wonderful because there was nothing else—as it should be; nothing else—that was essential! Wonderful, easy, infinitely easy! Oh, if only he could undergo, experience, feel what had come to him in the fields near Sanshino!

"Drive on, drive on, drive on!"

KONRAD STEIN

On the same day in Moscow, a man in a furry hare-skin cap, a torn, dirty overcoat of German pattern and with light blue Austrian leggings approached the house in which the German Soviet of Soldiers' Deputies was situated. He knocked at a door in the vestibule, read over the announcements and reports pinned to the walls and went up to the third floor.

In a room crowded with ragged people he took his place in a line. For half an hour he moved forward with the air of a man accustomed to waiting, tired and indifferent. Going up to the table he took off his cap. His hair was cut very short and across his head, from the right ear to the back, there stretched a broad scar, strewn with wrinkled, pink stitch-marks. He held himself erect like a good soldier and loudly clicked his heels when the man sitting behind the table lifted his eyes to him.

"I got left behind my troop train going home. Here are my papers. Please attach me to the nearest party. I should have . . ."

"Where was your train coming from?"

"From Semidol."

"How did you get left behind?"

"I was buying potatoes for my comrades. The train commander said we would halt for eight hours. I went to a little village about two to three kilometers away. At the same time the train took them away on some branch-line. Because of all this Russian confusion, while I was finding out . . ."

"Where was this?"

"In Ryazan. I walked a good half of the way on foot, as far as Moscow."

"Your name?"

"Konrad Stein."

Moving his finger over the lists, the man sitting behind the table lit a cigarette and said:

"Yes, it's here. It was at the end of October?"

"The train was loaded in Semidol on October twenty-fourth and departed on the twenty-fifth."

"One moment," said the man checking the lists and got up and went into the next room.

An elderly, bearded soldier with a Russian hood around his neck stared affectionately at Konrad Stein and indicating the scar with his eyes said:

"Well done. Shrapnel?"

"A French job," responded Stein, "in Champagne in fifteen."

"Well done," repeated the soldier. "Are you from Saxony?"

"Yes."

The door of the next room opened and the man with the lists in his hand called out:

"Konrad Stein, come in here."

When Stein came up with him he added:

"Inform the secretary that you spoke to me."

And he stood in the doorway.

The secretary glanced at him cursorily and said:

"You can go, Comrade."

Then he turned coolly to Stein:

"In what camp were you held?"

"In the Tomsk camp."

"Until when?"

"Here are my papers. They have all the details. Kindly . . ."

"I beg you to answer my questions. We are in a foreign country which until recently was at war with us and our duty is to help one another. We are all dying to go home, but not all of us have equal rights to go first."

"Yes, but I was already put on a train."

"I know. When were you taken prisoner?"

"I am seriously ill, you can see." Stein pointed to his scar.

"When were you taken prisoner?"

"In February, 1917."

"Where?"

"Near Riga."

"Until when were you held in Tomsk?"

"I don't remember exactly. The spring of this year. I have, do you see?" Stein again pointed to his head.

"However, you said exactly when you departed from Semidol."

"That's written down in my papers."

"How did you come to be in Semidol?"

"Six men escaped from Tomsk—including me."

"How did you get through the front?"

"The Reds received us well and helped us get to Semidol."

"And the Whites?"

"We avoided the Whites."

"Did you take part in the Civil War?"

"No."

"Are you a private?"

"Private first class."

The secretary rose and went to the farther door. Reaching it, he swiftly turned and asked:

"And you weren't acquainted with a certain zur Mühlen-Schönau?"

The private first class wrinkled his brows, raised his eyes to the ceiling and hemmed and hawed.

"No, I don't recall him," he answered calmly.

"What's your name?"

"Konrad Stein," said the private first class.

The secretary went out.

Then Konrad Stein rushed to the door through which he had entered, stopped for a single moment, held his breath, listening, and then deliberately grasped the door-handle.

In the room full of ragged people there was no one at the table. From a telephone booth came someone's high, angry shout.

Konrad Stein placed his papers in the bottom of his cap, pulled the hare-skin down over his eyes and began to make his way toward the exit. To the bearded soldier with the hood around his neck, who had looked at him so affectionately, he said in a bored voice:

"I'll go and take a smoke while they are messing around with their papers. . . ."

And quietly he went down the stairs. On the street he slipped around the corner, rushed to a streetcar stop and was lost in the shabby crowd.

That night a swiftly moving man with a large white head ran out of the darkness and up to a freight train crawling from Moscow to Klin. After letting the squeaking train go by him, its couplings clanking, he fastened himself to the nape of the last car near the buffer, under the blind eye of a red lamp.

ENEMY AT THE GATES!

The staff headquarters were illuminated and people were wandering running and dashing up and down the begrimed well-worn staircases. Telephone bells erupted through the wide open door and a wheezing, exhausted voice shrieked every minute:

"Hullo . . . to take a message . . ."

"He says to take a message . . . at the telephone to take a me-ssa-ge!"

A sleepy man was swimming in tobacco smoke and a heap of papers in a high circular room. Spitting on his fingers, he was sorting and moving cards, bills and papers.

He raised an enamel teapot to his lips, sucked from the chipped spout, then for a long while bulged his eyes—with their fat lids and colorless pupils—and again began moving bills.

"When were you told to come?" he asked Startsov, without leaving the bills.

"At nine."

"And what time is it now?"

He had gone all to seed—his mustache had crept into his mouth, his cheeks sagged onto his lower jaw, his long hair curtained his forehead, eyes and ears—but his hands were indefatigable, sorting the cards, bills and papers.

"Stop," he cried to the departing Startsov, "it's here! It's on the French Embankment."

Startsov took a paper, stuffed it in his cuff and—past the people wandering running and dashing up and down, through the cacophonic crackle of bells and the wheezy shriek: "To take a me-ssa-ge!"—emerged on the square.

Over the palace streamed the irregular paleness of dawn, but the palace itself, the Alexandrovsky Park and the unbent horseshoe of headquarters formed a solid gray wall, chopping off the crossed paws of automobile headlights.

Andrei was enveloped in fog. He took long, confident strides, encouraged by the cold wind which crept inside his collar and sleeves.

He was in a hurry to get to work and he believed that everything in the world would become simple and clear if he began it. It seemed to him that the feeling which had lifted him off the ground, as the wind a scrap of paper, was concealed somewhere quite nearby and was on the point of bursting into him in order to whirl about once more within its coil. How could he know that his following wind was blowing away from the shore he was trying to moor on? How could he know that from the moment he crossed the threshold of the rain-blinded house, his every day would constitute a mountain between him and his simple, tangible aim?

He opened the dampened door and went up the staircase with its stair-carpet saturated in mud.

In the large hall burned a feeble electric light. Its ruddy

light fell on a long row of card tables arranged along the windows.

"*Sa-la-vat!*" Andrei heard the harsh, guttural word.

He turned around. In the corner, on the lid of a concert piano, lay a man face up with a telephone to his mouth.

"*Salavat! Salavat!*" he yelled, so that his stomach quivered and his legs twitched.

Andrei looked into the far corner of the hall. It seemed to him that no one was there. But in the pale light struggling through the window he suddenly made out the silhouette of a soldier. A bayonet stuck up above his head in a straight distinct line. The soldier stood beside a shapeless black mound which grew out of the floor. Andrei went closer. On a high dais with hanging folds of material stood a coffin, covered with wreaths. The soldier on guard was sleeping soundly.

"The publisher of *Salavat?*" cried the man on the piano and immediately began to ram harsh indistinct words down the telephone. Then he jumped off the piano and said, already addressing Andrei:

"These bastards, they still haven't sent it down to the truck!"

"What?"

"*Salavat!* The newspaper, the devils! And what do you want?"

"I don't know if I'm in the right place. I need the chief. . . ."

"The chief? There, over there."

And a short finger indicated the far corner and the coffin to Andrei.

"Is he dead?" asked Andrei.

"No, of course not, that's someone else! There, look, the door."

The red light running over the walls leaped onto Andrei's chest, fluttered over his face and slipped down to the floor. By the fireplace on a large carpet sat three people, their legs folded under them. A black man with high cheekbones and oiled straight hair plastered down, twisted his head sharply toward Andrei and asked in a sing-song Eastern accent:

"What do you want, Comrade?"

Andrei came closer and offered his papers.

"Good. We need a man like you," said the black man and pierced Andrei with his keen eyes.

The two others squinted momentarily at Andrei and sighing loudly began to hum a monotonous song.

"If you want to wait you can wait in the other room."

"Are you sending me to a unit?" asked Andrei.

"Why to a unit, why to a unit if I say that we need a man like you?"

"But I am expressing a desire to go to the front and not to stay here."

"Dear Comrade, I am also expressing a desire that you stay here. This is also the front and not something else."

"I want to go to the front units, Comrade. I was sent here for that."

"How talkative, how talkative, my dear boy!" exclaimed the black man and showed Andrei a satisfied, dazzling smile. "Then I am informing you that this is a front-line unit; at this moment the front-line can be in Petrograd itself. Do you have a weapon?"

"A Mauser."

"Go and clean your Mauser."

"It's oiled, there's no point in cleaning it."

"How talkative!"

The black man jumped to his feet, slapped his thighs and went up to Andrei. He was slim, lithe and narrow-shouldered and suddenly there sounded in what he was saying a seriousness which was intensified by the incongruous accent. He said:

"Young Comrade, the revolution knows what to do with you, with me, with this or that person. Neither do I want to sit in this room, cold, high, five miles from floor to ceiling! The revolution knows that I, a chief, must be here, by this lousy fireplace. Wait in the other room. You will help bury the dead commander."

He clapped Andrei on the shoulder.

"We need a good burial—he was a good red commander!"

An orderly entered and stood in the doorway. The chief strode to meet him and suddenly a cascade of uncontainable guttural cries descended on the orderly and seemed to knock him off his feet; he took a step backward and sat in an armchair. Then the black man rushed toward him, shook him by the shoulders, struck him in the chest and began to pull at his waist. The orderly stretched out a short-fingered hand toward the chief, with the palm turned upward, the chief slapped it and dashed to the fireplace. There his two comrades were still rocking and humming a song. He growled something to them and they turned on the orderly and yelled a short word. The orderly got up, uttered the same word and went out. Then the chief went up to Andrei.

"I said to him, why do you give my mare a white saddle-cloth? I'm not in the white army, I'm in the red army; give me a red saddle-cloth, a red star, a red saddle. What's white for?"

He burst into joyful laughter and stretched out a hand to Andrei.

Andrei grasped this hand—tenacious, strong and dry—pressed it and turned toward the door. When he had taken several steps he stopped in the middle of the room and his face reflected the black man's transparent, joyful and crafty smile.

He began to work.

Telephones, packages, papers, telegraph reports, some books and records, some actors and quartermaster-sergeants, something suddenly cold like a hard frost, creeping through the door and over the parquet, or easily soiled, like the silk shade over the lamp, someone's sorrows, someone's joy, stable-hands, lecturers on the history of primitive culture and division medical officers, young ladies in rabbit-fur coats and artists in felt boots, something immense and suddenly something trifling—all this whirled him up and made him giddy, like a longboat, and he swam, sank and scrambled out in order to swim and sink again.

He came to his senses at dusk, in a crowd of high-cheekboned men surrounding the red coffin; he was by the coffin itself, beside the chief who was black as mourning. The hall, illuminated by charcoal lamps, decorated with paneling, Gobelins and heavy pictures, hummed with a

well-known melody. But the song was being sung in a staccato language which grated like a woodcock, and the
melody had become as drear as the steppe. It seemed
to Andrei that the dry slanting eyes on these high-
cheekboned, immobile faces, forged out of copper, were
closing and blinking much too often.

He went out onto the embankment where sticky blackness was clinging to the blind, gloomy houses. He stood on
the road a while indecisively, turning his head from side to
side, then pulled his cap down and strode toward the
Liteiny Bridge.

At night a new branch of the staff began work.

Banging about on walls, fences and posts were telephone
wires hung up with tape and string. On them tinkled the
wooden labels of the Winter and Smolny division staffs from
the Petropavlovskaya Fortress.

The manuscript of the dispatch was written on two sheets
in indelible pencil with no corrections. When the first had
been covered with a steep formation of letters a voice,
which was immediately caught up and drowned by a telephone bell, rapped through the door:

"Copy!"

The second sheet ended with the paragraph:

> Under the present circumstances, when the units of the
> 2nd and 6th divisions are putting up practically no resist-
> ance to the enemy, thus acting detrimentally to the rein-
> forcements moved up in their support, it is to be expected
> that in the very near future the enemy will break through
> the Nikolayev Railroad. The resources of the Petrograd
> fortified region are inadequate for battle and its defenses
> have not been repaired. In view of the extremely serious
> threat to Petrograd, which has been created, I request you
> send at least two brigades of seasoned reinforcements to the
> region of Tosno at least in order to preclude the possibility
> of an advance by the enemy from the Gatchina side toward
> Tosno and to forestall his intention of seizing Petrograd.
> From today army headquarters are transferred to Petrograd.

"Copy!"

This was the first dispatch of the new army headquarters to the headquarters of the northwest front.

The communiqué from the front that day read—second from last paragraph:

After stubborn fighting our troops abandoned Gatchina in the direction of Yamburg.

Last paragraph:

In the region of Luga under pressure from the enemy our units are retreating to a line along the Windava railroad.

In houses there are staircases confused and unfrequented; pantries where, besides cooks, only mice go; barns, coach-houses and attics with doors which are closed even to dogs; passages, storerooms and the dead ends of corridors.

It is on these staircases, in these barns, in these attics, that lips whisper more distinctly and fists begin to show under coats. The neglected state of the coach-house, the silence of the barn, the emptiness of the corridor, where the most dangerous witness is a spider surrounded by the dusty, empty-bellied corpses of flies—these put courage into souls whose lot it is to tremble.

The lips whispered distinctly:

"From every window, flags! National flags!"

"From every attic, fireworks! Magnificent, festive fireworks!"

"From every basement, the shouts of the liberated! Joyful, ecstatic shouts!

"Around every corner, flowers! Fragrant, luxuriant flowers!"

"From everywhere! Everywhere!"

The lips whispered in attics and pantries of the fireworks, shouts and flowers, as if in answer to a command which stood the petrified capital on end. Fists were brandished in coach-houses and barns, in defiance of the summons pasted about the streets, which was persuading citizens that the gigantic city possessed sufficient machine guns, grenades, rifles and revolvers and that to destroy the White

Guardists only a few thousand men needed to decide not to surrender Petrograd.

A few thousand men decided.

But the Liteiny, as Andrei found it, seemed not to know this.

In the viscid darkness of the avenue, people flattened by the fog dragged sacks, bundles and baskets behind them.

They scurried to the sides and clung to the battered, hole-ridden streetcar, whose sagging buffers tore up wood-blocks and stones from the roadway.

Their panic-stricken eyes grasped the fearless words from scraps of a new order on the walls:

TO WORK!

EVERYONE TO THE RANKS!

SOUND THE ALARM, ENEMY AT THE GATES!

They nimbly picked up their bags again, tucked up skirts which were flapping in the mud and scattered in a line along the streetcar tracks.

They were saving themselves.

And suddenly, among these fugitives delirious with impending disaster, Andrei caught sight of a woman crossing the street with the measured tread of a clockwork doll. The woman was walking under an umbrella. She had a shawl wrapped around her and her dress was tidy. Folding her umbrella deliberately she bent her head and entered a doorway. Andrei followed her.

Above the door, beneath a gloomy lamp, he read:

> COME IN AND LISTEN
> TO THE WORD OF THE GOSPELS.
> WE INVITE YOU.
> ENTRANCE FREE TO ALL.

Behind benches set out as in a theater, in the semi-darkness of twilight, were crowds of kneeling women. A broad-shouldered man was speaking from a school desk. His words were distinct but were not linked by anything except his voice—sleek and slinking, matching the preacher's quiet movements.

". . . An active conscience is necessary to us in order that man settle not comfortably on the false feather beds of this life. And I know that my redeemer liveth, as it is said by the prophet Job. Brethren and sisters, eternity is guaranteed to us, we shall stand behind Christ. Because it is said in the Epistle to the Corinthians: *For Christ our Paschal Lamb is sacrificed for us.* Let us pray together, brethren and sisters, of our grief and our daily needs . . .

The speaker crossed his hands on the desk and laid his head on them. The black groups behind the benches swayed and grew still. Someone's muffled voice began to mutter something indistinct. Then sporadic words wriggled out of the muttering and began to wash around the room:

"Dear Lord, I am a poor woman. . . ."

"Lord, my daughter is frail. . . ."

Suddenly in the wash of cries and sobs Andrei made out a strangely familiar voice. He listened to it as he stepped forward, looking for the speaker. Right by the desk he distinguished a head thrown far back. The pince-nez on its nose trembled and was slipping downward, flashing rainbow sparks, while the head went higher and higher with each word:

"Lord! Forgive my son Lev and set him on the right path. . . . Son Lev . . . My Son Lev, who robbed his father and relatives, oh Lord. . . . And my second son, Aleksei . . . Lord . . ."

Someone choked in a spasm of weeping and shrill wails immediately began to spin over the bent, twitching heads in black shawls.

And only one head was still, like a stone: the head of the preacher lying high on the desk, with its broad back toward the brethren and sisters.

How did Andrei get in here? What urge had led him to follow the woman who resembled a clockwork doll? Where

was she now? Was it possible that—featureless, inaudible
—she had appeared in order to jolt Andrei from the path
which was so easy and cheering to follow?

He rushed to the exit. The insistent letters of the placard
collided with his eyes:

GO AND SIN NO MORE!

Away from here, away! Into the avenue! Into the avenue!
Into a cauldron of gray overcoats, into the line of march,
an eternal march—yes, would that this march were eternal!

A face with lips stretched to a wire slashed Andrei like a
knife with its keen gaze and turned toward a red soldier
running behind it:

"We'll still see!" heard Andrei.

"We'll still see!" cried the red soldier and laughed with
pleasure, overtaking his comrade at a trot.

"We'll still see," Andrei threatened someone and suddenly the sourish smell of bread was wafted to him, the smell
was hardly perceptible, but it acted on the heart like a
drug. Andrei looked about him in order to decide where to
go. Thinning fans of people were moving toward him. Their
faces were flat and sallow. Andrei caught the glance of
someone's colorless eyes. Behind their torpid, motionless
stare he caught sight of the savage pangs of hunger. And
at once something heavy fell upon his shoulders and he
staggered.

Hunger, hunger was marching down the whole avenue!
—it seemed to Andrei. All this confusion, all this running of
human bodies, all this endless marching of people in gray
overcoats was a marking time, a march around the black
skeleton of hungry death!

Hurry to a secret corner of your hovel, home, home!
Where there's a thick slice of bread.

In the case which Andrei had brought from Semidol
there was still a lot of bread. So much that it would have
been enough for a whole evening and a whole night. But
the case had remained on Shchepov's leather sofa. Andrei
had recalled this only twice during the whole day and he
knew that he would go to Shchepov, that there was no-

where else to go. But it was terrible to think that the time had already come to beg a night's lodging.

He wrenched himself from the spot, and the avenue carried him over the familiar dank, wooden cobbles.

In the house which was to become his shelter Andrei awaited Sergei Lvovich on the stairs, by the door of Shchepov's apartment.

But Sergei Lvovich took his time.

He was returning slowly from the communion of evangelical Christians, his hands folded behind his back, and he would stop before the ruined houses shaking his head. In his walk, which had been conditioned and broken by time, there still lurked the trace of a pensioner: he did not hurry but carried his worthy person of the fourth class without fuss or bother.

Before going to his apartment Sergei Lvovich called on the chairman of the house committee.

"How are you," he said, taking off his cap and sitting down. "For digging trenches a pound of bread is due. I came to ask if the bread has been allocated to me yet."

"But you didn't dig," replied the chairman.

"My apartment dug, according to the list. It doesn't matter who dug for the apartment. I am the tenant of the apartment, therefore, legally, I should be assigned a pound of bread. Besides, this is no time . . ."

And Sergei Lvovich tapped a cigarette against his thumb nail.

Petersburg made preparations to receive an eminent guest.

The eminent guest, preparing to enter the capital, lingered in the imperial summer residences. But his messengers and runners had already approached the capital's gates in order to ascertain whether the capital was ready to receive and honor its guest. The messengers and runners rarely returned from the gates to the summer residences because Petersburg—the city of imperial traditions—could never be caught unawares and because the capital knew exactly how to behave toward the ambassadors of eminent guests.

Petersburg made preparations to receive the eminent guest.

The institutes for the nobility—the Smolny and Kseninsky —experienced in the reception of eminent and extra-eminent personages, once proud of their past and now confident in the future, honorably placed themselves at the head of the capital's trembling anxieties and indefatigable labors. It was necessary to bedeck the whole city. They had to decorate the entrance, to erect triumphal arches, raise up rostrums, line up guards of honor, unfurl standards and well-deserved banners.

In every window there must be—flags! From every rooftop—fireworks! Around every corner—flowers!

Ah, a beautiful paper streamer is cut from barbed wire. And from its resilient ribbons the daintiest bows are tied in the buttonholes of the impresarios. And surely tapering shells, loaded with shot, will scatter like bright, gay confetti? And are not these fat bags full of wet sand convenient for building pavilions? Once upon a time the corks of matured *vin sec* had popped in such pavilions, but is the wailing crackle of a well-oiled machine gun inferior to corks?

The noble Smolny wove and cut a barbed streamer and the noble Kseninsky produced fantastic pavilions out of bags full of sand.

And now everything was ready and the confetti, bound in steel cases, calmly awaited its hour, and heads in red kerchiefs looked out from the pavilions and it remained only to pull the fuse on the eight-inch gun on the Ligovka in order to salute the entry of the eminent guest into Petersburg.

But the eminent guest did not enter the capital. He declined the honor. He had been misunderstood. He had not sought such a splendid welcome. He had never thought that his appearance would call forth such a fanfare. He had expected everything to be simpler. He saw that he was mistaken and he turned his back on the capital in order to depart forever—the poor, misunderstood, eminent guest.

But how annoying! What a warm welcome Petersburg had prepared for him!

Here is what the man with the croaking Eastern accent said to Andrei when time was found to utter something other than a command:

"The revolution needs a clerk. You know how to write—write."

Then Andrei yelled in a voice not his own:

"I don't want to write! I loathe messing about with bits of paper when men around me are fighting to the death!"

And the man with the accent replied in a calm voice, with a faint smile on his high-cheekboned face:

"Dear Comrade, why do you think that every man in the revolution has to fire a gun? Maybe your whole revolution is a paper one?"

And then, going to one side, he turned and added almost tenderly:

"The revolution doesn't like to be crossed. You must always be cheerful. . . ."

It is true that even at this time there were people who had not lost their gaiety.

The commissar of the division in which Andrei served was preparing to marry a pale little woman in a rabbit-fur coat. The commissar was hospitable, he liked people, his comrades and wartime brothers. And he wanted to make an occasion of his wedding, as is done in the steppes, out in the open, under the open sky. He did not have enough horses and he asked the division medical officer to lend him the plump little mare on which the medical officer rode about the city. The medical officer lent it: it was quieter in the city, the army had recovered and he could go about on foot for a day or two.

But a day or two passed and the mare was not returned to the medical officer. He was unable to meet the commissar and at last he thought of asking the commissar's wife about his horse—the pale little woman in the rabbit-fur coat.

"Mare?" said the woman in the fur coat with surprise. "My dear Doctor, but at that very time, at the wedding, we skinned it and shared it among our guests! If only you knew what guests we had!"

And she dissolved into laughter. . . .

If only Andrei had known how to laugh like that. Maybe his eyes would not then have sunk so deep and his walk would have been firmer and stronger? But every day disabled him, as a strong wind does a bird, and everything around him became strange and almost imperceptible.

And once, on a snowy evening on his way home, he stopped on a corner and looked around him in astonishment, as if he had been transported to these streets from another world. The wet snow was beating frenziedly against the brown, chipped walls. People, it seemed, were running about aimlessly and in nothing which surrounded Andrei could he discover the ordinary and simple meaning of a live city.

A girl with rags on her head, wearing a short dress and with something tucked under her arm, shifted from one long thin leg to the other beside a nailed-up door. Her face was not visible.

"What did you say, Citizen?"

A tall bony man fixed his empty eyes upon Andrei. His mouth was half open and water dripped onto his soaking shoulders from the loose brim of his hat.

"I believe you just said something?" he repeated.

"I did?" asked Andrei.

"You didn't say anything?"

The tall man came right up to Andrei's face and examined it carefully.

"Citizen, give me something for a piece of bread," he suddenly grumbled and his mouth opened still wider.

"Bread?" asked Andrei.

The man stood silent a short time, with face frozen and eyes bulging, then turned and quickly ran round the corner.

An old man went by, with his body bent forward and legs which dragged half a pace behind his body. His feet were wrapped in heavy wet rags and on the sidewalk behind him remained tracks like those of a mop. He stopped opposite the girl and asked her something. Then with a piercing cry she rushed to the other side of the road. Her long, thin legs flashed before Andrei with their naked knees gleaming wet. Andrei took several steps after the girl. She disappeared somewhere. A raucous clanging, at first muffled then sharp, increasing in frequency, engulfed the street. It was impossible to tell where it came from. Then suddenly a massive noise rolled over Andrei from overhead, from the sides, from out of the earth, and immediately died down, licking away the clanging which had engulfed the street.

At that moment someone ran up to Andrei and took him by the arm. He turned. The blind bull's-eye of a weak, dim and yellow headlight was staring him in the back. Vociferous womanish abuse sliced through the bedlam of hoarse bawling:

"The d-devil! I honked at him and he—a d-devil, that's a fact. . . ."

"What, is it you?" said someone's quiet voice.

The hand which had led Andrei, like a blind man, to the pavement remained outstretched. . . . Then Andrei understood something and wanted to thank someone, and like a blind man began to seek support with his extended hand.

And his hand encountered someone's thin cold fingers. He seized and drew them toward him.

"Thank you," he said.

A frightened trembling cry lashed him in the face:

"Andrei!"

He winced as from a blow, peering into the round black eyes which were before him.

"Andrei, is it you, Andrei?"

He rushed to the woman, seized her by the head—cold and plastered with wet hair—sought out her lips, pressed them to his own and became still.

"Rita," he said inaudibly, "how did you get here?"

"I came. I've been looking for you. . . ."

"Let's go, there are people here," he said, leading her into a side street.

And immediately the streets became distinct and everything acquired a sharp clarity.

"What nonsense," said Andrei.

Rita interrupted him hastily:

"What's the matter with you, you stood in the road like

a madman, I hardly recognized you. Are you unwell, Andrei?"

"Wait, you say you came to me?"

"Yes, Andrei. I couldn't go on any longer."

"Well of course you couldn't, you missed me too badly!"

"Andrei!"

"What about Andrei? What idiocy, what nonsense! And what if I'm going to the front today? And then, did you know I'd gone to the front? That I was at the front? How could you . . . No, this the devil . . ."

"Andrei . . ."

"Oh, cut it! What were you counting on? How did you know I was living here? What are you going to do?"

"I knew you were serving here. Why, two months went past. I thought . . ."

"And you thought I got four pounds of bread a day? You thought you'd conk out by the wayside somewhere? And finally, maybe I was dead? That is you thought I could have been killed? Well, if not killed, then could have died a hundred times from hunger?"

"Listen . . ."

"Well, where are you going now?"

"To your place."

He stopped, waved his arms and wanted to shout, but Rita forestalled him with a quiet, low groan:

"I've nowhere else, Andrei! . . ."

He breathed out the air with which he had been ready to shout and looked at her. Her eyes were moist and were embraced by the deadened blue circles of her lids. Her chapped lips twitched as though striving to pronounce some word.

"Of course, nowhere else," muttered Andrei, turning away from her but continuing to stand there.

"I wanted to tell you . . ." he heard that same groaning voice, falling away somewhere. He shuddered, then shivered with the cold, tucked his fingers into the sleeves of his overcoat and uttered the word which always cheered him:

"Nonsense!"

"I wanted to tell you why I came."

He didn't stir.

Then Rita leaned toward his arm and quickly said:

"I had to come. I'm pregnant."

Andrei jumped away and pressed against the wet wall. He stroked the slippery stone with his palms, his legs bent at the knees, and the tails of his damp, heavy overcoat trembled. He remained silent for a long time, his sunken eyes fixed upon some point above Rita's head. Then he whispered, barely audibly:

"How could you . . ."

"I'm not to blame, Andrei. . . ."

"No, no!" he exclaimed, breaking away from the wall. "How stupid! And in general . . ."

"Andrei!"

"No, no! I am saying, why didn't you say anything? That is, why didn't you say right away, as soon as I asked you?"

"But you didn't ask," she said in a wavering voice.

He laughed abruptly, extraordinarily, then seized her by the hand and led her quickly, almost at a run.

"What are we standing for? What were we standing for? What a fool you are! You should have . . ."

"But, Andrei, how could I have known that you . . ."

"That—what? What about me?"

She looked up into his eyes, bending her head somehow bird-like, and smiled without a word.

They walked along deserted streets, pressed closely to one another, and he carefully examined the road, walking around the loose stones and dully gleaming puddles.

Then he asked quietly:

"You're not cold, Rita?"

THE TANGLED BALL

Early in the morning Andrei bumped into the professor on the stairs. He recognized him by his size and by the movements of his head—short, twitching and frequent. And his face—it was possible to make it out on the landing, where the morning light had had time to gather—his face also twitched, cut up into little squares by deep transverse lines. He shook Andrei's hand and said in amazement:

"What miracles! You know, it's just unbelievable. As if you weren't alive but found yourself in some remarkable book. Day after day, page after page—from miracle to miracle."

Andrei listened, looking out of the window. To turn and look at this little man's winking eyes which flashed like tin-foil, while he continually contracted and expanded like a spring, was beyond Andrei's strength.

"An exceptional time!" exclaimed the professor, and moved closer to Andrei. "Tell me," he said insinuatingly, "you, yes you, young man, are you sure? Eh, sure? Just about yourself. When you talk to yourself alone, are you sure?"

He did not wait for an answer and exclaimed again hotly and hastily:

"I have no doubt, no doubt! I have never before experienced anything like it. It's something wonderful! I don't know why. Something is carrying me above the ground."

"I know that feeling," said Andrei in a hollow voice.

"You must certainly know! Even better than I! If I were in your place! Do you know I walked around Smolny a whole week. Walked and looked, only looked, nothing more. . . ."

The professor was silent for a moment, then began to laugh:

"Like a schoolboy on a date—every day at the appointed hour. And—do you believe me?—I go, I look at the house and I almost suffocate."

"But doesn't fatigue ever attack you?" asked Andrei dully.

The professor grew quiet.

"How can I tell you . . . of course. I am not a very healthy man. Although now even a healthy man . . ."

Furtively, almost guiltily, he looked sideways at Andrei.

"I heard that you have been joined by . . ."

And suddenly he quivered all over—from his short tiny legs to the minutest little swellings and squares on his face.

"I have been wanting to see you for a long time, in order

to . . . You see they brought me some flour from the country . . . some friends there, I used to . . ."

"No, why should you," said Andrei, scowling.

"I assumed that it was very hard for you now, with the arrival of your wife. . . ."

"Wife?" repeated Andrei and then answered himself: "Oh yes, Rita. . . . No, why should you, you yourself . . ."

The professor touched his arm with the roughened ends of his fingers.

"I give you my word that you will not be depriving me. I have a lot. I'll bring you some, I'll bring it, all right?"

He rushed upstairs and, leaning over the banister, kept shouting restively:

"I'll bring you some, I'll bring you some! . . . No point in being formal. . . . I'll bring you some!"

Rita would wrap herself in a shawl and perch with her legs up on the sofa, sitting out the gloomy evenings one after another. It was essential to husband the warmth, stored up under the shawl, and for hours she did not move.

She did not make a sound, but her face—white, with its cracked dry lips and smoldering motionless gaze—was visible from everywhere, from every corner, as if the room were filled with dim mirrors which reflected nothing but this face.

She did not turn around, but she saw Andrei as clearly as if she had been holding his head in her hands. And Andrei, sitting with his back to her, saw the fine features of her face, and the folds of her shawl, and her knees resting against her chin, and her hair scattered over the shawl.

They were awaiting the child.

It was supposed to appear in some indefinite, distant future. It was supposed to appear after it had sucked up the last drop of its mother's blood and after it had devoured the last drop of her fat.

Fat had once been carried about in barrels, bound with thick hoops; fat once used to lie around in unweighed and unmeasured lumps on counters, which it warped by its weight: cellars and basements were once crammed, jammed and stopped up with fat; stray dogs once did not eat fat, they had lost their taste for it—yes, yes, that same fat.

In order to receive a tiny piece of it weighing nothing, one had to wait for seven endless days. In order to store up one drop of it one had to husband warmth, to husband the insignificant strength of flabby muscles, while hiding inside a shawl, as in a cozy thicket. One drop needed for the child who would irrevocably appear in the indefinite future —who would appear as a freak, with soft, bending bones, with no nails on its fingers or toes.

For the sake of this freak, for the sake of this imperceptible, invisible fabric growing into a freak, Rita sat immobile, hunched into a ball, and Andrei was afraid to break the silence for fear of dispersing the warmth she had stored up.

But the silence was broken by Sergei Lvovich.

He flew into the room, folded his arms and said threateningly through his teeth:

"Sss-s-oo, sss-o-o!"

His pince-nez trembled and slipped downward. He threw his head back.

"Ss-so-o!" he repeated, tapping his sole on the floor. "So this is how you, Andrei Gennadyevich, have rewarded me for my hospitality? Not bad. It's in the order of things today. You think, in all probability, that you are dealing with a fool? You are mistaken, mis-ta-ken!"

"What's that?" said Andrei.

"Ah, you don't un-der-stand? You hadn't thought of it? You don't say? What innocence!"

"Well, say what the matter is!" shouted Andrei, pushing his chair away and straightening up.

Then Sergei Lvovich strode toward Andrei, thrust his hands determinedly in his pockets and poured out words long since prepared:

"You are very cunning, young man. You make use of every moment in order to augment your own budget at my expense. I have only to turn away and something of mine disappears. You are pleased to overlook nothing, like an old cook. You . . ."

"Why are you silent?" cried Rita.

"But what can he say? What can he say when just now, only a quarter of an hour ago, while I ran down to the shop, an ounce of my butter disappeared! I had no time to lock up, I hurried to the shop, leaving it in a basin on the table, in salt water, so big, a piece of about half a pound. I marked the top of it with little crosses. I always do that. I came back and I looked—the crosses were intact, but the butter had somehow diminished. I tried weighing it. An ounce short. Oh crafty, crafty, young man! Only I'm craftier than you. You were so good as to take a knife and cut such a slice from the bottom. It's floating, he says, the piece is floating, who will realize about the bottom if everything on top is all right."

"Andrei!" groaned Rita.

"Is that gratitude for the fact that I, you might say, picked you up off the street? Is that gratitude for the fact that, so to say, your wife . . ."

Andrei reeled as if someone had pushed him, went up to Sergei Lvovich, grasped him by the shoulders, turned him and led him out of the room. Sergei Lvovich not only put up no resistance but even hurried somehow, forgetting to close his mouth and turning sideways in the door in order to go through more easily. But once through the door he stamped his foot and screamed shrilly:

"Get out of my house, get out!"

Andrei closed the door and looked at Rita. Then he jerked open the door again, clutched his head in his palms and ran out through the scream which reverberated along the corridor.

On the staircase a cold draught bathed his face. He stopped. To return to the room for his overcoat and cap was impossible. He went up a floor higher and knocked at the professor's apartment. No one responded. He began to knock louder, listening closely to the knocks dying away in the apartment and getting lost in the silence. Then he began to pound the door violently with his boots and a heavy rumbling boomed along the whole flight of stairs from attic to basement.

Someone's voice sounded behind him.

"Are you looking for the professor?" he heard and turned around.

"Yes, for him."

"Doesn't he answer?"

"No."

"He's always home at this time."

"Yes, I know."

"Well, knock again."

Andrei knocked. He listened. Everything was still.

Behind Andrei a chain clinked and there appeared in the darkness a tall, slightly stooping man.

"That's strange, it's some time since I saw him," he said, and touched the door.

"Perhaps . . ." began Andrei.

"Perhaps, of course, perhaps anything," interrupted the tall man. "Let's go to the committee."

"Surely you don't think . . ." began Andrei again; and again the tall man interrupted him:

"Think? Of course I think. . . . Why not think?"

By way of the dark stairs and the narrow yard which echoed one's voice, by way of porches in which the wind whistled, they walked just the two of them—then three, four, five, dawdling and lingering everywhere, as if afraid to begin the business.

Then they knocked for a long time at the professor's apartment, listened, and knocked again. They asked one another when they had seen the professor for the last time, could he not have gone away somewhere or spent the night somewhere.

At last a blunt chopper with a battered blade ate into the jointure of the doors which crackled dryly as if ignited. And then as if according to a signal, they all began to interrupt one another with advice on how best to break down the door. But as soon as the lock gave way and it became evident that with the next effort the door would fly open, they all fell silent again.

Andrei entered the apartment second, behind the chairman of the committee. They went from room to room, fearfully and without speaking. They struck matches, looked for switches behind doorposts and tried to get some light. Again they lit matches, inspected the empty corners and went farther.

A pink light slipped out when they tried the door of the room farthest from the corridor.

"There we are," said the chairman and turned to Andrei, "we never thought to look at the windows from outside."

"But they're curtained," retorted someone.

"Well hurry up!"

The chairman opened the door with arm outstretched. All gathered cautiously at the entrance.

The dull light of the table-lamp fell in an even circle on the books, the floor, the bed.

The professor was lying on his bed with his head thrown back and his sharp, pointed chin tilted up. He was lying at attention and had become long, as if he had grown since he had last been among the living. The wrinkles on his face had been smoothed out, the little bumps and squares, so mobile and clearly etched during his lifetime, had disappeared: he had grown younger. On his smooth forehead lay a peaceful spot of light.

They all approached him quietly, examined him carefully and then dispersed about the room, not looking at one another. And since no one was speaking and there was nothing to say, Andrei remarked almost inaudibly:

"The mice have been up to something. . . ."

Then they all turned their heads and with interest began to examine a flour bag resting against the bookshelf. It was gnawed on all sides, the torn shreds of canvas were hanging down on the floor and narrow white tracks led over the parquet to the baseboard.

"That must be cleaned up," said the chairman and immediately three men rushed to the sack and dragged it out.

In the course of a year, maybe two, there occurred clashes, quarrels, fights, and even murder took place, although none of the culprits wanted to take such a sin upon himself. In the end it reached the consciousness of these people that they were living in a new era and that the world from that date rejected all that was past and already experienced. It was decided to found a guild on the basis of professional solidarity. True, this guild was doomed to a secret existence: it was impossible to mention its true aims even in front of the warden. But so much the firmer and stricter were its unwritten regulations.

The cemetery was split up into seven sections and each section was placed under the supervision of two gravediggers. Here it is necessary to say a few words about the cemetery itself, however unrewarding its description. The cemetery extended over a broad plain, behind a cheerless sprawling suburb, and its old part was overgrown with poplars. The church was barely visible through a thick screen of trees. The new sections were deserted, if it is possible to call an immense suburb of grave mounds deserted. Around the church clustered ancient mausoleums, towers and heavy gravestones.

But it was not a question of mausoleums or of splendid monuments. This section, once the most profitable, had in recent times fallen into decay, like a village graveyard, and in two years had received only one fresh corpse, and even that was profitless—it was the corpse of the cemetery's father-deacon, who had died of ennui.

No monuments had been erected for a long time, nor had crypts with towers been built. But crosses had still not gone out of use and crosses, precisely crosses, had helped the gravediggers become aware of their own nature and found a guild for the systematic protection of their interests in the transitional era.

Crosses, as, by the way, is well-known, are cast-iron, iron and, for the most part, wooden. Cast-iron ones are unsuitable for anything practical. They are essentially junk, like stone headstones, monuments and towers. Fortunately, cast-iron has become legendary, together with classy, or class, funerals, and the cross reserves have been reinforced in recent years only with iron and wood. Forged iron crosses with tight scrolls like church railings are no more practical than cast-iron. On the other hand, hollow crosses made of sheet iron, decorated usually as imitation birch wood, are easily adaptable for use in the home. Without any special preparation anyone can make a chimney joint out of them for their iron stove, or a samovar chimney or a convenient drain. There were a good many such crosses in the area of the sections some distance from the poplars, and given an intelligent use of them the supply could have lasted a long time.

The difficulty of apportioning the sections among the members of the guild sprang from the fact that the number of wooden crosses in each part of the cemetery was not equal. Therefore the guild was forced to undertake considerable preliminary labor in taking inventory of the property left behind after the old regime. But in the process of this work new difficulties were revealed because, unlike other areas of public life, in the area of cemetery affairs the old regime was not rotten, so to speak, all through, but only partially, although in the final reckoning more rotten crosses were found than sound ones. However, their now awakened conscientiousness assisted the guildsmen to come to a wise decision: two rotten crosses were made equal to one unrotten one—on the calculation that one stout log gives as much heat as two rotten ones.

When the foundations of the society had been thus laid, the gravediggers proposed to the cemetery sexton that he entrust them with guarding the crosses which were being wantonly plundered.

The sexton consented. After that the devastation of the graveyard was accomplished systematically and there reigned among the gravediggers that philosophical contemplativeness which was long since noted in this profession and which is completely characteristic of it alone.

Two days later, after the death of the professor had been discovered, a shabby young student came to the graveyard and made inquiries in the office as to how they could speed the burial of a man long dead. In the office they began to talk about the system of receiving orders for coffins and graves, about registrations, bookings and turns. It ended with the student being sent to the cemetery to look for the gravediggers. He met one of them and told him his business. The gravedigger named a price which horrified the student.

"And who is the dead man?" asked the gravedigger.

"A scholar," replied the student.

"It must have been from hunger?"

"No, not from hunger."

"If it wasn't from hunger then there must be something to pay with."

"That's the point, there is nothing. If there were I wouldn't haggle."

"Cheaper than that's impossible. If you can't, then take your turn, in about a week—or a week and a half. . . ."

"I haven't got that much money," said the student.

"We're not volunteers, we have our fee. . . . It's up to you."

"No, we can't pay that much money," repeated the student decisively.

The gravedigger thought a while and asked:

"D'you want a Christian burial or a civil one?"

"A civil one."

"Then it's dearer."

"Why is that?"

"How shall I put it. . . . From a Christian one you get some sort of profit: maybe they'll tell you to watch the cross, so's no one swipes it. . . . Well, d'you think you can do it? There's a shortage of firewood. . . . But a civil burial— what's the good of that? You bury 'em and that's that. The other day we buried an airman, and on his grave they put an oak propeller from his plane. What can you get out of that, out of a propeller? You can't rip anything off it, it's like iron. For the money you're giving, a civil burial's not worth while."

"What can we do?"

"For that much money a grave can be dug—at a pinch. But the burial's your own affair."

That is how it was decided: the gravediggers would dig a hole but the dead man would be lowered and buried by his mourners.

To show their last respects to the professor came four students, a lean red-bearded man who resembled a school-teacher, and the university porter.

The frost that day had partly broken and it was drizzling a fine gray rain, which seemed to come through a sieve. A knot of people, huddling from the cold and with a drooping wet red banner, awaited the coffin by the gate. The occupants of the house carried the coffin out, placed it on the cart, crossed themselves and gave orders for it to start. Behind the cart walked the students with the banner, the lean teacher-like man, the porter, Andrei and the chairman of the house committee. And since it was difficult to carry the wet banner they laid it on the coffin and from the jolting it clung tightly to the lid and stuck on like upholstery.

When they were filling in the grave, Andrei stood to one side, looking over the numberless mounds with occasional crosses. He heard the rain-washed clods of earth fall into the trench and he heard the noises of their falling become shorter and sharper as they came closer to the surface of the ground. And it seemed to him that the professor, who had appeared so unexpectedly in his life, had carried out of it some kind of last opportunity to talk of what was most important—of just what, Andrei hardly knew. But he had a kind of feeling that someone's cruel hand was holding him by the throat and he realized that it would not release him until he spoke out what was most important.

He left the graveyard last of all, stooping, dull, pierced by the twilight fog. He did not walk but dragged himself, almost crawling along the deserted, endless streets of the suburbs. He resembled a sick man who has been thrown out of the sick bay when he has hardly had time to get over his illness.

At home Rita opened the door to him.

"A soldier is waiting for you."

"A soldier?"

"Yes. He didn't give a name, says you know him. . . ."

"Strange . . ." said Andrei slowly and indifferently and went into the room, still the same as he had been on the street, worn out and dully dragging his drooping body.

A soldier was warming himself by the stove, with his face to the fire. His overcoat hung on a chair near the stove. He was sitting on his haunches and rubbing his hands. When the door creaked he raised his head, the light ran down from his forehead to his half-open mouth, which was surrounded by a fine circle of hardly noticeable wrinkles, and his lips twisted into a semblance of a smile.

"So here you are," he said and got up from the floor.

Andrei discerned his guest only when the light played on his lips. He seized hold of the doorpost. All softness in him disappeared almost immediately. From an enfeebled and stooping man he turned into a wooden statue, straight as a column. Rita entered and closed the door, pushing him away. He took only one step and again froze.

"How are you," said the soldier, going up to Andrei.

Andrei's hands started backward as if he wanted to cross them behind his back, then he threw a glance at Rita and quickly shook the calm, outstretched hand of his guest. The soldier also looked at Rita and bowed in her direction:

"I haven't the honor of knowing the name of . . . your . . . ah . . . She was very kind. Here you see, I'm drying myself. . . . I think, wouldn't it be better for us . . ."

And he said evenly in German:

"It will be more convenient for us not to speak Russian."

Seemingly as a result of these unaccustomed clipped words of a foreign language, Andrei reeled and asked swiftly:

"How did you find me?"

"I saw you on the street. I'd recognize you among a battalion of soldiers. Then I followed you."

"Why haven't you left yet?"

"That's a long story."

"What do you want from me? Why have you come?"

Andrei squeezed these questions out of himself with such a strain that he seemed to be trying to suppress a desperate cry with them.

"I could have counted on a more enthusiastic welcome," replied his guest and his screwed-up eyes slid over Andrei's face.

"Undress, you're wet," he added condescendingly and shrugged his shoulders. "How agitated you are! I look at things more calmly. Once and for all I said to myself that I could die at any minute. I am prepared for the very worst —for death. Therefore I am always calm. What can be more dangerous than death?"

"It's probably so, if you love nothing in life," muttered Andrei, unbuttoning his overcoat.

He hung it on the back of a chair, moved it closer to the stove, slowly, leisurely, taking care with every movement, and sat down.

"How is it you didn't go away?"

His guest lowered himself beside him.

"I reached Moscow with great difficulty. About a month went by. I made my way alone. In Moscow I decided to make use of my new name for the first time. It didn't turn out to be quite suitable. I don't want to say anything bad about its former owner, but someone compromised this name before me. I must confess," grinned the guest, stroking Andrei with his laughing gaze, "I must confess that I thought at one time of you. . . ."

"Did they find out?" asked Andrei in a whisper.

"They found out," said the guest.

Andrei leaped up, rushed to Rita and mumbled in a terrible fright:

"They found out, my God! Rita, they found out! Rita, understand, they found out. . . ."

Rita was sitting on the bed as always, in her shawl, with her chin on her knees.

"Andrei," she said, darting toward him and freeing her hands from the shawl, "I don't understand, what do you mean? I beg you. . . ."

"Ah, you don't have to understand," he groaned, rushing back to his chair, "you don't have to understand anything! Have they really found out?"

The guest was silent for a while, then, as if dawdling on purpose, hesitating and pausing, he said:

"However, your self-control didn't last long. You would have been caught long ago in my place. I, as you see, remained safe."

Andrei seized him by the sleeve:

"But tell me, God damn you, tell me! Did they find out?"

"Here, better this way," said the guest and his mouth again grimaced the semblance of a smile.

"They found out," he said disdainfully, "but I can't say with any certainty what exactly it was they found out.

Probably it became known to them that I was passing myself off as someone else. But who I am in reality they can only suppose. As far as you're concerned . . ."

"My God," groaned Andrei again.

"As far as you're concerned I can say nothing. At one time I thought it was you who had compromised my new name. But then I decided that this would have been risky for you."

"Risky?"

The guest looked intently at Andrei.

"Yes. Even if you had wished to give me up in order somewhat to ease your own situation. Then I remembered that you are a Russian. To give up and to betray are not in character for Russians, as far as I have studied them."

"I have no inclination to philosophize on national themes. I would like you to say what you think . . . what in your opinion . . . what is known. . . ."

"Ha, ha! How well you began and how mixed up you end! You want to know whether the role that you played has become known. . . ."

"Well yes, yes! The role that I . . . isn't it all the same?" interrupted Andrei. "Tell me!"

"Judging by the fact that you are strolling peacefully about such a large city, they don't suspect you of anything. In general it seems to me that the affair was managed successfully. I am almost sure of that. In any case, here they included me in a troop train without any obstacles at all."

"What? You were . . . you named yourself?" cried Andrei and seized the shoulders of his interlocutor.

"That's to say not myself. . . ."

"Konrad Stein?"

"Calm yourself, my dear friend. There is no danger at all from that direction. Konrad Stein no longer exists."

"Doesn't exist?" Andrei started back.

"Konrad Stein is dead."

"I don't understand a thing!"

"Now listen. In Moscow everything could have come out. I got out in time. I found myself in Klin, from there I went to Tver. There I did casual labor. I had a comrade, a wonderful guy, a Berliner. We slept all over the place, we had no

fixed address. We lived wherever we could get work. Nowhere were we actually known. So that when this Berliner
died, everything came out of itself. I took his papers and
gave him mine."

Andrei sat silently, seeming not to listen.

The guest looked into his eyes and, as if he had just realized something, said:

"No, it wasn't that at all! Who do you take me for? I
forgot to say that this Berliner went down with typhus. I
looked after him for a week and a half. A wonderful guy."

Andrei rose.

"That means that the affair of Konrad Stein ended with
his death?"

"In all probability."

"That means we're quits?"

The guest leaped quickly to his feet, hunched himself and
slowly spaced the keen, cold words:

"No, we're not quits yet, Comrade Startsov."

"What do you need from me?" cried Andrei again.

The guest shook his head, arranged his face into an affectionately mocking smile and, going up to Andrei, took
him by the elbow.

"My dear friend, I speak like that because I feel myself
obligated. You have done everything that a kind heart
could do. But we're still not quits. I promised to deliver from
you a letter to your fiancée. I consider it my duty. I have
even remembered her name: Fräulein Marie Urbach, from
Bischofsberg, isn't it? Why are you silent? It seems I was not
mistaken? Fräulein Marie Urbach, isn't it?"

Andrei covered his face with his hands.

"But you see I mislaid your letter. That is I didn't mislay
it, but gave it to this dead Berliner together with the papers
of Konrad Stein. . . ."

"You've gone out of your mind!" said Andrei hoarsely,
gasping for breath. "You know if they find my letter together with the papers of Konrad Stein . . ."

"Well, what's the matter with you, to whom will it occur
to link your name with Konrad Stein?"

"Don't make fun of me! Don't you dare to make fun of
me!"

"I am saying what I think."

"The papers will certainly be sent to Semidol, to Kurt! Then Kurt will understand everything immediately!"

"I hadn't thought of that, I must confess. . . ."

"Listen, you . . . devil. . . . Listen! Find someone else to play the fool with! Don't forget that you are in my hands. . . ."

The guest wagged a protruding finger before Andrei's eyes.

"But I advise you, too, not to forget that you are in my hands. Yes . . . But whatever our disagreement," he expanded into a smile again, "surely you can feel that I am eternally grateful to you and am ready to repay you however you like?"

"How was it you couldn't think of . . ."

"I was joking, my dear friend; believe me, I was joking. I gave only Stein's papers to the dead man. Nothing more."

"Do you still have the letter? Give it to me, give it!"

"No. I tore up the letter so as not to harm you accidentally in any way."

"Ah, I don't believe you, I don't believe a single word!"

Andrei ran from corner to corner, clasping his head with his hands and rocking it as if in pain. The guest followed him with screwed-up eyes and said slowly, seeming to spear his words like bait on a hook:

"Why are you worrying, my dear friend? Is it really difficult to write another letter? It will afford you the pleasure of talking an extra time with your beloved. I give you my word that as soon as I return home I'll seek out Fräulein . . . Marie Urbach—that's it, I think?—I'll hand her the letter and tell her all I know about you."

"Do you know Marie?" asked Andrei, suddenly ceasing to run.

The guest fell silent and looked point-blank at Andrei. "No."

"Don't tell her anything about me," said Andrei, coming face to face with his guest.

"But you yourself asked me."

"And now I am asking you not to do it. Don't seek out Marie. It's not necessary."

The guest again fell silent, then clapped Andrei on the shoulder, nodded to Rita and began to laugh.

"We completely forgot about the lady. I understand you perfectly. But you are worrying for nothing. Fräulein Urbach will learn nothing of this."

And he nodded to Rita again.

"Let's talk business," said Andrei, stepping in front of Rita. "Why did you come to me?"

"Let's talk business," echoed the guest in Andrei's tone of voice. "I came to spend the night with you. Tomorrow they are sending me with the troop train. I am avoiding being with lots of people."

"Good. Give me your word that you will leave me in peace for good."

"I give you my word."

Andrei left the room with long strides.

"Sergei Lvovich," he said, going to the landlord's room, "a comrade has to spend the night with me. It's essential. I'll put him in the next room, on the sofa."

Sergei Lvovich wrung his hands.

"Stop," continued Andrei insistently, "no objections. He must stay. It'll be no good otherwise. Do you hear? And—mum's the word. Not a peep to anyone. Thank you."

He turned and went out, not noticing that Sergei Lvovich was covering himself with quick, frightened crosses.

Andrei led his guest into the next room, showed him the sofa, shut the door and returned to his own room.

There he stood motionless for a few seconds, passed his hand over his head and wiped his forehead, cheeks and neck. Then he clenched his fists and said to himself:

"He knows her, he knows, he knows!"

He staggered, went to the bed, laid his head on Rita's knees. Then he closed his eyes.

Rita embraced his head and bent over him. A burning drop fell on his lips. Not moving his lids, he asked quietly:

"What is it?" and licked his salty lips. "If only we could live again from the beginning. . . . Unravel the tangle, follow the thread back to the fateful hour and act differently. Completely differently . . ."

Rita sobbed loudly and laid her cheek on his shoulder.

"My darling, darling . . ."

"What is it?" he asked again.

"Who is this man, tell me? What did you talk about?"

He did not reply for a long time.

It was quiet; behind the window sounded distant rumbling noises. Slowly, unwillingly, the electric light went out.

Andrei turned his head, buried his face in Rita's knees and—to the knees, to the dress, to the close warmth of her legs—he said: "That I can't tell anyone. Not anyone."

A CHAPTER ON
NINETEEN FOURTEEN

CUPID'S CENTRIFUGE

"Belegte Brötchen!"*

"Warme Würstchen!"†

"Bier, Bier, Bier, gefälligst!"‡

"S-s-simplicissimus, Berliner Tageblatt, Lustige Blätter!"§

"Woche, Woche, Woche!"§

"Bier, Bier, Bier!"

"Belegte Brötchen, warme Würstchen!"

"Zigarren, Zigarren, Zigaretten!"

"Kladderadatsch, Kladderadatsch!"§

"Einsteigen!"‖

Light blue sheets of cigar smoke tremble under the roof and gently enshroud the buzzing voices. Voluminous stomachs, perspiring bald pates, white skirts, bared brawny elbows, and large rounded breasts beneath laces and crochet-work sway smoothly in their seats.

Behind the windows the portly fatherland sails by, bathed and blessed by the sun.

In Erlangen the magnificent, buzzing, bedizened train spilled out into the station and flowed down along the narrow street to the other end of the town.

Andrei and Kurt separated from the crowd and went into

*Sandwiches.
†Hot dogs.
‡Beer, beer, have some beer.
§The names of newspapers and magazines, etc.
‖All aboard!

the university park. Here it was quiet, warm shadows lay on the paths, and ash and oak trees screened the sky. On their trunks gleamed yellow polished plaques with Latin inscriptions, and similar plaques stuck up on poles rammed into flower beds. It smelt of the well-fed, satiated earth and —from somewhere—of fresh oil paint.

"Do you have that peaceful feeling," asked Kurt, "which puts you at rest—the feeling of being at home? We are content with trifles because they are our trifles. I assure you I'm glad I came here. A nice, foolish holiday, a nice, foolish habit. Once again I look at this ash tree here, so old, tumble-down and spongy. The fungus on it was as high as my waist last year. Now you can see it's crept higher. . . . But there's the entrance to the dissecting-room. Let's go, I'll show you the museum."

From the door leading into the park, the cool, sweet smell of iodoform drifted over the ground. In the room they entered stood a large galvanized trunk, which had been placed in a niche in the damp wall. Its lid was slightly open.

Kurt opened it. Lying in the trunk were human legs and arms with the skin stripped off, pieces of muscle turned blue, white bones with sinews pulled off, like bast; and purple, black and grayish entrails—intestines, liver, lungs. In a corner of the trunk, illuminated by the daylight which penetrated through the door from the park, two heads huddled together. The back of one head had been scalped and the skull seams ran over the head in a thin, blood-stained, jagged line. The neck of the other head—hairless and sturdy—was embraced, tie-like, by the swollen blue arm of a child. Here and there little piles of some powder were turning yellow.

"Let's go," said Andrei.

Kurt looked silently into the trunk.

"Let's go, you'll suffocate here."

Kurt lowered the lid and, smiling, quietly took Andrei by the arm.

They passed through a light, spacious room, set out with tall narrow tables, covered with glass. The tables were washed clean, the floor shone and a slight chilly draught, smelling of camphor, wandered from door to door. The semi-darkness of a vaulted corridor led to a broad stair case. On the landing sat a caretaker beside a small table. He took off his cap and asked:

"Do the gentlemen wish to see the museum?"

Then he moved forward.

Glass cases stretched one behind the other. In the cases glass jars were drawn up on glass shelves according to height and diameter, with human organs prepared in surgical spirit. Glass, spirit, and blue, gray, red pieces, threads, fibers and fragments of the human body were all that filled the high, spacious halls.

The sun poured unchecked through the clean windows; and over the walls, ceiling and floor, over the dresses, hands and faces of the people hovered fiery, multicolored spectra, refracted by the cases, the shelves, the jars and the spirit.

Suddenly the caretaker stopped, put one foot back, thrust the thumb of his right hand between the buttons of his uniform and opened his mouth deliberately:

"The embryological section. It has the highest number of specimens in the whole world."

Here the yellowish fragments of foetuses were swimming in small jars hardly distinguishable from one another in size—a whole assembly of unborn souls. Then there stretched tight rows of tadpole-like manikins with thin little legs and web-fingered hands against their stomachs. At the end—in jars the size of buckets—children were regarding their little knees, just like those which mothers see by their beds when they wake after delivery. Farther, in another hall, pieces of brain showed dully in the sun and behind them, under a special glass case, a human head was settled on the bottom of a broad glass jar.

It had a low forehead, and right across it went the stitches of a carelessly sewn scar. The brown eyes were open and the pupils were distended and fixed on some point situated, in all probability, directly in front of them. Over its upper lip and on its cheeks short, dark, thick hairs were sticking out in different directions—they had been shaved no more than a week before his death. And the

whole face, the chopped-off piece of neck and the ears
were dark blue. Beneath the case stood a plaque:

THE HEAD OF THE RENOWNED MURDERER

KARL EBERSOCKS

(THE LAST PUBLIC EXECUTION

IN NUREMBERG)

"My father was present at that execution," began the
caretaker, placing one foot backward, "and if the gentlemen wish . . ."

"Listen," said Andrei suddenly, "what the devil exactly
are we looking at all this for?"

Kurt threw back his head.

"This is a celebrated museum."

"I came here for the carousels not for corpses."

"We've got time for the carousels too. But this
museum . . ."

"To the devil with the museum, to the devil with Karl
Ebersocks, I want air, sunshine!"

There is lots of air in Erlangen.

To inhale it, sitting on a balcony with a pipe in one's
mouth and with a cup of coffee before one, is a pleasure of
which only small towns can boast.

At midday, when the peaceful shady side of main street
is clearly revealed and when rugs, pillows and mattresses
are hanging from every window, the Erlangen balconies
are occupied by students half lying in sloping armchairs.

From the university park drift the light scents of flowering
trees and from below come coolness and moisture from the
lively stream. The sky has ascended infinitely high and
the little town feels easy, pleasant and comfortable. The
roads and sidewalks are deserted.

"Heh-heh!" sounds a loud voice from a balcony. "Heh-
heh! Erich! How are you getting on after yesterday at the
casino?"

"Don't laugh, sonny: during the night my waist grew five
centimeters. . . ."

"Ha-ha!"

And now from balcony to balcony, from one end of the street to the other:

"Heh, heh, friend! What are you cackling about?"

"Erich is now a surgical case: he's had an expansion of the waist!"

"Ha-ha!"

"Fraternity Alpha is against a radical operation. Try using a bougie."

"And what do you prescribe for slight hoarseness?"

In the narrow side streets, from house to house:

"On main street they're looking for second-hand trousers; waist—a hundred and fifty centimeters."

"Ha-ha!"

Behind the balconies in low, curtained, carpeted rooms diligent landladies are applying boot polish to their boarders' shoes. In the university laboratories and offices caretakers are unhurriedly rinsing test tubes, retorts and flasks. In the spacious hall they are putting away rapiers, sabers, swords and spadroons and placing them in mounts.

"Heh-heh, Otto! What d'you say about our Erich? . . ."

The lacy, flashy and décolleté'd guests were still proceeding down main street toward the stream. But there was no noise and the tendrils of tobacco smoke on the balconies quietly ascended the smooth walls.

"How peaceful, how infinitely peaceful," said Kurt.

He was walking with uncovered head, slowly, lovingly examining every nook and cranny, as if seeking something long since lost. Andrei was silent.

Not a single one of the walks which the friends made in the years to come was as voluntary or as aimless as the trip to Erlangen. That is why we are in no hurry to run ahead and why we are walking joyfully step by step along the street, to the end of the town, over the bridge and farther—onto the hill, covered by a dense grove of trees. Who knows, maybe this walk is a last respite, which only death can exceed.

The hill, wrapped like a head in a shawl in thickets of lindens, birches and maples, was spinning in a living funnel of sound. Sounds elbowed one another on the spot, flew from side to side, curled snake-like around the trees and spread underfoot. Here were all the instruments thought up by east and west, made by hand and in the factory: mechanical ones, wind ones, stringed ones and percussion ones. And they piped, growled, honked, chattered, sang and wailed all simultaneously, and without stopping for a single moment. All the operettas and operas, mazurkas and waltzes, marches and gallops ever composed in the world, not counting solemn oratorios, sad cantatas, rhapsodies, minuets, polonaises and songs—they all strove with the greatest diligence and improbable fortissimo to announce their presence here, on this hill, which was covered shawl-wise with thickets of linden and maple.

And the hill was spinning, spinning.

On the top of it, along the length of an avenue, were crowded side-shows, panoramas, movie-shows, hypnotic cabinets, swing-boats, shooting galleries, strength-testing and sports halls, pavilions with horoscope readers and grottoes with fortune-tellers. Every person at this fair was jammed into the crowd like the wadding in a shell and was indisputably glad to be able to turn his head in all directions.

"Oh, most lovely ladies, most honorable gentlemen! I call on you to make a superhuman effort: stop before me for only two minutes. The effort must be made in order to hold off the pressure of the rams striving to take your places. You won't want to yield your places to the rams, gentlemen! One minute's attention. You see before you suspenders, whose modest appearance leads simpletons and yokels to despair. But we know that true virtue is always modest. Look, I stretch these suspenders with all my strength, I rip them, I tear them with my teeth like a lion from the Hamburg zoo, I tie knots with them, I chop them with an ax, look—ach, a-ach, hah!—I lift a weight of twenty-five kilos with them! Look—they only become more elastic, softer and pleasanter, not changing their color, their strength or their attractiveness in the least. Wait, wait! I put them in water, I soap them, I scrub them with a brush. . . ."

"Come here, come here, young lady! Here is a parasol whose mission is to protect your incomparable skin from the sun's heat. Let's try pouring water over it, let's try turning it inside out, let's try breaking its handle, let's try pushing a finger through it—in vain! Napoleon the Great used this kind of silk to make a dress for his second wife—his favorite wife, as has been established by the science of history. If this parasol is rolled up with an expert hand, it becomes as thin as a sewing needle, through the eye of which the camel entered the kingdom of heaven. If your grandmother had seen it, not the camel of course . . ."

"O-la, o-la! Here are people ready to swallow what they're told by any old windbag! Thank God the trees protect you from the sun. Why spend money on parasols? On the other hand, the Erlangen town council has thrown all the dust off its streets into your open mouths and it wouldn't hurt you to wash them out with genuine lemonade, with ice and pure sugar. . . ."

"My dear people, in the name of civilization and good relations between allied German monarchies—just half a minute's attention! A small gold chain, invented by a professor . . ."

"How long have women been wearing pants with suspenders? That's enough of listening to this suspender-merchant, the devil take my after-dinner nap. . . ."

"It's beginning, it's beginning!"

"You will see a man who has been fed all his life on old leather soles. You will see demonstrated . . ."

"Five hundred marks to anyone who can prove that his own hands have touched a midget smaller than Pondi-Rondi-Kax, height nineteen centimeters and weight . . ."

Purple-faced barkers, streaming with sweat and saliva, drink a shot of liquor and again bawl out hoarse yells, pumping the veins on their necks and foreheads full of heavy blue blood.

"It . . . is . . . be-ginning!"

"It . . . is . . . be-e-gin-ning!"

The shriek of parrots, the roar of performing donkeys, phonographs, organs, barrel-organs, bands, orchestrions, pianos and solitary, piercing violins. But above all this is the howl of human voices, a howl unparalleled and incomparable, a titanic howl. Because man has to drown all noises, all the racket, all the roar of machines, instruments, animals and birds. Because it is essential on this wonderful once-in-a-year holiday—a capital holiday, a summer holiday, a holiday of love—it is essential not only to sell, not only to show things off but also to laugh, to be witty and to make declarations of love.

Oh yes, declarations of love.

For this one has to yell in the very ear of one's beloved, as if on a bell-tower in full peal.

But surely true passion was never contained in an elegiac piano?

Ah, passion! Ah, youthful, cruel, impetuous passion!

To sit in a carriage smothered in carousel braid, to sit, cuddled up, one's whole body pressed to that lacy, hot, full-breasted, made-up, slightly sweating girl whom one has just met, bumped into, made friends with a moment ago in the crowd, where every person is like wadding in a shell, to sit—ah, ah, no!—to fly, to skim, to spin, as if in the clouds. Here is a dark semi-circle—a tunnel, black as pitch—no one will see—a second, another, another; here's day, blinding, bright; under one's feet—people are looking, pointing with fingers, laughing; here's darkness again—there's no one, only her—which?—unknown, spun round by the carousel—a second, another, another—light, day, people; and into the tunnel again!

Has humanity invented any other machine which could rework the hearts, souls, glances, kisses—all this raw material of love—into such a crystal condensed product of happiness as does the carousel, Cupid's Centrifuge?

All these swing-boats, all these bucking staircases, and endlessly running tracks, and roller-coasters—none of them produces even a small degree of the happiness produced by that one-and-only, the carousel. Genuine happiness—that state of heaven on earth, of real whirlwind passion (beware of imitations!)—is the monopoly of the carousel.

Rejoice, O gaudy, braided, multi-colored, constellated one, combining the gallop of horses with the smooth rocking of boats, forever obedient to the voices of the barrel organ in your eternal round—rejoice!

WHEN, IN FACT, THE WORLD WAR BEGAN

Swaying and rocking, carried from sideshow to swing-boats, from swing-boats to booths, Kurt and Andrei abandoned themselves to the crowd, to its recklessness, to its caprices. Like born loafers they could not have said how much of their time was taken by barkers, traders, clowns and gentlemen in crumpled frock-coats, who dignified themselves as professors of neurology and psychiatry and who personally dragged out painted sleeping somnambulists onto the platforms of their booths.

When the current had carried the friends to a place where they could freely move and breathe, they looked at one another and burst into laughter. Sweating and crumpled they looked like people caught in a torrential rain. Kurt exclaimed delightedly:

"Look, Andrei! These people with long mustaches or with gray hair, these fathers, mothers, and maybe granddads and grandmas, they are all children who prize a toy above all else. Such a holiday . . . such naïve gaiety . . ."

"Wait," Andrei stopped him, "what's this! What's this, Kurt?"

"An Aunt Sally."

Andrei rushed forward, then seized Kurt by the arm and pressed his whole body to him, as if seeking shelter and defense.

"What's the matter with you, what are you doing?"

A dense, steady roar of laughter came from before a small booth. A solid group of men alternately backed away from the barrier and then hurled itself toward it. At a distance of eight or nine paces from the barrier disheveled, battered human heads stuck up on iron rods. Above all of them were fastened plaques with the names of criminals, whose heads had once been punished by justice and which had now been turned into stuffed dummies by the wrathful hand of the showman.

The game was very simple. One had to hit a head with a large ball of rags. The ball knocked the head backward. It fell down and disappeared behind a canvas counter. A skinny, pale-faced boy ran behind the counter, replaced the target immediately and returned the ball to the proprietor's feet, while the latter, at the barrier, collected a small fine for every miss.

The work went on without intermission: the balls flew from the barrier behind the line of targets and back again; the proprietor changed marks, gave balls to the contestants, yelled at the lad and took pulls at a tankard of beer; the public roared with laughter, gave encouragement and jeered, retiring when a sportsman put back his arm and rushing forward once he had hurled the ball at his target.

A head, sticking up in the center of the targets—with the stitches of a carelessly sewn scar on its low forehead, with bulging brown eyes in a dark blue face, covered with short, shaven sprouts of hair—this head attracted the particular attention of the public and ball after ball flew at it. Hurled backward, disappearing, it rose again and again on its elastic iron rod and dully fixed its senseless brown eyes on the roaring, sweaty crowd.

They addressed the head affectionately, unceremoniously, familiarly:

"Karlkins, Karly-boy, Karly."

And above it hung a plaque:

THE FEROCIOUS MURDERER

TERRIBLE BANDIT

DAYLIGHT ROBBER AND

RENOWNED TORTURER

OF WOMEN

KARL EBERSOCKS

THEY CHOPPED THE ROGUE'S BLOCK OFF

IN NUREMBERG

"What is it?" cried Andrei again.

"This is sport," sounded calmly right by his ear.

He did not understand at first who had uttered these

words, nor did he realize immediately that they had been spoken in Russian. Did that mean that Russian words also had burst from him?

"Let's introduce ourselves. I'm a student here, my name . . . however that's not important. You and your friend caught my fancy: I've been watching you gape at this babel a long time."

The crinkled, slightly tired eyes looked mockingly and calmly, the mouth twitched as if into an uncertain smile.

The student shook Andrei and Kurt by the hand.

"Are you German?" he addressed Kurt with interest. "Excellent, we'll talk in German. Your friend was so stunned by this showman's diversion that he even turned pale."

Andrei tried to look Kurt in the eyes and say:

"At any rate children don't amuse themselves that way."

Kurt pressed Andrei's elbow as if to soothe him and examined their new companion.

The latter said, without caring whether his voice was audible or not:

"Sport, as is known, is physical education. But how much wisdom the showman has displayed, joining use to edification. Exquisite! That way you not only stretch the muscles of your run-down militia-man but you also give an edge to his moral sentiment, strengthen his consciousness of right and so on. And to prevent all this from being deadly dull, they gild the pill with the most piquant of hints: a torturer of women, and not merely an ordinary one, but—renowned! Here you have it—reptilian wisdom! What prospects for the imagination of the shop-assistant from Tietz's store! There's not a single Japanese picture could so titillate his fantasy as this brief little line: renowned torturer of women! The main thing is that this whole affair is imbued with the idea of patriotism, the idea of educating citizens in the spirit of nationalism."

"Really repulsive!" shivered Andrei.

"Ha-ha, if I weren't in a good mood," laughed Kurt, "I'd thrash you, friend."

"What for?"

"For your generalizations. A charlatan has set up a trap

for fools and you chatter something about nationalism."

The student frowned and shrugged his shoulders. A smile hovered about his face the whole time but its expression remained elusive. He seemed to be chuckling at his own words and deciding to himself whether they believed him or not.

"You look fine. You are probably a student, perhaps an artist? In short there's nothing to be expected from you. I mean you are dreamers. But I am a sober man, though I don't mind a drink now and then. Let's go over to the hill, to the restaurant. And finally give up this habit of walking along paths. It's quicker and less crowded through the trees. . . . I have been, my friends, in five universities, and have been thrown out of four. It's not a question of universities, however, but of the fact that within a short time I have lived in four countries and learned to spit on all of them. So that it's difficult to accuse me of favoritism. I am an international swine. And if your hands are itching I'm ready to continue my generalizations so as to be beaten for everything at once. Okay?"

On the grass slumped tired people, jacketless, hatless and in the shade of open parasols flung down on the ground. The friends had passed the trees and found themselves again among an idle crowd of revelers.

Here, on a broad plaza, sprawled the restaurant. Rows of long tables and benches stretched the whole length of the plaza and mounted in regular steps to a tent, which was being besieged by a starched cavalcade of waitresses. Guests adhered to the benches as a flock of roosting rooks to the branches of a lone tree. The tables were packed with earthenware beer mugs. Stout waitresses with mugs threaded on their fingers and raised overhead elbowed their way to the tent which sheltered the barrels of foamy liquid. Flower and paper streamer sellers leaned over the customers' shoulders and smiled into their faces as if all these people were their lovers. Overhead, caught in the branches of trees, tangled and curled, hung multicolored paper streamers, rocked and broken by the impact of newer and newer paper snakes. Here laughter held sway.

The friends sat down at a table on the upper part of the plaza. Their companion appeared between them, turning first to one and then to the other, trying to make himself heard:

"Here's the ABC of biology for you: if some organ is not exercised over a prolonged period of time, it loses its capacity to fulfill its functions. In my opinion they attack the organic theory for nothing. The laws of biology embrace in essence the entire psychic life of peoples. Europeans substituted the duel for blood revenge and the duel has taken the form of fencing: one scratches one's enemy's cheek with a rapier and one is satisfied. Or else, still better: you get a slap in the face, the judge fines the offender—and the insult is washed away, you are at rest. That is because from generation to generation we have not been exercising the feeling of revenge. Gradually it has atrophied."

"What are you trying to convince us of?" asked Andrei.

The student took a drink from a mug of beer and suddenly his face grew pinched, darkened, aged, his smile disappeared and he said tiredly:

"Of nothing. I was cheered by the naïveté with which you gaped at the sideshows. And then your fright at the Aunt Sally. Nothing more."

He stared at Andrei intently.

"Especially with you, a Russian. I raise questions—only. Didn't Rome occur to you when you first saw Germany? Do you understand? Such prosperity, such splendor, such plenty, such satisfaction. Insufferable. I feel that beneath the soil of this entire country, beneath the consciousness of this entire people lie whole layers of repressed impatience. Everything around is so satiated, so overflowing, so crammed, that a discharge is necessary, essential, inevitable. In everything around me I hear a breathing of terrific potency. And I see this potency growing, being fed constantly from without, like a battery being charged with electricity. Do you remember the faces of the sportsmen? Were you terrified? And have you thought what power stands behind that amusement? They are exercising it in such an innocent fashion in order to direct it later to wher-

ever necessary. Do you realize where it will be directed? Do
you realize? Do you feel how this power makes the earth
tremble under you? Do you feel what kind of eruption it
will be?"

"What are you talking about?" cried Andrei suddenly.
The student seized his arm.

"Eruption," he repeated hollowly, "can you feel it?" And
he nodded his head downward, at the tables to which the
revelers clung like rooks to branches.

"Look!"

A student had clambered onto a bench one row below
where they were sitting. A gaily colored fraternity cap was
perched on the back of his smooth pink head. He was jacketless and his shirt sleeves were rolled up. Behind him stood
a girl with a basket of paper streamers. He took a ring of
streamers from the basket, wound the end of the ribbon
around his finger, spent a long time measuring his distance
and aiming, and then directed the ring toward a table
lower down. On the way the ribbon became entangled with
the strands of a streamer hanging down from a tree or
collided and intertwined with a ribbon coming the other
way or became stuck in the branches of a linden tree without having unwound. The student lowered his hand into the
basket without looking, took a fresh wheel and used all
his skill to evade the tangled web of obstacles with a new
throw. He was entering into the spirit of the thing and was
incensed at every failure. At last he succeeded in hooking
a ribbon onto the rich curtain of streamers which separated
him from his target. He pulled it down onto the heads of the
customers amid general laughter. The battlefield was his.
He spread his legs wider, took a whole bundle of streamers
and opened brisk fire.

His target was a girl. She was sitting with an elderly,
respectable lady with the bearing of a mother or an aunt.
The first ribbon to reach its object fell on the girl's shoulder.
Without haste she threw the ribbon on the ground. As if
there weren't enough streamers here! They rained down
from above and rustled underfoot like shavings in a car-
penter's workshop. The tiny ball of the second ribbon struck

her on the hand. She flung the ball away impatiently. The third descended gently onto the table in front of the lady's face. The girl took the precaution of removing the ribbon to one side and, as she chatted about something, involuntarily wound it around her finger.

Then the student pulled the ribbon tight and jerked it very carefully. The girl lifted her head and her eyes ran along the aerial conductor until they collided with the student's face, just breaking into a smile and gleaming with sweat. She grinned and with a brief movement of her hand snapped the conductor.

Kurt and Andrei laughed. Their companion's face again grew youthful and a diffident smile played over it.

"Do you know," he said, "that students call this holiday the gynecological season? No? It's an instructive story. One professor beginning his course here announced: 'It's a great pity we are starting work in the winter semester and in the initial stages will be deprived of the beneficent material to which the embryological section of our museum owes its world-wide reputation: two or three months after the Erlangen fair we have more than enough material.' Are you surprised? Is this incomprehensible to you? The professor knew what he was talking about. Once a year phalanxes of women descend on this eternally hungry burg. They are awaited here by students and soldiers. Do you think they wait for women in vain? Within two months a certain percentage of all these blue-eyed brides, wives, cousins and sisters will arrive once again in Erlangen to recline in the beds of the university clinics."

"You're exaggerating and you're morbid, friend," said Kurt.

"I'm exaggerating? Morbid? Oh, you romantics! D'you want to bet that this fellow here won't get his way before this evening's out? Look, look!"

Around the student standing on the bench clustered flower sellers. Between him and the girl at the lower table stretched a new streamer ribbon. The student was putting his lips to the end of the ribbon grasped in his fist and the whole of his bulky body expressed an irresistible urge for the girl. He selected a flower from a basket thrust at him, imprinted a kiss upon it and dispatched it with the flower seller to his lady. Then he lifted his beer mug over his head and drained it in a few gulps. The girl accepted the flowers, raised them to her face and, unobserved, darted sly glances at the student. The latter momentarily intercepted them and expressed his delight with looks and gestures which embarrassed her.

"It's great, it's really great!" laughed Kurt.

"Look at his figure," cried the student, "why he's terrifying! Try and interfere with him, distract him for a single minute and he'll fall on you with the ferociousness of a slaughterer, he'll crush you! And in doing this he'll experience the greatest satisfaction, because he's brimming over with the greatest impatience."

"Are you talking about this fellow?"

"I'm talking about all of them."

"You're crazy!"

"Ha-ha! Are you artists? I knew it! You squat here and there on your canvas stools and it never once enters your head that you are sitting on a volcano. Ha-ha! One fine day it will blow you to pieces, together with your fine études, umbrellas and stools, like a bottle of soda in the sun. A horde of fellows like this will trample your complacency underfoot."

"Maniac," pronounced Kurt, moving away from the student.

"Wait," said the latter, throwing his legs over the bench, "there's an idiot I have to see. I'll come back immediately and finish my line of thought."

"Don't bother," replied Kurt.

"I want to din it into your head—not yours, not yours, my friend, but his, my fine-souled countryman's—that . . . I'll tell you later what . . ."

He spun round and disappeared in the semi-drunk, noisy crush of human beings.

"Let's go," said Andrei and anxiety crept into his glance as it rested on his friend's face.

When they had descended to the sideshows and everything around them whirled, creaking and squeaking in unison, Kurt said:

"Of course he's sick, that guy."

And a little later, with a wan smile:

"Let's enjoy ourselves without him, eh? . . ."

That night on the station, amid the crush and the quarrels of people climbing into the cars, exhausted by the sun, the carousels, liquor and the crowd, Kurt again fell into fond contemplation, stirred by the looks, the laughter, the songs and the night.

"We won't get into the train anyway, Andrei. Come, let's finish the holiday in the old style: we'll find an inn, spend the night, and tomorrow at dawn we'll go home on foot, to our amazing, our beautiful . . ."

Kurt did not finish. His gaze fell on a pyramid-shaped young tree, sticking up by a table at the end of the hall.

"But that guy," he growled, "the one who came up to us today was certainly right about something, God damn it!"

On the table behind the pyramid-shaped young tree stood a bright yellow suitcase. On a leather sofa behind the suitcase sprawled a student, embracing a young girl and pulling her toward him. A few hours ago, on the hill in the fair restaurant, they had been linked only by a ribbon of paper streamer. Their eyes roamed lazily, flashing fire. The student waved a hand in the air, not even a hand, not even the main part of his hand, but the fingers alone, held tightly together and erect. This gesture—condescendingly affectionate and careless—was directed at the elderly and respectable lady—at the mother or aunt of the girl. The lady stood a little way off, preparing to leave, and she shook her head—it was impossible to tell whether reproachfully, sympathetically or encouragingly. Her hat had crept to one side and the curls which had fallen out from under her hat were wet. The student mumbled appeasingly:

"Adieu, Frau Mama, adieu!"

Andrei and Kurt made their way out onto the street.

Across the square marched a gang of rowdies, seven in all, arm in arm, forming a solid chain, staggering to right and left. With high voices they sang in unison:

Die Männer sind alle Verbrecher,
Ihr Herz ist ein finsteres Loch;
Die Frauen sind auch nicht viel besser,
Aber lieb,
aber lieb
*sind sie doch!**

DICHTUNG UND WAHRHEIT

"Without the slightest effort you are carried back hundreds
of years. You are no longer living in civilization. The imagination recalls the minutest details of the past with ease.
Just don't resist it, put no obstacle in its way, do not confine
it to this evening. . . . And, watch, you are already an
apprentice, you are hurrying to reach the town before dark;
you know, you see, you feel it. Rumors of it circulate
through taverns and inns, people tell stories about it in a
whisper, songs are sung about it. This is a wonderful old
town with good masters from all the noble guilds, with the
marvelous church of St. Lawrence, which is under the jurisdiction of Strasburg Cathedral itself; with wonderful foun-
tains, a superb market and excellent grilled sausages.
With every step you are closer to your goal and with every
step your tiredness decreases. You climb onto a hill—and
before you, encircled by a high wall, turrets, trees and flowers, sprawls the town. You see the gates and you want to be
sure of entering them before the sun disappears over the
horizon. You run. But suddenly a disturbing, doleful melody
hangs suspended in the still of the evening. A tall thin man
is walking in the opposite direction. His hair is disheveled,
his eyes half closed. He is piping a monotonous air on a
shepherd's flute and walks lightly, practically sliding along
the road, like a lunatic. What's this, what's this, Andrei?
Behind him a layer of road curves up, like the crest of a
wave which can't reach the shore. It is gray, this layer, it is
swarming with some kind of beings. Andrei, they are rats,

*Men are all rogues,
Their heart is a deep pit;
Women are not much better,
But they're nice, they are nice, nonetheless!

rats! They spread over the road in a solid avalanche and scramble over one another, with motionless black beads of eyes, with snarling snouts. Stop, stop, don't move! They will go round you, they notice nothing, they see nothing; they want only one thing: to hear the doleful piping of the man who summoned them onto the street from their nests and barn cellars and led them behind him into the fields. Hurry —they are closing the town gates behind the rodent horde. The sun has set. You are cool, your tiredness has slipped off. You enter the town. . . ."

"You enter the town," Andrei chimes in, "and you are immediately surrounded by the anxious faces of artisans, servant girls and young lads—those same citizens who guffaw so loudly at singing contests and who sob so bitterly at seeing the Passions of our Lord Jesus in the mystery play on the market square. They are scared, they devour you with their eyes, they wish to know for sure if you have heard of that strange youth who appeared among them in the town at dawn that day. But you're not from here? And probably you've come from far away, have seen a lot and know a lot. So this morning a young boy appeared, known to nobody. He's as white as paper, his skin transparent, he's thin and so weak that he can't take five steps. He has beautiful blue eyes and extremely long hair, probably never cut and soft as down. Judging by his height he's about fifteen, but he's as helpless as an infant. His glance terrifies you— it is so pure and innocent a glance. That's probably the way angels and martyrs look. But most terrifying of all is that he doesn't know a single word, as if he had only just been born. Now look, you've come from another town, from Halle, from Frankfurt, or else maybe from the Rhine itself. Haven't you heard about this youth somewhere? Is it true that a scoundrel kept him in a dark cubbyhole and since his birth he's never seen a human face or heard a human voice?"

"And you are already scared, too," says Kurt, putting his arm round Andrei's shoulders, "you yourself are as agitated as these good people; your heartbeats have fallen into tune with the town's heartbeats, you are drawn into its life and you live it as if you had been born and brought up here. . . ."

The friends are walking swiftly, in step, along a straight road closely paved with stones. Along the sides stretch rows of short-boled apple trees, with luxuriant crowns and, inside, globes of half-ripe gleaming yellow fruit. Their legs are covered with a fine grayish dust, but their walk is still light and brisk. Ahead, behind a sloping hill, a light, smoky shroud hangs in the sky. There is the city. The friends look in that direction, and at the sky, raising their uncovered, shaggy heads.

"You breathe with the breast of this town. It wraps you in its being, like a dream. Everything accomplished here is accomplished within you. You live from wonder to wonder. . . . A lad playing by the Church of St. Lawrence said: 'The devil take me!' In a twinkling there's the devil, in an instant the lad is wriggling under the devil's arm, the lad is underground and in the ground there is only a hole. Can you really be indifferent as to what the devil's horns were like, and to what his tail was like, and to how he smelled? And can you really resist running to the castle to see with your own eyes the traces of horse's hooves on the wall, where one had jumped the fortress moat and carried a robber away? . . ."

The friends halted. Directly beneath their feet the road swam smoothly away toward the patches of bright square fields. The new city girdled the old in a dim circle. Five towers, broad and bulky, surveyed the environs. Over the crowded dark houses which had grown upon its indestructible stone breast, the pink castle lay like a crown of the centuries.

"Nuremberg!" broke from Kurt's lips.

"Nuremberg!" repeated Andrei.

They stood motionless, their whole bodies straining forward, like travelers in the desert before an unexpected well. Then Kurt seized Andrei by the hands, drew him close with an abrupt, hasty motion, looked into his eyes as if he wanted to pour all his ecstasy into Andrei, and they embraced.

"Forever!" said Andrei.

"Forever!"

Hand in hand they suddenly burst into a long wordless cry and ran down to the city.

It was evening.

Descending the staircase from his mansard, Kurt met an officer. The officer was young and agile, and ease was proclaimed in his bearing. He saluted:

"Can you tell me where the artist Herr Wahn lives?"

"What can I do for you?"

The officer ascended a step higher, came face to face with Kurt, smiled and almost exclaimed:

"Ah, so it's you yourself! I recognized you from a self-portrait—you remember, the little pencil drawing?"

"You . . . you . . ." mumbled Kurt and suddenly turned to go down the stairs. But he immediately changed his mind and jumped two steps upward. Then he again dashed downward, looked at the officer, shook his out-stretched hand and, precisely, like a soldier, he replied:

"Very pleased, Herr Lieutenant."

"Evidently you are in a hurry. I beg you to call me simply von Schönau. Perhaps, just a few minutes in all . . . I shan't delay you. And please—simply von Schönau.

"Very pleased," repeated Kurt and pointed aloft with his hand.

"I found you without any particular trouble," said the officer, going up the stairs, "although my agent, with whom you have done business up to now, assured me that it was generally impossible to find your studio. Ha-ha! I am afraid the good man wants to preserve a barrier between me and you. By the way, how much did you receive from him last time by way of an advance?"

"Five hundred marks."

"You don't say! It does him honor, ha-ha!"

Kurt opened the door and let the officer in first.

"Is this your studio? You don't say! So this is how modest truly great people are."

"I am very grateful, Herr von Schönau, but . . ."

"Right, I'm joking. I wanted to get to know you. The good man with whom you did business probably told you that I

value your talent. I would like it to be simpler, without
ceremony. I am terribly glad that I found you. You know I
like artists in general. By contrast everything with us is so
complicated—introductions, etiquette—while you are simple.
Tell me. Is this your new canvas? Turn it around, turn it
around, there . . . that's it. This is billed against the advance, what? Ha-ha!"

"Excuse me, Herr von Schönau, but I've already promised
this picture to someone else . . . actually, to the city council of Nuremberg. . . ."

The officer sat in an armchair and leaned forward, his
elbow resting on his knee. His face narrowed, his broad
forehead, striped red by his cap, expanded, his mouth was
outlined clearly and sharply. He looked at the picture.

"What were you saying there?" he said softly.

Then he tore himself away from the canvas:

"Did I seem to hear you talking some rubbish, Herr
Wahn?"

Kurt strode over to his guest and his voice became heavy.

"I was about to thank you, Herr von Schönau. . . . I
also wanted to return the advance. . . ."

The officer quickly got up and threw out his hand, abruptly, like a gymnast:

"Give it to me!"

"Unfortunately, at the present moment . . . I . . ."

"You are talking nonsense, dear Wahn. I give you the
opportunity to work. I don't hurry you. You can paint one
picture in three years. Go ahead. I'll provide for you. I make
you no conditions except one: the pictures know only one
way out of this studio—into my collection."

"That's rotten!"

The officer's mouth was clearly and sharply defined and
his words, like his mouth, were clear and sharp:

"Herr artist understands that an officer is talking to him.
An officer proposes, an artist agrees or refuses. Do you
refuse?"

"My God! But you are depriving me of what's most important, you are taking my . . ."

"I am doing you an honor. Are you acquainted with the

catalogue of my collection? Van Dyck and Rubens, the
French, ending with Cézanne, and the Germans up to
Klinger. I have reserved for you a whole wall."

"No one knows me. I work. . . . I work. . . ."

Kurt grasped the back of the sofa, knocked his legs on
some stretchers and said tensely, as if dying from thirst:

"I work for you!"

"You don't say! Wahn, Wahn, you are mad, like a genius.
You want to pave your road step by step, while I promise
to assure your future for you in one motion. No one knows
you? Well, I shall make it so that the whole world knows.
I'll do that."

Kurt fell onto the sofa.

"But this canvas, just this one. I beg you. I wanted to see
it in the city hall. The Court of the German Museum—that's
ours, Nuremberg's, close to us. . . ."

"Wahn, quit talking rubbish! It would displease me to
leave you in a bad frame of mind. And besides . . ."

The officer's forehead again expanded, the red stripe
from his cap grew pale and disappeared. He looked at the
painting.

"Good. Very. How pleasant to watch your progress.
You know . . ."

The officer rose, went up to Kurt, took him by the shoulders and looked into his face—as if into the face of a soldier
—encouragingly.

"You know you're the best artist of your generation. Why
you're not much older than I am, eh?"

Then he looked around the room again, took a visiting
card from his pocket, wrote several words on it and said
youthfully, as before:

"I'm here in passing. Terribly glad I found you. Here,
take it, maybe it'll come in handy. And good-by. I'll definitely invite you to my place, to Schönau. You'll see what
wall I've reserved for you. Definitely. Good-by."

The officer shook his hand, his uniform rustled briskly
and cheerfully, and he noisily closed the thin glass door
behind him.

Kurt sat motionless.

From below, from the street, rose the evening chatter of

the workers returning from the factory. One could hear bicycle tires swishing over the pavement. Dusk hid in the corners of the room. The canvas on its easel shone red.

Kurt felt a small card in his hand. He lifted it to his eyes. In pencil:

> *Put 200 on the bill for the*
> *"Court of the German Museum."*

In printing ink:

LIEUTENANT MAX VON ZUR MÜHLEN-SCHÖNAU
(MARGRAVE)

Then Kurt jumped up from the sofa, tore up the visiting card, ran to the window and threatened the street with his fist.

With heavy breathing the hissing words crept out and foamed:

"I ha-a-ate him!"

Rosenau lies in a depression, and in Rosenau there is a pond. As a result of this pond's dampness, of the juicy grass of the lawns and of the dense crowns of the white willows, it is cool in Rosenau.

And when twilight used to fall and sultriness weighed heavily upon the town, people used to flock to Rosenau.

Because, this summer, thunderstorms were passing over Bavaria.

They gathered at nightfall and descended furiously on towns, roads and fields. At dawn the sky would clear; the days would be sweltering, close; in the evenings clouds would drift up and at night, torn to pieces by the storm, they would collapse onto the ground. . . .

Man set about correcting the madness of nature. Set up lightning conductors, laid out drainage, invented the umbrella.

Proud man!

When the first drop of rain falls like a cold herald upon the earth he feels his bald pate with his palm, opens his umbrella and his face reveals not the slightest trace of dismay: beneath the umbrella walks this monarch of nature.

No dismay at all. No anxiety, no haste, no fuss. Life—is harmony. And the homeland of harmony is the homeland of Bach, Mendelssohn, Liszt, Haydn. At every step you meet men who are incapable of distinguishing c-major from a-minor. But anyone knows that Haydn and Mendelssohn came from Germany. And everyone, like a true-believing Hellene, believes that the seven tones of the musical scale correspond to the seven colors of the spectrum.

Life is harmony, in which every cigar is a known tonality, and the orange tile of roofs, the button of an air bell, the leather cuff of a woman sausage-seller, the comb in the hair of a waitress—these have a known timbre, pleasant, proper to them alone and assigned to them alone.

Tap a knife against the coffee cup of a Berlin tavern. It will give out the same tone as a coffee cup from any tavern in Hanover—or Dresden, Stettin, Lübeck. Substitute the inkwell of a Bautzen *Stadtrat*.* It will not even occur to the worthy burghers that they are dipping their pens into other people's inkwells.

Why Bautzen, why Herliz? And the forty kilometers separating these neighboring towns?

Oh, even if four hundred, five hundred, even a thousand!

But these are the inkwells of Stadtrats. And not of professors, friars and officers.

Life is harmony.

And to live means not to destroy harmony. At all ages and at all times, in all professions and in all ranks, in no matter what social sphere—to sound with the proper and assigned tone. . . .

Thus this summer, when thunderstorms were passing over Bavaria and sultriness weighed heavily upon the town at twilight, they set off in the evenings for Rosenau, for the cool of the pond.

The men took off their jackets, hung panamas and hats (you get a special holder as a free gift from Tietz's) on their vest buttons, took their umbrellas and walked.

And from their first step, as soon as they put their feet down, jackets off and hats hung on buttons, everything was

*Alderman.

accomplished to a rhythm and measure dictated by harmony.

Thus: the men.

Behind them—simultaneously: wives, daughters, mothers-in-law. All in white blouses, with purses and umbrellas.

And in front—the little sons: hatless, in "Robespierre" shirts tucked into short pants. Well, these were without umbrellas. At the first peal of thunder—on the double, march, home! And the "Robespierres" would dry out and be ironed the next day. . . .

They sat stolidly at a small table for a long time. Imperturbably they listened to the orchestra. They joined in Strauss, they were moved:

"A good composer, prosit!"

The sergeant-major conductor led them with parade ground precision. He turned to the applause—once, twice, thrice. And he bowed as much as he was permitted by army regulations and his collar.

The flautist got up and changed the number on the board —"4."

At this point every family—in patriarchal precedence—looked at the program:

"Four? Schumann, a potpourri of songs."

"Ah, Schumann!"

"Yes, of songs . . ."

"An excellent musician, although—Austrian? Prosit!"

All to this rhythm and this measure.

But the night before the thundercloud was to hang and then break over the town, the accustomed and comfortable rhythm was broken.

The proper and assigned timbres, which were invariably pleasant after the cool of Rosenau, after Strauss and Schumann, were pierced by words which dispersed the harmony, as a thunderstorm does the sultriness.

People crowded together at the crossroads, lashed by torrential rain, like birds battered by the wind, like sheep deafened by the thunder.

They opened and closed their umbrellas. They unbuttoned and buttoned their collars. They took off and put on their hats.

But they did not move. They were waiting for the lightning.

And when it darted thievishly over the rooftops men fixed their eyes on the tatters of telegrams pasted onto the walls to be blinded again and again by the word:

ERZHERZOG!*

Then they broke away from the spot, lashed, battered, deafened by the storm and the torrential rain, and again rejoined the crowd huddled on the crossroads, and again they were blinded by the word:

ERZHERZOG!

And again they did not move: they were waiting for the lightning.

Thus everyone: of all ages, of all professions, from every walk of life.

Because from this night, blinding them with the word:

ERZHERZOG!

the old harmony ceased to be and—dismayed—the people rushed to seek a new one.

Wet through to the skin, Andrei made his way through the familiar outskirts of the city to the house where Kurt lived. Under the impact of the gusts of wind, the gaslights expired and came to life again. Andrei lit a match and looked for the doorbell. About three minutes later a weak voice from above crept down to the street:

"Is that you, Herr Wahn?"

Andrei ran back from the door into the middle of the pavement.

"Excuse the disturbance, Frau Maier. Isn't Kurt at home?"

"Ah, Herr Startsov! Good evening. We thought Herr Wahn was with you. He went away a long time ago. There was some officer here."

*Archduke.

"Officer?"

"A young officer."

"And Kurt went away with him?"

"No. The officer went away earlier."

"Then where's Kurt?"

"Really, you frighten me, Herr Startsov. How should I know where he goes? He slammed the door so hard when he went out that my crockery bounced in the kitchen."

"Excuse the disturbance, Frau Maier. Good night!"

"Good night, Herr Startsov!"

The white spot in the attic disappeared, the window was closed. Andrei stood motionless for a few moments. Then he said quietly:

"An officer."

Then he returned slowly, through the outskirts which had led him to Kurt's place.

At home he undressed, rubbed his chest, back and stomach with a dry towel, changed his underwear, opened the windows, got under the bed clothes and fell asleep immediately, as if he had tumbled into a pit.

In this pit he distinctly saw:

In a limitless perhaps snowy expanse hangs a man's head. Round about all is quiet and motionless. Suddenly a student materializes out of nothing with a fraternity cap on the back of his smooth pink head. The brown eyes in the man's head are open, their pupils are fixed on the student.

"Adieu, Frau Mama!" says the head and winks at the student. Then the student runs away a little, spreads his legs wide and raises his hand. Where did those cloth balls come from? The first throw misses. The second also. The balls fly half a centimeter to the right and left of the head. The head shifts its gaze to Andrei and opens its blue lips to say something. But it disappears for an instant behind a ball and it rocks and wobbles as if in deep thought, then suddenly tumbles on its back and flies somewhere down below. And at that same instant the snowy limitlessness vanishes and a grandiose stone staircase grows up before

Andrei and the head rolls down it with metronomic regularity, striking loudly against every step in turn, now with its face, now with its back:

> boom—bom
> boom—bom. . . .

But its gaze remained irremovably fixed on Andrei's eyes, although there must be, there must be moments when Andrei cannot see this gaze, cannot!

> boom—bom
> boom—bom. . . .

Andrei jumped out of bed. He was all covered with sweat and his mouth was filled with a salty dryness. He pressed his head with his hands. He listened. Clear strokes resounded loudly in the street. Andrei rushed to the window and lifted the curtain.

In the fresh post-thunderstorm dawn innumerable horseshoes were clattering over the cobblestones. Particolored pennants fluttered in the air from the points of cavalry lances. Sitting stiffly and prancing in the saddles were highly polished dark green uniforms, stuffed with solid broad-chested bodies. Over the black-lacquered squares, which capped their helmets, flitted the uncertain shadows of the morning sky.

In front of the cavalry seated on raven horses marched the regimental band, blazing with the burning brass of trumpets. The big drum shook the peace of the sleeping streets.

Andrei sank down onto the windowsill and covered his face with his hands.

People recalled that kings existed on this earth.

Their actual existence suddenly became obvious after the blinding word:

ERZHERZOG!

had burst into the harmony, broken the rhythms, distorted the measures and disfigured the timbres.

It turned out that kings did not live only on the pages of

magazines and reviews and in the display windows of photographers. It turned out that kings did not only travel, transfer from winter to summer residences, smile in portraits and annually celebrate their anniversaries. It turned out that kings lived not only in history and geography books —that is, only on school benches. No!

Kings *really* lived. Kings indeed possessed skulls which were affected by bullets in exactly the same way as the skulls of their subjects. And the kings shouted so well that their voices were audible in regions very far removed from their residences.

And goodness, what a lot of kings were suddenly discovered! Every day, every hour they came crawling out of their residences, like beetles out of cracks. Finally they had drifted into every corner of the newspapers and the time came to place a limit to this kingly confusion.

Enough listening to dissension, enough pondering this muddle, enough spoiling one's eyes on all these notes, memoranda, expressions of will and manifestoes, enough!

Is it not clear yet where the sense of duty calls you?

Obey this sense—the sense of duty! Only it, nothing else!

It will bring you onto the street, into the crowd, and the crowd will sweep you up on its shoulders, as a wave sweeps a chip upon its crest. And you will hurry to the house of the Serbian trade consul and the sense of duty will squeeze from your insides a howl of indignation. And then you will beat a stick against the locked front door of the consulate, until a *Schutzmann** comes up to you and explains that you are mistaken if you think the law allows you to damage doors. And then the feeling of duty will draw you along the streets to the house of the Italian trade consul and you will sing the national anthem and cry *"Vivat Italia!"* until a Schutzmann comes up to you again and advises you to go home, because it's getting time for the policemen to arrive and it will be necessary to stop the noise. And although the sense of duty and a hoarse throat are modifying your ardor, yet you will still shout and be indignant and be angry because—can life really sound with its old harmony after a

*Constable.

refreshing storm? Can we really be fated not to experience a wonderful, long-awaited change? Can there really be again that blessed, grave, harmonious world? Oh, never! Not for anything! Change, change, change!

We demand, we wish, we thirst for change!

Then obey your sense of duty!

The crowd raged at the front door of the Serbian trade consul and in the crowd were Andrei and Kurt. But they did not see one another. Because, if you regard the crowd, confined between the sides of the street, as a rectangle, then Andrei was at one end of the diagonal and Kurt at the other. And this second end of the diagonal came right up to the front door of the consulate, while the first was where people stood who were not imbued with a sense of duty or—from nature—were altogether without one.

The mechanics of popular crowds in town streets has its own laws and these laws, of course, cannot be broken by such a superficial phenomenon as human friendship.

And when the crowd turned and went back to the house of the Italian trade consul, Andrei found himself in front of the procession and headed it as far as the first side street. There he whisked around the corner and—by way of the outskirts—rushed to Kurt's place.

Learning from Frau Maier that her lodger had not been home since morning, he went to his room, sought out a scrap of paper on the table and with a brown pastel crayon which came to hand wrote in thick letters:

What's wrong with you, Kurt? I called twice. I'll come tomorrow morning. I'm exhausted.

                          Andrei

The following day the sun rose two and a half minutes later than it had the day before. For the rest, the dawn was not the least bit remarkable.

As always, cyclists appeared in the streets about seven o'clock in the morning, with sacks and baskets upon their humped backs. Their tires hissing, the cycles rolled under Kurt's windows to the right and left.

Those which rolled to the right carried the workers of Johann Faber in their saddles.

As always the workers stacked their bicycles in a spacious garage, in racks, and climbed up to the cloakroom. There, each one opened his locker—with a separate lock beneath the number and name of the workman—took off his jacket, unbuttoned his cuffs and celluloid collar with a dicky and, hanging all this in the closet, donned a burlap blouse.

At seven o'clock they all stood in their places.

At seven o'clock foreman Maier began the second shift at the non-stop furnace.

Measuring apparatus and radiation pyrometers were located in the next building where, motionless behind gauges, tables and meters, sat men who squeezed out one more division on the social test-your-strength machine than an ordinary foreman. Aerial cables, bells and telephones connected these people with Maier and he carried out their commands like a sailor the signals of a control tower.

He had only a vague conception of the readings taken by the motionless men sitting behind the pyrometers in the next building. He knew only the signals born of their will, and by the signals he was able to tell confidently what serial number was being heated in the furnace.

He had faith in the signal tower—and also in the fact that behind the hatches and screws, behind the reinforced concrete wall, the space which was the furnace could be heated to 1,300 degrees.

To 1,300 centigrade.

He had faith in that, did foreman Maier.

Daily at midday the workers went to the washbasins, gave their due to the factory soap and factory towels, put on their celluloid collars and cuffs and went to the garage for their bicycles.

On this day they went to the hand basins at ten o'clock in the morning and did not take their bicycles.

At ten o'clock in the morning two men entered the location of the non-stop furnace.

"Listen Maier," they said, "we're going on the street today. We're against war. Let's go together."

"Against war?" repeated Maier. "That's good. But I have a furnace."

"That's true, Maier, you have a furnace. But we thought that besides that you had a head as well. . . ."

Maier shot up his eyebrows and chewed as if he held a pipe in his mouth.

"But I'm telling you I'm against it."

"Then let's go."

"And the furnace?"

"Then let the workmen go."

Maier went away into a corner, took some tobacco from his pocket and mumbled in a low bass:

"I know nothing. . . ."

But in a quarter of an hour a ruffled man in a calico smock burst through the door and shouted straight at Maier:

"Maier, are you here?"

He smiled distractedly and immediately flew outside.

Then Maier went up to the telephone mouthpiece and said calmly:

"Send me two men with shovels. Mine have vanished somewhere, devil take 'em. . . ."

And a quarter of an hour later a man carrying a placard out through the factory gates:

WE SOCIAL DEMOCRATS ARE
AGAINST WAR!

was approached by a police inspector who took the pole from his hands and, giving the placard to a Schutzmann, said:

"Take this rubbish to the station."

Behind the man from whom they had taken the placard wavered a loose, amorphous crowd. Behind the inspector, etched against the cobblestones, stretched an even line of Schutzmann uniforms. For the space of a minute the crowd looked at the uniforms. Then it began to thin, then it melted and the last of the crowd—he who had carried the placard out onto the street—quietly returned to the factory yard and closed the iron gates behind him.

This was at a quarter to eleven.

And at this hour Andrei came for the third time to the house where Kurt lived.

He stopped at the door to catch his breath. His glance fell on a rolled-up scrap of paper lying on the pavement under Kurt's window. Something urged him forward. He bent down, picked up the paper and opened it.

Torn, crushed, the note scrawled in brown pastel crayon ended with the word:

Andrei.

FLOWERS

Maier was wearing a knitted jacket with small pockets on the breast. From one pocket to another ran a small chain. From his mouth—toothless, pleasant, surrounded by the grayish bristle of his mustache and beard—descended a long pipe. The bowl lay on his stomach. His stomach was stout, not because Maier lived well and ate lots of ham, but simply because Maier was going on sixty and his stomach, which had labored sufficiently over potatoes, salads and liverwurst, had sagged a little.

Maier had been a foreman eighteen years, but he still could not permit himself the luxury of heating all the rooms of his mansard, and the largest of all (facing southeast) he rented out.

And now, after dinner, having lit his pipe, Maier went in to see his lodger—a dreamer, a fool, and in general a fine fellow—the artist Kurt Wahn.

The fine fellow was standing at the open window, looking down at the street.

"Things are really moving now," said Maier, raising his pipe with his lips.

The fine fellow did not respond.

"I dare say the business'll be more drastic than in seventy one. . . ."

The fine fellow stamped his shoe on the floor.

"When you think of it . . ." began Maier again and clicked his tongue: "Ts-ts-ts-tsk . . ."

The fine fellow asked without turning round:

"What's new, Herr Maier?"

The landlord sucked his pipe and sat down on the sofa, moving some dusty stretchers away from him.

"Every trade has its own logic which can be understood if you look closely enough. I look at your trade and I understand nothing. When will you tell my wife, Herr Wahn, that she can sweep the dust out of your room? . . . New? Still the same: only foolishness."

"Is duty, according to you, also foolishness? Indignation, anger—also?"

Kurt turned round, beat his chest with his fist and cried:

"When right here it's boiling, on fire?" and again turned to face the window.

Maier puffed out some smoke.

"Last night I didn't sleep, Herr Wahn. I was thinking, Herr Wahn. So much so that my wife wanted to put a mustard-plaster on my feet. These are the thoughts that came to me, Herr Wahn. I have been standing so many years at my furnace, you know. My friend—the artist Herr Wahn, who won't allow the dust to be swept out of his room —goes out of town in order to draw from nature and then he paints pictures. No one has insulted me or my friend and we have nothing to feel insulted at. And suddenly . . ."

"The nation, Herr Maier, the nation, the people," cried Kurt into the window.

"I understand, Herr Wahn. But I was thinking, Herr Wahn. . . . Perhaps I should have listened about those mustard-plasters: that would have drawn the blood away from my head. I was thinking, is it made that way? Why must I feel insulted by . . . ?"

Kurt interrupted:

"There are occasions when it is impossible to think. You will forgive me, Herr Maier, but someone has slapped you in the face and all you do is philosophize."

"I learned about this along with you, from the newspapers on the second day by telegraph. But when it was delivered, this slap in the face, I was sleeping peacefully with my wife."

Kurt broke away from the window, ran up to the land-lord and grated in a suppressed voice, his head shaking:

"I requested you, Herr Maier, not to talk to me about this subject!"

"I didn't think you were such a hothead," replied Maier and raised his pipe with his lips. "I didn't even want to raise that subject. You yourself asked me what's new. I wanted to tell you what happened to me today, before dinner. . . ."

Maier opened the lid on his pipe bowl, pressed the to-bacco down with his finger and sucked at the pipe.

"This morning I was called to the telephone. Someone said: 'At dinnertime go to the office.' I went. The second director, Herr Lieber, came to meet me, stretched out his hand and said: 'The management has instructed me to ex-press to you, Herr Maier, gratitude on its behalf for the fact that you exhibited a sense of duty in not leaving your post at the time of the disorder which took place.' I said to him: 'Herr Director, but you know, the furnace, you know it. . . .' At this point someone brought him some papers and he asked what they were. They told him it was a list, a list of fines. Then he took a pencil out of his pocket— in a gray casing, our patent, the last word you know, Herr Wahn; the lead comes out automatically, no pressing or screwing necessary, automatically—leafed through the papers and I saw sheet after sheet, sheet after sheet, but I didn't count them and I was looking at the director's hands. Such long, such white fingers. Believe me, Herr Wahn, I was only thinking that I had never had such fingers, not even as a young man, and that it had nothing at all to do with work, it's simply that my fingers were completely different from birth. Herr Director turned over the papers and ran his pencil lightly over where necessary, and again he gave me his hand and spoke on behalf of the manage-ment. I shook his hand—a hand completely free of bones— I said that the furnace, well it . . . and all that and couldn't think about anything except fingers. That's how it ended. I went through the yard, took my bicycle, turned the pedals with my foot and then, suddenly, I said to myself: 'Wait, old Maier, wait! Why, you've done it dirty, you've done it dirty for sure, if you got thanked, when the whole factory, all the workmen . . . ' "

The artist's eyes slowly wrinkled, he shook his head and asked:

"Admit it, Herr Maier, are you a socialist?"

Maier took out his pipe, blinked at the bright window, trying to see into his lodger's face, and smacked his soft mouth, then he smiled uncertainly and got up.

"Your jokes used to be more successful, Herr Wahn."

And went out.

Kurt looked out of the window.

With a swish of tires bicycles were rolling to the right and left along the licked white street. Sacks and baskets stuck out from the riders' humped backs. Above the handlebars pipes swayed like pendulums, every now and then throwing out puffs of blue smoke behind the smokers. The puffs dashed after the sacks and baskets, hung onto them, streamed out into white strips and disappeared. The bicycles overtook one another, gathered in small bands, and crawled apart in a line, emerging hurriedly from behind houses and bunching into a dense black flood at the ends of the street.

At this point a yellow bicycle sailed into the road, wobbled, and turned right; it had tall handlebars and a rider who sat as if he were in an armchair, straight and still: Herr Maier was going to Faber.

And so for a quarter of an hour: overtaking one another, gathering in bands, crawling apart in a line, disappearing in the dense black flood at the ends of the street—bicycles, bicycles, bicycles. And when a quarter of an hour had passed and no one was late, because nothing had happened, the road was emptied. A woman wiping the sweat from her face was driving a pair of sinewy dogs harnessed to a cart. The dogs had their mouths open wide and in the mansard high above the road one could hear their labored breathing. A monk in a brown cassock with a hood, and a tasseled, tightly twisted belt around his waist, beads in hand, his head lowered, dashed across the road.

Kurt looked out of the window.

"War."

Who said that?

"War."

Whose was that voice?

"War."

Why here, on roads planted with apple trees, shaded by cedars, nurtured, cherished, beloved, why here?

"War."

In the noisy grumbling of the turbines, submerged in the foliage of white willows, in the creaks and rustles of the sluices, letting caravans of barges through—why here?

"War."

Our homes planted with flowers, our fields soft under the new harvests—and our factories, our factories, our factories, those cathedrals where from childhood we have celebrated mass day and night! Why, why?

"War."

Apple trees and cedars, flowers and turbines, fields and sluices, and our eternal mass to the factory—these are in our bones, in our muscles, in our hearts—and we don't want it, don't want it, don't want it!

"War."

Kurt ran down the stairs, ran across the street and jumped onto a streetcar. The streetcar sped to the center, to the old city. The center, the old city, with its buses, bars, squares and streets, Polish churches, cafeterias and castle from the Middle Ages, was speeding nowhere.

It was too quiet, this city, it almost dozed, preserving the peace of its stone skeleton of the Middle Ages. The bars and cafeterias rattled their knives and glasses but not too loudly, and the buses considerately muffled their engines in order not to disturb, to destroy the pleasant doze of earlier times.

And now, aroused, frightened, the awakened city had in a few days, in a few hours, to catch up with the twentieth century. It had to catch up with it in order to keep its Middle Ages skeleton in one piece. This was screamed out by the newspapers—morning and evening ones, conservative and Social Democratic ones, liberal and clerical ones, rich ones, poor ones, large ones, small ones, ones with readers and ones without, illustrated ones, special ones, traditional ones, ones for Christians, ones for housewives, ones for servants and ones for gentlemen officers.

Correspondents have already been sent to the frontiers, the publication of four new war novels has been announced, the first military communiqué has already been received—in bold type on the front pages of all newspapers: Christian, social democratic and so on—in bold type, the first military communiqué:

> Yesterday, at four p.m., near the village of Fanoir, southwest of Metz, our border patrol ran into a French reconnaissance detachment and attacked it. The Frenchmen, returning our fire in vain, were put to flight.

Oh, oh! They've already been put to flight!

Oh, they don't know how to shoot properly!

"Have you read?"

"And have you read?"

"Have you heard how a French spy, dressed as a monk . . ."

"Do you know that the Russians long ago . . ."

"Oh, we were far too good-natured and our patience . . ."

"They seized him and—what d'you think?—he turned out to have gun cotton in his mouth. . . ."

"Damn it, although he was writing to our Kaiser, yet at the same time . . ."

"She had the passport of a simple schoolmistress, but when they searched her . . ."

"Dirty cowards, they'll run away at the very sight of our helmets!"

"I assure you, the most good-natured appearance: light-blue eyes . . ."

"I would have guessed right away!"

"Hold it, hold it, ho-old it!"

"Special te-le-gra-ams!"

"Spe-e-e . . ."

". . . gra-am!"

"Read, read!"

"Aha-a! . . ."

"I told you, I told you! . . ."

"Have you read?"

"And you?"

"And you?"

Oh, oh! They've already been put to flight!

Oh, they don't know how to shoot properly!

Today at five in the morning in the region of Rot a young man was detained, calling himself . . .

A cab-driver, top-hat cocked on the back of his head, swaying on top of his high box, was waving a telegram in the air. A driver, holding the steering wheel with one hand, was stuffing a telegram up his sleeve. A *Schutzmann* having walked ten steps away from the crossroads was squinting at the telegram stuck on a window. A cyclist without dismounting bought a telegram from a puffing lad. In restaurants, taverns, cafeterias, streetcars, overhead, in hands and pockets, on the floor—telegrams. In windows, on walls, in display windows, in the air—blown by the wind—telegrams, telegrams, telegrams.

"Special te-le-gram!"

"Spe-e . . ."

". . . gra-a-m!"

It was as if a strong wine were being poured through the city and the people were choking on it and swimming, drowning and disappearing in the wine.

Kurt crushed a white scrap of paper strewn with chopped words into a ball. Then he smoothed it out, slid his sharp eyes over the distinct lines, crumpled the paper again into a tight ball and shouted:

*"Ober!"**

He paid and ran out into the square. There—amid the noise and vibration of the city choking, drowning—he suddenly stopped in the middle of the sidewalk. People went round him, bumped into him, looked back at him. He noticed nothing. He was looking over the heads, shoulders, hats and umbrellas straight in front of him, in the direction

*Waiter.

he had just been walking. Just as suddenly as he had stopped, he turned around, cut across the square and boarded a streetcar. Breaking away from the human crush on the pavement, a man ran across the square toward the car. The car was moving. The man speeded up, leaped onto the running board, entered the car and looked for someone.

"Kurt!"

Kurt looked at the street and crushed the white scrap of paper in his hands.

"Kurt, Kurt! . . . You saw me?"

Kurt turned away and thrust his hands into his pockets. His mouth was closed tight, his delicate upper lids pressed down by his brows.

"We've nothing to say to each other."

"Kurt!"

"Listen," began Kurt.

But the one who had called him by name clutched his head and whispered:

"So you were running away from me?"

Kurt sank down on a bench. His lips were trembling, his eyes reddened. Any moment he would smile, or cry, or even shout.

He said, also in a whisper:

"I hate you, Andrei. . . . I have to hate you! Go away. Farewell. . . . Go away!"

"You are contradicting your reason, contradicting your heart!"

"Heart? Heart?" cried Kurt and rose from his seat. "Go away, leave me. There's nothing to say. Go away! Otherwise I'll shout it over the whole car—who you are, and you'll be . . ."

"Shout away, shout! I shan't take a step!"

They stood face to face, not taking their stubborn eyes from one another, and their faces were pale, distorted with the strain, covered with sweat.

"I'm waiting."

Kurt was silent.

"Good-by, Kurt. You will come to your senses, I know."

"I'm not a hypocrite. Good-by," said Kurt, turning away from Andrei.

Startsov jumped down from the car.

Along the street a newsboy on a bicycle flew toward him rending the silence with his hoarse wail:

"Special te-el-e-gram!"

"Spe-e-e . . ."

". . . gra-am!"

The houses roundabout were quiet and deserted, flowers yellowed and curled in open windows, mansards hung over the other stories and buried the stillness of the streets. People had gone away from here to the churches, they had gone away, run away, sped away, in order to see with their own eyes how the city, asleep for centuries, was being aroused to war and glory.

Andrei walked quietly—through the outskirts, through side streets hiding in the irregular crooked rows of old stone dwellings. There was no need to hurry. There was nowhere to hurry to. Behind were years which you could not have back and which were not necessary, people who would never be as they had been, never. Was it not all the same, no matter where? Was it not all the same, wherever you went? And would you reach anywhere?

The crossing over the road to Fürth—the first and oldest road in Germany—the crossing over which Andrei had passed so many times was being guarded by a patrol of soldiers.

Had Andrei noticed that these soldiers were wearing greenish-gray uniforms with matted buttons, knapsacks of calf-hide, helmets in canvas covers and cartridge belts on either side of the stomach? Had he noticed that the soldiers were in battle order? And that people were looking at this order from windows, doors and pavements? Did he see how the handkerchiefs, umbrellas, hats and hands waved and jumped in the windows of a train crawling through to Fürth and did he see, scattered at the feet of the soldiers in battle order, flowers, cigars, cigarettes—and again flowers, flowers, flowers? Did he see how majestically the soldiers in battle order tilted their heads back and did he see what a smile descended from their lips to the handkerchiefs, umbrellas, hats and flowers? The soldiers in battle order did not pick up all the flowers thrown at their feet, but only stuck a single rose in the bands of their rifles and in their waists by the cartridge belts. Can you really gather the flowers spread by the fatherland in the path of an army in battle order? Did Andrei see all this?

What did it matter whether he did or not?

Andrei walked with his head lowered.

On the light scrubbed staircase by the door of the apartment he lived in, men in long black overcoats and derbies stood motionless. There were five of them. They were noiseless. Andrei first noticed the men when he was already inside the circle they formed.

A pale-faced close-shaven man with a kind look in his bright eyes raised his derby and asked:

"Herr Startsov?"

"Yes."

"Be so kind," and he opened the unlocked door in front of Andrei.

"Perhaps Herr Startsov will show us his things?"

Four of them took off their derbies, overcoats and jackets, unbuttoned their cuffs and rolled the sleeves of their striped shirts to the elbow. On the narrow belts of the men who undressed, sticking to their ribs in pale yellow holsters, hung tiny Colts.

A CHAPTER
OF DIGRESSIONS

LEGENDS—GOSSIP—FACT

The Villa Urbach lies in the mountains not far from the border of Bohemia. It is surrounded by pines—violet in the evenings, reddish-brown at midday. The stones on the peaks of the mountains are bare, with sharp edges. Seen from afar the mountains seem to be piled up with old broken furniture. However, on one peak, in cowls and with hoods thrown on their backs, the Three Nuns bow toward the east. One has her beads in her hand: this is curly pink heather creeping out of a crevice in the rock. Along the valley winding to the Villa Urbach runs a white highway, beside it a narrow-gauge railroad. At the point where the valley rests against the sloping foot of Mt. Lausche lies the reddish sooty roof of the station. From above, from the round-breasted summit of Mt. Lausche, the valley, the highway, the strip of railroad and the station would fit into the hollow of a man's hand. The whistle of the trains heard from here is like the chirruping of sparrows. Here slumbers the echo, buried in the deep softness of pine needles. On the other hand, every sound in the valley makes its way seven times to the feet of the Three Nuns. Toward evening, when peasant carts are hastening homeward for the night along the highway, not even a desperate daredevil will sit at the feet of the Three Nuns.

There are no legends concerning the Villa Urbach. It is known only that it was previously called von Freileben, until the last bearer of this name married a man with no occupation, who was not a nobleman at all—Urbach.

If there were a need to and worse came to worse, it would be possible to invent a legend about the Villa von Freileben as well. But there is no need.

To the north of the Three Nuns stand the ruins of a Capuchin monastery. It was struck by lightning at the moment when the monks had enticed two young beauties from a neighboring village into the monastery wine cellar. All the Capuchins were burned to a cinder. Both the village beauties—saved by a miracle—remained alive: Providence had protected innocence for the edification of Christians. This was asserted by the villagers who won these beauties. Here follows the story of what a fight set in among the suitors of the whole district over these girls: everyone wanted to come into contact with Providence through them. But now is not the time to linger over the story.

The point is that the peasants had no need of legends. Before the Capuchin order had arrived here, the castle, which had Christianly served the humble brethren, had been for long years the residence of the possessor of a small margraviate, zur Mühlen-Schönau. The ancestors of this knightly line had once been close to the Vatican and twice had equipped expeditions to the grave of our Lord. During the Thirty Years War they had sat it out, like bats, behind their castle battlements. Afterward they pillaged Protestant Saxony. Then, quietly, they declined. Cardinal Sebastian sought a refuge with the margraves for an impoverished order of Capuchin brethren. The margraves gave up their residence to be used as a monastery, and notified all the Catholic monarchs of this act. Only woodlice and spiders have remained in the castle to the present time.

To the west of Mt. Lausche, almost on its slopes, nestled the new castle—smaller, better natured and younger than the ruins. Here were transferred the knights' ancestors, relinquishing the wood-lice and spiders to the Capuchins. Here were preserved the reliquaries of an old landed family. Here grew up its last scion—a taciturn, smooth and fair-haired little boy, Maximilian-Johann von zur Mühlen-Schönau. He grew up under the supervision of a guardian and before the eyes of the peasants—the descendants of those who had twice attempted to help their Lord God by rescuing his grave from the heathens.

That is why in these places they had no need of legends. That is why, when you looked at a peasant from behind, as he planted his feet down like a house, it seemed that resting on his back was the heavy burden of the centuries, with their knights, their monarchs, their cardinals and their monks. If it had not been for this back—how would you have known whether in the castle library—west of Lausche —there lay a beautiful volume which had turned green: *The Heraldry and Family Tree of the Line of Landed Margraves von zur Mühlen-Schönau?*

What can you say after that about the Villa Urbach? Gossip, gossip—oh yes!

An incomprehensible man this Herr Urbach! Perhaps in some other country he would not have attracted attention to himself. But in Germany, in Germany . . .

First of all: what did he do? Landowner. Good. But why had he not once peeped into the dairy, or inspected the cattle-sheds, or made arrangements for haymaking? He had a manager? Good. It was unwise, of course, to entrust a large farm to a mere servant, but a rich man could permit himself a great deal. Only why had Herr Urbach never once taken account of his confidential agent and why did he send him to his wife—Frau Urbach, born von Freileben? Perhaps Herr Urbach was in government service? A member of the *Landtag**? Nothing of the kind. Perhaps a scholar? But then he would have been called professor. Perhaps a writer? In that case it would have been known to every gendarme. Simply a rentier? But really, did a rentier lead that kind of life? A day at the villa, a day in town, a day at a resort. Spent nights in the mountains, slept at dinner, or else stayed in his study for three whole days. The way of life of a genuine rentier had been established by a whole consilium of professors. A rentier did not live, but greeted incessantly. They said that Herr Urbach was drafting some

*Provincial Diet.

projects or other. But what kind of projects nobody knew. People just talked.

No, Herr Urbach was an incomprehensible man. Frau Urbach would never have married him if . . . In short she was still Fräulein von Freileben when her son had been born. Furthermore she was lame in one leg: she had had that since childhood. But she was a sturdy, strict and virtuous woman and not to bow to her when she was passing along the highway was somehow awkward.

They had children. That little boy with whose appearance in the world Herr Urbach was unexpectedly blessed, and a little girl named Marie. It is strange how severe and just is fate. The elder child took after his mother. Heinrich-Adolf—not Urbach, of course—Heinrich-Adolf von Freileben was the heir and descendant of the line. Marie . . . well, what can be said about that little wench?

Gossip, gossip—oh yes!

Ask any peasant—she was known throughout the entire district. She turned up everywhere and always unexpectedly, like a ghost. It was truly a bad sign if Marie ever ran into someone else's yard. After her appearance some kind of trouble was sure to happen on that farm: a horse would fall sick, or a reaper would break, or—at the very least—the milk would go sour. Once Marie had stopped for some reason by the church. At that time the organist was coming out.

"How do you do, little girl," he said.

And then Marie looked at him with such eyes that he immediately felt an itching in his nose. And what do you think—well, the organist came down with a cold and sneezed so much at the Whitsun service that all you could hear from the choir were tchoos and atishoos!

And once Marie peeped into the *Forstamt's** window. The latter was sitting sorting his papers and writing odds and ends.

"Ooh," said Marie, "how many papers you have! Don't you get mixed up in them?"

"No," answered he, "that's why I'm a Forstamt, to see

*Forestry superintendent.

that things do not get mixed up. But you go away from here and don't interfere."

"Well," said Marie, "now you're getting mixed up!"

And ran away.

And the *Forstamt* made such a mess of things from that day that an official came from town and ordered him to be removed right away.

It was as if nothing less than a demon had settled in the wench, and she had been born in an evil hour. . . .

But just as there was no need of legends in these places, because every stone was overgrown with legends, so there was no need of gossip about Marie, for the story of her childhood was full of accidents and secrets, whose telling perhaps would have been more unexpected and terrible than all the gossip.

Marie had been three months old when death first came after her. Herr Urbach brought two doctors from the town and the doctors did not leave Villa Urbach for nineteen days. The child was dying for nineteen days. She was quiet, almost soundless, and only once in twenty-four hours—in the evenings—did she flare up with fever, like coals, and then slowly cooled down during the night, taking on the grayish pallor of ashes. Her eyes, at times as clear as an autumn stream, would suddenly rest on her father and then Herr Urbach would rush out of the house and wander in the mountains. The doctors consulted one another, wrote prescriptions and explained something to the child's father at length, then went upstairs to the rooms reserved for them and sat down at a chessboard. Fast messengers sped to the pharmacy with prescriptions, brought back compresses, thermometers, baths, then sat in the kitchen and made leisurely calculations as to how much the child's funeral would cost the master.

Marie was dying. That was evident not only to outsiders —to the doctors and the servant—but also to the father. More and more often he disappeared in the mountains and returned stealthily, listening to the silence of the nursery. Frau Urbach awaited her daughter's end without leaving her room.

On the eighteenth day one doctor grew tired of losing at chess and he went away, promising to send his colleague from town. On the nineteenth, the second doctor announced that he could be of no use.

And on that day, in the evening, when the child's stiffened little body glowed crimson with the fiery tints of the fever, a cry sounded in the nursery. It was brief, helpless, and forcefully recalled to everyone the pitiful squeak with which, three months before, Marie had appeared in the world.

"A good sign," said the nurse, "the child has been born a second time."

Herr Urbach began to sob.

"It seems to me," said the doctor taking his leave, "that in spite of the difficulty of diagnosis, the treatment we applied was absolutely correct."

This hour defined forever the place which Marie occupied in the family: she became the darling of her father, and her mother took a dislike to her. Of course this was bound to happen sooner or later, because a son was growing up in the family—Heinrich-Adolf—with the name of Urbach but with the blood of a von Freileben. But it happened precisely from that moment when Marie was born a second time.

She was helped by the goat's milk with which they began to feed her after her illness. When she learned to hold things and her father gave her toys, Marie in company showed no curiosity toward the toys—and only when she was left alone in her baby-carriage would she set about examining her toys.

At nine months Marie learned to walk. Her father accidentally saw this happen. The child was sitting on the floor surrounded by toys. Her nurse went out. Watching her go and seemingly making sure that there was no one in the room, Marie stretched out her little hands to a chair. Groaning and straining, she got to her feet and began to shift her disobedient little legs, which were fastened together. Going round the chair. Marie decided to take a few steps without support and started toward the bed. But immediately she fell and bumped the back of her head on the floor. Herr Urbach involuntarily took a step forward. Marie raised herself up with difficulty, tried to stretch out her arm and reach the back of her head to rub it, could not reach, prattled something to herself under her breath and looked around her. The chair stood behind her, the bed before her. In order to hold on to the chair it was necessary to take two or three steps backward. To the bed it was farther. Marie decided to reach the bed. At first she got on her knees. Then with great effort she placed her knees under her stomach and rested a little, standing on all fours. To lift her head and at the same time tear her hands from the floor was more difficult. Marie could easily have crawled to the bed on all fours, but she had decided to get to her feet and she was bound to have her way. One little hand broke away at last from the floor and dangled in the air. Then the whole weight of her little body went on to the other hand. It was impossible to stand up. Then Marie squatted down, got her breath back and began the whole job from the beginning. Again her little legs were brought up under her stomach, again she took a little rest, again one little hand began to wave in the air. But her legs suddenly bent at the knees of their own accord and Marie found herself on her haunches. Then she leaned her hands on her knees, struggled, straightened up, and without taking her hands from her knees shifted first one and then the other leg. Having assured herself that she was able to move along, Marie thrust out one hand in front of her, straightened up still more and with a wobble toddled forward, forward, almost as far as the actual bed. Here she tore her other hand away from her knee, clasped her palms joyously, quacked like a duck and fell on the bed, digging her fingers into the blanket.

Then Herr Urbach rushed over to her, lifted her high over his head, and shouted something incoherent.

But Marie, usually quiet, suddenly burst into irresistible tears, as if bitterly offended that someone had eavesdropped on her in her solitude.

After that, no matter how they taught Marie to walk, how they forced her to stand on her legs, every time she sat

down and remained motionless as a stone—until she was a
year old, when she walked confidently and without any
help.

THE STONE MARGRAVINE

Soft, rotten pine needles underfoot, regular rows of mast
timber, heather-covered cliffs, mountains piled up all
around, the castle ruins, the valley girdled by the strip of
railroad and the smooth, sloping foot of Mt. Lausche—
these were Marie's nursery.

The house and its furniture were burdensome to her and
she accounted winter the greatest unhappiness in her life.
But even in winter Marie lived in the frost, in the wind, lived
for skis and skiing down the mountain, for running and
sliding over the frozen slippery rocks. She ran and slid like
a goat, clambering over the steep cliffs, clinging to invisible
projections, swiftly and noiselessly. They said truly that she
had taken after her wet-nurse—a butting bully and jumper
who had exhausted everyone's patience.

One autumn Marie disappeared. For a whole day she
could not be found and in the evening the Villa Urbach
sounded the alarm. Men were sent in all directions. In the
village they questioned the children who were friendly with
Marie. No one had seen her.

Darkness covered the forest leaving no trace, paths
went off into the night, a fine rain hung like cold screens
between the mountains.

The whole village was aroused. Peasants seized lanterns
and split up into parties and had only just moved off in
different directions when a young laborer dashed in from
the high road at full gallop. His horse was lathered, the
hay in the cart was straggling and he himself was drenched
in sweat, trembling, and unable for a long time to talk
sense about what had happened to him.

It turned out that when he had been traveling along the
highway and had passed the Three Nuns, a terrible noise
had suddenly descended on him. It had seemed to the

youth that the mountains had moved out of place and an evil spirit had been laughing and howling after him. His horse had bolted and he had only just been able to stay in the cart, remembering Lord Jesus and all the prayers he had been taught by the friar. And behind him there had been a whistling and grinding and laughter and howling. Apparently Beelzebub himself was then celebrating his birthday.

It was not so easy to discover men who would agree to go at night to the Three Nuns. Herr Urbach himself headed the courageous peasants. He knew his daughter well indeed if he decided immediately that she would be nowhere else than visiting the devil!

One should have heard the concert *he* gave on that accursed evening! A roaring and crashing rolled through the woods around, as if a thunderstorm were scorching the pines and hurling them to the ground. The mountains hooted and groaned, monsters were clawing their breasts to pieces. And on top of all this—the night: it was pitch-black—you couldn't see a thing, and the lamps, you could bet, would be put out by the rain. Only the man who didn't give a damn about saving his soul would go out there to the Three Nuns on such a night.

Courage stayed with our "heroes" exactly as far as the strip of railroad. They refused point-blank to cross it and go out on the highway. Herr Urbach chose one of the better lanterns and made a detour to the cliff. He had not crossed the highway and come abreast of the Three Nuns before the noise suddenly died away. At regular intervals the brittle clang of a banging sheet of iron rolled down from the summit. It did not echo here even once.

Herr Urbach shouted:

"Marie!"

"Ah-ah," came in reply.

"I am waiting for you below!"

"I'm com-ming!"

The iron could be heard clanging against stones and rumbling. And gradually, moment by moment, a peaceful and even silence settled in the mountains.

Rumpled and spattered with raindrops, Marie slid quickly

over the wet stones and appeared in the yellow circle of lamp light. She laid a finger to her lips and, like a conspirator, shook her head:

"Only, Papa, don't tell anyone it was me. The tin stayed up there, on top. Tomorrow I'll come here again and bring another sheet."

"Tomorrow you'll be in your room all day."

"No, Papa, we'll come here together. You've got to sit on the top, at the very feet of the Nuns."

"But I said you'll sit under lock and key."

"Oh, you! I'm telling you: it's so terrible there that you can't resist it. You'll fall down with fear for sure!"

She laughed, seized her father by the hand and ran skipping along in front of him, as if he were not leading her home but she him.

That was the last prank to leave no trace on Marie.

In the spring she began to pay attention to her village friends. It was necessary to test their fidelity, to choose the most reliable, determined, taciturn and steadfast. It was possible to rely on only three with a light heart. These were thirteen- to fourteen-year-old lads, broad-shouldered, sturdy and with such choice large round eyes that when Marie told them frightful stories it seemed to her that these eyes were just about to jump out and roll away. Furthermore they had heard one or two things about the stone margravine, who had been buried many hundreds of years ago in the castle. It was not difficult to persuade them to undertake secret excavations in the monastery ruins; they themselves pestered Marie and had decided long ago who would flee where when the margravine's treasures had been discovered in the castle vault.

Not just anyone would have been clever enough to organize properly such a delicate matter as the search for treasure.

Marie knew what had to be done.

One day she brought her friends to her father's study. The boys were piled with books, maps and plans from the closets and shelves.

"Here! Look! Here it's written in English: four hundred years ago the margraves discovered an ossified margravine in their family crypt. When they tried to take the valuables off her the lid of the coffin snapped tight shut of its own accord and it proved impossible to open it. . . ."

"Here's a document for you. Here it's in German. You yourselves can read German: 'In fifteen hundred and sixty the margraves gave their castle to the order of the Capuchins.' Do you see? Read: to the order of the Capuchins."

There was no denying it: it was there in black and white: the order of the Capuchins. And the year—with extraordinary exactness: 1560.

"It's true all right," said one accomplice.

"Aha!" said Marie and they were all frightened.

"And look in this book. You see, here there's a picture too: the old castle zur Mühlen-Schönau. And it says that the coffin with the margravine stands under the ruins to this day. Understand?"

All of course understood perfectly. Yes, and it was impossible not to understand when Marie displayed before her accomplices an extraordinary learning, reading not only in English, but also in Dutch and even in American, and unrolled some kind of reddish sheets, huge rolls of documents and illuminated maps. Here, then, was something to make your eyes pop out!

"Now to work!" whispered one accomplice.

"Oh, no," announced Marie, "now I shall do some studying."

This word rang out solemnly and all agreed that to get down to work without studying was impossible.

"Who's been rummaging in my documents today?" asked Herr Urbach in the evening.

"What do you mean? What do you mean?" Marie took fright and bent her father's head to her lips. "Those are all manuscripts revealing the secret. . . ."

"You should be occupying yourself with arithmetic and not secrets."

But the secret was discovered.

The secret was discovered in the forest, not far from the ruins, and was contained in the plan on which Marie had marked all the underground passages of the old castle, the place where excavations had to be carried out and the burial vault of the margravine. On that day belief in underground treasures became a certainty.

"Swear, repeat every word after me," whispered Marie, raising her hand.

And the conspirators pronounced:

"We swear that we shall reveal our secret to no one on earth. We swear that we shall work until we find the stone margravine. We'll work like beasts. We'll work like oxen. May we be burned by fire and tried by iron. We swear that not by a single sound shall we betray one another. We swear that like brothers we shall share the treasure, without quarreling. We swear that we'll get spades, a lantern and some rope. And we'll obey Marie in everything. Amen."

"Wait," said Marie, when the oath had been pronounced, "I don't like the end, and you must repeat it."

All raised their hands a second time and said:

"And we shall obey Marie in everything and for all our lives. We swear, we swear, we swear. Amen."

"Right, now that's good. We can get to work."

And they got to work.

The first ascent to the ruins was limited to an investigation of the area. A ledge was found, strewn with earth and covered with moss, tall and steep. It was decided that this was the entrance to the vault.

The following day they started the excavations. The work extended over three days. In the mornings, when glassy dewdrops still shone on the undergrowth, the three conspirators with spades stolen from their fathers' barns crept up to the ruins, each by his own route. There, having met and exchanged gloomy looks, they selected one for guard duty. Two got down to digging. The soil was loose, the roots and stumps which the spades encountered crumbled into dust from a light blow and there were no stones, yet the work went slowly. When the sun had climbed high over Mt. Lausche the guard heard the prearranged whistle. Marie was bringing her friends breakfast. This was the best moment experienced by the treasure seekers. Ah, what tasty things were to be found in the pantry of the Villa Urbach! And what an appetite our laborers had worked up by ten o'clock in the morning! For an Edam cheese it was worth plying a spade!

Marie questioned her friends like an officer his soldiers, went round the excavated ledge on all sides, tapped a spade on the ground and shouted:

"Do you hear it hum?"

"It hums, o-o-ooh!" responded the conspirators.

"We'll soon reach it."

"We'll reach it!"

Strangely, they really did reach it.

On the third morning when, after breakfast, they had resumed digging, the trench suddenly fell away under their feet into a pit. They jumped back in terror. They exchanged looks. Carefully they tried to dig the earth around the gap. And they emitted a joyful frightened kind of bird-like squeal: the clods of earth raining into the pit were striking hollowly against the firm invisible bottom of the vault.

"Rope!" commanded Marie, selecting a sharp-edged stone from a pile of excavated earth.

Everything that happened after that took place as on a ship's deck—briskly, precisely and smoothly.

Out of the rope and stone a plumb was made. With the plumb they measured the depth of the pit. A dead tree was rolled up to the pit and thrown across the opening. A loop was tied at one end of the rope, the other was secured to the cross-beam.

Marie crawled into the loop, took the lamp in her hand and threw a triumphant glance at her friends. Her little face was the picture of determination, her mouth was slightly open and her lips twitched greedily, unevenly. She sat on the cross-beam, she dangled her legs into the pit, she gave the command:

"Lower!"

The boys dug their feet into the ground and stretched the rope tight. Marie jumped off the tree and her head—marked out clearly against the black wall of the trench—disappeared underground. The quivering string of rope slid away into the pit, the brave lads fixed their eyes on the yawning blackness of the hole and caught their breath with the same fearful caution as that with which their trembling hands were letting the rope run through them. But then it slackened, waved in the air and fell, and from underground floated a muffled and barely audible:

"Come here!"

And when the conspirators had hung their heads over the opening and their eyes had made out in the depths the dim spot of the lantern and Marie's face, indistinct and terribly pale, they again heard the muffled unfamiliar voice:

"The vault! Come down, get the spades. I'm going ahead."

They saw her pale face vanish under the ground and the dim light thinned out, faded and disappeared in the darkness. Then they pulled the rope out of the pit, went off to one side and began to deliberate about whom to lower into the vault.

And at this instant the earth trembled beneath them and over the mountains, from peak to peak, rolled a heavy groan: the excavated ledge slipped away underground and in place of the pit which had swallowed Marie gaped the deep jaws of a crater.

Another instant and the conspirators bolted in all directions. Behind the ruins in different directions could be heard the crunching of twigs and the scattering of small stones. Farther and farther.

Stillness.

Thus death came after Marie a second time. . . .

The oath taken by the treasure seekers was not broken. True, they were not tried with fire and iron, because the spades forgotten at the excavations had betrayed all the accomplices without their denying it, but bitter hours fell to their lot. And how can one know which was worse: their fathers' fists, which they had been experiencing for a long time past, or the loss of the treasure, of which their dream had been dissipated with the first evening glow of sunset? Because, when, in the evening—ten hours after the landslide —the peasants had dug into the catacomb and Marie was crying in her father's arms, her first words were:

"The margravine's not there. . . ."

The lantern with which Marie had descended into the

vault was glimmering hopelessly. She was clinging to it with both hands. Her face was soiled and grave. Tears rolled down it in slow rivulets.

"Silly, silly," said Herr Urbach, "you should have asked me in the beginning; the margravine lies in the new castle."

Thus was Marie born a third time.

It coincided with her thirteenth birthday, and to this coincidence the peasants attributed the change which took place in Marie.

She became taciturn and sluggish, the abruptness disappeared from her movements, she still remained a child, but the features of an adult were about to absorb everything childish in her. She repulsed everyone she met. Especially frightening was a certain ominous obstinacy in her eyes, and a single thought—harsh and restless—gave a perpetual coldness to her gaze.

From that time the rumor spread about Marie that from her it was a short distance to the devil himself and that it was better not to cross her path. It was then, precisely then, that the *Forstamt* experienced the inexplicable occurrence with his papers and the respected organist by courtesy of the little wench sneezed his way all through the Whitsun mass.

An old coachman who in his time had cut the throats of innumerable chickens, geese and ducks suddenly refused to carry out the obligations of a warrior. It cost a great deal of thorough pestering in the kitchen before he related what had happened to him in the barn the last time he had tried to cut a goose's throat. He had only just settled himself on a chair with the goose pressed between his knees and had been waving his sword over its neck, when Fräulein Marie ran up to him and announced her desire to cut the goose's neck personally. Yes, yes, personally! How had he felt hearing that? Or course he tried to talk her out of it, begged, threatened even to complain about her. Nothing doing! Marie had grabbed hold of the goose's neck and kept repeating over again: let me, let me. Finally she had practically torn the sword out of his hand and brought it down on the goose's neck. She had not succeeded in cutting the goose's head off, but the blood had spurted out like a hose and the goose had broken loose from the coachman's hands. The bird had been a large one and strong. Two or three flaps of its wings and it had soared up under the roof and begun to rush up and down and across the barn, bumping into rafters and doorposts and throwing up a moaning throat rattle. It had been all covered in blood and the blood had dripped from it onto the earthen floor in heavy black drops.

Yet Marie had stood motionless by the lintel and followed the expiring bird with a kind of deathly frozen gaze. And when the coachman had noticed this gaze he had rushed headlong out of the barn. He was terrified to recall Marie's eyes or to go into the barn where he had seen them. And to cut a bird's throat now was simply beyond him.

Soon after the history of the goose Marie abducted Adolf's favorite cat.

Ah, yes, Heinrich-Adolf. But to talk of Marie means to say nothing about her elder brother. They lived apart, in enmity, in separate rooms in opposite parts of the house. They had separate teachers, separate likes and separate dislikes. Marie was the daughter of Urbach, Heinrich-Adolf the son of Frau Urbach, born a von Freileben. They were united only by name and the dining room. The dining room more than the name. They were strangers.

Adolf, perpetually fussing over animals, immediately noticed the disappearance of his favorite—a sleek fat angora cat.

In the whole house doors slammed, voices resounded through the passageways and corridors, Frau Urbach herself used her cane with its rubber tip to raise covers and counterpanes and looked under furniture and beds. Adolf squealed and sniveled, stamped his foot, rushed from one room to another and finally ventured on a sortie into his father's half of the villa. There, stealthily and holding his breath, he made his way up to Marie's room and, after hesitating at the entrance, hurled the door open with all his strength, flew into the room and turned to stone.

From the bracket of the wall-lamp at the head of the bed, suspended by its throat, its tail between its legs and the long soft fur on its back torn and scratched, swung the cat. Its paws twitched, above its bared teeth its shining bristly whiskers trembled, as if being tickled, and its stomach had sunk convulsively back to its spine.

Adolf did not see Marie. He rushed to the cat, lifted it and began to pull at the string, which had cut into its neck and become entangled in its fur. He was gasping for breath—red and wet with tears—and he hissed curses, stamped his feet on the floor and spilled a small dish of milk standing on the floor. Then he cried piercingly: the cat, recovering its breath, had dug its claws into him. A servant ran in.

Marie was nowhere. . . .

That evening she stood in her father's study and with her moist sharp eyes she followed him from under lowered brows; as if expecting an attack and ready for it she was all bunched up, tiny, like a little wild beast.

Herr Urbach was pacing from corner to corner, scratching his short hair, slapping himself with his hands as if seeking something in his pockets and groaning, hardly forcing out:

"A-a-ah!"

For the third time he stopped before Marie, wrung his hands and asked:

"What's the matter with you, Marie?"

She jerked her sharp little shoulders high and without dropping them exclaimed in terrible surprise:

"Well, I'm telling you, I would have given it milk, the objectionable little beast!"

"But why did you do such a vile thing?"

"I wanted to see how it would die. . . ."

"My God!"

Herr Urbach slumped into an armchair. His arms hung like cords, he fixed sightless eyes on the lampshade and he sat long and soundlessly, not budging a finger, not moving an eyebrow, thinking.

Frau Urbach had told him not only about Adolf's cat. The occurrence in the barn had also been known to her. She had known of Marie's tricks in the garden, bloodthirsty, repulsive. She had insisted, demanded, ordered that Marie be dispatched somewhere to a boarding school, to an asylum, finally—there are such institutions for juvenile criminals! It is impossible to bring Heinrich-Adolf up in the company of a degenerate girl!

"Shut up!" Herr Urbach had then cried.

Closed curtained doors, windows, the tap of a rubber tip on the floor, wails, reproaches, threats, humiliating, senseless, nausea-inducing hysterics. Yes, yes, hysterics by the virtuous, sturdy and strict Frau Urbach.

Marie, hiding in a corner, silently watched her father.

He roused himself, sought her with his gaze and in a changed—hardened, constrained—voice said:

"What's to be done, what's to be done, Marie? I always wished you well, was your friend. What's to be done?"

He got up and banged his fist on the table.

"This autumn you'll go to a boarding school."

He turned to face his daughter.

"I never put restraint on you, you know. Now . . . it'll be better this way. . . . Go to your room."

Marie left her ambush and moved uncertainly toward the exit. When she had opened the door she stopped and looked at her father. He again stood with his back to her. Lightly and impetuously she dashed over to him, stood stock still beside the armchair, carefully touched his jacket and whispered:

"Good night."

Without stirring he repeated:

"Go to your room."

Then sharply, almost jumping, she turned around, slammed the door on the run behind her and fled along the corridors.

She lay in her bed until late that night, still dressed, leaning her elbows on the pillow and looking under the table where her long abandoned black-faced dolls, donkeys, babies, teddy bears and monkeys lay scattered about on their backs and stomachs or stuck out upside down. Marie was waiting all the time for the puppet-monkey to turn its snout to her and take pity:

"Poor Marie!"

But the glove puppet kept quiet.

Frau Urbach was sitting at her needlework when her husband came into her. He stretched out his hand and said quietly:

"Forgive me for having been abrupt and rude. I have decided to treat Marie as you advise. . . ."

"That is entirely sensible," replied Frau Urbach and laid the tips of her fingers in her husband's hand.

When he had kissed his wife's fingers Herr Urbach sank down beside her on the sofa. The house was plunged in silence. Frau Urbach's bad leg was resting on a stool embroidered with pearls. The bone knitting needles moved softly, restrained by the fluffy wool of the knitting. Herr Urbach looked hard at the firm profile of his wife, which was bathed in pale light.

"How cruel you are," he said, "how cruel!"

"Go away from here," she replied after a short silence.

He got up and snapped his fingers.

"I would do that without your invitation. . . ."

The glove puppet remained silent. The monkey's lower jaw unfeelingly stuck its sparse gray little beard in the air and its reddish-yellow amber eye goggled ardently at the moon, which was looking at the toys under the table. Not one movement, not one sound out of the whole bunch of living—of course living—souls and treasures.

Poor Marie!

She jumped up, pulled out the glove puppet from under the table and, banging its head on the windowsill, hurled it into the garden.

"Make eyes there at your stupid old moon!"

Then she lowered the shutters, and the darkness saw something wrapped in a blanket twitching on the bed.

In the morning Marie was awakened by her father.

"Get up. Do you want to go to the seashore?"

She jumped up on the bed and the blanket slid off her; still hot from sleep, flushed, disheveled, she squeezed her father with all the strength of her tenacious arms and breathed in his face:

"I'm not angry at you. I know it wasn't you who thought up the boarding school. Well, it's true—it wasn't you? . . ."

FOOTSTEPS BECOME FIRMER

Space, space and light.

The wind was blowing prickly, burning sand from south to west, from the smooth yellow board of the shore out to sea. The sluggish crests of the low waves were stroking the peaceful water; then they would run onto the sand, fluff it into curls, comb it out, color it with something red and roll back to the sea in a transparent mica shroud. The strip of red would turn pink, become suffused with yellow and then disappear.

The clouds turned from side to side, drew out and then set: they were looking at the sea. A dense blueness was falling out of the sky, speeding faster and faster, rippling in countless blue dots; and then the ripple of dots, silently bouncing off the water, rushed upward to the clouds, and beyond them into the unfathomable blueness, into the sky.

The smooth yellow board of the beach was resting against the horizon in the distance and to run and run and run there was beyond one's strength—endless. From behind a shining line, a strangely distant line—how could the human eye suffice?— perhaps of the sea, perhaps of the sky, against the wind in the intervals between gusts, were wafted the smells of some kind of resinous and salty crust, then fish, then fresh new milk.

If you screwed up your eyes and whirled around on one spot and then forecast what color you'd see if you opened your eyes facing the sea—you could never guess! Dove-gray, light blue, steely blue, dark blue, and somewhere a spot of gray, and over there turquoise, and over there green.

Oh, to speed along the beach, head back, hands thrown upward, or spread out as for an embrace, bare feet hardly touching the red hot sand, offering one's body to its prickly needles, hurled by a wind which burned and bored through to one's very bones! In the ears—the brassy sighs

of the water; somewhere behind the eyes, in the head, in
its depths—indignant, burning—unfading sparks, flaming
strips and threads of light.

At midday Marie was walking along the shore, along
the very edge of the quiet waves running up on the beach.
The sand, filled with warm water, softly gave way beneath
her feet and her footsteps pressed out shallow hollows
around themselves which momentarily showed white and
then immediately filled with thick dark moisture. The tidy
beach, adorned with flowery cabins, was left far behind.
The curly dark-green bushes got closer and closer to the
water. Beside three broom bushes lay the moldering, half-
smashed skeleton of a sailing boat. Short juicy grass crept
along where its ribs stuck into the sand and on it a large
spot showed bright red. Marie stole up to it, stepping noiselessly over the sand.

Under the broom sat a fair-haired boy in a red bathing
suit, with his bent back toward the sea. On a bare patch of
sand between his outstretched legs he was fashioning something out of cockleshells, with his head bent and hardly
moving, noticing nothing around him.

Marie approached so closely to him that she could see
his hands—thin and white, like sand—moving the shells,
and fantastic grottoes, fortresses and bastions grew up in
front of him. She stood a long time behind the boy and then
stealthily went away, without giving herself away by a single careless sound or movement.

By the sea Marie gathered shells: they lay in a wave-
shaped strip along the shore, a few paces from the water, dried out by the sun, aired and moistureless. But to
build something out of them, even the most simple thing,
was beyond Marie's powers. Cockleshells spilled out of her
hands, slipped off one another, rolled down, and no trick
succeeded in welding them into a whole or in making them
hold. Marie trampled the shells into the sand.

Then she returned to the broom and stole up to the boy.
The fortresses were enclosed with rocks; from bastion to
bastion stretched little paths of red gravel, and grottoes disappeared into the grass. It was a whole world!

And then—one, two!—a leap into the very middle of this

world: swift feet landed on grottoes, fortresses, bastions, then on the sides—sand, grass, cockleshells—with a noisy crunching—and a desperate cry.

The boy ran off, turned around. He had cried out in fright—not because he was sorry for his skillful construction of shells; and now, standing some way off, he marveled at his fright. When she had spotted him Marie put her hands behind her back and waited. She waited for opposition, for tears and defense from a boy who had amused himself, like a girl, with such useless trifles as playing with cockleshells. But, strangely, before her stood a youth—she only now perceived how big and strong and calm he was —not thinking of tears or of defense. His wide bright eyes looked at Marie with a lingering gaze, his mouth was barely parted, and he remained silent.

For a second it seemed to Marie that she had seen his face somewhere before. She stared at him more closely and suddenly remembered that she was naked, that she had run off into the sea without her bathing suit, that he was the first person she had met since running out of her cabin and that she was separated from him only by light and air. She gritted through her teeth the words she had prepared earlier:

"Just try and touch me!"

But the youth did not move—he continued looking at her with that same lingering gaze, and this gaze took her all in from head to foot.

Then Marie rushed toward the sea. . . .

She caught sight of the wide bright eyes later, in the station tunnel of the noisy town—when she was returning home with her father—and it made her incomprehensibly glad and afraid. The eyes did not collide with hers— the meeting was momentary—but she had time to see that above them hung the long peak of a military cap. The whole way back she tried to recall where that face had first occurred, with its barely parted mouth and lingering bright gaze. And then, when the familiar pines had already flashed by, when the train had been inspected from on high by the Three Nuns and the tiny locomotive was shrilling like an angry sparrow in the blackened station—

then the face with the barely parted mouth suddenly appeared before her.

A sleek blond Junker came up to Marie, clicked his heels and said hastily, turning pale:

"We are acquainted, I believe . . . on the beach. . . ."

Marie blushed and clung to her father's arm.

"I'm from here, Schönau . . . we're neighbors. . . ."

Marie glanced at her father, quickly jerked her arm away and asked:

"From the castle . . . over behind Lausche?"

"Yes, to the west . . ."

Marie took a resolute step forward.

"Tell me, the margravine, the stone margravine . . ." she caught her breath and was unable to finish.

"Yes, in the new castle. Do you want to look? Come."

Herr Urbach approached a stout elderly man standing a little off from the Junker and raised his hat. . . .

How did those two days pass, stretching in an eternity between the sooty station in the mountains and the forest paths to the west of Lausche? How did the hours manage to go by while actually standing motionless day and night? How did an end come to this slow torture, when at every instant something should have happened, at every moment someone's call should have sounded and in every second some question was hidden?

But the end came and then the moments, minutes, hours sped along the paths and raced past reddish-brown pines, amid the scent of resin and the scrunching of soft pine needles.

"You came?" asked the bright-eyed Junker, and it seemed to Marie that he was choking with fright.

"Don't be afraid," she said encouragingly, "let's go straight there, to her. . . ."

The castle was quiet in the park where the Junker had awaited Marie; along the old walls lay hillocks of spilled lime overgrown with grass, the doors and passages were low, the sounds of their steps flew off to the sides and grew into a rumble somewhere deep within the walls.

"Oh, this is a real castle!" said Marie.

But the inhabited rooms were almost the same as in the

Villa Urbach—only everywhere hung pictures in heavy dark frames, while the windows stole and stifled the light. And Marie was in a hurry:

"Come, faster, faster!"

And then at last Marie was walking along a vaulted corridor, with a lamp in her hands, down firm steep steps, between cold damp stone walls.

"To the right," she heard the voice of her companion and he seemed to be terribly far away from her, although his breathing was here—behind her back, quite close.

"Bend lower now. . . ."

An iron door with a semicircular top, a rusty bolt—no lock, no secret—creaking hinges, heavy disobedient panels and a steep descent without steps.

"Jump. Can you see the floor? Now to the left, there the third. . . ."

"What third?"

"The third tomb from here. These two are stone—therefore empty. The coffins are underneath, in the ground. But this is a coffin."

"A real one?"

"Yes. Now I'll lift the lid."

"And she's here?"

"Now you'll see. . . ."

The lid came up easily, slipped, revealed the head of the coffin and fell across the coffin with a loud bang.

Marie took one step, then another, stretched the lamp as far as possible in front of her and leaned over the bulky lid.

In the coffin, surrounded by fine dust—on the dust as on a pillow—lay a hairless head. The face was pale yellow in the light of the feeble lamp, the lids were deep-sunk, the nose was almost transparent, straight, with slight curved wings of nostrils; the mouth was half-open and the teeth—even and young—did not gleam, but showed a dull yellow, like the forehead, like the chin, like the well-curved neck which was almost hidden in dust.

"She was only seventeen," said the Junker, "like me. . . ."

Marie looked round at him—he was standing behind her back—his face was pale, even pale yellow, like the margravine's, and the mouth—his mouth was half-open and his teeth were exactly the same. . . .

Marie took another look at the petrified face, chilling in the yellow light.

"Beautiful," she whispered.

"They have been showing her for a long time if anyone wants. Here, look."

He thrust a hand into the coffin, took a small hammer on a long turned handle out of the dust and tapped it against the margravine's head. The head echoed the blows shortly and hollowly and the hammer fell softly and sank into the dust.

"Just like stone."

A row of low headstones slipped away into the darkness, the black vault hung in an egg over the crypt; knights, courtiers, margraves, kept silence in the ancient dampness of stone and earth.

"But the treasures . . . you took them off her?" whispered Marie.

"There were no treasures . . . not for ages. . . ."

What's that? He seemed to smile? No, that was fear twisting his face. What was he afraid of? How pale he was! He was paler, paler than the margravine. His eyes had grown still, he was hardly breathing. What was the matter with him, what? He stretched out his arms to Marie, he embraced her, his half-open mouth came quite close to her lips, he . . .

"A-a-ah!"

Marie struck him in the chest with all her strength, the lamp trembled and winked in her hand, she turned around and ran off to the exit to the iron panels of the tall door, climbed into the corridor and ran and ran. At a turning which branched out to either side Marie stopped: why, he had remained in the darkness; there it was as black as . . . then, underground—he wouldn't find the way out . . . funny! And she laughed and shouted:

"Yoo-hoo, alley-oop!"

Then he walked silently before her, obediently carrying the lamp, protectingly lighting every projection, turn and step. By the exit to the park Marie said:

"I'll go alone. Good-by."

But out of the park, when the lime-splashed and tear-stained walls had gone from sight, she shouted:

"Yoo-hoo, alley-oop, yoo-hoo!"

And she laughed and laughed, as if sensing that this laughter had to last a long time, that in the evening at home her father would say to her:

"Marie, the day after tomorrow you go to Weimar, to Miss Ronny."

"Then that means it's true?" Marie would exclaim.

"What's to be done, what's to be done, Marie?" Herr Urbach would say and would lock himself in his study.

MISS RONNY'S BOARDING SCHOOL

The boarding school occupied a spacious house surrounded by a high iron fence with gilded spikes and with stone globes on the gates. Across the garden, paths of concrete slabs, closely laid and gleaming from hot water and scrubbing brushes, led from the entrance to the door. The garden walks were sprinkled evenly with gravel; lace girdles of yellow and blue hoops inserted alternately embraced the lawns and flowerbeds; the multicolored suns of glazed globes shone forth from planed poles stuck into the flowerbeds; a gnome with a wheelbarrow in his hands laughed cunningly, his head flung back and his earthenware shoes dug tightly into the clipped turf.

The house stood stately, well-groomed and buttoned up, shining in the sun like a *Schutzmann's* buttons, with the brass and nickel of its window handles and locks, of its polished bell-cup and its massive board on the door:

MISS RONNY'S BOARDING SCHOOL
for noblemen's daughters

A small mirror, focused on the entrance, sparkled on the frame of the window nearest the entrance door in an iron zigzag-like holder. Behind the window with the mirror, the gloomily draped and always quiet study of Miss Ronny lay concealed. Next to it extended the other rooms of her apartment; in the far corner—a classroom, across the corridor—the servants' quarters, the kitchen, storerooms and a locker-room. The upper story was occupied by classrooms, a gymnasium and a spacious *dortoir*.

The boarding school's mode of life had been established by Miss Ronny once and for all and it was just as straightforward, firm and exact as the iron railing, as the locks on the windows, as the paths and glazed globes in the garden. Every person that came within the bounds of Miss Ronny's dominions walked only along the clear and level line marked out by the directress, sat on chairs reserved for her, breathed at appointed places and smiled at the stipulated moments. Here there was indulgence for absolutely no one. The teacher of English and the cook, the class mistress and the gardener, the directress herself and the dancing mistress, bore different functions, but they submitted to a single inflexible regime. In the regulations of the school, the noblemen's daughters were not equal to the chambermaids who cleaned their bedroom after them, but an infringement of the regulations was punished with uniform severity both toward boarders and chambermaids.

"Fräulein," Miss Ronny would say to a guilty pupil, "you are mistaken if you think that I shall send you back to your parents out of exasperation. Go to the class mistress and tell her to shut you up in the locker-room for three hours."

Miss Ronny found that the boarding school was well run only when its whole system reflected her way of life with complete fidelity.

When she got up, Miss Ronny would take a cold bath, do exercises, rub herself with towels, put on her working dress, say her prayers and commence work. And she demanded that all who lived under the same roof with her, when they got up, should—in the absence of baths—pour water over themselves, do exercises, rub themselves with towels and say their prayers. Even the gardener—an old man of about sixty—assured Miss Ronny that he followed Müller's system in the mornings and changed his underwear exactly as he was directed—on Wednesdays and Saturdays. Miss Ronny was able to check the female servants personally, and here deception was out of the question. Except for the gardener and the teachers who came to give lessons at the boarding school, that is after the exercises and rubbing, there were no men in the house at all.

The twenty pupils—always twenty, no more and no less —were under the unwearying supervision of the directress; and nothing could be hidden from her, just as nothing happening in the entrance could escape being reflected in the little mirror affixed to the window of Miss Ronny's study.

After dinner, dancing and prayers the teachers checked their watches, and it seemed that the very sun closely watched the country excursions and walks taken by Miss Ronny's boarding school.

Twice a winter the school girls visited Goethe's house, and beforehand Miss Ronny read extracts from his biography in class, agreeing that it was possible to utter this man's name beside the name of Shakespeare.

In spring and autumn they went outside the town, and then Miss Ronny listened suspiciously to what the natural science teacher was saying about the pollination of plants.

Once a month there was a walk in town. And every week they visited the church where they listened to the sermon and joined in singing with the organ.

There was a daily walk inside the garden, along the walks and paths some way off from the railings, around the smiling gnome and the globes shining in the flowerbeds, and it lasted three-quarters of an hour. They walked in pairs, without haste, without looking back, circling and going dozens of times past one and the same point, and in front of them went the class mistress, her neck drawn up and her hands folded on her stomach, while behind, Miss Ronny imprinted her unbending soles on the gravel.

"Fräulein," she would say, calling a pupil by name, "halt. I noticed you tear a twig from a poplar and throw it on the lawn. Thus you committed two bad acts. Name them. First . . ."

"First I tore a twig from a poplar. . . ."

"And second . . ."

"And second I threw the twig on the lawn. . . ."

"Have you nothing more to say?"

"I beg your pardon, Miss Ronny."

"Pick the twig up off the lawn and take it to the waste basket."

Oh, the educational system employed by Miss Ronny was recognized not only by pedagogical authorities, but also by society and even high society. It was irreproachable, this system, and the boarding-school girls understood this perfectly.

It was perfectly understood by Marie when, having put on her cape, pinafore and oversleeves, she suddenly lost her face, her voice, even her look; and misty, pain-obscured, as if they had never existed, there suddenly crept into her memory the monastery ruins, the summit of Lausche, upon which the sun was clambering, the sharp-edged cliffs, the mountains with crests piled up like broken furniture, the gloomy crypt of the margraves—and in it a pale frightened pleading face with barely parted mouth.

From that minute Marie felt, even to the point of physical discomfort, that iron corset into which the boarding school's life had been constricted and into which she herself was now constricted. And she sensed that her childhood was over. She looked closer at the forms constituting the practice of the boarding school, tried stirring to the right and left, moving forward and moving backward—each time causing herself pain and provoking the outbreak of forces immeasurably more steadfast than she. She looked closely at the corset tightened around the people to whose power she had been entrusted, at its laces, bones and hooks, and she found that to tear it, break it, destroy it, or even merely loosen it, weaken it—was impossible. And then she became reconciled to it and, without the slightest difficulty, as if she had been born to it, with her own hands, accustomed to opposition, willfulness, caprice and freedom, she put it on herself and convinced everyone that she felt fine.

"Fräulein Marie," said Miss Ronny once, "I notice that you are too thoughtful and not very sociable. You should be a little more animated."

When Marie became slightly more animated Miss Ronny could no longer find anything in her which deserved correction and before Christmas she wrote on her certificate:

perfect behavior, excellent marks,
application and attention,

and before the summer holidays:

model behavior in the school and excellent marks.

Her exceptional place among the pupils came easily to Marie, in any case incomparably more easily than it came to her father. The belief that this was she, his daughter, took the following form. He was suspicious and guarded—and perhaps offended—because he considered he had not deserved such a perpetual, deferentially cold manner from Marie. Did he never see revenge in this for the severity with which he had treated Marie? How can one tell? On the other hand, Frau Urbach became openly well-disposed toward her daughter and responded graciously to her respectful curtseys.

Thus two years passed.

But in the third, in Weimar, during the school's walk along quiet streets, past private residences resembling the school, with gardens behind iron railings and gnomes smiling in flowerbeds, a young officer came swiftly across the street and up to the sedately advancing couples, to the first couple walking behind the class mistress, to the pupil Marie Urbach.

"Marie!" he exclaimed.

"Max!" she replied and her companions saw how her eyebrows went up and how the blood rushed to her cheeks.

"Herr Lieutenant!" spluttered the class mistress.

"One moment," said the officer and went toward Miss Ronny.

"My esteemed Lady, will you permit me to talk with my cousin, Fräulein Urbach?"

"But, Herr Lieutenant, in the school there are hours set aside . . ."

"That's quite right, my esteemed Lady. But I am passing through, have only an hour, and it is essential for me . . ."

He suddenly saluted, said "thank you" as if he had received assent and hurried over to Marie.

In all, there was one minute of confusion, when the ranks of the schoolgirls broke and tangled, when someone lifted an arm, someone laughed, someone sobbed, when the class mistress had an attack of unprecedented coughing, when the whole procession disintegrated and even Miss Ronny took two unnecessary steps forward and one unnecessary step back, because at that moment a fierce struggle occurred within her between her respect for the uniform of the Saxon army and the necessity of observing the established order of the school.

But by the second minute the officer had already exchanged a brief word with Marie and offered her his arm, and they walked across the road laughing and quickening their pace. And then everyone saw how Marie leaned against the officer's elbow and shoulder and everyone heard her as she turned round and said loudly and gaily:

"My God, Miss Ronny, how like a woodpecker you are!"

And then still louder:

"Adieu, adieu, girls!"

And after the word "girls," it seemed to Marie's friends that, departing on the officer's arm, it was not a girl in oversleeves, cape and pinafore but a young woman, lissome, buoyant, and beautiful. . . .

The lieutenant had hardly lied to Miss Ronny, saying that he was passing through Weimar and was there only for an hour: he seemed to sink without trace, once around the corner, and Marie with him.

Where she was gone for three days and two nights remained known only to her.

On the third day Herr Urbach was sitting in his study in his old Bischofsberg home when he was handed a visiting card:

LIEUTENANT MAX VON ZUR MÜHLEN-SCHÖNAU
(MARGRAVE)

This little word in parentheses printed in smaller type in
the corner of the large rectangular card had been thought
up long ago by von zur Mühlen-Schönau and it did not at
all indicate that in Germany the splendid title of Charles'
times had been resurrected, but only that one should not
confuse the descendant and heir of a margravian line with
some Baltic barons or others accidentally bearing exactly
the same name.

The lieutenant came with Marie, who was dressed in a
new costume which made her more shapely and more striking, with a new hair-style and with a new look in her
darkened aroused eyes. She sat in the drawing room, as if
making a visit to a little-known house—without removing
her hat and pulling the glove of her right hand half off.
The mirror standing behind her chair made her uneasy and
she soon turned to look in it.

The lieutenant remained in her father's study about five
minutes, then they passed through the drawing room and
Herr Urbach, looking sideways at his daughter, growled
without stopping:

"Welcome!"

Then the lieutenant returned alone to the drawing room,
kissed Marie's hand and said:

"Everything is settled. You will remain here, I shall return to Schönau. I'll come tomorrow at midday. . . ."

Von Schönau's proposal, sudden and categorical, Marie's
flight from the boarding school—where she had been "of
model behavior and with excellent marks"—but most important, of course, the proposal—of a margrave and not
of some baron or other—and most important, of course
. . . in short, Frau Urbach was disarmed and flattered. All
this so shook her conception of what was permissible and
decent, so blunted her powers of observation, that the mother's attention was not even caught by Marie's strange costume and manner, while the father was crushed and shut
himself in his room.

That evening Frau Urbach recalled that Marie, coming home for holidays, had frequently gone to Schönau and had talked a great deal about the pictures in the castle collected by the margrave's guardian. Evidently it had not been merely a question of pictures. Frau Urbach was satisfied.

Herr Urbach, pacing about his study, recalled only one thing: that new, unaccustomed dress which he had seen on Marie when he had said "Welcome" to her. He rang and ordered a briquette to be brought and the fire lighted, although young summer languished outside the windows.

The following day at midday, Lieutenant von zur Mühlen-Schönau came accompanied by his guardian—a well-combed, stout, acutely bowed retired colonel—and the guardian confirmed the proposal made by the lieutenant. The betrothal was set for two years ahead, when Marie would be eighteen.

This fell in the spring of nineteen sixteen.

A CHAPTER ON
NINETEEN SIXTEEN

LANDSTURM

If the neck is cut from a bottle then the latter's form will
resemble a small-caliber artillery shell with an exploded
cone. The bottle can be painted with silver paint and the
portrait of some general or other can be stuck upon it. A
thing like that is good to put on the piano or sideboard—
it ornaments the room and makes it cosy. Housewives soon
guessed the secret of making glass shells: they began to
break bottles, to buy silver paint and postcards with pictures of generals and to use this economical method of
preparing decorations. As a result of this, the demand for
shells fell off considerably and the manufacturers were
obliged to change their machines; some of them took up the
manufacture of silver paint, others began to print postcards with generals. As far as bottles were concerned,
pre-war over-production made itself felt. On the other hand
other areas of industry, protected from the competition of
housewives by the technical conditions of their production,
expanded widely and flourished for a long period of time.
Thus, for example, the manufacture of brooches and pins
in the shape of 42-centimeter shells, done up with a red,
white and black border, attained exceptional proportions.
China factories were induced to expand, thanks to the out-
put of crockery with pictures of the members of the happily
reigning imperial family. The producers of packaging experienced an era of storm and stress; boxes and cartons
were pasted, wrapped or embroidered in the national col-

ors. By the second year of the war their whole production was supplied to the customer in a completely patriotic form, from laxative at the drug-store to a horse's collar at the saddler's.

This was an unprecedented flight of fantasy, this was ascetic devotion, this was the height of unanimity.

By this time Andrei had moved to Bischofsberg.

He lived feebly, dully, tiredly. The world surrounding him was an unshakable thickness. It washed over Andrei like water. He could move about in the thickness, but its density was everywhere the same. He was permitted to breathe but he was unable to move his shoulders in order to spread them and breathe more deeply. He breathed through a reed pipe which led out through the thickness to the air, as a native hunter breathes when hiding in a lake.

Since the day he had parted with Kurt in the Nuremberg streetcar he had been governed by the inevitable. He suddenly saw himself as a piece of grit between enormous masses of moving, machine-like inevitabilities. In essence it was a reversal of attitude from that which he had had previously. For had it not seemed to him then that the sun was warm only because his will was free? Now he took a beggar's delight in warmth and light. . . .

Bischofsberg was not the worst place on earth. Like any city it consisted of tailors, policemen, booksellers, monks, bakers, dentists, professors and streetcar drivers. Bischofsberg was an old city and in an old city there have to be people of various professions, predominantly honorable ones. At least that is what the powers of Bischofsberg thought, extending their benevolence even to the Social Democrats.

"I ask you," said, for instance, the secretary of police, "as if a man were only a Social Democrat! Why, besides that, he's a brewer, or a glazier or a messenger. These are all completely trustworthy professions comprising a certain part of society. Therefore, I am in complete disagreement with the point of view of the Stuttgart police."

Here the secretary opened the *"Stuttgart Town Police News"* and read:

On Monday at seven-thirty in the evening, supporters of the radical Social Democratic party of both sexes attempted to organize a political demonstration. The procession left the Karlsplatz and proceeded along the Dorotheenstrasse to the Charlottenplatz where it was brought to a speedy end. The male and female leaders were arrested. The population of Stuttgart took no part in the procession. . . .

"Of whom then, one asks, did the procession consist, if the population didn't take part in it?" exclaimed the secretary.

Such liberalism on the part of the secretary of police was—through the smallness and orderliness of the city of Bischofsberg—known not only to officials but even to Social Democracy itself, and—as God is our witness!—the latter became more and more brazen every day. It reached such a pitch that the hairdresser Paul Hennig, an old member of the party and treasurer of the Society of Friends of Choral Singing, sitting once with a clique of Social Democrats, in everybody's hearing, praised his lodger—a Russian student, exiled to Bischofsberg at the beginning of the war.

"I assure you," growled this shameless man, "my Russ is the mildest creature and if they were all no worse than him we'd have thrashed 'em long ago and they'd be helping us whip the French. . . ."

Instead of keeping a more vigilant watch over his lodger and inquiring into his true intentions (he must have had some kind of intentions!), Paul Hennig was taking advantage of the indulgence of the powers that be to sow confusion and doubt among the people. No, it was positively necessary to be on one's guard not only with foreigners but also with a certain element of one's countrymen. Perhaps the Stuttgart police were not without reason in removing the whole Social Democratic party? Look, if you will, at this hairdresser, Paul Hennig. . . .

But is it not time to silence the Bischofsberg burghers and relate all with our customary impartiality?

Every day at nine in the morning Andrei went out

through a tall old door with cracked carving and dilapidated ornament scrolls on its doorposts. Three paces away Paul Hennig would stand in a white coat, with his hands crossed behind his back. Bursting with morning freshness, his face would shine like the newly polished brass basin which hung over the entrance to his shop. Hennig would break into an encouraging smile and say so the whole street could hear:

"Every man has his duty, isn't it so, Herr Startsov?"

"Yes, yes," replied Andrei, "good morning, Herr Hennig."

On the corner behind the turning of the theater alley the tobacconist, dressed in a soldier's uniform, shifted from foot to foot beside his shop. Farther on, the hunchbacked daughter of the tailor was sitting in front of the next door. The pink baker's wife peeped out of the neighboring window. Then came the narrow tulle curtain-covered windows of the café. Then the jeweler's, the greengrocer's, the library.

The square had only a few people on it and its city hall was gloomy and cold. A streetcar carefully rolled down a small hill. The driver looked at Andrei: he knew him certainly, just as Andrei knew the streetcar driver, the Schutzmann on point duty, the tobacconist, the tailor's daughter, the old messenger who smoked his pipe on the move, or the ragman who picked up paper in the streets with his long iron tongs. Every stone on this route, every live creature, every look and every shout had long been known, long exhausted, long studied, like the nails on one's hand, like worn out shoes, like the patterns and spots on the ceiling above the head of one's bed. Right there, in front of the entrance to the police station, at the half-open door of the public rest-rooms, Auntie Maier, with the invariable stocking in her hands, cast a stony look at Andrei, muttered some word in a deep voice and again leaned on her knitting needles.

A graying official with patched elbows and a pin in his tie probed Andrei with a frowning eye from under his brows and asked:

"Well?"

"Fifty-two."

"Good."

And he disappeared behind a bureau.

Then one could go home.

Halfway, Andrei met a small hurrying man with a wrinkled dry face. He quickly pulled a hand from his pocket, raised his derby a fraction off his bald pate and smiled with innumerable little wrinkles around his fine white lips:

"Bonjour, bonjour, bonjour!"

He uttered his greeting in a gabble, three consecutive times without fail, and the smile disappeared from his face just as swiftly as his fine lips came together. His hands were bandaged from wrist to finger tips with woolen rags: he had strained his tendons practicing the accordion, but he could not abandon his work because he had nothing to do and because he did not know how to do anything else.

This was Monsieur Percy, a Belgian citizen and musical clown.

Monsieur Percy lived in the same corridor as Andrei and —for six months now—day and night, chromatic scales had been cascading from his room and galloping down the stairs. Not counting these scales, Monsieur Percy was not a noisy man, he was even, on the contrary, wordless, quiet and inconspicuous. In the mornings Andrei would meet him on the street or in the corridor and Monsieur Percy would greet him in a gabble, raising his derby slightly.

"Bonjour, bonjour, bonjour."

Only once had Monsieur Percy offered his hand and shaken Andrei's hand—once, on a raw windy evening in the corridor, which was lit by an old gas bracket full of holes.

"I'm homesick, Monsieur Percy," said Andrei.

"Russians love homesickness," he replied. "I was in Russia, I know. Lodz, Riga, Libava, Dorpat—a fine country. And everyone drinks. . . ."

Monsieur Percy laughed.

"Today is my birthday, therefore I have also been drinking. Vile cognac. In general I don't drink. My profession won't allow it. For the same reason I don't get homesick."

"You are joking?"

Monsieur Percy bent toward Andrei and, moving only his

lips, with his face hardened like a mask, said without pausing:

"A clown jokes only in the ring; the Russians understand that very well. I have been in Morocco, Algeria, England; with the Austrians, the Swedes, the Russians, the Germans; I have seen the world. Now at nights I think how unhappy the world is, how unhappy people are if they can laugh at Monsieur Percy's jokes. At night I close my eyes and look at people—they understand nothing; Monsieur Percy sees them in Algeria, in Stockholm, in Vienna, in Bischofsberg, all simultaneously—they do not see Monsieur Percy, they think they are the whole world, and that the whole world is bigger than this, look, than this. . . ."

He touched his derby reverently with his index finger.

"This is bigger than the world, here is the whole world, believe me, Monsieur, the whole world. . . ."

"Let's go into my room."

"Oh, no! Russians like to feel homesick and then to talk about it. I'm a Belgian. During the day I work, at night I close my eyes—oh-oh, old eyes, Monsieur Percy!—and look at people. I see you also, I am fond of you, very fond."

Suddenly he started back, uncovered his bald pate for a second and ran down the stairs, shouting once only:

"Bonjour!"

This was his first and last conversation with Andrei.

The last because that night the Belgian citizen and musical clown Monsieur Percy was taken and escorted to an unknown destination.

Among the documents removed during a search of the Belgian citizen Monsieur Percy's room and presented to the *Stadtrat* of the town of Bischofsberg was an exercise book in a blue paper binding, with a picture of the Belgian national flag in the left corner of the cover by the spine. The exercise book was adorned with an inscription:

In memory of an engagement without contract.
The critics' reviews of a gala performance
without my participation.

The text consisted of newspaper and magazine cuttings

neatly pasted in and supplied with careful references as to source. There were no commentaries anywhere. Separate paragraphs were circled in ink. Probably they seemed the most remarkable to Monsieur Percy. At least some of them caught the attention of the Stadtrat and he marked them with red pencil. Here they are:

If Jesus of Nazareth, who preached love for one's enemies, wished to descend once more to earth he would, of course, become incarnate in the German fatherland. And— how do you suppose—where could you meet him? Surely you do not think that he would proclaim from a church pulpit: sinful Germans, love your enemies? I am sure not! No, he would be in the very first ranks of our warriors, battling with implacable hatred. He would be there, he would bless the bloody hands and the death-dealing weapons; he himself, perhaps, would seize the chastising sword and drive the enemies of Germany far beyond the bounds of the promised land, as he once drove the merchants and moneylenders from the temple of Judea.

(Volkserzieher)

The front of a pay-sheet from the textile mill "Concordia" in Bunzlau:

S A V E   B R E A D !

With every tiny piece of bread saved you are helping your husbands, fathers and sons in a difficult war.
Every lump of bread saved is
            a shot at England,
at our traditional enemy!
Every crust of bread saved shortens the war!

The reverse side of the same sheet:

THE TEXTILE MILL "CONCORDIA"
OF BUNZLAU

Wage for 57½ Hours		*M. 9.91*
Deductions:		
Hospital fund	M. .28	
Insurance	.12	
	M. .40	— .40
	Netto	M. 9.51

From now on no one is able to avoid the logical conclusion that *appeasement* would be a *catastrophe*, that war has become the sole possibility. Until now the reply to a challenge has been a matter of honor, the means to an end, but from now on war becomes an end in itself! The whole nation will as one man demand *eternal war!*

(*Münchener Medizinische Wochenschrift*)

Breed hatred! Breed respect for hatred! Breed love for hatred! Organize hatred! Down with childish fear, false pride before brutality and fanaticism! Let there be in politics, in the words of Marinetti: more slaps, less kisses! We dare not hesitate to announce blasphemously: our assets are faith, hope and hatred! The greatest of these is hatred!

(*Councillor of medicine, Doctor V. Fuchs,
senior doctor of Baden State Psychiatric
Hospital in Emmendingen*)

The Stadtrat sat over the blue exercise book until the dead of night, reading one clipping after another. There were lots of them, they were pasted in without any order and people, images, ideas, anecdotes poured over the Stadtrat like rattles from the sack of a Father Christmas—deformed, brightly painted, distorted, circus-like. The Stadtrat sharpened his red pencil with a small knife and then imprinted on the blue cover in sharp letters:

The notes collected in this exercise book do not comprise state or military secrets, since they appeared in print. However, the tendentious choice of newspaper reports indicates the hostile feelings of the collector toward Germany and could in the right circumstances fall into the hands of the enemy. Therefore I consider it necessary to hand the Belgian citizen Percy over to the military authorities.

In the Society of Friends of Choral Singing, Paul Hennig, the hairdresser, sang bass. Basses in Europe are rare and Paul Hennig had reason to consider himself a man out of the common run. His consciousness of this made him restless and restlessness brought him to the Social Democratic Party. Here he came to final belief in his star and became the noisiest man in Bischofsberg. When, in the evenings, he had closed his barbershop and called on Andrei to talk politics, every piece of poor furniture in the room, which resembled an arena, was momentarily turned into a machine tool. All around it hummed and crackled and rang and jarred in answer to the rumble and roar and roll of the barber's bass voice. Hennig filled the whole arena with himself.

"Nonsense, all that's nonsense! The Junkers don't understand that we are moving toward socialism. They don't un-der-stand!"

"How?" asked Andrei.

"Oho! You don't understand either, dear Andreas?"

"I see that we are living at the expense of what was saved in the past."

"Andreas, Andreas! War! Do you understand?—War!"

"What's it got to do . . ."

"Wait, wait! Hennig will develop his thought for you. You have no mental discipline—you Russians. Wonderful people. I say wonderful people, you Rooussians! Bismarck was right, the old man, right. He said: don't quarrel with the Russians, the Russians are the natural—understand?—the natural allies of the Germans. Hennig is developing the thought of the old man and he says: wonderful people! But you have no mental discipline. In the Society of Friends of Choral Singing, where I am treasurer, I said right out: we are moving toward socialism!"

"Through war?"

"Oh-oh! Through war! Andreas, you are beginning to think with discipline, that's thanks to me! Ha, ha, ha, don't be angry, Andreas! Precisely—through war. How? War will teach us how to distribute—oh!—to distrrribute goods and bypass—oh!—bypass the capitalist apparatus!"

"Bread coupons?"

"Oh-oh!

"And the other countries?"

"Other countries?"

Paul Hennig broke away from his chair and raised his voice two tones. The machine tools around the corners of the arena hastened to jar and ring with all their might.

"We will teach the otherrr countrries to distrrribute their goods and bypass the capitalists. But first, in order to do this we'll brreak, we'll brrreak them—we Germans!"

"Yes but if . . ."

"Wha-at?"

Hennig raised his voice another two tones.

But at that moment the door opened and a long painted pole entered the room. At first it hesitated whether to turn left or right, tried to bend toward the floor, then rose to the ceiling and, describing a parabola, began steadily to enter the room.

" 'But if,' you say?" droned Hennig good-naturedly, immediately lowering his voice four tones.

At that moment the pole was followed by the barber's apprentice who, tucking the pole under his arm, stumbled into the room, ginger-red, rough and puffing like a locomotive. Behind him trailed the peacock tail of a half-unfurled flag.

"Well, Erich, whom have we thrashed?"

"The Russians, Master."

"Ah, poor guys," said Hennig, taking the staff and leading its end toward the window. "How unlucky they are! Look, Andreas, at the other countries! It doesn't concern Russia, of course, our socialist affair. But then I'm not talking about Russia. . . ."

The apprentice opened the window, unrolled and threw the flag out through it, then began to thrust the staff out. It was long and heavy and it was difficult to insert in the iron sleeve beneath the window. The apprentice slowly lowered the staff on a rope while Paul Hennig, red and puffed up, made efforts to direct the thick end of the pole into the sleeve, barely managing to throw out jerky powerful arguments:

"It seems that we socialists are aiding imperialism, but in fact it is aiding us . . . that is a good parrt of socialism—distrrribution. . . . Erich, to your right, to your right . . . lower it a little . . . we have the most numerous party . . . after the war we'll have a socialist . . . Erich, leave it, it's okay! . . . a socialist experiment. . . ."

A cold draft came through the window and perhaps because of that Andrei felt chilly. He hid in the far corner.

"I understand. But then your distribution won't stop the war?"

"We must brreak the enemy, then war will stop."

"Yes but if . . ."

"No 'if,' Andrreas! They must be brroken. The rest is rrubbish!"

Hennig clapped Andrei on the shoulder, breathed cheap brandy into his mouth and said:

"Do you know what discipline is? Andrreas, you Russians don't know what it is. . . ."

He shook Andrei's hand and went out after his apprentice.

When thousands, hundreds of thousands, millions of noble burghers sat in their drawing rooms and sang the praises of discipline, they no longer knew what it was. Since the time when, as youths, they had met it joyfully, fifteen to twenty years had passed. In the meantime they had had time to languish on double mattresses, to grow half-dead cactuses, to confirm their daughters and to acquire the works of Goethe with gold spines.

Thousands, hundreds of thousands, millions of noble burghers this year constituted the Landsturm. The calf-skin knapsack which the Landsturm carried on its back seemed inordinately heavy to it and the straps which sank into its fleshy shoulders—inordinately sharp. The Landsturm was dragging behind it double beds, cactuses, confirmation presents for its daughters and the gilded works of Goethe. This was too much weight for a war.

"War needs bone and muscle," said a certain military leader.

The sergeant-major instructing the Bischofsberg Landsturm understood this maxim very well. He taught the Landsturm formation. March, march, march! Run, fall, crawl, and again—run, fall, crawl! Then for a change: march, march, march!

The fat had to be knocked off the Landsturm—backsides, stomachs, backs. These were unsuitable for war.

After training far out of town the clumsy fat men, disguised as soldiers, returned to their barracks toward evening.

The sergeant-major remembered that the noble burghers had a great propensity for comfort. He heard habits rattling in their knapsacks. He saw each of them on a soft sofa with a pillow on it, embroidered in satin-stitch:

Nur ein Viertelstundchen!*

On the walls hung postcards splashed with plaster of Paris, the door to the balcony was ajar and peeping through it were the branches of a pruned pear tree. Tobacco smoke extended to the branches in a tiny stream.

"Squa-a-ad!" commanded the sergeant-major.

Oh, all those pictures had to be cleaned out of the memories of the noble burghers, together with the fat of backsides, stomachs and backs!

"Si-i-ing!"

Silence.

"Squa-a-ad halt!"

The Landsturm halted.

"Why don't you sing?"

Silence.

"Squa-a-ad atten-shun! Right face. About face. Quick march!"

And out of town again, into the fields. Again run, crouch, fall, crawl. Then march, march, march. Then home.

A Landsturm is unquestioning.

In the town on the old spot, on precisely that spot where the command had first been uttered:

*Just a quarter of an hour!

"Si-i-ing!"

Silence.

"Squa-a-ad halt! Right face, about face, quick march!"

And again the fields.

The Landsturm was collapsing from exhaustion but the Landsturm was unquestioning.

And in the town, already dark with the night, on the same spot:

"Si-i-ing!"

And then a hoarse voice, intermittent and breaking, struck up a song and it was taken up by voices similarly breaking:

I-ich hatte ein Kama-ra-aden. . . .

"No 'if,' Andreas! You Russians don't know what discipline is!"

THE PARK OF THE SEVEN PONDS

Two winters had passed since Marie discovered what war was. War was incessant activity filling the blood with feverish energy, it was walking along a tightrope over a gulf full of fluttering banners, raging torchlights, brassy trumpet voices and victory cries. War was victory. This was its meaning. Incidentally, whole books written about the meaning of war were fanned out on round tables in Frau Urbach's drawing room. In these books everyone might find a completely accurate explanation of why it is really essential from time to time to organize a war—from the point of view of positivist philosophy, or Christian dogma, or Darwin's theory. (Mesdames, have you read *Origin of the Species?* Ah, the struggle for survival, the law of nature—very simple!)

Marie had not once looked in the books set out on tables in her mother's drawing room. But if she had accidentally discovered that the majority of these books had not been

*I used to have a comrade. . . .

cut she would not in the least have been surprised, because war above all was incessant activity, which explains everything and justifies it by itself, without books or interpretations. Thus an actor who fills seven parts in three acts does not think about the nature of the theater, but merely changes his costume.

War was activity. When, within a span of ten days, twelve fortresses were taken and twenty-eight towns occupied in Poland, a cloud of soot hung over Bischofsberg from the torches and lanterns. A commission composed of high school students, under the direction of the teachers' union, counted the flags decorating public buildings and private homes during this period. The town was split up into sections. When the commission had completed its work and announced that there was an average of 9 1/37 flags on every inhabited structure in Bischofsberg, a puffing elderly man ran up and wailed: "You've miscalculated, miscalculated!" It turned out that this man, in checking the commission, had personally counted all the flags decorating the town and had obtained the figure 9 1/29! The Bischofsberg Social Democratic newspaper did not fail, of course, to taunt them on this account and announced that the commission had dropped the patriotic value of Bischofsberg 8/1073.

If one does not count the work done in wartime in factories, fields and mines by people who are absorbed by this work in peacetime, then what astonishing energy war awakens in people who usually take only a small part in productive labor. There is no point in discussing armies employed every second in destroying the most powerful human beings individually and in groups. This kind of activity has always attracted attention. It is much more instructive to turn our gaze, for example, to the Berlin Union of Innkeepers, which dedicated several business conferences to a discussion of the question whether it was proper to rename hotels "inns"? In fiery debates the renaming was rejected because, taking advantage of the absence of unbiased linguists, the proprietors voted that hotel was a word of German origin.

In the Emmendingen hospital experienced personages

were shown a man who had worked out a project for a statistical bureau to register meetings called as a result of war activities. Among the materials collected by this man was the protocol of the Conference of the Union of German Confectioners, at which they had debated the question: Is it patriotic to eat fancy cakes? This had been resolved positively, since the bakers had established that confectionery wares were made predominantly out of sugar, eggs, raisins and almonds, without any expenditure of wheat flour requisitioned by the authorities. It is known that when the decision became public property six thousand German confectioners' shops became filled with joyful patriots. . . .

Above the entrance door to Frau Urbach's drawing room hung an oak plaque with a carved couplet:

Wir stehen in Ost und West
*Wie Fels und Eiche fest.**

The couplet corresponded to reality. Its strength, however, did not consist in this but in its being a program of action, a simple understandable "must." Its power over people was concealed in the invisible imperative with which the oak plaque was imbued. This was felt and understood by everyone. This was felt and understood by Marie from the first hour of the war. And she submitted to the subtle command, which did not offend one's pride, but rather flattered it. She blossomed out into activity.

She ordered from Berlin eleven special flagpoles which were fixed to windowsills and flags three yards long to fit them. Gradually it was discovered that Germany valued even its down-at-the-heel war allies more than its dreamy standard bearers desired. The collection of imperial linen had to be reinforced by the allied national colors. This took time, not to speak of the fact that nearly every day one had to choose a combination of eleven flags from seventeen in order to decorate the house façade with them.

Frau Urbach was the patroness of a refreshment stand on the Bischofsberg station. Train-loads of soldiers followed each other through Bischofsberg every two or three days.

---

*We stand in east and west
As firm as rock and oak.

To give soldiers flowers and patriotic mementoes imprinted on Bristol board, to feed coffee to a hundred, at times two or three hundred, ill-bred men, to provide them with cigars and at the same time smile and say something pleasant about the fatherland—such work can be done only by a person dedicated to the idea.

Marie used to help Frau Urbach. Here on the station, in the crush of clean-shaven wide-mouthed young men, in the racket and roar of brassy voices, in the flashing of sturdy foreheads and heads, Marie experienced a feeling as if she had been carried into a hand-to-hand struggle in a glorious battle. The contact of elbows, the almost palpable adhering glances, the flowing elusive ribbon of smiles and that eternal refrain:

"Hey, there are fine girls in Saxony!"

Who could maintain indifference and coldness in such a flood? Who would not sip its beating frothing foam?

And suddenly Marie grew bored. It happened in early spring, the wind had just grown a little warmer and the trees had thawed out. For the first time in six months Marie did not go to the station. A band of her friends, who poured the soldiers' coffee on the station, ran to see her from all parts of the town—anxious, wide-eyed and chattering like magpies. Marie was in good health, nothing in her life had changed, she was the old Marie. But she was bored. She did not know why. The magpies chattered, adjusted their skirts, cajoled, remonstrated, finally made her feel ashamed and made fun of her. She insisted:

"I'm bored!"

Strangely she herself did not guess the cause of this boredom. Sitting in her room and going over in her head the events of the past few days she decided that in fact there had been no events and that this was the trouble. She recalled that the troop-trains to whom they had given mementoes and coffee had lost their color and were silent. In the gray line extending past the servers no laughter was heard. Recently a shortish Landsturmer had addressed Marie with the words:

"Pour me a hot one, my girl!"

Her hand had shaken and she had looked at him more

closely. The soldier had been puffy, his short mustache had been streaked with gray. Marie had taken a glance along the line of gray overcoats. Gloomy faces with lines dug deep into them had swayed indifferently under the gaslight. It had occurred to her then that these people had remained where they came from: only their shells swayed here on the station.

This incident had been so trivial that it was surprising how it sprang up in her memory now, when Marie was looking for what had bored her. Equally unexpectedly she recalled the yellow faces of the women crammed in the school corridor, where bread coupons were distributed. Marie was employed twice a month in distributing bread coupons and not once had it occurred to her to take a closer look at the people swarming in the corridors. And again, not long before, when she remarked to someone:

"Can't you be a bit nicer?" a screech came from the far corner:

"You're nice only because you're full!"

Then Marie raised her head and met dozens of desperate twisted eyes. The women standing round the table were strangely yellow, as if their skin was colored not by blood but by bile. Among them were young girls, but it was possible to tell their youth only by their eyes.

"Hey, there are fine girls in Saxony!"

This was just as trivial as the incident on the station and also explained nothing. A file of emaciated women and puffy soldiers alternately fell away and sprang up again in her memory—but it was clear that all this had come to mind only now, when Marie tried to think about her boredom.

The second recollection had not retreated even a step from her for a long time now, but was it conceivable that this was responsible for her boredom?

However, did she not recall everything in detail?

In the last month before spring there was a snowy day, matched by frost—the last winter day in the reddish light of a low sun. A kind of sweet smell floated about the streets,

as if from a fresh basket, and people loudly called to one
another as they trotted along the sidewalks:

"Hey, it's nippy!"

"Oho-ho!"

A sled flashed through the square to the accompaniment
of stormy cries. A band of small boys sped along behind it.
The huge thermometer on the city hall stood stiffer than
usual: they had cleaned it with gasoline that morning. In
such sunshine, with one's feet breaking the scented weight-
less snow, one wanted to think that the world was peaceful
and forgiving, that people had gathered in gay towns and
villages to look one another in the eyes, to shake hands
and to cheer each other with a joyful cry from round the
corner:

"Fräulein Marie! Your nose is redder than a tomato!"

"Fräulein Marie, don't fall on Weberstrasse, it's a real
ice-rink there!"

Oh, no, Marie would not fall on Weberstrasse. Marie was
not afraid of the cold! She dashed along with such force
that it seemed she could have gone over an impregnable
glacier. Through the sharp frost, cutting her flushed face,
with her hands thrust deep in her sleeves, she ran as far as
the station. Two or three passengers were jumping up and
down on the snow-dusted platform. A toy, ice-covered locomotive, puffing in embarrassment, leaped out from behind a turning.

"To Lausche!"

It was a working day and the cars were empty. The
neighborhood seemed unfamiliar—and perhaps that was
why snow-covered Lausche came forward out of the distance so quickly. The hoods of the Three Nuns had grown
into a huge cap, hanging over the cliffs in a dazzling ball.

Imprinted on the narrow path running to the summit of
Lausche were the solitary tracks of a man's feet. Marie ran
up as far as the first slope of the mountain and took a short
rest. The man's tracks turned to one side while the path
wound upward beneath an undisturbed carpet of snow,
and to scatter it was as enjoyable as blazing a new route.
The frosted scent of resin floated amid the tall rows of

pines, which were weighed down by snowy overhangs, and the peace and quiet in which Lausche was locked filled Marie with light gay strength.

With the agility which had once caused Frau Urbach so much trouble, Marie cleared ledge after ledge. Suddenly her leg turned under her, she slipped on a rock and tumbled down a good dozen yards. In falling she raked the snow with her back into a fat snowdrift and, growing instantaneously, it fell over on top of her and spattered her face, chest and arms. She cried out joyfully, loudly, as from the caressing cold of splashes when bathing. At that moment, like a blow against a frozen pine, a strong voice rang out above her:

"Careful!"

She jumped up and shook the snow off. Youthful eyes looked at her from behind a tree. They seemed to her to contain more gaiety than anxiety.

"Are those your tracks going along the path there?" she asked.

"Yes. I wanted to find a shorter way and turned off to the side."

"Are you headed for the top?"

"Yes."

"This is the shortest way."

"But also the most dangerous. Did you hurt yourself?"

"It's nothing."

There was nothing more to talk about. It was necessary to part. However, it was possible to walk together.

"It's a nice day today," he said.

"Yes."

"Are you also going to the top?"

"Also."

Thus it was evident that their way was the same and that they were going the shortest possible way.

"Will you sled down the mountain?" asked Marie.

"I don't know."

"Afraid?"

"I've never done it."

Marie turned to look at him. His legs were covered tightly by thick stockings and took strong regular steps in time with his loud calm breathing. He held his head high, not looking at the ground under his feet. He looked frankly at Marie.

"I feel good today. I rarely get out of town," he said.

"You're not from here?"

He laughed.

"Are you a Czech?" asked Marie in a tone of voice which made this word insulting.

"Worse!"

"I thought so. People like you are needed in the war. But you stroll around as if nothing were happening. Are you a Russian?"

He laughed again.

"Yes."

Marie quickened her step. For a few minutes they were silent. Then he said:

"The situation is becoming awkward. It could be saved only by a police official, isn't that so?"

"That's vulgar."

"I didn't mean to offend you."

"We have much more chivalry than foreigners think."

Marie suddenly stopped.

"What gave you the right to consider us all informers? Is it bad for you here, for you, our enemy?"

She moved forward again. Then her companion said:

"It's sad that we've forgotten how to live simply. Perhaps we never did know how. Behind the partitions and annexes nothing is visible. Why did you have to question me as to who I was? Is it really impossible without that to walk side by side, as we are doing now? Around us is snow, pine trees, quiet. We are linked by nothing other than this snow, this quiet and the piece of road which we must traverse together. We'll traverse it and forget. Chance. Why seek what isn't there? If I had turned out to be an Austrian or a fellow countryman of yours you would have looked differently at me. But would anything around us really have changed? Everything would have been just as simple."

They stopped on the last ledge of the mountain. From here the summit was not much higher. To the west a broad clearing through the forest dropped away, as if on a thread. Through it one could see, like the sides of a triangle toward the base, a relay of pine plantations going away, covered by the snowy blueness of the valley, and a chain of crooked mountains. The sky sheltered the whole expanse with its peaceful blue.

"I grew up here," said Marie. "There on that hill a pine tree used to hang like a toadstool. That's the first tree I ever climbed. Behind that toadstool is the castle Schönau. Do you see the black roofs? To the right is the highway, the border is there."

"The border?" he repeated. "So close?"

Marie squinted at him:

"Do you feel close to home?"

"The Czechs are there."

"Oh, yes, solid with Czechs!"

"Can't we forget about that?"

She was about to move closer to him but stopped immediately, as if forcing herself not to listen to his words. Then suddenly she cried loudly:

"To the top, quickly!" and holding on to the tree trunks before her she lightly and tenaciously took the slope, like a roe-deer.

On the tidy platform on top, long low-slung sleds stood in a sedate row. A grim keeper, ponderous as a mass of stone, slowly rolled out of a board hut and looked at his guests. It was an unseasonable hour and there was no one else on the mountain besides the keeper. A smoothly rolled, well-cleaned road traveled down to a turn in a steep curve. It was protected on either side by barriers of snow.

And Marie cried loudly again, cleaving the benumbed air:

"Enough hesitating! Let's go!"

She chose a sled, pushed it to the slope with her foot, sat astride it and grasped the rings bent onto the front of the runners.

She was surrounded by the air which she had breathed in childhood. The crumbling rocks were piled up in confusion, like broken furniture; there were the thickset dry-barked trees, whose every branch seemed an old friend; below was the mutilated checkerboard of roads and clearings. Every stone on these mountains made faces at Marie and she remembered its nickname, knew its secrets. How sad that the accomplices in her pranks were not beside her —the broad-chested, wide-eyed village lads! How good it would be to command them, to shout and give orders! Where were they now, the dear bumpkins? . . .

Marie quickly looked her companion over.

"Settle up with the keeper and sit down. Quickly . . . Sit closer to me. Stretch your legs out in front. Like this. Hold on to me with your arms. Properly. Tighter, still tighter, otherwise you'll fall out. I'll steer. Let's go!"

And now a jolt, another jolt, now an accelerating smooth sliding, now a swift run—and now before one's very face, over one's head, the icy snow barrier of the turn which a moment ago had seemed such a terribly long way off. The barrier descended on one's head, a stinging white dust sealed the eyes, gushed in an irresistible fountain from somewhere underground and suddenly ceased; and an even wind like sharpened steel rang in one's face, rushing upward, up the mountain which soared to the sky. The turn had passed long ago, the sled had already left the ground, a straight drop—endless a second before—had already flown into another turn and snow barriers had descended on one's head.

"Hold on!" cried Marie and felt how a broad hardened body had grown into her back and an icy circle of crossed arms into her chest. And also, as if from a distant peak, through the cold and whistle of the dust, in spite of and in opposition to the cutting steel of the wind—a whisper, almost warm, flowed into her very ear:

"Ho-old on your-self!"

And then she saw to one side a white blizzard smoking from a strong masculine leg furrowing the road—a higher and wilder cascade than her leg was raising. . . . "Ah it's all the same—let him think he is steering! Down, down, down the mountain, into the abyss! . . ."

Then at the sloping foot of Lausche they shook themselves, cleaned their hair, collars and ears of the melting sticky dust and laughed.

Probably they talked of something here, just as they

talked in the tiny room of some inn, where they were regaled
with pungent grog and a cheerful open fire. But Marie did
not remember a word of these conversations. However, one
word—funny and unusual—remained in her memory. Taking
leave of her companion far from the station she asked:

"What is your name?"

"Andrei Startsov."

"Startsov? How do you spell it?"

The wind grew warmer and the trees thawed out. At
such a time an open window does not ease the breathing.
And unless one moves, flies constantly with the force of a
stone breaking away from the mountain—the dense March
days will squeeze the throat, will suffocate one.

Boredom came together with the warm wind, unexpectedly, at the height of the activity, and with every hour became more unbearable. And because Marie could not guess
the cause of her boredom—perhaps simply out of boredom
—she wrote Andrei that she wanted to see him.

He waited for her in the Park of the Seven Ponds.

In the thaw the park had become muddy, the streetcars
came up to it empty, the deserted avenues showed uni-
formly black. But from the melting of the snow and the imperceptible timid rustle of some beings or other, scents of
animation roamed over the earth and to breathe them was
as tormenting as looking from a height into a ravine.

Andrei stood on the right-angled junction of two avenues.
Marie was supposed to come along one of them. That was
Bismarck Avenue—four rows of lindens pruned into upturned coffee cups. The road, as smooth as a bowling alley,
joined the town to the park. The other avenue curved to
encircle the park and its turning was fifty yards away from
where Andrei was standing.

He caught sight of Marie at the appointed hour. She was
walking quickly, keeping so close to the straight line of tree-
trunks that she seemed to be seeking cover behind them.
When her face became distinguishable it seemed to Andrei
that she was smiling. He walked back to the inner side of
the avenue which encircled the park. The rustles, which had
been almost inaudible till now, suddenly cohered into a

broad rolling rumble. It grew and expanded somewhere in the depths of the earth, as if the thawing roots were violently compressing the soil. Andrei saw Marie's steps quicken. She was almost running to the park. Surely the tremble and rumble of the earth, which was filling Andrei with incomprehensible anxiety, had not rolled as far as her? It continued to expand, this underground rumble, it changed to a clearly audible noise, it seized and shook not only the ground but also the air, it rolled on in an invisible avalanche, at any moment it must crush Andrei.

It is inexplicable why he did not move from the spot. He waited for Marie motionless, as if petrified.

And then, when Marie was quite close to him, he caught sight of the avalanche. It crept around the turn in the avenue, fifty yards from where he was standing. The rumble agitating the earth was raised by hundreds of heavy feet.

Marie had only to cross the road in order to stretch out her hand to Andrei. At that moment the avalanche rolled up to the junction of the avenues. Andrei had time to notice how Marie's eyes rested on the approaching procession. Then it separated them.

It was headed by armed Landsturmers, marching depressedly and slowly, scowling and grim. Behind them came close ranks of soldiers. The four in the front rank held on to the overcoat straps of the Landsturmers. Those behind laid their hands on the shoulders of those in front.

The bluish-gray crumpled overcoats had been made by a single tailor and their cloth caps had been stretched on a single block. But the steps of the swaying bluish-gray soldier mass were not the steps of soldiers. Their feet were dragging heavy torn remains of boots and scuffing over the ground, hardly lifting off it. Men staggered from side to side, crowded together and stumbled into one another. Their hands were stretched constantly upward, groping in space and leaning on the backs and elbows of those walking in front.

Andrei noticed one soldier especially. His head was turned to one side and bobbed on its long neck as on a thread. He seemed to be listening to what was approaching him with every step. His face was drawn into a grimace and his mouth clamped shut so firmly that his jaw muscles bulged like cheekbones. Inside the black circle of his eyelashes his immobilized eyes were glassy. In them swam the shadows of branches hanging over the avenue.

The soldier was blind.

Then with an immeasurably brief glance Andrei took in the crowd creeping past.

The faces of dozens and hundreds of men seemed to him one face. And when he looked closely at it he cried out.

It was the face of Karl Ebersocks, as he had seen it in the Erlangen museum and then in his dream, when the purple head had been debating—should it fall or remain on the staircase. But—horror of horrors!—down the face of the murderer, who had ascended the scaffold with open eyes in order to look shamelessly at people after death from a museum spirit jar, down this face tears were flowing!

Andrei no longer saw the crowd. Before him somewhere quite close, at the distance a human breath can reach, swung the head of Karl Ebersocks. The executed man's blue lips shivered, opened and as in a dream, uttered:

"Italians. Captured near Trieste."

Then he winked through his tears and added:

"The gas is called Yellow Cross. An excellent brand."

The voice seemed sad to Andrei. Was it not because the puny escort of the blind men was speaking?

He had stopped beside Andrei in order to light his pipe and spoke several words out of sociability and sympathy. Then he ran to his place, pressing to his back a long, Russian-made rifle.

And the silent procession flowed uninterruptedly along the avenue and numberless hands groped in space. The downcast Landsturmers bringing up the rear of the crowd lightly prodded the stragglers and then they trod on the heels of those walking in front and threw back their heads as if listening to what approached them with every step. Probably they had already made out the blows of an ax constructing camp huts.

The tear-stained face of Ebersocks dissolved in the March twilight air. The noise of the scuffling boots died down, changed to an underground rumble and was absorbed in the rustles of spring's reawakening. The Park of the Seven Ponds awaited the evening.

Then Andrei looked around.

On the other side of the avenue stood Marie, leaning against a tree with her eyes closed; she seemed to be bound to the trunk and her hands were hanging helplessly. Andrei rushed over to her, tearing himself forcibly away from the piece of earth which had held him petrified. Marie opened her eyes and Andrei grasped her hands. They were cold and trembling, as if feverish.

"Our meeting . . ." began Andrei.

Marie wanted to smile.

"I can't," she replied, "today. . . ."

Then she pushed herself away from the tree and squared her shoulders.

"I don't want to talk today. . . . I can't."

She pressed his hand.

"Perhaps I'll write to you again."

She turned and went where the streetcar had stopped, empty at this time.

He followed her with his eyes.

MORE FLOWERS

That summer two sea powers met for the first time in the open sea. Battleships created to destroy and to perish, pining from inactivity and too much armament, left their nest on the same day at the same hour, like magnetic needles of opposite poles. The meeting place was where Skagerrak Sound flowed into the North Sea. The hour of meeting was the hour of fate, when winds cease to blow and planets stop and men put on clean shirts. Victory was assured for both squadrons, because both squadrons were considered the most powerful in the world and because the powers whose squadrons met in the Skagerrak considered themselves the most powerful powers.

All powers always consider themselves the most powerful; it is essential to them that every company nag thundering with his rusty trappings should feel like Tamerlaine.

In the Skagerrak, naval England defeated naval Germany and naval Germany defeated naval England. Defeated in this battle was logic—the least mighty of powers. It was defeated by both winning sides—England and Germany, with the exception of those sailors whom the water had washed out of the Skagerrak into the North Sea.

It was explained to the German population with diagrams that the sea power of Great Britain had been irreparably damaged and that this had been extraordinarily fortunate because Germany's losses were negligible. The English newspapers for their part proved with charts that the German fleet could be considered nonexistent and that this had been achieved at the cost of essentially trivial losses on the part of Great Britain.

Thus at the time of Skagerrak Bischofsberg had every reason to organize a festival. It had even more reason in that it was expecting the arrival of His Majesty the King of Saxony. This did not happen often and it was a historic occasion for Bischofsberg. It was necessary to surround the eminent visitation with dignity and splendor. And since every eminent visitation is timed to coincide with some event, although His Majesty the King of Saxony was visiting Bischofsberg simply to shoot roe-deer in the mountains, naturally his arrival was linked with the victory over naval Great Britain. And he was honored and hailed as the real genius of the Battle of Jutland. . . .

But this is a whole chapter in the history of the city of Bischofsberg; while the chapter we are writing is dedicated to flowers. There are few in our novel and they are loved by young girls who are indignant at writers for talking about the Landsturm and war, strikes and kings, instead of discussing betrayals and embraces, love and flowers. It is sad to think that not a single young girl will have read the novel as far as these sympathetic words. But if a tender soul, tired out finally with troop trains, revolutionaries, Social Democrats and kings, should accidentally open the book at this page she will find here our solemn promise to talk throughout the chapter only of flowers, of flowers alone—fragrant, besprinkled with pure dew, chaste and living flowers! . . .

The king was met on the station by the military authorities. From there he was supposed to pass in state to the city hall and there receive the civilians. After two hours, benevolent societies were supposed to be presented to His Majesty.

It must be admitted that the Bischofsbergians experienced a certain disillusionment on that historic day. An inordinate quantity of starch had been used up on giving petticoats, shirt-fronts, cuffs and collars a ceremonial appearance. They expected to see His Majesty in medals and ribbons and stars, surrounded by his retinue and palace guard. But the king came in a jacket and Tyrolean felt hat with a grouse feather in it. They provided him at the station with a capacious old-fashioned phaeton, harnessed to a pair of stupid horses. He sat down next to the Ober-burgermeister and the iron rims of the kerosene-washed wheels rumbled along the main street. At the sight of such an entrance the starched subjects occupying the sidewalks forgot to take off their hats. Schoolboys surrounded the phaeton and sped along the road with shouts and exclamations. His Majesty good-humoredly flicked the ash of his cigar onto the small boys' noses and encouraged them to climb onto the steps and hang on the springs.

"Look," said one burgher to his wife upon seeing his sovereign, "he's wearing a jacket like our son-in-law Hans's. . . ."

Thus was the hero dimmed in the consciousness of a citizen deeply devoted to him.

On this day of victory over naval Great Britain and of the King's arrival in Bischofsberg, at the moment when the last collars were being ironed and the last boots cleaned, Frau Urbach ran through her drawing room exclaiming:

"Marie! Marie! Marie!"

She was so agitated that she had forgotten to take her cane with the rubber tip and she was limping very noticeably. She almost choked, crying:

"Marie! Marie!"

And when she flew into her daughter's room she burst out without pause for breath:

"Where are our flags, Marie? What does this mean? Where are the flags?"

Marie was buttoning her dress with her hands thrust behind her back. She was uncomfortable and there was a pause before she replied with a question:

"What's happened?"

"The flags, the flags! Our flags aren't hung out!"

"Why are you coming to me about it?"

Frau Urbach clutched at the back of a chair.

"Did I hear you right, Marie?" she mumbled.

"I'm saying I don't know why our flags aren't hung out."

"Perhaps you don't know why they should be hung out?" Marie raised her indifferent gaze to her mother.

"Frankly speaking, no."

Then Frau Urbach sank down onto a chair. Incredible! A half an hour ago this absurd person had been talking to her completely sensibly!

"We only just agreed, Marie . . ." began Frau Urbach, taking in more air and settling herself more comfortably: it was necessary to restore her shattered equilibrium.

But Marie interrupted:

"I assure you that nothing has happened. I'm getting ready to go to the station and then to the town hall. Your instructions will be carried out precisely. You had better get dressed, otherwise you'll be late."

"But the flags, the flags!" exclaimed Frau Urbach.

"As far as the flags are concerned, I beg you to entrust this work to someone else."

Marie unexpectedly burst into laughter:

"Well, entrust it to Papa, for example! That's right! Papa will hang out the flags with pleasure, even if it were every morning! That will be mag-ni-fi-cent!"

Frau Urbach rose slowly. Her head was flung back, her eyes fixed. Her figure was monumental—in its wide flaring heavy dress, with a raised and stiff right arm. Her whitened, tensely compressed lips gave vent to a distinct whisper:

"Remember once and for all, I do not permit your father to make fun of me, nor do I permit you."

She turned and went out of the door like an insulted heroine on the screen—majestically and almost as noiselessly.

In her own room Frau Urbach sat in the armchair a little while, fanning herself with her handkerchief. Then she rang for the chambermaid and ordered her to hang out the flags. Then she began to dress. . . .

What happened three hours later in the great hall of the city hall, where the benevolent and other societies were presented to the King, deserves the most detailed description. Such a description was done by the *Bischofsberg Morning News,* where the curious reader will find the whole ceremonial and, incidentally, a beautiful speech proclaimed on behalf of the guilds by a member of the Union of Hairdressers and Treasurer of the Society of Friends of Choral Singing—Paul Hennig. Here we shall relate only one insignificant detail, about which the editor of the *Bischofsberg Morning News* remained diplomatically silent, proving that he was truly on top of his responsible position.

Not long before the moment when His Majesty, accompanied by the Ober-burgermeister, Stadtrats and his adjutant, going from one deputation to another, approached Frau Urbach, she had looked round to reassure herself once more that Marie was standing behind her. A few minutes before that Frau Urbach had seen her daughter making her way to her through a crowd of dressed-up Fräuleins and Fraus.

And now His Majesty the King was standing face to face with Frau Urbach.

With particular pleasure the Ober-burgermeister said:

"Frau Urbach, born von Freileben, Patroness of the Refreshment Center, Chairwoman . . ."

Frau Urbach sank into a deep curtsey.

His Highness stretched out his hand to her and interrupted the Ober-burgermeister.

"I have already been informed about you, madam, at the residence. The Friedrich-August medal is awaiting you in Dresden."

"*Majestät,*" said Frau Urbach and again sank into a

deep curtsey. Having risen and seeing that His Majesty continued to smile kindly, Frau Urbach said:

"*Majestät*, permit me to present my daughter, Fräulein Marie Urbach. . . ."

She turned her head to the right and met someone's astonished and embarrassed gaze. She turned her head to the left and saw a strange frightened face. And suddenly the feverish words scorched her décolleté:

"Fräulein Marie isn't here!"

"You can't find your daughter?" she heard. "My God, is the King saying that?"

"*Majestät*," whispered Frau Urbach.

"It's nothing," laughed His Majesty, "something worse happened to me today: they've called me a sea-dog here, but it makes me sick to cross the bridge over the Elbe. . . ."

Frau Urbach still found the strength within herself to smile at the King's joke, found the strength to offer him her hand. Then she turned to the dressed-up Fräuleins and Fraus, cast a hasty look at them and was practically carried out of the hall. . . .

If Frau Urbach's glance had fallen on the flowers, which this chapter is supposed to be about, they would have wilted with compassion.

The hour at which the war began had been born under the sign of stations. Mountainous, excavated with underground passages, strung with bridges and crossings, braided with iron tangles of rails, eternally trembling and wailing—stations made the war. Like gigantic vacuum cleaners they sucked innumerable specks of dust into their smoky muzzles, collected them in generators, pushed them along pipes and spat them out into war. Once called to life, not for a second did their groaning steel breast cease to breathe and their every breath sucked in and blew out human dust.

At the hour born under the sign of stations people collected on roads covered with coal-dust, flooded with grease and oil, roads which led to war. And people strewed these roads with flowers and the petals of red roses scattered over the iron tangles of rails, so that the coal-dust, grease and oil became invisible. Soldiers in battle order stuck roses into their rifle barrels and behind their cartridge belts and behind the flaps of their knapsacks, and trampled the roses on platforms and rails with their heavy thick-soled boots. Can you really gather all the flowers strewn by the fatherland in the path of an army in battle order?

The army in battle order poured into the generators and sped along the pipes in order, like gas which mingles with the atmosphere, to burn up in war. And the soldiers—inflamed by the iron groan of the stations, aroused by the raving of the crowd, exultant, young—took the cars by assault, decorating their walls with funny drawings:

"Here's a Frenchman for you, conqueror of the universe!"

"Here's Serbian Peter after his Vienna campaign!"

And the thick letters of a fat white inscription gleamed white on every car:

TO PARIS!

TO PARIS!

TO PARIS!

This was the hour when the scent of roses drowned the acrid smell of oil and the stink of coal-dust. . . .

When Marie came with Frau Urbach's instructions to the station, it had just met the King and was about to begin its normal way of life: war. A draft company of the Landsturm was leaving for the front and a group of recruits was crawling about the crossings, tunnels and rails while waiting for travel orders. As always, shunting was going on and the station shook with a steel tremble.

The Landsturm, parting with its wives and children, had decorated its rifles with flowers. These were stunted little carnations and sweet peas which had lost their smell—because the roses which had once strewn the path of the army in field dress were all gone and because roses were too dear for the wives the Landsturm was leaving.

A bored recruit, tired of waiting, a clean-shaven flat-faced lad, was loafing along the sidings. Here it was deserted, the station had drawn everything live into itself, the station had only just met the King. Patrols of restless locomotives were grinding about the sidings. Out of boredom the recruit stopped by a freight car, out of boredom he picked up a piece of chalk which was lying on the ground beside the rails, out of boredom he began to draw the chalk over the side of the car:

TO PARI . . .

A voice as piercing as a whistle lashed him on the hand: "What are you scrawling there? Who'll clean up after you?"

The boy turned round. A car cleaner was walking along the rails. Her face shone with grease, her hands were black. He wanted to answer something. After all, he was a soldier, he would be shoved off to the front soon, he would fight, while this smudgy old girl would get all dirty at the station just as before, and it wouldn't be a bad idea to cuss her in some sergeant-major lingo. But the recruit was bored, he was tired of waiting, and the air around him was weary of the iron groans, and the sun itself was pining away like the recruit. The chalk stuck to the car in a white blot as the result of a heavy blow and the recruit's heels furrowed the sand of the path as he trailed off to the station.

The cleaner wiped the car off with a greasy rag and her lips whispered something, but the words could not be made out above the grinding of the locomotives. Perhaps she felt sorry for the recruit? Perhaps her husband had gone away in a car with a thick inscription:

TO PARIS!

and had not come home? Perhaps she had even come to hate Paris?

The station did not know this; the station was making war.

Human specks of dust floated in the tunnels, on crossings and through the halls. Among them Marie. She had fulfilled Frau Urbach's instructions and was about to return to town to go to the city hall. But on the platform, which still breathed with the solemnity of the king's welcome, she was detained by the Landsturmers departing for the front. This is how it happened.

The command was given to entrain.

The noise from the blessings and the weeping, from the clink of bayonets and the scraping of ammunition rose up to the glass roof of the station and fell, as if knocked down by a gust of wind. Gray men streamed off to the cars and silently stood along the line of them, not taking their eyes from the people remaining at the station windows. Across the platform, from the cars to the station, stretched the gazes of hundreds of fixed eyes. And if it were not an innate characteristic of man to see the slightest breach of homogeneity in a mass, this leave-taking would have stamped itself as any other mass movement:

"The crowd is moving."

"The public applauds."

"The people are praying."

"The mobilized men are taking leave of their wives."

But the homogeneity of the mass had been violated and people suddenly saw what was happening in the world, something they had never seen before.

A swarthy clumsy Landsturmer did not obey the command and stayed in the crowd that had come to see them off, at the front of the station.

He stood with his hands resting on the shoulders of a pale-faced woman, piercing her tired gaze with dry eyes. He had an obvious advantage over his comrades because his wife's eyes were blinking right in front of him and because the last kiss was still to come. Perhaps out of envy someone shouted:

"Well, kiss her already, Tiny!"

And he kissed her.

He bent his long arms at the elbows and his wife's pale face came impassively and softly close to his chest. He bent his head, his overcoat collar stuck up over his bent back, and his knapsack slipped heavily down to his waist as he placed his black mustache against his wife's perspiring forehead.

And she asked:

"What shall I tell our little one?"

"Tell our little one . . ." he began, straightening up.

His hands slipped from her shoulders, hung and waved in the air, then with an effort began to rise to his head.

"Tell our little one . . ." he repeated more loudly. And slowly began to sit.

"Tell our little one . . ."

Suddenly his hands clutched his head, his helmet jumped up and fell on his bent back, onto his knapsack, and rolled to the ground. He sat on his haunches, his hands on his knees, and he wailed:

"Our lit-tle o-one!"

And again, more forcibly and more drawn out:

"Our lit-tle o-one! . . ."

A noncom ran up to him hastily and shouted:

"To your place!"

The Landsturmer quickly got up and, not looking at his wife, not picking up his helmet, went toward the car bareheaded.

"Cover up!" shouted the noncom.

But it was too late.

Hundreds of hands stretched out from the crowd standing at the front of the station, across the platform, toward the line of gray men by the cars, and hundreds of wails hurled men's names into the air:

"Paul! Karl!"

"Robert! Paul!"

And they were answered by the coarse, hoarse broken voices of the men:

"Maria! Anna!"

"Elizabeth!"

And the hands stretching forth from the crowd standing in line with the building met the hands stretched from the cars.

Then the commanders pretended that the order to entrain had not yet been given.

In the room formerly occupied by Monsieur Percy lived a noncom from the volunteers. He was noisier and more sociable than Monsieur Percy, wore extraordinarily high collars and on his belt, instead of a bayonet, a small Finnish knife. The Finnish knife was in fashion and the noncom followed the fashion, was well-mannered, patriotic within reason, read Wilde in translation and called him, like everyone else, "Vilde." He himself was called Dietrich.

That day he had invited his sergeant-major round for a cup of tea. A cup of tea was a custom of foreign origin, it had about it something English, something Russian; and in the very word "tea" Dietrich seemed to hear a certain liberalism, especially that day, the day of the English fleet's destruction.

Dietrich's guests besides the sergeant-major were Paul Hennig, his lodger Andrei Startsov and Fräulein Lissy.

Dietrich bent over and addressed each of his guests in turn, offering them cakes. The sergeant-major's short fingers were plucking at the strings of a zither, the instrument whimpered and complained, the musician's face—spotted like a currant cake—was smiling sadly. Fräulein Lissy, a round plump little brunette, was making eyes and trying to please everyone at once. Paul Hennig was evidently shaken, and, like a man who has experienced something out of the ordinary, seemed unlike himself: he had grown quiet, lowered his voice and shrunk within himself. But gleams of pride wandered over his slightly sweating face, which was as shiny as a brass bowl.

"The very concept of an international," he said after a long pause, "presupposes the existence of different nations, oh!"

"Very true, very true. Have a cake," said Dietrich.

"I know what I'm talking about. Bebel has this."

"Did he really talk with you so long, Herr Hennig?" asked Fräulein Lissy hardly audibly and her plump elbows and shoulders twitched in a ripple of dimples.

"He said: from the Guild of Hairdressers? and offered his hand. I replied: exactly so, Your Majesty, from the Guild of Hairdressers, and shook his hand. You have a powerful voice, you read the address well, he said. I replied that I was in the Society of Friends of Choral Singing and had sung *Wacht am Rhein* in the town hall that day. Then he asked: perhaps you belong to some other society? I said right out: Your Majesty, I am a Social Democrat."

"And he said nothing?" exclaimed Fräulein Lissy.

"He has no prejudices, our king," remarked Herr Hennig condescendingly. "He bowed and went away. I bowed to him also. Then I went off to have a drink with the boys and they approved my having announced who I was straight out."

"Very good!" said Dietrich. "Herr Sergeant-major, play something else. Fräulein Lissy. . . ."

"Ahh, play, play," begged the little brunette.

"Of course it was good," pronounced Herr Hennig, sprawling back in his armchair. "I'm telling you that our national characteristic is honesty. I announced honestly: I am a Social Democrat."

"As far as I understood," said the sergeant-major sadly, tearing his eyes from the zither and looking at Andrei, "Herr Startsov was saying that it wasn't at all right for Social Democrats to be presented to the King. Isn't that so?"

Hennig's voice became a little firmer:

"Andreas is a good fellow, but he doesn't understand that honesty is our national characteristic. Andreas is a nihilist—a nihilist!—he doesn't recognize tactics, tac-tics!"

"Have some cakes," said Dietrich, disturbed by the stormy wave of the barber's bass.

But suddenly Herr Hennig adopted a sympathetic tone:

"There is a great deal of love in Russians. I've long wanted to say that. What's the sense of such love? Tactics, Andreas, tactics! Why do we love our fatherland? Because we hate its enemies. Love appears after hate! Hatred cements love! When people hate the same thing, then love comes. Andreas wants to love—and doesn't know how, doesn't know how, damn it! I noticed that long ago. Why? Because he has nothing to love, because he loves everything equally. A nihilist! He doesn't understand that you have to hate what men do as well as the men who do it. . . ."

Herr Hennig sighed and stretched, as after a good pork chop. He was satisfied with the style of his speech and wrinkled his eyes at the transparent clarity of his philosophy.

Andrei filled his chest with air and surveyed everyone with his eyes. Dietrich's face was distorted into a pleading smile: he was suffering from a premonition that his cup of tea would be darkened by unpleasantness. The sergeant-major dejectedly hung his head over his zither. The little brunette was wearily propping up her eyelids and her look spoke of simpler and pleasanter things than quarrels.

Ah, these were good people—the noncom Dietrich, his sergeant-major and Fräulein Lissy! What could one say to them, when with their every motion they prayed for silence? Did they really not understand Andrei? Good people, good people . . .

Andrei emitted a heavy breath from his chest and stood up.

"Excuse me," he said, "I'll be back in a moment."

He walked along the dark corridor, bent over and hanging his head. If someone had met him here he would have seemed an old man, dragging behind him a load of many years' torments.

He did not ponder the fact that the door of his room stood wide open. He closed it to and went toward the bed when, from the semidarkness of the corner, from the sofa, he heard the barely audible words:

"What's the matter with you?"

He turned and stood for a long while, peering into the corner, at a vague spot resembling someone's face.

"Are you ill?" he heard again.

"No, it's nothing," he replied.

"Why are you holding on to your head?"

"Am I really holding it?" he asked, lowering his hands. And suddenly he cried:

"It's you?"

The silence which cut off this cry constricted Andrei with excessive heaviness. He bent still farther and against his will a short pitiful groan escaped him. But at the same moment the silence was broken by a ringing almost ecstatic voice:

"Yes, yes, yes!"

Andrei rushed to the sofa toward a white dress, toward

slender extended arms, toward a brightened suddenly distinct face.

"Marie!"

He seized and squeezed her hands so hard she grimaced from the pain and bit her lip in order not to cry out.

"Yes, yes, it's me," she mumbled, attempting to seat him beside her and he crushed her hands awkwardly and roughly, and it was impossible to tell what he wanted to say through the noise of his breathing. Then he sank down on the sofa.

"I had to come."

"You had to, of course, had to," seconded Andrei and his words were confused and scattered, like flying chips.

"I knew, I was waiting . . . you had to, of course, was waiting . . ."

"I wanted to for a long time. I couldn't help coming. . . ."

"Couldn't help, I was waiting for you. . . . Good, good . . ."

"Do you know why?"

"Of course, of course!"

"But why?"

"I was waiting every day."

"I thought for months about coming. You are unhappy, you have made me unhappy."

"I?"

"Since we met I have been pursued by unhappiness. On my heels. I have only to go out of the house to see something which destroys my peace of mind. Like that time in the park. Those blind men prevented me sleeping. They kept filing past me as soon as I closed my eyes. Do you remember how they were holding on to one another? How they stretched out their hands in front of them? And their heads back, remember?"

"They kept listening for something."

"Yes, yes! And I have been listening for something since, as if I had gone blind, my eyes replaced and I didn't know how to look with these strange eyes. Do you know what I think?"

Marie stopped.

"Strange eyes?" repeated Andrei.

"Your eyes," she said, staring at him as if verifying her idea.

"Mine? Maybe."

"I'm sure. That's certainly it. I've lost something. Everything was simple before . . . and necessary. . . . After our meeting in the mountains . . . solitude . . . And not a moment's peace. At every step! Just now I was rushing around the town, around the streets, I don't know where. At the station I saw them leaving for the front. I had seen soldiers off a hundred times and not once had I guessed that I was seeing condemned men! When the soldiers placed their feet on the car steps it seemed to me that they were ascending the scaffold."

Andrei said softly:

"For three years I have been watching executions. Men are dying every second. We are all standing in a line before the scaffold. And I am thinking more and more often about the executioner."

"Fate?"

"Men, not fate."

"What men?"

"You and I. Everyone."

He moved closer to Marie, took her hand, passed his palm over it, felt its warmth and smoothness and said even more softly:

"We have condemned ourselves."

"We?"

"We should have thought how we were organizing the world."

Marie rolled against him and asked with childlike simplicity, confidingly and abruptly:

"How have we organized the world?"

Now the time has come to keep our solemn promise to talk of flowers in this chapter. It is necessary to do this, essential to do this, without wasting a single word or a single line. Because at this time Marie became a woman in love. And because for many pages we shall be separated from descriptions of youthful, impulsive and disturbing emotions, or of tender sorrow, or of the charm of words whose sense is as distant from their meaning as war is from love.

Andrei and Marie talked of war. They talked of war while their hands were coupled: squeezing, feeling and caressing fingers, palms, wrists. They spoke of life crushing and trampling people, of the fact that people themselves were to blame for this and their faces grew flushed from their irregular breathing. They said that the world was soaked in blood, blood that was flowing over the earth in an endless river, that death was walking among the people up to its knees in blood—and their lips met of their own accord, moist, salty from the onrush of blood. They spoke of the end which would ruin and destroy everything—and laid the beginning from which everything springs. They were young, they were strong and of all that they talked about they remembered only that they loved one another.

Andrei stood up—swift, erect, shivering, as after a night on the bare spring earth—and turned the key in the door.

Perhaps Paul Hennig had been right, saying that when people hate the same thing then love comes?

His Royal Highness had graciously permitted Ober-lieutenant von zur Mühlen-Schönau to wear a soft cap at all times—even on inspections and parades. The Ober-lieutenant's skull had been trepanned and a part of a splintered temporal bone had been taken out. The operation had been performed three times, the Ober-lieutenant had borne his sufferings like a soldier; for nearly six months his reason had teetered on the border between light and darkness, but the doctors were skillful, youth was strong, and the Ober-lieutenant recovered. From the back of his head to his right ear ran a glossy pink scar, but the Ober-lieutenant's face sparkled with the colors of sunrise, as if reflecting the tints of the ribbons decorating his uniform. He was the most remarkable man in Bischofsberg, most remarkable after Ober-lieutenant Adolf Urbach, who had received the order *pour le mérite*. But that was luck: Adolf Urbach had traversed the whole of Belgium, had been one of the first to enter Maubeuge, was in Sedan, fought near Verdun—and not even a single scratch! Von Schönau had gone successfully as far as Northern Champagne, had dislodged the French from a reinforced sector and immediately, on the first job, in the first half-way decent skirmish, a mere splinter had put him out of action, and right away sick-bays, hospitals, resorts, consultations—soft, creeping, irksome murk. To an officer bandages, bed linen, compresses and clysters are offensive. An officer commands, slashes, enters the fortress, blows up arsenals, organizes inspections and receives medals. Ober-lieutenant Urbach was the most remarkable man in Bischofsberg, because he had the order *pour le mérite*. Ober-lieutenant von zur Mühlen-Schönau had only two iron crosses—first and second class. But Urbach had not once been on leave whereas von Schönau was strolling about the evening streets of Bischofsberg and everyone saw him—a wounded cavalier of the iron cross of the first and second class and of other medals, whose ribbons gaily decorated his uniform with the colors of the sunrise.

"Girls, girls! He went round the corner!"

"He's gone into a café!"

"I vote we go buy some cakes!"

"But if he's going to drink coffee?"

"Sit at the next table!"

"He has such eyes!"

"And the mouth?"

"Ah, the mouth! . . ."

"How lucky she is!"

"Who?"

"Marie."

"In her place I'd . . ."

"He's looking! He's smiling! Let's go!"

In the evening the city seems unfamiliar, mysterious, populous. At every step the store lights disguise a man. Now he is gloomy and enigmatic, now affectionate and artless, then sorrowful, then joyful. If you want to pour your happiness into your muscles and bones, to test it by touch with your palm, go out onto the street at the time when the street lamps and shops have just lit up, run through the bevies of girls dreaming on the sidewalks, stretch your legs with Lovelace, the idler and man-about-town, shun the busy careworn person — and you will seem to have the whole of life grasped in your fist and you will be free to drink it in one gulp or to spill it onto the road. . . .

When Marie returned home from Andrei's place, creeping stealthily along the promenades, Ober-lieutenant von zur Mühlen-Schönau was strolling in the city hall square. It was good as usual to hear whispering around him, to feel the gaze of passers-by on his chest, to reply to the urgent bows of schoolboys and the saluting of soldiers, to know that people going in the other direction would turn around and look after him. The uniform helped him bear his flushed body lightly and erectly, his saber bounced ever so slightly on his resilient thigh and it was pleasant to hold it easily with two fingers. Every tenth or twelfth glance of eyes going the other way seemed to him to be inviting and tender, and somewhere in their temples, as if from wine, floated circles, sometimes black like painted eyelashes, at others scarlet like lips.

He went into a shop with pictures exhibited in the window, walked along the rows of canvases and frames, gaily screwing up his eyes against the lights of the reflections and the work of home-grown artists, leafed through some gravures and ordered them set aside.

He did not walk out of the shop but flew out—red, impetuous, wreathed in scent from his freshly perfumed uniform. His saber scraped against the door, knocked against his spurs, his legs walked springily over the asphalt—and here he was again in the gentle spell of the evening hour, among the smiles, whispers and glances.

A bearded, round-shouldered Landsturmer, putting on speed in the presence of the officer's uniform which had gleamed unexpectedly in the crowd, clumsily waved his arm.

"You almost knocked my nose off, old fellow," said von Schönau with a faint smile, stopping the soldier. "You should be kept in barracks. Salute according to regulations."

The Landsturmer turned around and went several steps off. Passers-by stopped. The bearded man, digging his soles into the asphalt, moved towards the officer and threw up his elbow.

"Back!" shouted von Schönau.

The public quickly gathered on both sides, forming a corridor through which the soldier marched freely. He was obviously a bad, perhaps the worst soldier, and his movements were pitiful, he walked like a bird, thrusting his nose forward with every step. It was just like an operetta.

"Back!" commanded von Schönau, suddenly becoming hoarse.

The schoolboys tittered, looking servilely into the officer's face. One girl wrung her hands in delight. The Landsturmer creaked his boots a third time and waved his arm still more disgracefully.

Von Schönau choked down some word or other, his veins bulged over his collar, he was stiff and tense.

At that instant someone shouted loudly from behind: "Shame!"

Von Schönau shuddered and suddenly saw himself—a hero of Champagne, a cavalier of the iron cross, an officer of the Saxon army—before a crowd which awaited an outcome worthy of the uniform, the title, the medals. In a minute the whole town would know how an officer acts when the word "Shame!" hangs suspended like a slap in the face over a hushed crowd—the whole town! In an hour—all the newspapers, in a day—the whole country! Now, without losing a second, in the hush, in view of everyone, for hundreds of eyes and ears, it was necessary to decide what to do, necessary to find a way out.

Von Schönau strode up to the Landsturmer standing with his hand pressed to his head and said distinctly:

"Did you hear how the people branded your attitude to the service? A good lesson. Go!"

Then he turned and, bisecting the crowd, cutting into its hum of approval, glided swiftly and springily along the pavement.

He was going to see Marie.

The evening lights seemed to have dimmed, lost their luster, grown cold, people seemed to look at him—the hero of Champagne—discontentedly and the soldiers saluted reservedly and unwillingly.

He regretted having participated in such a ridiculous scene and he was chafed by a feeling that he had somehow been insulted. He could not get rid of that loud shout echoing in his ears: "Shame!"—and could not forget the moment when he had taken this shout to apply to him. Of course, it had not been that, it could not have been that. The man who had shouted—oh to have seen his face! What was he like? Did he genuinely feel the same as he, the Ober-lieutenant? A soldier like that Landsturmer shames the army. Shame, shame! But my God, how boring it was in the streets of this little town! And what tiresome, gray unpleasant burghers! If it were not for Marie he would not have stayed here a single hour. But with her, with her it was fine.

He entered her room, quietly closing the door behind him, and said, peering into the dusk:

"You're not busy?"

Marie jumped off the sofa, hastily adjusted her dress and was silent. Vague words rose in her throat but she was incapable of uttering them.

"What a stupid affair!" exclaimed von Schönau and carefully fumbling in the darkness perched himself on the edge of the sofa. He told her about the clumsy Landsturmer who resembled a bird, about how the army was getting worse, that discipline was falling off, that clumsy pigeon-toed bearded fellows were no good even as cooks.

"Yes, but you know that's Germany!" interrupted Marie and it seemed to her that all the furniture had suddenly become full of attention, was standing on tiptoe and pricking up its ears.

"M-yes . . . hmm-m . . . very likely. B-but I'm talking about the army. . . . It's not quite the same. When this lout behaved in the way he did, someone from the crowd shouted 'Shame!' "

"Was that referring to the soldier?"

The margrave jumped to his feet and glanced at the door: it was tight shut. Then he folded his arms on his chest and began to walk about the room.

"I think I understand your meaning. But do you really think that I wouldn't have cut down on the spot any rogue who dared to insult my person. . . ."

"O-oh, of course! I don't doubt it for a minute! Why, an officer has no alternative."

"No alternative? . . . However, let it go. You're in a bad mood today?"

"Yes."

"A pity. . . ."

He went up to the sofa and stretched out both arms to Marie. She hid in the corner.

"A pity. I wanted to remind you that we must hurry. . . ."

"Why 'must'? . . ."

"Marie!"

"Forgive me."

"The commission has pronounced me fit. I have been posted to the eastern front."

"In that case, why hurry?"

"Two years ago. . . ."

"Ah, two years! . . . I could still think it essential two hours ago!"

He suddenly seized her head in his palms.

"What happened, Marie, two hours ago?"

Was it possible, in the darkness settling in the corners of the night, to see the reflections of two resolutions alternating in Marie's eyes? Dusk became darkness, her sight became accustomed to it, but it could not overcome it and her gaze wandered to the window, reflecting whitely the combined lights of the deep streets.

Marie submitted to the movement of the hands pressing her head, laughed softly and said in the voice which subdues a man:

"Silly. I myself don't know why I'm so crotchety."

"Then when?"

"No, no. I was only answering your last question."

"But I might be sent away any day!"

"Isn't it all the same whether you depart with a ring or without a ring?"

"For me, Marie, you understand, for me it's not the same. . . . Well?"

She stood up. Von Schönau moved swiftly after her and suddenly, losing all his directness and precision, the Ober-lieutenant hung over the end of the sofa in a kind of crumpled ball.

"Well?"

"I don't want to."

"Marie!"

"Does the indefiniteness bother you? Do you feel awkward in front of outsiders?"

"I love you."

"I know."

He rose, the new flexible uniform straightened him, he inlined his head:

"I see that it is impossible to talk to you today. Goody." In the doorway he turned. "Perhaps you will come to chönau?"

"Perhaps."

And now she was alone again. Her hands flew quickly to the air and stretched over her head; she rose on her es—slim, light, inaudible, and her breath floated out with quiet rustle, in keeping with the night. She lay down, e was surrounded by the soundless furniture, indistinuishable in the darkness, and the room seemed to her rangely similar to Andrei's quarters. . . .

The Ober-lieutenant went to the station. On either side lances, smiles and whispers were exchanged, his chest ore the iron crosses first and second class as before, but e felt cold, his saber got in the way of his feet, the surounding lights were dim and miserable. He took a ticket o Lausche and sought out an empty compartment.

FLIGHT

The citadel stood silent and impregnable. Its old stones were purplish-blue; between the flagstones which encircled

its base in a narrow path struggled green mold and fungus: the flagstones were not trodden by human feet.

Old-fashioned little houses fearfully goggled their tiny windows at the citadel and backed away from its overpowering gloom, forming an extensive circular square. But people had grown used to the citadel. As children they had flipped coins beside it, had climbed on one another's backs from the foot of the foundations, had daubed the ancient stones of its walls with chalk and paint. At that time the city scales and hay-lofts had been situated in the citadel and the purplish-blue fortress had resembled an old toothless bear which had turned over to bask in the sun.

In wartime they had cleared the scales out of the citadel and had carried away the hay, bars had been placed over the windows under the roof, a striped sentry-box had been erected at the entrance and—ten yards from the narrow path—a rope had been stretched around the citadel. For a short while the Bischofsbergians looked unfavorably upon their tame old bear being turned into a sullen forbidding wild beast. Then they got used to not being able to linger by the citadel, to the guard being changed in the sentry-box every six hours and to criminals sitting under the roof behind bars. They stopped noticing the fortress.

And then one day, exhausted by the sun, when life was dragging along like a hearse over sandy ground, a protracted wail hung over the square:

"O-o-o-oow! . . ."

Passers-by stopped, turned their heads, raised their eyebrows, asked themselves:

"Mmm-ah! What can that be?"

The wail fell on the square a second time, rolled by in a frightening breeze:

"O-o-o-ow!"

It became clear that the voice was coming from the citadel. One burgher darted from the pavement, raised his hand and shouted:

"There, in the window!"

All heads turned to the citadel.

"Where, where?"

"Under the roof!"

People gathered unexpectedly quickly. They ran out of their houses, rushed to the rope barring the fortress, clustered in a crowd and spread out singly, throwing back their heads, shading themselves from the sun with their hands, not taking their eyes from the window under the roof of the citadel.

"O-o-o-oow! O-o-o-ow!"

Through the broken window a hand was thrust out between the bars. Its fingers alternately opened and clenched into a fist, and in the sunlight one could see black rivulets of blood flowing from cuts down the white body: the fist was scratched and a sleeve of dark blue soldier's cloth was waving in a fringe at the elbow.

From behind the bars the wail burst unabatingly:

"O-o-o-oow!"

Someone in the crowd recognized the fringe of uniform and cried out:

"A German soldier!"

And immediately the troubled word fluttered and flapped its wings over their heads:

"A soldier! A soldier! A German soldier!"

Someone's penetrating voice, almost a squeal, flew up over the roof of the citadel:

"What happened there, friend?"

But in reply that same desperate wail floated over the square:

"O-o-o-oow!"

Andrei stood a little way off from the crowd, his teeth clenched and his whole body straining upward to the citadel. It seemed to him that some terrible force was constantly dragging the wailing man away from the window, the hand was clutching at the air, at the light, at times disappearing behind the bars, then being thrust outside again. He made out the fingers firmly grasping the bars, one rung below where the hand projected. Distinctly, exactly, as if the wall had parted in front of him, he saw the imprisoned soldier hanging with his right arm braced against the bars and with his left, free arm catching at the light and air beyond the wall, at liberty. Suddenly he seemed to see some men or other hanging on to the soldier's legs and beating him on the back, trying to tear him away from the bars. He was on the point of wailing with the prisoner at the whole square.

At that moment short ringing little sounds echoed in Andrei's very ear:

"Bonjour, bonjour, bonjour!"

Andrei turned. A small derby was lifted slightly over a wrinkled, immobile, mask-like face.

"Monsieur Percy!"

"Yes, Monsieur, it is I. They have decided to shut me away in this hole."

Monsieur Percy pointed his finger at the citadel.

"It appears to be good fun up there," he added and screwed up his eyes at the hand writhing under the roof.

Andrei looked about him. On either side of Monsieur Percy two young soldiers stood frozen beneath their rifles. The crowd's consternation had affected them and, astonished, bewildered, they had forgotten their duty. Next to Monsieur Percy, his hands folded behind his back, swayed a man in a knitted jacket. The grayish bristle of his mustache and beard, long unshaven, gleaming with fat, made his smile soft and tender. The smile broadened, illumined his bright eyes, revealed his worn-down yellow teeth, and suddenly a quiet voice splashed Andrei's face with tender warmth:

"You don't remember me?"

"Master Maier? You?"

Master Maier took Andrei's hand and lightly pressed it—kindly, like a child's.

"Not Master Maier," he said, quietly as before, "but an enemy of the fatherland. What's to be done? I always said that dirty piggishness would result. I'm accused of politics. Perhaps it's politics that I'm against war? What do you say?"

"How did all this happen, Master? How did you come to be here?"

"Very simple. The whole trouble is that I was surrounded by dirty piggishness. How are you getting on, dear Herr Startsov?"

"Tell me rather, what's happened to Kurt?"

The disturbance on the square had settled down, but the crowd did not disperse. The prisoner's hand had disappeared, the broken window behind the bars gaped black and empty, the wail could not be heard. The escorts composed themselves and one of them—younger and livelier—shouted at Andrei:

"Don't talk!"

"Why have you stopped?" said the other, prodding Monsieur Percy's elbow.

"Adieu," said the latter, raised his derby and moved off toward the citadel.

Master Maier managed to nod his head to Andrei and say:

"Herr Wahn has been a prisoner a good year now, in Russia."

Then he got into step like a soldier and walked shoulder to shoulder with Monsieur Percy. The escorts took a more comfortable grip on their rifles.

Andrei saw them approach the gates of the citadel and stop in front of the guard. A low wicket gate, cut into the large gates, opened slowly and swallowed up Monsieur Percy, Master Maier and the soldiers. The wicket did not close for a long time. An officer came out of it, marched carefully over the flagstones of the path encircling the citadel, stopped opposite the crowd and, raising his hand, lashed it with a brassy shout:

"Please disperse! Nothing special has happened. The prisoner became mentally ill and has been sent to the hospital."

The heads of Marie and Andrei were bent low over a round table. Spread out on the table was a plan of the Villa Urbach and neighboring estates. Marie was drawing a pencil over the plan. Her hair descended in tangled curls onto the plan and the yellow light of the lamp hanging over her head passed through them in a dim web of dots. The dots trembled on her hands and on the colored drawing of the plan, the pencil now stopped at a certain point, now crept over the broken lines.

"From here it is twenty minutes," said Marie, "and you will come out at Forest Post Number Seven. From there go left, westward, along the road."

"Wait, I'll mark it."

Andrei sketched a curve on a small scrap of paper and bisected it with a thick line.

"Westward. Then?"

"After ten minutes you'll see a ditch to your right. This is the frontier. But you can't cross it here: there are always people there. Go straight to the crossroads, here, you see? This is the frontier post. Our soldiers are here. And farther —straight, straight. The frontier bends away from the road here toward the north. I think that after three-quarters of an hour you can turn off into the forest and cross the frontier just here. I know the peasants always cross here. It's a God-forsaken spot and you need only be careful as you go."

Andrei rose and began to walk about the room. When he came close to the lamp it was evident that his face was careworn.

"Tell me, Marie, am I right?"

"Yes, you are."

"You understand that nothing can be done here?"

"I do."

"Here my every step is hindered. I'm simply in no condition to make a start. I'm an outsider. And I can be inactive no longer. I must escape, I must!"

"But, Andrei, that's already decided!"

He rushed to her, pressed her to him, looked into her eyes and his look was heavy with distrust and a kind of melancholy fear.

"It's hard for me to part. For the first time on this earth I feel at home. Marie, do you hear—at home, loved! I'm afraid that if I leave you you'll think. . . ."

"Quiet!"

"But I can't bear this citadel any longer! People stifle me, people's voices, even the good in people. . . ."

"It's decided, Andrei. Decided! We'll meet again afterward."

"Yes, yes."

They leaned again over the table, arm in arm, and ran their fingers over the plan. Then Andrei said:

"What's Kurt like now? He's gone through a lot for sure. It seems to me he must change."

"Certainly," answered Marie, "to judge from what you've told me, he's a fine fellow."

"So, it's decided?" asked Andrei again.

"Decided. . . ."

It was so good for the memory to resurrect every turn of the paths and roads known so well, to talk about the forest lodges, cliffs and pines which Andrei had to encounter.

A chill horror seized Marie when she named the way stations extending through Bohemia from the frontier to Reichenberg. As if she had thought up a new prank with the gay friends of her childhood. As if she were undertaking explorations for an enchanted treasure. As if the plans of the Villa Urbach and neighboring estates had been stolen from her father's study. What in life can replace the sweetness of agitation which a secret brings? . . . But on the dim stairs, before leaving the ridiculous old house with the room resembling an arena, Marie leaned against the cool damp wall. She had to allow her lips to cool, which still tasted of kisses. She had to wait for her heart to calm down. She had to decide for herself once and for all: why, why now, when love had only just come, when her first unbearable pain had not yet dulled, why was Andrei fleeing?

Fat ducks waddled around Forest Post Number Seven. Andrei heard their gurgling quacking a long time before the brown post lodge appeared at the end of a narrow ridge. The farther he penetrated into the mountains the sharper became his hearing. He had known the noise of the forest before, incessantly rolling and merging into one. Now this noise splintered into an infinite number of sounds. The cracking of bark, the breaking of branches under the weight of perching birds, the clicking of ripened pine cones, the creaking and groaning of old dead trunks; some kinds of very faint rustles became distinct and loud, as if each of them sounded in a profound silence. His hearing removed the screens from trees, stones and bushes and Andrei saw what had been hidden from his eyes. His face was calm. He walked regularly, evenly, heavily, like a peasant returning home from the town. He carried only a canvas bag on his back and a stick in his hand.

A girl nursing a baby stood by the entrance to the lodge. She wrinkled her eyes at the passer-by, measured him from head to foot with that look which is bestowed on a person in deserted, remote places and adjusted the baby in her arms like a woman.

"Good day," she said.

"Good day," replied Andrei and turned left onto a straight smooth road.

After a quarter of an hour he caught the wheezing groan of a barrel organ. Andrei forced himself to move his feet as regularly and heavily as before. He did not know what was awaiting him at the crossroads to which he was drawing near, but for several nights now he had fallen asleep with the thought that in flight one must meet any surprise with equanimity.

"Be prepared, be prepared," he kept saying to himself, stubbornly digging his thick unbending soles into the ground.

Behind the trees flashed the gray back of a Landsturmer. Then a massive guard with a rifle at his feet appeared suddenly and was outlined majestically against the reddish background of tree trunks. A second soldier sat on a smoothly sawn stump, his rifle leaning against a neighboring tree.

On the road crossing Andrei's path, beneath a black, sharp-clawed, coarse-feathered bird nailed to a post, a blind old man was turning the handle of a barrel organ. The barrel organ was turned toward Germany, but its wooden leg was resting on the national soil of Austria. It was a moving evasion of the law which forbade the collection of alms in Saxony, the appeal of poverty to implacable order. What honorable and noble patriot would not smile at a tune lightheartedly sung by grateful Vienna? And what can be expected from this carefree Vienna besides lightheartedness? As long as Vienna does not violate foreign customs and laws she is pleasant and nice.

Andrei stopped in front of the organ grinder. He looked at his face, dulled by indifference, at the shiny round sun of his bald skull, at his closed quivering eyelashes. But the frontier guard standing outside his field of vision stuck in his memory more firmly and distinctly than the organ grinder whom he examined intently. He could not have said what kind of face the soldier had nor what kind of hands. He was a frontier guard towering two yards away from a fugitive. Andrei saw neither his look nor his movements, but he would have recognized him among thousands of other soldiers whom he had never seen. Is it really possible ever to forget the man in whose hands one's fate has rested?

Andrei took a purse from his pocket, obtained an iron coin, slowly approached the post, placed the coin in a cap lying turned up on the barrel organ and turned back. In passing he cast a glance at the second soldier sitting on the stump. He had not looked at him before, but he knew that the soldier had not stirred while he was looking at the organ grinder. He felt as if he were seeing with his back.

He said, addressing no one in particular:

"Good day."

And walked on.

A heavy voice overtook him:

"Good day."

He realized that he had been answered by the soldier sitting on the stump.

And suddenly a joyful, reckless and humorous march showered out behind him, running up against the trees and bouncing back from the stones. He changed his step and, in time with the music, swiftly and freely moved ahead.

A shallow ditch extending along the road, overgrown with moss and bilberry, gradually bent away to the right, disappearing quicker and quicker into the forest. The road went downhill, easy and straight. All was quiet and limpid. Three-quarters of an hour later, without looking back, Andrei turned to the right and was hidden by the dense pines.

He knew that the frontier guards had been taken off the Austrian side. The master always looks after his servants, but why should the servants look after their master? Their interests are violated by the very nature of the things which create master and servants.

From the frontier left behind by Andrei to the nearest railroad station was no more than six kilometers. Andrei's plan was simple. He intended to ride through to Prague, from there to Salzburg and Innsbruck, then—to the Swiss border on foot. For such a journey only one thing was necessary: decision. It had been stored up by Andrei over two years and he felt already free as he approached the station building.

He took a ticket to Reichenberg. The car was spacious, the train dragged itself along unwillingly like all local trains which have grown decrepit from endlessly rattling over a short boring section. A brisk late afternoon breeze blew in the window, the words reaching Andrei had a new sound which mingled strangely with something kindred to him, almost completely understandable.

And people seemed subtly close, accessible and simple, so much so that their thoughts showed through the bars of their shaggy eyebrows. And even their slightest movements were strangely significant with a coarse, somehow clumsy, simplicity.

That peasant there with the old-fashioned haircut sitting by the window and wiping the sweat from his steep white forehead with his handkerchief. That unobtrusive sick old man there, yawning without ceremony. That thickset dried-up man there who had just flung open the compartment door and come in, with a direct incisive look in his deep eyes. There was something open and likable about him. He came up to Andrei. He probably wanted to sit on the bench beside him, he did not take his eyes from his face—they really did cut, those eyes, they were actually frightening, repellent! What an arrogant and ominous look! This man was of a different breed, had different bones, he was inaccessible and cruel. Danger, Andrei, danger! Andrei was prepared for any emergency any second, he knew in advance how to meet an emergency when he came face to face with it. However, could it really have come so soon, so pitilessly soon and so matter-of-factly?

"Your papers?"

"Papers? I am returning home to Reichenberg. I was going as far as the station. . . ."

"Don't you have any papers with you?"

"With me no, I forgot. In Reichenberg you can easily find out . . ."

"I can do most things easily. I am doing my duty."

Two tall soldiers appeared in the doorway. They were lean, thin-legged, with narrow straps drawn around them. Their lips were drawn tight, like the straps. The thickset man transferred his eyes from Andrei to the soldiers and walked on down the car. . . .

The end.

Really so soon, so pitilessly soon and just like that?

Oh, no! Andrei had not crossed the border! Around him were the same people whose voices and laughter he had fled: a dense thickness was washing over every atom of his body. He could stretch out his arms, turn his head or hug the wall. But to square his shoulders in order to breathe with his whole chest was impossible for him. The pipe through which he was permitted to breathe had become still longer, the air was being drawn into it still more slowly and his chest was working with its last strength. No, this was still the same people, the same country, where everything was immutable and solid, like an iron bar dug into the earth and covered with cement—Germany!

However, one had to think more precisely and not yield to the temptation of generalizing where generalizations suggested themselves. Was it thinkable that in Germany events could happen like the one which awaited Andrei on the station at Reichenberg?

Andrei was taken from the train and delivered to the station. They were a long time seeking out the military commandant in the excitement and noise. They found only his assistant on the point of leaving for town. Because of the lateness of the hour it was decided to postpone the questioning of the detainee from the train until morning. The station cell turned out to be occupied by prisoners and a good hour went by finding a place for the newly arrested man. A place was found in the customs warehouse a little way off from the station.

It was a small room in a squat house, with a window looking on to a sparse, withered garden.

The arrested man was padlocked in and a guard was ordered to watch the window on the garden side.

The night was dark and soft, as nights can be only in August when the corn is ripening and apple trees split from the weight of juicy ripe apples. The bent back of the motionless guard showed in the window, but behind it the tree-tops showed purple, illuminated by the light of a signal lamp; above the trees dim stars quivered in a black abyss: their sparkle was blotted out by a cloud of smoke and dust which had not yet settled on the ground.

The guard stood still for a long time. Then he began to walk back and forth past the window. The hubbub of the station died down and the soldier's steps were clearly audible. Gradually they became regular, dying away and ceasing when the soldier came to the ends of the beat he had set himself, and becoming loud when he walked past the window.

Andrei touched the window frame. It moved noiselessly. Probably the window had been standing open for a long while. He thrust his head out and looked closely at the soldier. The latter walked to the corner of the house fifteen paces from the window, looked around the corner in the direction of the station noises, then turned back. Andrei closed the window, let the guard pass and again looked outside. To the right it was no more than ten paces to the end of the house, and on the garden side there was a bed of shrubbery.

Andrei listened to the soldier's steps again. The main thing was not to disturb the methodicalness of his movements. Then it was necessary to take advantage of that brief moment when the guard was looking at the station. There was nothing else to consider. Luck would either save or ruin him.

It saved him.

Andrei opened the window when the soldier had moved five paces toward the far end of his beat. Andrei sat on the windowsill, crawled quietly on his stomach and hung from his hands. It remained only to calculate the timing of his leap, which had to coincide with one of the guard's last steps. The leap would not be difficult, the ground was no more than half a yard away. And suddenly the piercing whistle of a locomotive somewhere quite close to the window soared and flew into the night.

Andrei let go his hands, fell to the ground and dashed into the dark thicket of bushes. Their thorns were sharp, the pain from their blows and scratches fierce—but only iron could have halted his flight.

The whistle still deafened the neighborhood—overwhelming and crushing, like a hurricane. And when its echoes had passed into the invisible recesses of the night Andrei was on a huge stretch of waste land which rested against a railroad embankment. He ran across it and walked quickly along the tracks. . . .

Of course it was another country in which Andrei found himself—a country of simple-hearted people, clumsy, close, almost kindred. . . .

But it was no simpler to escape through this country than through any other. But enough of this—is it ever simple, is it ever safe and easy to escape? Escapes are made by heroes and there are so few heroes in this world. It is all right to escape over familiar roads. Unfamiliar ones are difficult and harsh.

Andrei knew only one road in this country—the road which had brought him here. And he escaped along it—back toward the frontier.

At school Ober-lieutenant von zur Mühlen-Schönau had been taught to keep a diary. And he had become accustomed to note down a few words every day in notebooks, which were placed in a pile in the drawer where he kept deeds, settlement documents and a moldering volume: *The Heraldry and Family Tree of the Line of Landed Margraves von zur Mühlen-Schönau.*

The Ober-lieutenant opened his new notebook with the following entry:

I am again bidding farewell to the Penates. An unconquerable force has been preserved in the past. I listen to the silence of things. It is more comprehensible to me than a commander's order. I am sure that I shall not die soon. I am destined to bring our line to an end. It must rot away. I am its last fabric, doomed to destruction. I shall be pushed in a wheelchair, fed, washed, until I crumble to pieces. Fate intended my grandfather to grow rich. The line which was then numerous is doomed to gradual extinction. Grandfather's wealth will enable me to rot alive. I am exactly rich enough for nothing to interfere with the loneliness of my death, so that I will die among the silent ruins of the past, as a symbol. This is in store for the line. The fatal wound which I sustained in Champagne, fatal for any man—proved to be only serious for me. But this wound is enough to render me, toward the end of my life, an idiot. I shall be an idiot, legless and repulsive. I shall be pushed about in a wheelchair. This is in the nature of things. The ancient fates which nurtured my line will look upon its end.

In a few days I go again to the front. The knowledge that these native walls will look upon my death fills me with courage. I am convinced that war does not menace my life. But this certainty is tormentingly dull.

Late this evening, while walking in the park, I came across a man trying to find his way. When he noticed me he tried to hide behind the trees, but I caught up with him. He looked exhausted, he has probably been on the run several days. I demanded his name. He announced that he was a prisoner and would not say another word. I shut him in the vault. Let him come to his senses. In the morning I shall question him. He's probably big game.

Andrei awoke from the cold as if he had been suddenly plunged into an ice-hole. He could hardly drag his arms out from under his head. He was all cramped up like bark stripped from a tree. From the moment he had been dropped onto the smooth stone flags in the basement he had fallen asleep, as if stricken senseless. Having awaked he felt the flagstones. Their smooth surface receded into the darkness. He crawled to either side, sometimes with his arms stretched out in front of him, sometimes lifting them over his head. Then he stood up. His hands collided with stone. Right-angled slabs like those which paved the floor hung overhead in a sloping arch.

Andrei made several sharp movements with his arms in order to warm up. An incomprehensible rumble sounded behind him. He stopped moving and listened. The rumble approached steadily, as if heavy articles were being rolled some distance away. Suddenly it ceased, its hollow echoes dying away in the darkness. Heavy abrupt footsteps, replacing the rumble, stopped somewhere not far from Andrei. Then came a grumbling of rusty iron, a lock chimed like an old clock and light cut into Andrei's eyes like lightning. Through a new wave of rumbles set up by a low voice Andrei distinguished the words:

"If you please, sir."

He climbed out onto a high step, bending his cramped legs with difficulty. A young soldier looking like an orderly, with sleeves rolled up to the elbow and in soft slippers, led Andrei through a series of corridors and small stairways into silent dusky halls, hung with weapons, pictures and knightly equipment. Then he knocked at a low door and asked loudly:

"Shall I bring him in?"

Andrei walked into a spacious room, stopping before a desk crammed with frames and a heap of glass trinkets. All around hung pictures, as in museums, in three to four rows, on iron shelves stretched along the white walls.

The Ober-lieutenant was sitting behind the desk, squeezed into a flexible uniform and facing the door.

"You can go," he said to the orderly.

Then he inspected Andrei with his bright, open eyes.

"Now that you have rested," he said smiling, "perhaps you will tell me more about yourself?"

Andrei shrugged his shoulders.

"I think," continued the Ober-lieutenant, "that the hospitality shown you by this house obliges you to a certain courtesy."

"The hospitality of the house?" exclaimed Andrei. "You presumably mean the hospitality of the basement?"

"You must forgive me that little subterfuge. It was provoked by a desire to extend and, so to speak, to secure your stay here."

"I should not want to embarrass you with my presence," said Andrei and stared intently at the Ober-lieutenant. He had to force him to change his tone. Otherwise it was impossible to understand his intentions.

"However I need not worry," added Andrei, turning his head to the wall, "hospitality is characteristic only of savages. I could not waste your time even if I wanted to."

The Ober-lieutenant lifted his eyebrows and compressed his always half-open lips. But his former smile immediately smoothed out his face. He felt fresh and healthy. The day was cloudless. The sun had already risen over the trees and was gently warming him through the open window. A spirit coffee-pot was sniffing at a little distance from the Ober-lieutenant on a round table.

"Ha, I noticed even last night that you were infected by polemics. Probably as a result of the failure of your enterprise? But you should give more details about yourself in your own interests."

"You're questioning me out of curiosity," said Andrei, "it's all the same, nothing will change: someone else will decide my fate."

"That's the whole point," exclaimed the Ober-lieutenant, seemingly overjoyed that their conversation had come to the most important thing. "Who will decide your fate is the whole point. Therefore I am questioning you to the point and not from curiosity. . . . What are you looking at there?"

"A picture," said Andrei.

"It depends on me how your future turns out," said the Ober-lieutenant coldly.

"How?"

"How?" repeated the Ober-lieutenant threateningly and began to space his words impressively. "I can hand you over to the authorities as a prisoner of war or as a spy. You don't seem to me to be a naïve man. Fugitive and spy have dissimilar nuances, is it not so? That's the first thing. The second is that I can hand you over either to the military or to the civil authorities. Do you sense the difference? What are you looking at all the time there?"

"I know that picture."

"You can't know that picture!" cried the Ober-lieutenant. "I beg you to look at me when I am talking to you!"

Andrei glanced at him.

"I know that artist."

"You can't know either that picture or that artist," shouted the Ober-lieutenant and banged his palm on the desk. "I can see right through you! You won't get away from me! You made the wrong choice: I am the only one who knows that artist!"

"His name is Kurt Wahn," said Andrei quietly.

The Ober-lieutenant jumped up and leaned over the desk toward Andrei.

"Kurt was working on that picture before the war. I don't think he finished it."

"Are you acquainted with Kurt Wahn?" asked the Ober-lieutenant, and his lips parted like a child's.

"I wasted weeks in his mansard. We were friends."

The Ober-lieutenant recovered from his surprise.

"Sit down, please," he said, pointing to a high leather chair and sitting in his own seat.

"Kurt was intending to present that picture to the town council of Nuremberg. How did you get hold of it?"

The Ober-lieutenant was silent and looked at the picture.

"Strange," said Andrei, "this is the second incident reminding me of Kurt after two years of not hearing of him."

"Do you know what has become of him?"

"He was taken prisoner, taken to Russia."

The Ober-lieutenant rose and took two long steps to the window. Then, without turning, he said softly:

"And you are Russian?"

"Yes."

"You were friends," said the Ober-lieutenant, thinking of something, "and fate came between you. That is sad. We esteem friendship. This feeling is highly developed in us. *And* the feeling of sorrow."

He turned, looked at Andrei, at Kurt's picture, approached the table, and with unexpected affection offered:

"Do you want a cup of coffee? I was very discourteous in forgetting to ask you whether you had had enough to eat. You look very exhausted. You were probably . . . a long time on the run?"

"I am full," said Startsov, sitting on the chair, "but I haven't drunk for a long time and coffee will warm me. I haven't been able to get warm yet."

The Ober-lieutenant poured out a cup of the coffee which he had not touched yet and offered:

"Have some cheese."

'Cakes, please have some cakes,' Andrei recalled the bent-over, smiling Dietrich. He took a big mouthful of coffee and held his breath as he felt the hot liquid flowing through his body and burning its way until it became painful.

The Ober-lieutenant was strolling from the window to the wall and saying:

"I consider Wahn a major talent. He is persistent, stubborn and merciless with himself. Every new picture of his is a step forward. I decided to collect them and then at one sweep to show Germany a new German artist. It's true, though, that the French have influenced him too much."

"A good influence," interjected Andrei.

"It demoralizes Germans," said the Ober-lieutenant. "Only the theme comes naturally to us. That can be seen in our literature as well as in our industry. We work out only the idea. The French are carried away by methods. That is the Gallic nature. They know how to maneuver but they don't know how to organize an advance, nor do they even know how to retreat. Their revolutions became classics. But what has France become as a result of these classic revolutions? A lawless oligarchy. The revolutions of the French are maneuver, method. The French can have a Cézanne but they will never have a Beklin.

"Beklin?" exclaimed Andrei, clutching his head. "Beklin? But that's an outrage!"

"I agree he's a bad artist. I am talking of him as the best exponent of a theme. He places an idea before the viewer as no one else."

"Klinger does that even better," said Andrei, "but then that doesn't prevent him from being even less gifted than Beklin."

"On the other hand, that very ability is what makes Lenbach a genius," cried the Ober-lieutenant.

He spoke with an abrupt movement of one hand, unbuttoning the collar of his uniform in order to turn his head from the picture to Andrei more easily.

"I am deeply convinced of this basic difference in the national characters. Therefore I say the French can harm Kurt Wahn but not help him. For his theme he must find his own methods and not borrow them from the French. He has his own road. Look, this wall here is his work."

The Ober-lieutenant dashed over to the pictures, seizing a polished pointer, and began to explain Kurt Wahn's manner of painting, going from one picture to another. He forced Andrei to approach the paintings and led him by the sleeve around the room in order to reiterate some thought of his by pointing to the actual pictures.

Then he sat, somewhat tired and preoccupied, laying his hands out on the table and examining them with a lingering look.

"Kurt Wahn did not understand me," he said sadly. "It seemed to him that I was depriving him of fame. He was sure that his pictures were being wasted in some tiny village. I wrote to him that one must not irritate the public with frequent appearances. Every exhibition of an artist should be a surprise. He did not believe in my sincerity. That was fatal."

The Ober-lieutenant again reflected.

"Fatal," he said more quietly, "because his distrust of me was instinctive. We are of different blood."

He looked searchingly at Andrei.

"You are his friend. Therefore you also distrust me."

Andrei wanted to say something, but the Ober-lieutenant shook his head and closed his eyes.

"It's not in our power. I sometimes envy people like

Wahn, or, perhaps, like you. They know no one beyond their father. Solitaries. It must be very easy for them. They make decisions always for themselves, for themselves alone. But for people like me everything has been decided long ago by grandfathers, ancestors, history."

The Ober-lieutenant rubbed his hands as if washing them.

"Now we must finish our business," he said. "I can help you out. Do you have any documents with you?"

Andrei took a yellow sheet folded into four from his side pocket. This was the only paper he had taken with him. The Ober-lieutenant opened it.

Stadtrat of the city
of Bischofsberg

CERTIFICATE

23 August, 1916. The Russian subject, Herr Andrei Startsov, born 17/XI/1890, has permission to walk on Lausche.

Stadtrat,
Police presidium

"You cannot complain of your inhuman treatment," said the Ober-lieutenant with a smile. "But why did your walk drag out so long? Where were you for three whole days? Trying to escape?"

He laughed.

"Home through Austria? Ha-ha! I shall get to Russia before you do: I'm being sent to the front soon."

He again fell silent, leaning back in his armchair and examining Andrei.

"Do you want me to help you out?" he asked, frowning.

Andrei suddenly remembered the last hour with Marie in the room concealed by soft, soundless darkness. Such an hour, when there is nothing but touch and the whole world is enveloped by human warmth—such an hour he had been waiting for all his life. And now, finding himself again somewhere near Marie—not to see her, not to touch her face?

"Help me," he said in a trembling voice, "if it is possible. I am ashamed of this childish affair."

"But why?" laughed the Ober-lieutenant, "such an out-break in heroic!"

He took his pen and with sharp letters traced a lattice of words on the paper:

> I certify that the Russian subject, Herr Andrei Start-sov, was discovered in an unconscious condition near the castle zur Mühlen-Schönau and, in view of his weak health, has remained with me during the course of three days, the which has caused his failure to appear before the proper authorities.
>
> Ober-lieutenant
> von zur Mühlen-Schönau

He handed the paper to Andrei and, as he was bidding farewell, grasped his arm:

"In reality it was my duty to hand you over to the authorities. I violated it. You know what it means when a German violates his duty? Good-by."

He rang and commanded the orderly:

"Take Herr Startsov to the road for the station."

On the day of his departure the Ober-lieutenant noted:

> *Yesterday Marie came unexpectedly. I was aston-ished by her buoyancy and said so. She did not cease thanking me for something, even after I had told her I was going away. I could not understand what the mat-ter was. We strolled in the park and, as in the past, she again spoke a lot about our future. I was sorry to let her go. But she was in a hurry and caught the next train back. Today I said good-by to my pictures and helped to put covers on them.*

Poor Ober-lieutenant! He was covering up his pictures and did not know how long they would be covered up. He was looking into Marie's eyes overflowing with joy and did not understand what they were thanking him for.

What if he were told how Marie had reacted to Andrei's story of the officer who had so hastened their meeting?

"Zur Mühlen-Schönau?" repeated Marie to Andrei. "Yes,

I've heard of him. He's our neighbor. But I'm not acquainted with him. . . ."

What if these words were related to him?

Would our novel even then have to overcome endless digressions and dismal, lengthy stretches about war?

A CHAPTER ON
NINETEEN SEVENTEEN

WHOM WAS GENERAL-FIELD-MARSHAL
VON HINDENBURG THINKING OF?

This house was satisfactory.

It could not fail to be satisfactory. Its windows sparkled in the sun so brightly that they seemed to have in them not panes of glass but crystal polyhedra. It was moderately gray because it was faced with cement, moderately pink because the cement had been mixed with red lead, moderately white because the ledges and moldings on the façade were neatly plastered.

This house—with its hundreds of sparkling windows, with its heavy cathedral-like door, covered with a smooth skin of brick-red tiles—this house was moderately pleasant.

Any moderately pleasant house is, of course, satisfactory. Like a man who stands in his place in a tie, cuffs and pressed trousers, with his hair combed down on his head, in stout shoes and with a timely smile on his face. Such a man is pleasant, such a man is satisfactory.

So was this house.

It stood at the point where Bismarck Avenue began, just where the Stadtrat had placed it and just where the only Jewish city councillor in the whole of Germany, Herr Otto-Moses Milch, had wanted to see its façade. Just where it was passed every Sunday at four thirty p.m. by the most respectable burghers of the city of Bischofsberg, walking to the Park of Seven Ponds to listen to the evening concert by the military choir.

The most respectable burghers used to walk past the moderately pleasant house and, every Sunday at four-thirty p.m., they would cast their eyes beneath the brick-red skin of tiles, where the moderately large letters read:

THE

CITY COUNCILLOR

OTTO-MOSES MILCH

MUNICIPAL

SURGICAL HOSPITAL

Then the burghers in morning coats, with tightly rolled umbrellas, in debries and light-colored vests, began to say that the victor in the World War would be the one who had the strongest nerves, as General-Field-marshal von Hindenburg had so rightly said.

"But I say, Herr Assistant, we've been talking too much and are on the path reserved for bicycles!"

"Oh, yes, Herr Privy-councillor, you're quite right."

And they turned back and turned onto the path for pedestrians. Bismarck Avenue was divided into three branches and at the beginning of each branch stood signs on solid posts:

BICYCLES ONLY

PEDESTRIANS ONLY

HORSEMEN ONLY

These came right at the beginning of the avenue, opposite a path paved with tiny pebbles, and pointed like arrows to the entrance of the surgical hospital. And the society of the three solid posts was shared by no less solid iron rods with neatly lettered plaques:

DROPPING PAPER
OR FRUIT PEEL FORBIDDEN

DOGS MUST BE KEPT ON A LEASH

NURSES WITH CHILDREN ARE FORBIDDEN
TO SIT ON THE BENCHES

DO NOT BREAK BRANCHES OR
KNOCK OFF LEAVES

DO NOT DIG UP THE PATHS WITH
STICKS AND UMBRELLAS

CYCLISTS!
SPEED LIMIT 12 KILOMETERS
PER HOUR

HORSEMEN!
ONLY WALKING AND TROTTING
ALLOWED

And then several notices in very small print with paragraphs, points, heavy type and italics. Beneath them the
signatures of Stadtrats, the Police Presidium, the Society for
the Protection of Plants.

The burghers in morning coats and with tightly rolled umbrellas walked along the branch for pedestrians and said
that the victor in the World War would be the one with
the strongest nerves.

Linden trees, level and round like upturned coffee cups,
forming four identical rows, merged into the bluish Park of
the Seven Ponds. On both sides of the Avenue, at a respectable distance from it, cubes of stone dwelling houses
dug themselves sturdily into the ground. The moderately

pleasant, cement-faced house sparkled with the polyhedral crystal of its windows. The burghers walked along the branch for pedestrians, the regimental adjutant jogged along the raked path for horsemen, and along the maca-damed strip for cyclists, at twelve kilometers per hour, rode the senior intern from the Otto-Moses Milch Surgical Hospital.

In front of the burghers, going to listen to the evening concert by the military choir, walked their wives with little packages and boxes in their hands. In the little packages and boxes were cakes and cookies which were to be eaten with coffee to the music of Mozart and Schumann.

Thus it had been a year ago, thus it had been three years ago, thus it had been ten years ago and probably thus it was forty years ago when the four rows of lindens had been planted in honor of Prince Bismarck.

The world was solid, the world was strong, and the old man Archimedes was a great jester with his lever for turn-ing the whole earth upside down.

Whom was General-Field-marshal von Hindenburg think-ing of when he spoke of strong nerves?

The burghers in morning coats and with tightly rolled um-brellas, walking along Bismarck Avenue, remembered si-multaneously the ten rules which they had composed for this Avenue. And if one of them forgot some rule or other:

DO NOT DIG UP THE PATHS WITH STICKS AND UMBRELLAS

---

another would remind him of it.

"I understand, Herr Post Office Secretary, that there is a revolution in Russia, but how can one possibly permit min-isters to be imprisoned?"

"Whom was General-Field-marshal von Hindenburg thinking of?"

The world was solid, the world was strong, the world was satisfactory.

But in front of the burghers walked their wives. Two years ago they had still carried in their little packages and boxes sandwiches of Westphalian ham, almond cakes with whipped cream and the thinnest salami, which some idiot had named Italian. Two years ago it had still been possible to listen to Mozart, drinking in the music with sweet coffee and nibbling at crumbly *streusel-kuchen*. And only a year, only one year ago it had been possible to spread one's good ration of bread with genuine fruit jam!

But this can be discussed only with old friends. And speak softly, very softly, so that even your husbands don't hear, so nobody hears! Like this, in a whisper:

"Frau Eisenbok, have you heard?"

"What, Frau Busch?"

"It has blossomed. . . ."

"Blossomed?"

"Yes."

"When?"

"I heard yesterday."

"Is it sure?"

"Yes, Frau Busch."

"They say it hasn't blossomed for forty-five years."

"The whole town's talking about it. Do you know its history? It's over four hundred years old. At that time an old man lived with his son in Annaberg. The son was dissolute. He even went so far as to say there was no God. His father decided to prove to him that God existed. They quarreled for two whole years. Finally the father said: 'I'll take a young linden and plant it with its roots in the air; if it takes —God exists.' So he did it. And the linden took and grew with its roots in the air, higher and higher until it covered the whole of the old cemetery at Annaberg. The last time it blossomed was in seventy-one."

"That means, soon?"

"Sh-sh-sh . . ."

"Frau Eisenbok, what hair style are you wearing?"

"Quite smooth, of course."

"That means, that's also true?"

"Sh-sh-sh. Recently I was at the theater and looked downstairs: almost all the women had this hair style."

"I saw the same at church."

"But when everyone, everyone to the very last, in the whole of Germany!"

"Only then, Frau Eisenbok?"

"Only then, Frau Busch. And don't forget—quite smooth and a parting in the middle."

"Yes, yes, a parting in the middle."

Thus, in front of the burghers walked their wives, on Sundays at four-thirty p.m., going along Bismarck Avenue toward the Park of the Seven Ponds.

Perhaps the burghers did not know all that their wives knew?

But no, the world was strong, the world was solid, and old Archimedes was a jester.

Look, look, you burghers in morning coats and with tightly rolled umbrellas, look how moderately pleasant the cement-faced house is!

This house is satisfactory, it cannot fail to be satisfactory, cannot, has no right to, does not dare to break the rules which have been once and for all established for it by the Ministry of Public Health, the Stadtrat, the senior doctor and other lawful appropriate authorities.

It does not dare.

However, be calm. Whom was General-Field-marshal von Hindenburg thinking of when he said that the victor in the World War would be the one whose nerves were strongest?

In front of the burghers walked their wives. What were they talking about?

"Sh-sh-sh!"

A young nurse was writing a letter. Her hands were trembling and she was not aware of what she was doing, did not see what she was writing, only shivered at the cry which hung suspended in the ward and with her left hand, without stopping writing, patted a wounded man's burning cheek briefly and fearfully, not daring to lift her eyes to him.

And she wrote to the wounded man's wife to come and see him, wrote the name of the city where the wounded man lay, and the name of the hospital and the number of the ward. The nurse did all this so as not to hear the cry, be driven insane by the cry, forgetting the paragraphs, points, bold type and italics of instructions and rules, explanations and orders.

And the wife came.

She came in the evening, went through a door to which was nailed a neatly lettered plaque:

NO ADMISSION TO THE PUBLIC

---

traversed some staircases—dark, light, and half-dark—and found herself in the room of the nurse on duty. And when the nurse informed her of the regulation barring her from the duty room, the woman went out into the corridor.

Here she was blinded by the light on the polished concrete floors, the whitewashed walls and the innumerable window panes, sparkling like polyhedral crystal. It was easier for her to look out of the window at the far end of the corridor which revealed the sky and the round tops of the lindens. She looked there and did not see who showed her the way to the ward where her husband lay. She only seemed to hear a man's hand, which was raised to show her the way, tinkling and creaking like a vending machine in which a coin has been placed. And she rushed down the corridor in the direction which the hand had indicated.

She was met by two orderlies with a stretcher. Behind them walked people all in white, dissolving in the light of the concrete walls and ceiling.

The woman seemed to hear them saying loudly at first, then shouting:

"Where are you going?"

"Where are you going?"

And then, it seemed also:

"Turn around, you there!"

But she had already disappeared through the door she had been looking for and the people in white, dissolved in the light of the cement, walls and ceiling, swept on behind the stretcher.

This was the first wife during the war to have a meeting with her husband in the moderately pleasant house which could not fail to be satisfactory.

She stopped at the entrance.

The ward was quite small. Two beds stood against the walls, one on either side. The window between them shone prim and new and through it, far ahead, rolled the sky, duller and sadder than the window, with clouds darker than the whitewashed walls. Looking out from under the blanket of the left bed was a clean-shaven, freckled, greenish-yellow, melon-like face. Its eyes were closed and the thin colorless corner of an eyebrow fidgeted up and down on its forehead. On the pillow of the bed to the right showed the black, broad, round back of a head. It was immobile.

The woman cried:

"Albert!"

Then the melon-like face winced, opened its eyes, moved its eyebrows quickly but with an effort, as if repulsing an importunate fly. Then it moved its woolly caterpillar-like lips:

"He doesn't hear. He's deaf."

And lingeringly, with a petulant sigh:

"Why's that, d'you think? . . . Oh stick it up your . . ."

But the woman, without taking her eyes from the round head, cried again:

"Albert!"

Her body swayed forward but her legs remained in one spot, as if screwed to the concrete, and for a moment she remained suspended, like a tightly bound man who has been pushed. But immediately her legs broke away and slid over the concrete after her body, which darted to the cot.

"Albert!"

The round, broad, black back of a head slowly slid into the pillow and in its place, as in a revolving panorama, came a face.

"Albert, Albert, Albert! Al-be-e-ert!"

In front of the woman wandered eyes—without pupils, blue-black, with fine purple veins, like enameled saucers cracked with age. Wide open, round, they revolved like those of a child that has not yet learned to look, ready almost to catch at the necessary point and stop in order to see.

The woman clasped her husband's head in her hands and screamed:

"Al-be-ert! Can you see, can you see me?"

Then the wounded man opened his mouth, clicked his teeth as if biting off some air, and in an excited hoarse voice howled:

"Write to my wife, write to my wife! Martha Birman, at Teufelsmühle in Lausitz, my wife! Tell my wife to come. Martha, Martha!"

"Albert! Albert! I'm here, here, Albe-ert!"

"My wife, Martha Birman, in Teufelsmühle . . ."

"Albe-e-ert! Do you hear, do you see me? Albe-e-ert!"

"Write to my wife, do you hear? Martha Birman, in Teufelsmühle . . ."

She threw herself on her knees before him, plucking at his head, swallowing the tears which flowed into her mouth; and gasping for breath, coughing, hiccuping, she screamed:

"Albert! I'm here, here, me, your Martha! Merchen, yours, yours, here, here! . . ."

He wailed in a voice torn by shouting, circling his wide-open, blue-black eyes like old enamel, without pupils:

"My wife, write to my wife!"

Then she pressed her wet lips to his face and calmed down.

And he, weakened, whispered to her:

"It's dark, completely dark. I can't see. Write to my wife, I beg you, my wife Martha Birman, I'll tell you the address. Write her to come. Before I die. If you agree pinch me twice so that I know, twice. I have no arms or legs. Before I die, I beg you, my wife. . . . Pinch me twice. . . ."

The woman scrambled to her feet and swiftly wrenched the blanket from her husband. He lay closely wrapped in bandages, short, round, like a barrel.

She plunged away toward the other bed, covering her face with clenched fists.

The greenish-yellow man with the melon-like face said:

"A real pity, eh? Why's that, d'you think . . ."

And now, one after another, ceiling-white figures flew precipitately into the ward.

"Here!"

And when they took the woman by the arm she shouted piercingly some word or other.

And she no longer heard the wail:

"My wife, Martha Birman, at Teufelsmühle, in Lausitz . . ."

And no one heard the woolly lips, like a caterpillar, of the man with the melon-like face whisper:

"That's right."

That evening, as usual, the senior intern of the City Surgical Hospital named after City Councillor Otto-Moses Milch called in at the tobacconist's and bought two cigars. Then, as usual, he sat on Bismarck Avenue and smoked one of the cigars. Then, on arrival home, as usual, he took off his coat and collar, put on a pink dressing gown, filled a clay pipe and sat at the table. He opened a thick, bound notebook and wrote in small handwriting:

Experimental research on a system of communication for war invalids completely without:
1) any limbs,
2) sight,
3) hearing.

He leaned back on the pillow of his armchair, puffed out some smoke and closed his eyes.

WHAT USE TO A MAN ARE THESE EMPTY DAYS AND HOURS

Cobbled streets are washed this way.

Short-legged men in tarpaulin pants and tarpaulin jackets flood the smooth cube-shaped stones with a broad jet of water, which spurts in a sparkling fan from the nozzle of a sprinkler. Then they rub every cube long and hard with brushes of steel wire. The dirt rubbed off by the brushes

is washed away by a new jolly, fan-shaped shower. Manure
is dug out of the cracks between the stones with iron hooks
fixed to sticks. The cracks are washed out with a strong,
thin jet of water—without the sprinkler. Then a brisk dense
shower is driven over the cobbles, from one pavement to
another, as in harrowing—up one strip and down the next—
farther, farther, on the heels of the men in tarpaulin pants
and jackets, who drag a fat hose, bloated like a full boa
constrictor. And then, when the lusterless, scrubbed cobbles,
slightly damp in the cracks, stretch for two or three blocks
—they take a bristly roller over them on fat-rumped shaggy-
hooved horses and that smooths and perfumes the cube-
shaped stones as the barber's round brush does a crew-cut.

Oh, that is how they washed the roads even in little far-
from-rich Bischofsberg! And little far-from-rich Bischofsberg had an extremely sound cistern with a dense shower, an
extremely harsh brush-roller, and sticks with iron hooks,
and a fat hose, all in wooden rings protecting them from
injury.

The concrete paths leading through yards from the gates
to the houses with tiled dates set into them:

ANNO 1898

---

were washed by women in tucked-up skirts, with thick
calves, in wooden clogs without backs or heels. They
washed them with soapy water and pieces of bast and
wiped them dry with burlap mops.

The women in tucked-up skirts with thick calves doused
the walls of the houses with hot water, from their base to a
man's height. And these women used a patented polish to
clean the door handles and keyholes, the plaques on the
gates with the residents' names and the brass knobs on fence
posts and railings.

Oh, that is how they washed and cleaned the concrete
paths, houses and railing knobs even in little far-from-rich
Bischofsberg!

And when of a morning the good old sun rose up from
behind the misty summit of Lausche, Bischofsberg glowed
pink, like a girl who had plunged into a cold stream after

sleeping. Perhaps for only one hour in twenty-four, one morning pink hour, Bischofsberg basked and stretched itself —lazy, sluggish, but already awake—stretched itself, blinking at Lausche. At this hour the washed cobblestones, the path tiles, the door handles, the knobs on railings and fences, the house walls and the slippery skins of their roofs, all glowed pink. At this hour the Church of John the Evangelist, pink too, would sway in the sky and suddenly the machicolated tower of the gloomy town hall would show up. Up the black velvet face of its old clock climbed a burning gold hand, ever higher and higher, ever closer with its flashing blade to the golden dot at the top. Look, it has almost climbed up, it has straightened out, it has reached! And into the pink bathed body of the little city would sink the sleepy, unhurried chimes:

> Z-zon-ne,
> Z-zon-ne,
> Z-zon-ne,
> Z-zon-ne!

The sun.

And now if at this hour, the only hour in twenty-four when Bischofsberg basked and stretched, blinking at Lausche, if at this hour the big bell on the Church of John the Evangelist broke into song—who would not exclaim that Germany was alive, who would not whisper that she was beautiful, and who would not think that

Germany cannot change?

And suddenly . . .

"Listen, listen my dear Herr Editor! What will happen, what will happen to us, what will happen to Germany if it goes on like this?"

"Calm yourself, my dear Herr Doctor. Calm yourself. We are doing everything within our power. We must endure, and we will endure, we Germans."

"But Herr Editor . . ."

"Herr Doctor, it is already a quarter to twelve. Let's go to the city hall."

The square had donned a dim belt of gas jets. They were

spreading white tablecloths of light on the ground. Over there a Landsturmer's gray overcoat emerged from round a corner and dissolved in the darkness. Snatches of an operetta tune floated from a wineshop with multicolored stained-glass windows. A door slammed somewhere. Quiet.

And now the ancient, familiar, husky arpeggios on the city hall tower concealed in the night. A quarter, another, a third, a fourth. Now a pause, dead, like the square. Now the wheeze of a spring.

And now the sleepy, unhurried chimes:

> Z-zon-ne,
> Z-zon-ne!

Midnight.

And suddenly again: a quarter, another, a third, a fourth.

A pause. The wheeze of a spring.

And slowly, tediously, solitarily:

> Zz-zzon-ne!

The doctor said:

"It's dark."

And a little later:

"There's nobody."

"Getting on for two," replied the editor, "it's late. Putting the clock ahead no longer attracts the public."

"We . . . we seem to be rushing, seem to be in a hurry. . . . We are taking time away from the war. . . ."

"How do you mean?"

"During this hour no one was killed. In this hour we were closer . . . to peace."

"I have calculated, Herr Doctor, that by putting clocks ahead the state saves from six to six and a half per cent of its fuel a year. Do you know how much that is in exact figures?"

"Doesn't it seem to you that we . . . are worried, we Germans?"

"It's already late, Herr Doctor. Good-by."

Quiet. The lamplighter was going his rounds with a long

pole in his hands, clearing the round tablecloths of light
from the ground one lamp at a time. Two black hunched-
up figures melted into opposite ends of the square. The city
hall tower was invisible. But it was there. It was there. . . .

"Putting the clock ahead no longer attracts the public,"
the editor had said that night in front of the town hall. But
he did not say what had happened on Sunday after mass,
on the square by the Church of John the Evangelist. He
wrote a short article about it and put it at the beginning of
his news items; and everyone read it, those who were not
at the church and those who were. But it is better, always
better, to see than to read.

The church was enclosed on the bell tower side by a
light-colored pine board fence. Schutzmen in short cloaks
stood ten paces from the fence, silent boundary posts marking off the forbidden area. Behind their dumb sloping backs
swayed derbies, ladies' hats with black crepe, the red peakless caps of soldiers, the protective covers of officers' helmets. There was more black crepe than anything else. Black
crepe fluttered in the wind, fell in curtains to the ground,
flew with gloomy wings over the derby, the peakless cap
and the helmet, clothed shoulders, heads and backs,
draped faces and embraced sleeves like tenacious hand-
cuffs; it trembled, swayed, floated in the air—black crepe!
See, it had poured in a broad flood from the doors of the
church and now it was rolling in a quiet avalanche from
the portals, spreading over the square, flooding it, level,
gloomy, cold, like a burial vault. Faces with parted lips,
faces with wrinkles, parchmented and earthy, with folds,
tumors and scars; faces wreathed in curls of gray hair; iron,
smooth, rectangular faces with red veins; soft faces, round
as sunflowers—a whole pasture of faces on a rich background of black crepe sprang toward the bell tower of
John the Evangelist.

There, on short rafters, sticking out through the windows,
lay the greenish-gray body of the big bell, wrapped in
ropes to which tiny slow-moving men were clinging.

The avalanche of black crepe had rolled down from the

portals. The pastor appeared in the doorway and beside him the Stadtrat and other officials of the town, the Commandant of the town and the Commandant of the prisoner-of-war camp, officers, society presidents—personages whom Bischofsberg had always esteemed and whom it was impossible not to esteem. And then the little bell in the bell tower of the Church of John the Evangelist, which was never rung on Sundays, sent forth invisibly a thin agitated call, while the greenish-gray body of the big one lay silent on the rafters, its wide muzzle gaping up at the empty sky.

Then this muzzle moved toward the edge of the rafters, the little men disappeared in the depths of the bell tower, the personages whom Bischofsberg had always esteemed descended from the portals and stood behind the silent backs of the Schutzmen. The Stadtrat slowly unfolded his handkerchief and waved it above his head. The wide muzzle of the big bell moved to the very edge of the rafters and for an instant hung suspended over the abyss.

And the little bell cast its agitated penetrating cry on the wind, breathlessly, muddling, breaking its strokes as if pleading for mercy in the throes of death. And then a black shadow hurtled down from the top of the bell tower and dashed against the fence.

And it was just as if the ground had opened and the world had tumbled down.

And it became quiet so that one could hear the cry of the martins over the Church of John the Evangelist, because the call of the little bell had been broken off and everyone was silent. . . .

That day in Bischofsberg the men unscrewed their doorknobs and locks, took the brass knobs from their railings and fences, and the lightning conductors from the ridges of their tiled roofs, while the women in their kitchens and pantries put the copper mugs and saucepans, the brass bowls and coffee-pots, into a corner.

The day passed. And the night passed. And from behind the misty summit of Lausche rose the good old sun and Bischofsberg turned pink, like a girl bathing in a cold stream after sleeping.

But who saw, who saw at this hour, the only hour in twenty-four when Bischofsberg basked and stretched itself, blinking at Lausche—who saw at this hour the wrinkled shaven face of an old man, twitching and trembling, in the bell tower of the Church of John the Evangelist, as he stood under the piles which the day before had still supported the big bell?

"Doesn't it seem to you that we . . . are worried, we Germans?"

After the concert there will be a demonstration of the latest improvements in artificial limbs in the following order:

1) Riding a bicycle, ascending and descending stairs (artificial limbs patent "Phoenix" for legs amputated above the knee). Perf. Pfc. Max Fischer.

2) Working with a typewriter (patent "Forberts" for arms with amputated hands). Perf. N.C.O. Franz D.

3) Working with a spade, ax, rake, hammer, plane and saw (patent "Deutsche Würde" for arms amputated above the elbow). Perf. Pvts. Hans Leben, Hans Forst, Erich Echke.

4) Rolling cigars (patent "Deutsche Würde" for one arm amputated at the shoulder). Perf. Pvt. Otto Bach.

In conclusion a team of convalescents will perform patriotic songs and present a vivid scene—"The Blessing of Germany."

GOD

PUNISH

ENGLAND

The very end of the program with the rectangle surrounded by a black-white-red border had been bent back and it stuck up on the table among the spotty newspaper columns. The rectangle was as exact as in geometry textbooks, and the colors of the border were exact colors, as on an eye-hospital color-sheet—completely black, completely white, completely red. And words as exact as in mathematics were in level rows inside the rectangle:

GOD

PUNISH

ENGLAND

The sun streamed through the tulle curtains into the dining room, tangled with the opened sheets of newspaper thrown on the table, rippled in the wickerwork of the chairs, played on the crockery and knives, and the black-white-red border shone in its beam like the silk ribbon of a medal.

Frau Urbach spread some Camembert sent from Switzerland on a thin slice of pumpernickel, poured out some coffee and slid frowning eyes over the newspapers. She had already related how at a concert in the infirmary, organized for public benefactors, legless and armless men with the aid of the fatherland's technicians and orthopedists had brilliantly refuted the widespread misconception that a man having lost his limbs is a cripple unfit for work. And how the convalescents had fervently sung that ever charming Prussian hymn—*The Watch over the Rhine,* which proved without a doubt both the patriotic sentiments of the simple people and their musical abilities.

"Someone said very truly that a people able to sing like that cannot be a barbarous people. They sang beautifully!"

Herr Urbach sniffed and remarked:

"I read about the men on forced labor. One cannot hear them sing and not shed tears."

"Did some Russian write that?"

"I don't remember," replied Herr Urbach and looked at his daughter.

With this the conversation ended and Frau Urbach busied herself with the pumpernickel, Camembert and newspapers.

Suddenly she stared at a small announcement. Then she took the newspaper and extended it across the table:

"Fräulein Marie, mark off this here with a pencil, please."

Marie read:

HERINGSDORF

Sea and sun bathing. This rich
resort of the German sea, rich in old
forests, is open as in peacetime.

No infirmaries.

The resort administration will send a
prospectus free.

Season from 1 June to 30 September.

Herr Urbach threw Marie a pencil. She smiled, marked the announcement with a cross and stood up.

"If you are collecting curiosities, Mama, I can help you."

"Curiosities? I don't quite understand, Marie."

Herr Urbach thrust his head out of his paper.

"Something interesting?"

"Nothing special. Mama wants to rest a little from heroes."

"Ah," said Herr Urbach, "so, so."

"I find, Fräulein Marie, that recently you have been having some trouble in finding the right words."

"I don't feel that, Mama. Thank you."

And once more a curtsey, after which one feels like slamming the door, rushing to one's bed and biting the pillow, as it had once been in Miss Ronny's boarding school.

A quiet bell in the anteroom. Marie had been listening to bells for almost two years now. She had studied them and knew particularly well the morning, dinner, and evening rings. It would not hurt to look the mail over before the others. Why, you don't always receive letters which you are in no hurry to open. Not always the kind you think long about. Or like this one—wide, with no stamps, completely smothered in postmarks, seals, inscriptions, over the sharpened needle letters:

*To her ladyship
Fräulein . . .*

What had caused the street to become still and the clock on the wall to cease beating out its seconds? That damned curtsey! That apish genuflection had sent blood to the temples which scorched them like red-hot steel! And why only

before her mother? Not before anyone else, ever, only in
front of her! Vile, stupid, disgusting! She had to lock the
door, open the window wider, smoke a cigarette calmly and
quietly. How stupid! And in the last analysis wasn't it all
the same? Well, he's alive, well, so what?

What had it got to do with Miss Ronny, what to do with
her mother? Stupid!

27 April 1917, Russia

Dear Fräulein Marie,

*You understand that I am unable to inform you of
all the circumstances which have brought me here,
from where I am at last writing to you, nor of all the
feelings overflowing within me since I arrived here. I am
trying even in the present situation to find some worthwhile occupation, although not always successfully.
The desire to improve myself, and the constant memory
of you, Fräulein Marie, never leave me and this you
know has always been a source of strength to me. I
have embarked upon learning the Russian language,
which I think will help me come a little closer to the
people surrounding me; and observing them, I am
sure, can prove very valuable to a civilized man. Up
to now my attention has been arrested by one feature
of the Russians which they themselves characterize by
our conception of "kindness," or something very close
to it. Unfortunately I am prevented by space from giving you more details. I am also studying a small people named the Mordvinians, of Finnish origin. The
camp, whose address you will find on the envelope, is
situated in a remote region and surrounded by villages
populated with Mordvinians. I don't remember that
our scholars paused long over a study of this semi-
pagan tribe.*

*In places the snow has not yet melted here. I am
helping one of my friends collect a herbarium, which
he embarked upon when the snowdrops appeared. On
days off I practice drawing and could show you a
whole collection of sketches like those which I did with
you at Schönau. I miss my pictures very much. Would*

*you care to take a trip to Schönau and write me your
impressions? Especially of the pictures. I'd like you to
very much, Fräulein Marie! Please give my sincere re-
gards to your parents. Permit me to kiss your hand.*

Your deeply devoted
Max von Schönau.

And an abrupt broad flourish firmly supporting the
sharp-pointed lattice work of letters.

Sometimes different letters came, quite different. . . .

"Marie, why have you locked yourself in? Open up!"

"My head is aching, Mama."

"Yes? I have received information from the Red Cross.
The margrave is in an officers' prison camp. . . . Have
a look, I can't make out this ridiculous word! . . . Probably somewhere in Siberia. However . . . are you so
cruel? . . ."

"I have a very bad headache."

"Indeed, I see there's a whole stack of new books on this
shelf. I have to repeat the same thing over and over again
. . . perhaps you will write to the margrave nevertheless?
Here's the information."

Inaudibly, as on a motion picture screen, Frau Urbach's
dress rustled and, as on the screen, she closed the door
softly behind her.

Yes, a whole stack of new books. It is they—immutable,
mysterious—which steal life, and everyone says they enrich
it. But what happiness to feel oneself ravaged by their unseeing and unmoving gaze. How wonderful to devote hour
after hour, day after day to them, because—what use to us
are these empty days and hours?

The hour for which Marie lived came so rarely and the
days following it were lightless, flat and hollow. This hour
preceded the gas jets when it was hard to distinguish a man
from a woman through the stone loopholes of Bischofsberg.

Then Marie slipped by the dull-gray façades of old
houses, through the blind streets, which ran like black
spreading fingers from the city hall to the soundless promenades. Running across the street she avoided the orange
and milky-blue windows of shops and restaurants, stopped,

looked into the darkness, suddenly turned back and hid behind a tree. Then she walked softly, then practically ran,
and again glided along a smooth wall.

On Hercules Square, opposite the fountain, was a heavy
door, pitted by a baroque knife and the years.

Through it. Then up the staircase—sixty-seven stairs, two
at a time—thirty-four steps. If you came exactly—at eight in
the evening by the city-hall clock—a door was ajar on the
fourth landing. Through it. Through the anteroom, straight.
You were there.

Only at exactly eight in the evening by the city-hall
clock, Marie!

Only exactly, Marie!

FYODOR LEPENDIN

When they took the woman by the arms she uttered some
word or other in a piercing cry.

Of those who could understand this word no one made
it out.

And only the woolly, caterpillar lips of the man with the
melon face whispered:

"That's right. . . ."

He turned his head on its side and took a long look at
the round back of his neighbor's head.

His eyes began to blink, his colorless eyebrows fidgeted,
wrinkling his forehead and moving the tip of an ear. He
sighed. Then he drew his arms from under the blanket,
placed them under his head, began to roll his torpid gaze
over the cornices of the high ceiling. Then he dozed off.

Had this happened? And if it had, when?

He was sitting on the stove, his bare feet tucked under
him—all twisted up.

The hut was very hot—they were baking bread out of the
first grist; groggy autumn flies were warming themselves on
the bleached oven door and the hearth; beetles were crawl-

ing through the gray burlap cloths which covered the loaves on the bench. The cheap fuel crackled in the tin lamp standing in the brazier.

Father had taken four heavy sacks of new grain into town, had returned late, had sat a long time at table, sipped cabbage soup with mutton, sucking the bones and cut bread. When he had eaten enough he changed his seat from the bench to the bed, under the bed-curtains, and mother helped him pull his boots off. Then father sprawled out on the bed, scratched his head and groaned. He called mother:

"Let's go, shall we. . . ."

He sniffed around.

"Fine!"

Mother stood with her back to the bed, leaning on the table, and turning the pages of a songbook, wetting her fingers. She sang out:

"Wait, one moment. . . ."

From the pine bed, from the cradle hanging from the ceiling and from the walls came a spicy smell, like the smell of raspberry bushes. The ceiling was low, black and reassuring to sit beneath—it clapped down firmly on the smells of the hut, which having nowhere to go, nowhere to move, stayed thickly, densely, kneaded together—from bugs, bread, beetles, the stove.

Father said in a deep voice:

"Listen then: I spent a few kopecks in the general store. . . ."

"The Lord be praised," responded mother, extinguishing the lamp, and began to undress.

Had this happened? And if it had, when?

Fyodor Lependin stretched his swollen arms.

His dead neighbor—with the round black head—was laid on a stretcher, covered with a sheet and carried out of the ward together with the bed linen.

Lependin crossed himself.

And then his arms suddenly shot up. He lay a short while as if disbelieving himself. Then he seized the iron bar of

the bed over his head with his fingers and pulled. His arms
cracked at the elbows, the folds of his shirt at the shoulders
cut into his body. Lependin groaned. . . .

It had happened like this.

When they had repulsed a weak attack and it began to
dawn, the ensign commanded Fyodor Lependin of his section to adjust the periscope. The instrument had to be
raised, supported on planed boards and aimed at the Germans.

And then when Lependin, his head level with the ground,
was patting the trench earth down with his shovel, he saw
some legs sticking out of a mound about a hundred paces
in front of him. They were like scissors pointing to the sky
and the body to which they belonged was invisible behind
the mound.

In the trench it was quiet, the soldiers were huddled on
straw pallets in grayish sticky groups, sleeping.

Lependin placed his rifle beside the periscope, jumped up,
leaped over the pile of earth, began to crawl.

In the clearing before the trench, the spring haze was
like the smoke of dead camp fires. Lependin quickly arrived at the mound. The legs stuck straight up over it.
Their boots were those of a soldier, short, yellowish leather,
with tips on the heels and soled with rusty nails the size of
a finger.

Without getting up from the ground, under the cover of
the mound, Lependin took hold of one leg with both hands.
The leg began to give stiffly, like the sweep of an abandoned well. The soldier's foot was bent upward and the
boot would not come off. Lependin put his knee under the
heel and pressed on the toe-cap. Inside the boot something
cracked.

"Maybe he's not finished?"

Lependin crawled round the mound and looked behind it.
A white clean-shaven face smiled at him with bulging light-
blue eyes. By his temple, whose edge had dug into the
ground, lay his upturned helmet.

Lependin crawled behind the mound, spat on his palms
and set about taking off the boots. He was busy for a long

time, broke into a sweat and bloodied his finger on the heel-tip.

Ramming his prize inside his tunic front he looked at the legs suspended over the mound, at the socks. He pulled them off and stuffed them in his pocket, first removing the safety pins which had prevented him taking off the socks. One he dropped, the other he stuck in his overcoat, beneath the Cross of St. George.

He crawled back.

But he soon stopped, took out the boots, got a pencil out of his tunic, turned back the top of each boot, spat upon it liberally and, lying more comfortably, wrote:

Private Fyodor Lependin, Plat. 2,

Co. 4, 137th Inf. Branzukil Regt.

He hurried away.

And suddenly, when he had crawled almost to the trench, a funnel of earth-clods came hurtling toward him and fastened onto his feet.

Lependin's knees straightened, he threw his head backward and rapidly moved his elbows. But as if tied down, his legs would not move, and he spun on the spot like a wheel on an axle driven into the ground.

A ragged flock of carrion crows swiftly slipped away across the sky.

And the last thing Lependin realized was that only one arm, one elbow, was working.

Lependin came to from the steady jolts. A round back was swaying in front of him. The strap of its light-colored overcoat was double, with a dark button in the middle. The cap-band of the driver's peakless cap was narrow, the crown small.

Lependin cried out.

The driver turned round and spoke an extremely long word. Lependin did not understand it, understood something else, groaned.

He awoke later in a hospital. Weariness coursed through his body but he felt good, felt like eating.

He chose a face he liked and asked:

"Permit me to inquire, sir. I had some clothing, also boots, quite new, nailed. Are these in safekeeping or what?"

A thick-lipped man—doctor, or assistant perhaps, in a coat smeared with bloodstains—frowned and replied as if he had mislaid something behind his tongue:

"Vy does Ifan neet a cap if Ifan has no het?"

And that was all.

It was quite clear in his memory how they had cut off his feet in the field hospital. His arm had healed quickly—the shoulder hit was partly a flesh wound; they took the bandage off on the sixth day. When they began to make up the troop trains for dispatch to camps, Lependin began to shiver with fever. Their own officers went with the troops in freight cars, among them the ensign who had ordered Lependin to adjust the periscope. Here it became clear to Lependin that the ensign was to blame for everything—both for the fact that he, a private in the ensign's company, had had his feet cut off and for the fact that the Germans had stolen from him, Private Lependin, nailed leather boots with tips on them.

Lependin was sent to the camp in an ambulance car a day after the departure of the troop train. His fellow countrymen lay in the ambulance car, all heavily wounded, and Lependin, suddenly fearing that the Germans would remember and throw him out of the ambulance car, began to groan without feeling any pain.

It did not seem right to Lependin that officers lay beside him—unconscious, true, puny and in the same hospital linen as he was dressed in. They did not groan properly but at intervals and breathing out soundlessly, and Lependin was pleased that he groaned better than they did.

In the mornings the doctors came, followed by nurses who noted in little books what they were told. Once or twice a day they took wounded men out of the car and later brought them back to their old place—though sometimes the place remained empty. The train was going somewhere a long way off in short swift dashes, standing a long time at the stations.

One day at dawn Lependin ceased groaning. After the

morning rounds they carried him out to a neighboring car, brought him back after an hour, and at dusk he awoke.

The fever no longer affected him and groaning became boring. Soon Lependin discovered that they had cut off his legs at the knees.

On that day—overcast and long—the train stood by a gray brick wall, staring at it with all its windows. After dinner a nurse appeared in the car in a crimped headdress. Behind her came an orderly with a tray on which were steaming cups of hot coffee. The nurse distributed the cups on the little tables beside the beds. Lependin also received some coffee and was the first—the door had hardly closed behind the orderly—to start drinking. He had taken two mouthfuls in all—hot, thick and sweet, when alarmed voices sounded on the other side of the door and the nurse and orderly flew into the car. Her lusterless eyes bulging, the nurse snatched Lependin's coffee away, put it on the orderly's tray and ran down the car collecting cups from the tables. Her headdress shook like a hen's comb when it tries to fly. The orderly had no time to set the cups on his tray, stumbled, caught his knees on the cots and spilled the coffee. Then the door slammed as never before throughout the whole journey—and it grew quiet.

Toward evening Lependin was carried to the ambulance and that same night he was lying in the hospital of the Bischofsberg prisoner-of-war camp.

He had settled himself in and was already sitting in bed looking at his stumps as an infant sitting up for the first time looks at its own legs, when, in the news items of the *Bischofsberg Morning News,* over the signature "R" (and only the Herr editor signed himself thus), under the rubric, "The Court," appeared the following paragraph:

Frau Doctor Nebel devoted all her efforts to taking care of military troop trains. Her activities were carried out at the station under the supervision of Senior Nurse Neumann. This nurse heard from the orderlies that Frau Doctor Nebel, upon the movement through Bischofsberg of a train containing captured Russian officers, was alleged to have intended to contact them and offer coffee for their refreshment. They recounted that in answer to warnings she had said: "My God, but they are also people!" A consequence of this statement were the instructions of the Patroness of the Refreshment Center, Frau Urbach, to Senior Nurse Neumann to inform Frau Doctor Nebel that the Refreshment Center declines any further philanthropy from her. Senior Nurse Neumann did not limit herself, however, to simply conveying these instructions, but, expressing her indignation, joined to them insulting remarks about "lack of patriotism," etc. As a result of this she was summoned to court. Witnesses to the action were called, the questioning of whom, however, proved to be unnecessary, since the judge managed to settle the action amicably. After the plaintiff had announced that her care had been intended not in the least for the Russians but for their escorts and ambulance personnel, the defendant announced that in the face of such an assurance she expressed her regret at the words she had uttered and would take them back. The action was concluded and costs laid on the defendant.

Of course the prisoners in the camp hospital had no suspicion of this notice, and all of it—in its entirety—is an obvious digression from the tale about Fyodor Lependin. But then even Fyodor Lependin is only a digression from another tale—more terrible and cruel than this one.

He fashioned himself two short crutches and, for his little stumps, pillows like milk pails with pot-bellied sides, and began to wait for permission to leave his bed.

But he did not walk for long. Within a week he began to feel feverish at night and it became impossible to stand on his stumps, although he even rammed a wad of thick felt into his pails.

And just at this time the senior intern of the City Surgical Hospital named after City Councillor Otto-Moses Milch was conducting experiments with a new method of local anesthesia in the amputation of limbs.

Four soldiers needing amputations were dispatched from the prisoner-of-war camp.

Lependin had the rest of his legs cut off.

The senior intern was completely satisfied with his method of local anesthesia and smoked, not the customary two, but three cigars on the day of the operation.

If Private Lependin had been ill longer he might perhaps have occasioned still further service to science. But he recovered and was no longer necessary.

If Lependin had been a private in the Saxon, Bavarian or Prussian Army he would no doubt have been given metal artificial limbs of the patent "Phoenix," and the fatherland's orthopedists and technicians would have taught him to ride a bicycle and climb stairs. But he was a private in the Russian Army and it was proposed that he get by on his own means.

And he got by.

He wove himself a basket of the kind which is placed under broody hens, spread the bottom with rags and sat on them, fastening the basket to his waist with straps. Then out of birch he cut oarlocks, resembling Kirghiz stirrups, with rounded bottoms. He put his hands into the arcs of the oarlocks, rested them on the ground, raised his trunk on his arms and, rocking it, sat down a good step forward. Tired out, he wiped his forehead and said to a soldier watching his exertions:

"There, my boy, that'll even take you to Kiev. . . ."

He laughed and began to live the life of the camp.

1

To Herr Commandant of the Prisoner-of-War
Camp in the City of Bischofsberg.

It has come to the knowledge of the Medical Faculty that in the camp entrusted to your care there is interned the Russian Divisional Medical Officer, Sidorkin, who during the period of his captivity has gathered a particularly remarkable collection of the spreaders of various kinds of diseases (*pediculus et pulex irritans*). This letter is a request to you, Herr Commandant, to allow the said Russian prisoner to enter into correspondence with the Medical Faculty concerning the latter's acquisition of the above-mentioned collection.

                        Dean of the Medical Faculty.
                        Rector of the University.

2

To His Excellency,
Herr Commandant of the Camp, Major Bidau

                        From Russian interpreter,
                        detachment prisoner-of-war,
                 Non-commissioned Officer Sergei Gorka.

I consider it my duty to inform Your Excellency that the agitation of the prisoners of war in huts 7 and 8 and equally in the laundry, about which I have been told, is growing. I venture to draw special attention to Doctor Sidorkin, who is taking advantage of his favored permission to visit the huts and laundry under the pretext of collecting body insects for scientific needs and meanwhile employing his time in agitation, saying that Russia must fight until it conquers Germany and that is why the Russian people have overthrown the Tsar, who was for peace. And although his agitation is unsuccessful, because Russian soldiers want peace with Germany and its faithful allies, other senseless voices can be heard which want a revolution to occur in Germany and which allege that then there would be peace among all nations. However, Doctor Sidorkin does have followers. I will make a report on the above-mentioned voices should Your Excellency order it.

                        At your service,
                        Sergei Gorka.

3

To His Excellency,
Herr Dean of the Medical Faculty.

The Commandant's office of the Bischofsberg prisoner-of-war camp is unable to supply any information on the question of the imprisoned Russian Doctor Sidorkin's collection, in which the Medical Faculty is interested, since the said prisoner of war has been transferred to the fortress of Waldheim (Saxony). Permission to communicate with the prisoner should be sought from the Army commander of the corresponding district.

Camp Commandant.
Adjutant.

4

To the Commandant,
Bischofsberg Concentration Camp,
His Excellency, Major Bidau.

You are instructed to take all measures for the speedy distribution of 70% of the prisoners of war held in your camp among estates and peasant farms. I recommend that in doing so you give preference to small farms and avoid concentrations of more than ten prisoners in any one farm.

I await your report.

For the Army Commander.
Adjutant.

And at this time, during these years, there were days when fluffy clouds swept across the sky, when the wind tangled the grass and knocked off the linden blossom. There were nights when the dew fell transparent and icy, there were evenings when everything became still and only fireflies roamed the darkness.

Barbed wire, bayonet and butt, Mauser, Nagant, Smith-Wesson, mortars, grenades, bombs; cut-off arms, sawn-off legs, burnt-out eyes, pierced foreheads, riddled chests—and again barbed wire, again Smith-Wessons, again grenades, bombs, land mines!

Trenches, dugouts, shelters, huts, camps, barracks; hospitals, sick bays, infirmaries, lunatic asylums, lunatic settlements, lunatic cities—and again trenches, again camps, again barracks!

Abscesses on necks, eczema sores under armpits, scabs on knees, shingles, boils, clammy rashes on stomachs, blisters on hairless heads, running like rotten cheese—

PEOPLE, PEOPLE—

at this time, during these years, days occurred when one could hear the spring wheat coming up, and yet every morning, every morning the dawn came! . . .

The basket in which Lependin sat creaked, the straps crunched, his belt cracked with the strain. But his arms and stomach grew strong, hard as nails, and to lean one's oarlocks on the ground and throw one's trunk backward and forward was easy.

Because the ground was always close to his face, because he touched it—warm, like a body—every minute with his hands, Lependin grew cheerful and accumulated strength.

The gardener took a fancy to Lependin—it was his gaiety, his mutilation, maybe—and put the cripple in charge of his beds. He set him to look after the vegetables, to lay out the seed-bed covers and cloches.

Lependin weeded, dug, fidgeted about in his basket among the beds from morning till night—and among the greenstuffs, amid the sweet smell of the rotting soil, he sang a song:

> *The Jerries caught some riflemen,*
> *Threw the riflemen in camps,*
> > *Oh, rifleman-trifleman,*
> > *Russian bullfinch,*
> > *In a camp.*
> *The Jerries planted beets*
> *Fed the beets to Russkies,*
> > *Oh, they'll swell*
> > *From the beets,*
> > > *The Russkies.*

Oh, they'll croak
From the greens,
Our Russkies.

Once after dinner Lependin crawled out of the green-house, dragged himself through the garden and sat at the gates. Before him shone a brick-red, tiled roof, tall, steep and flat. He frowned at its gleam and lifted his head. The sky was pure and blue. He turned his back to the roof.

A field rolled away before him, cut up by varicolored strips of grain. Two stacks of straw sown the year before stuck up in the distance, ragged and dark brown. He looked a long while at the stacks.

Somewhere a cock crowed. A minute later another one answered him.

Lependin screwed up his eyes.

The sun was baking hot, the rustle of grain drifted from the field—stacks stuck up there, squat, tattered, almost black—the cocks' voices hung almost suspended in the sweltering air. Behind the gates a hasty drip poured musically into a barrel from a tap.

Yes, if one screwed up one's eyes: it was as in Starye Ruchi—water dripping from the gutters—as in Sanshino at midday—the cocks crowing, the grain rustling, unwanted stacks standing around. . . .

But if you opened your eyes would you really see the old pot-bellied mare plunging over the bumps and pot-holes, in a breech-band and with a yoke over its long mane? Or the wench, rustling her skirt hitched up to the hips, her himble feet kicking up clouds of dust in the ruts?

Along the road which cut across the field a small figure was swiftly approaching the garden gate. It was indistinct, light, as if it were not touching the road, and in the light from the sky, the green and the sun, it was impossible to tell whether it was a child, a young girl or a woman. At the point where the channel of the road developed into several branches, with one branch coming up to the gate, she stopped. Fragile, transfixed by the sun, she stood on a hill-ock, facing Lependin. Suddenly she swayed toward him, came up, almost running, took a pack of cigarettes from her skirt pocket, held them out to the cripple and said with difficulty:

"Ciga'ette."

And smiled, as if begging forgiveness.

Lependin showed his teeth, moved his eyebrows. Then she again slid into her pocket and in her delicate fingers gleamed a cigarette case, she opened it—

But at that moment a bicycle rolled noiselessly down the road, the spokes of the front wheel flashed as they flew up into the air and the black monument of a gendarme sank obesely to the ground. He adjusted the short-barreled Berdau rifle on his back, ran a hand over the smooth row of buttons on his uniform and said quietly, as if punctuating the first stage of a successfully completed maneuver:

"So."

Then he looked at the pack of cigarettes sticking out of Lependin's coat, at the girl who still stood with the open cigarette case in her hand, and asked with restrained severity:

"Your identity card, Fräulein?"

"I haven't got it with me."

"What is your name?"

"Marie Urbach."

The gendarme's mustaches wilted.

"A relative of Frau Urbach?"

"Daughter."

The gendarme raised his cap, his bald head glistened, he wiped it with his palm and rammed the straight vizor down tighter.

"All the same, come along!"

Marie moved off beside him. Suddenly, as if recalling the cigarette case, she offered it—open, full of cigarettes—to the gendarme. His hand had already trembled, his mustache gone up, when she—half childishly, half slyly—bragged:

"Genuine Russian ones!"

The gendarme choked on something, coughed, his hand jerked on the bicycle's wobbling handlebars and his visor slipped down on his nose.

Then Marie looked round.

Lependin still sat in his former place. Seeing her look back he became agitated, swayed forward, then raised a hand over his head and waved his oarlock in the air.

Lependin thought the little girl—or girl, or woman maybe, —smiled at him.

"Ah, you . . . you quiet one . . ."

A TACTLESS FEUILLETON

Marie entered the Stadtrat's office.

Variegated colors from the panes of a wide window piled gaily down upon her. The light soaking through the panes was cheerful, drunken and musical, like a kaleidoscope of carnival lamps. There, in a tangled web of zinc frames, were sculpted ruby, pearl and turquoise caps, berets, hats, camisoles, wigs, stockings, pants, belts, bags, shoes and vests. Arrayed in the flowery, motley, drunken garments were people bunched in flowery, motley, drunken groups around the sides of a solid beer barrel, shaped by an expert cooper. They were pulling—drunken, rowdy, full of beer, rent by laughter, fat-bellied, fat-cheeked—tugging at the sides of the beer barrel. They had dug their heels into the ground, linked their arms together—their arms collapsed onto their stomachs and their stomachs were practically bursting with laughter. There was a motley crowd of fat people to the right of the barrel, a motley crowd to the left. Come on then! Who'll win? Ha-ha! Come on then! And by the color of the stockings on the left and by the cut of the pants on the right it was clear to everyone that those were the Niederbachians and these the Bischofsbergians. And the matter was no joke, it was a matter of supremacy, of first place, perhaps, in the whole fatherland: for the honor of being named champion drunkard of one's beautiful homeland! Come on then, who would out-tug whom? Niederbach or Bischofsberg? Who whom? Ha-Ha! Pull, pull! And it was no flattery to name such towns as these first drunkard in the fatherland! All was drunken, motley, multicolored in the window of the Stadtrat's office.

But along the window extended the deep red desert of a worktable. In the middle of the desert, in a dark blue glass, there stood hopelessly denuded pen-holders and pencils, like the dying palm trunks of a dried-up oasis. Not far away a deep well sank into the soil—the single inexhaustible spring of the joyless expanses: an inkwell. Around the edges of the desert the movement of dossiers took place. In blue, white and green files, behind numbers, letters and dates, they moved from the west of the desert, where they were placed by a client, to the east, whence they were taken by a secretary. Only very few dossiers penetrated into the middle of the desert, and then they made a long halt beneath the meager shade of the dying palms: west of the glass with the pencils.

The Stadtrat sat in an armchair between the gay crowd of disputants for the beer and the deep red desert of his table. But the Bischofsbergians and Niederbachians laughed and exerted themselves behind his back, whereas before him stretched the desert, and he belonged to this and not to the gay drunkards. He was dry, humorless, colorless.

"Fräulein Urbach?" he asked and cut the tip off a cigar with a small knife. "I am not surprised at the incident which brought you here, about which the Secretary of Police has informed me. Sit down."

The Stadtrat lit his cigar.

"I know your esteemed parents and I know you. Nevertheless, I dare say, I should not be surprised if I had to talk to you about alleged high treason. Do you understand what I am talking about?"

The Stadtrat was silent for a moment.

"Evidently you are aware of the gravity of your misdemeanor. I am not speaking of what happened today. That was a natural consequence of all your preceding behavior. I am saying . . . You understand what I am saying, Fräulein?"

The Stadtrat noisily expelled some yellow smoke through

his nose and stretched out a hand to a dossier lying in the middle of the desert.

"The police has long had at its disposal information concerning your relations with a Russian."

He jerked his dry, colorless eyes up and rested them on Marie.

"Do you hear? Concerning your relations with a Russian."

The Stadtrat drew deeply on his cigar.

"Your silence, Fräulein, is above all discourteous. In this I see the fruits of your association with this, what's his . . ."

The Stadtrat leafed through the dossier.

"His name . . . Do you intend to answer? . . . I speak to you this way only because I respect your parents, above all your mother, Frau Urbach. Otherwise I would find ways to make you behave toward an official as it becomes you. . . ."

The Stadtrat lowered and softened his voice.

"Do you really fail to understand that your conduct is impossible? Think, Fräulein, of the position you are placing your parents in! Your mother, Frau Urbach, is a personage respected by everyone, received at the court of His Majesty, a bearer of decorations, honorary member of societies. Your brother . . . But the newspapers write of your brother as of a national hero! He is the only officer in the whole of Bischofsberg to have received the order *pour le mérite!* The only one in Bischofsberg! He distinguished himself at Verdun! He was one of the first to enter Maubeuge! Think! And suddenly . . . No, it is unworthy, it is disgusting! Out of duty to my position I must . . . But come now, surely your conscience tells you? Surely you feel repentance?"

The Stadtrat moved back from the table and exclaimed:

"Oh, but this is monstrous, mon-strous!"

Then he stood up, walked about his office, sat down again and said in the same tone of voice:

"I demand that you answer me: do you admit that you have committed a misdemeanor which shames the honor of German womanhood and the honor of your home, and do you promise me as a representative of the authorities to do nothing of the kind in the future? Answer me. . . . What does this silence mean? Listen, you! . . ."

The Stadtrat banged his fist on the table and shouted:

"You hussy! How dare you remain silent when I demand an answer? How dare you? I'll teach you, I'll arrest you, I'll publish your name, I'll shame you! You will be driven from your home, you will be driven from the town. Fingers —do you hear?—fingers will be pointed at you, you! Fingers, fingers!"

He ran along the colored window. Over his face—compressed like a fist, sinewy and smooth—flashed the multicolored lights from the windowpanes. He shrieked:

"Do you think I shall spare you? Do you think that I shall permit a worthless hussy who has stained her family to bring shame upon the honor of German womanhood without punishment? I'll put an end to your hanging around damned Russians, God damn it! Why you . . . do you know what you are? You're a prostitute, you're worse than a prostitute; she's more patriotic than you and she wouldn't permit herself . . ."

And suddenly, as if a flood of broken, deafeningly jangling glass had collapsed over the Stadtrat:

"Shut up! Do you hear, shut up!"

He almost fell into his armchair and was dumfounded.

And Marie, erect, drawn up, as if encased in a steel uniform, walked to the door with crisp steps, opened it, went through corridors, through the hall where the Secretary of Police loomed at his desk, through the reception room— and out into the street. And there, unbending, still just as crisp, with head up, passed people as if walking over them, without hiding—

For the first time during these years without hiding— straight across the square to the low door with the baroque carving, and farther, up the stairs, higher, higher, not once—

—not once looking round—
to the door beside which her heart thumped so.

In the Stadtrat's office, impregnated with a delicate invisible scent, appeared the Secretary of Police.

"Herr Stadtrat?"

The Stadtrat started, seized a dossier lying to hand, laid it in the middle of the table—west of the glass with pencils —and said:

"I have released her for the time being, Herr Secretary. At the moment I am going through the newspapers."

And the Secretary melted away silently, like a small puff of steam in the frost. And the Stadtrat read:

DROP 10 PFENNIGS IN— YOU WILL SEE A WAR!

In Berlin in the arcade of the "Metropole" theater there is a slot machine panorama. Little Frenchmen in blue coats and little red pants are defending a fortress. Against them little toddlers in gray are scattered about in trenches and dugouts. Truly delightful! Especially if you think that any passer-by can easily convince himself how nice, actually, a world war is. However, what kind of a slot machine would this be if it did not promise still greater thrills? At the top of it is an aperture. Oh, how it yearns for a nickel coin! Over the aperture there is an inscription:

DROP 10 PFENNIGS IN— YOU WILL SEE A WAR!

In Berlin they take care of everyone! For ten pfennigs everyone can have his own small war. Put a small nickel coin (if the worst comes to the worst an iron coin will do) into the aperture—in a wink, as Berliners say, the thing's under way: cannon begin to pop corks, soldiers set about stabbing, slashing, shooting—sheer delight! Before you have had time to look round, all the French are slaughtered or taken prisoner, and the Germans enter the fortress. And then—what kind of slot machine would it be?—all return to their places. It is pleasant that this story can be always begun over again. Drop another coin in—the guns immediately begin to roar, the soldiers set about stabbing, slashing . . . and finally—everything is as it was before. And so on, until all the nickel is used up. Thus it was and thus it could be for a long time. In Paris, probably, there is also such a slot machine, because in wartime good taste is international. Only there, of course, everything is the opposite: there the Germans are shot and taken prisoner, and then all return to their places.

Recently one soldier returned from the front and passed through the arcade. He looked at the slot machine and, since he was accustomed at the front to strong language, cursed it. But since, besides that, he was also a journalist, therefore by profession an inquisitive man, and had also decided to write something on this subject for a newspaper, he put a nickel coin in the slot machine.

And a miracle happened! The battle did not begin! The cannon remained silent, the soldiers thought neither of stabbing nor of slashing nor of shooting. Shaking, kicks. Nothing moved. The slot machine was broken.

Some passer-by, glad of a free spectacle and deeply deceived in his expectations, wanted at all events to call the doorkeeper. He insisted on his little war, paid for by someone else, he wanted most definitely to see blood! But the man who had inserted the coin declined.

For although he was a journalist, therefore a man who does not believe in miracles, still it seemed to him, from a close scrutiny, as if the Frenchmen and the Germans were looking at each other quite amicably.

"Leave it," he said seriously, "Perhaps this ought to happen some time?"

He said "Good-by" and left.

The Stadtrat folded the newspaper and rang.
An attendant entered.
"Listen," said the Stadtrat, "this newspaper—you see it? —don't get me this newspaper any more."

A CHAPTER ON
NINETEEN EIGHTEEN

THE ROAD

An old maddened dog, biting itself in its frenzy, rolled over on its back at its last gasp. With its dry tongue it began to lick the wounds on its haunches and with its bloody muzzle replaced the entrails which had fallen out of its ripped open stomach.

And incense smoked around the dog and the little bells of censers overflowed about his ears and obsequious fathers, cardinals and priests proceeded in decorous concord, and rabbis intoned their thousand-year-old incantations and angel voices filled the benumbed air:

> *and peace on earth . . .*
> *good will to all men . . .*

And the dog groaned from its death pangs and its blind eyes were veiled with a cloudy tear.

That is how men received peace.

It came unexpectedly, although it had been expected every minute, day and night, in their waking and in their sleeping. It brought with it all that it was able to bring after Antwerp, the Marne, Champagne; after Trieste, the Carpathians and the Mazurian marshes. It was as soft-hearted as Verdun and as magnanimous as Brest-Litovsk.

But it brought an end to some periods and opened others. The last sheets fell from the calendar stitched together by the shot at Sarajevo and the time came for parting and good-bys.

For Andrei it came shortly before peace, when he was
informed he could return home. It was bitter—that hour—
filled with yearning, as is the steppe wind with the scent of
wormwood. But within it there lurked an elusive freshness,
as there lurks in the sultriness of the steppe wind the disturbing coolness of the sea.

Why is it impossible to speak of feelings as naïve and
moving as a child's prattle? Who laid an interdiction on
tender sighs, on forget-me-nots, on a chaste warm kiss?
Who dared to say that sensitivity is more trite than cruelty,
at a time when the lover's whisper is rarer than the slain
man's groan? . . .

Marie was saying farewell to Andrei.

They sat embracing in the room which had turned from
a prison into freedom for them, and to leave it forever was
as terrible as thinking of separation.

Their eyes rested on the familiar things and everything
was dissolving before them in some kind of vacuum, like the
future which faced them.

And in order to frighten the most terrible of all away
from them, they repeated incomprehensible, incomprehensible words to one another:

"Of course we shall meet."

"Of course, Marie! Why, everything's going perfectly."

"I don't doubt it for a minute, Andrei."

"I'm sure, Marie, I'm absolutely sure!"

Then burning cheeks came together, fingers fondled disheveled hair and the hushed room echoed their restrained
harmonious breathing.

"Write on the way."

"Definitely, definitely."

"As soon as you arrive."

"As soon as I arrive."

Far below the open window splashed the solitary jet of
a fountain—old, green, worn down by water and crumbling
with age. The tinkle of water echoed in the far corners of
the square and was painfully regular and melancholy.

"I'll come as soon as you get settled."

"I'll get settled quickly, very quickly, Marie."

"Well what do you think, in six months, or . . . ?"

"What do you mean, Marie! Two months at the very most . . ."

"That means in two months I can get ready?"

"You must be ready, Marie, every day. You know it'll soon be fixed, I'll let you know by telegram."

"Telegram?"

"Of course!"

"I'll always be ready."

And again they looked silently in front of them and the long familiar things disappeared into nothing and hands felt and picked at the flowers thrown between their legs on the sofa.

And suddenly Marie broke away from the sofa, turned to face Andrei, pressed his head in her arms and said shortly:

"It's time!"

Andrei reached out to her, embraced her, wanted to get up but failed to keep his balance and toppled her on top of him. And thus they remained without moving for several minutes: Marie—with his face pressed in her hands, he—clasping her bent body with large benumbed hands.

Then he loosened his hands, freed his head and looked into her eyes. She seemed not to see him. He said in a smothered tone:

"Marie, perhaps . . . perhaps it would be better for me not to go away . . . to stay with you?"

She thrust herself away from Andrei with such force as if she wanted to shake him, and joy and fear, alternately, showed in her glance.

"Andrei," she almost shouted, "you have waited so long for this hour!"

"Oh, yes . . . Endlessly long! But, Ma-rie! To leave you . . ."

"How—leave?" she interrupted. "Why, we shall meet very soon. . . ."

"Of course, I am chattering nonsense," he said quickly and began to move, to hurry, as if the time had come to rush off somewhere immediately.

"Of course nonsense. Faint-heartedness. You understand, at that minute it seemed to me that we . . . that I would never . . ."

He looked at Marie.

Her lids were tight shut and a gleaming thread soldered her lashes like lead.

He rushed to her.

"Mari-ie!"

He picked her up in his arms, carried her over and laid her on the sofa, lay beside her, wanted to kiss her, but his head fell on her face and their tears—swift, hurried—mingled.

The crushed flowers fell from the sofa and after them the separate petals drifted slowly to the floor.

Paul Hennig entered more noisily than ever and his voice was louder than usual.

"I must tell you, Andreas, that your constancy astounds me. But nothing is eternal in this best of all worlds, be it a hundred times. . . . *Andere Städtchen—andere Mädchen,** as they say . . ."

"Quit it, Herr Hennig."

"Differing in the political sense we naturally have to differ over the question of women, ha-ha! . . . But I tell you, Andreas, I am somewhat sad that you are leaving. Whom will I persecute? And besides that the world's getting more and more troubled."

"You calculated that everything would develop for the best."

"Andreas, Andreas! In the first place you are going away and I have no basis for hiding from you . . . well yes, that in certain respects I share your views. In the second place I see that . . ."

Hennig hemmed and slapped himself on the thighs.

"Let's talk straight! Our patriotism is something artificial! The hell with it—it commands respect of course. But . . ."

"To me it is repulsive."

"Love for one's people . . ."

"Not its love for the people. I've talked to you about this a hundred times. Not its love for its own people but its hatred of others."

"That I'll never understand. But I respect your point of

*A girl in every port.

view. Although it's impractical. You will be convinced that
to hate someone is a necessity of human existence. But I
respect . . . I respect you, Andreas. Have you already
packed your things? All your riches? Ha-ha, a church
mouse, Andreas, what?"

"Yes, I'm ready."

Paul Hennig sighed.

"To see people off is generally no good. To meet them
is better."

He turned round and bellowed with such force that a
decanter jingled on the table:

"When this room is left empty where shall I go, to the
devil to talk politics? I've got shivers running up my spine!"

He fell silent for a minute, drummed his feet on the floor
and took a newspaper from his pocket.

"And it is just now that the trouble is starting. There was
none of that before. Before it was different. We must hold
out—and we will hold out, we Germans! Oh! That's how it
was before. Now they've started sniveling."

"I've been repeating that to you for two whole years."

"Nonsense, Andreas! You are just as blind as I. You
maintain . . . I'd do better to read it to you. . . ."

Herr Hennig unfolded his newspaper and moved to the
lamp.

"I'll read an announcement, very simple, at thirty pfennigs a line of nonpareil, as the newspapermen say. Listen:

"A German soldier of good family, having lost a leg in
the war and as a consequence of this abandoned by his
fiancée, seeks a fellow unfortunate as his life's companion.
Ladies with missing or maimed lower limbs, but with a
kind heart and good character, are urgently invited to
take compassion on a noble broken soul in a mutilated body,
and in complete confidence and with an indication of their
family status and state of health to write to Box E. 8155,
Advertising Department, *Bischofsberg Morning News*.

Herr Hennig maintained a solemn pause and stood up,
holding out the newspaper in his hand and shaking it in
majestic wrath:

"This grandiose world event is truly teeming with new

forms of life. A mutilated warrior, a faithless fiancée, an unknown cripple who must assuage the sufferings of an unfortunate and soften the cruelty of perfidy—what inexhaustible material for a competent dramatist!"

He froze with the opened newspaper over his head.

"That's unimportant, Herr Hennig," said Andrei.

"That moved me. I am a man with a heart, Andreas, I understand delicate feelings. I have never once told you that Monsieur Percy is always in my mind. He was a harmless man and played the accordion, but they took him and shut him up in the citadel. That is touching. Politics—I understand only too well. But besides politics there is the human Yes and the human No. We've begun to snivel, that means we have reached the human No. . . ."

Andrei went up to Hennig and took his hand.

"It's time for me to go. Good-by, Herr Hennig. Thank you for everything, thank you. It also saddens me to part with you."

He drew Hennig to the window. They stood silent, looking at the square.

"Four years here, two there, three somewhere else—that's how life goes. It always seems to us that we are about to begin really living, that we have only to wait until something is over, to reach somewhere. And then we look back —it turns out we were down the mountain long ago, having passed everyone long ago. It turns out that here—don't be angry at my words, Herr Hennig—here in this prison, I was really living. And now I am leaving someone dear to me."

"I know, Andreas. I hope we may meet again. Good-by."

Herr Hennig suddenly choked, turned to face the wall and coughed.

"Dam-nation . . . what a cough and . . . hoarseness . . . Kcha-kcha-a! Yesterday in my part I was supposed to take top E—I couldn't hold it, kcha-a!"

Andrei went to the table, put his hat on his head, his bag on his back, took his case and looked round. On the floor beside the sofa lay the faded trampled flowers. He swiftly bent down, picked up one of them and put it in his pocket.

"From her?" asked Herr Hennig.

"Yes," replied Andrei, "from her. All the best, Herr Hennig!"

In a tiny little Polish place on the war-razed Russian frontier, a troop-train was being made up of sick and injured prisoners. Men unfit for work were being combed out of camps and hospitals and driven here, unhurriedly, as herds of weary cattle are driven.

The days stretched out, long and gloomy, and men became dejected by the whistles, by the lazy clank of iron on the tracks, by the waiting. What can be more depressing than a freight car uncoupled from a train and abandoned on a dead-end siding? Sooty engines of antediluvian construction pushed cars around the sidings for whole days, rolled about from place to place, coupled and uncoupled, and hundreds of times crawled indifferently after the cars like weathervanes moving in the wind.

The depression was lightened occasionally by the arrival of a new party of prisoners. Then long interrogations began, followed by jeering:

"Hey, look at 'em, how they've spread themselves! Give 'em Russia right away! Oh, no, brothers, you feed the Polish bugs first and then we'll see. Maybe you'll croak before Russia?"

"You came here like you was on a drunk. Before you had time to sneeze—the German had you. But get back—what a hope! . . ."

"And how did you get caught, on a gun-carriage, eh?"

"You and I, pal, both had our mugs beat in!"

"It's a long way to Russia, you'll never make it. The Germans own everything around us now, the Pole's under the German now."

"This is a lousy place. A real shit pile. We've been sitting here three weeks without moving."

Little by little they became reconciled, got used to one another and waited for fresh parties.

Once or twice a week crowds of Jews and Poles were driven through from the East—tattered, dirty, hemmed in by

their escorts' bayonets as by railings. Through the railings
one could see their hunted eyes, and jaws moving perpetually, as if chewing the cud.

"These poor people have turned all black, they're going
rotten."

"They're kaput now, boys. They're sending 'em right to
the Rhine to dig coal in the mines. The mines there are
twelve miles deep, takes a whole day to get down. The
heat there in that Rhine's enough to fry eggs. You can easy
see why the coal burns all the time there."

"Our boys that were sent there—we haven't seen 'em
since."

"Kaput! Because it's impossible—fire, you see."

"Nonsense, young fella. I was in the mines myself, it's
nothing like that."

"Where were you? Where? Perhaps you were back on
the Don? But I'm telling you about the Rhine. The Frenchman took the German's mines away and the German's
kaput without coal. That's why he's gone into the ground,
into the Rhine. He spares his own men such work, but sends
all sorts of proletarians there, our people, too, if they're
not crippled. I'm telling you the truth, brother!"

The men driven from the East shivered as if from cold,
looked pitifully at the prisoners chewing beets, and moved
their jaws in time with them, licking their dry lips. But they
were not kept long and were sent farther west.

In the party which arrived on the day of the troop-
train's departure were Andrei and Fyodor Lependin.

Andrei and the three civil prisoners with him were met
with silence.

Lependin immediately made himself at home, scurried
among the cripples and found a fellow-countryman.

"Us? Us?" he bellowed, creaking his basket and banging
his oarlocks, "they'll move us right away, take my word for
it!"

"Will they really, loud-mouth? Well, we've been kicking
around on the floor almost a month."

"Take my word for it! Right away! It's the end of our
tribulations, my boy, it's finished! It's all under the plow.
Now we're going home, there's land a-plenty for us, take

whatever you want. Whoever needs meadowland, whoever forest, whoever land for plowing—as much as he needs according to justice. Work, live, farm, you can shove it all!"

"Yes, but what the hell's the use of land to a legless man like you?"

"Huh, fool! Why how can you say what's land for, like that? You a peasant or tradesman or something?"

"We're from Penza."

"A fathead! You can see right away. So what about no land for the peasant now?"

"And what about you, you going to plow on your ass, with no legs?"

"Huh, fool! Why should I plow!"

Lependin plucked at his fellow-countryman:

"Tell the fathead what we have in Sanshino, in Ruchi, tell him!"

"We're from Semidol," said his fellow-countryman, "we've got mostly fruit, orchards, gardens, too, and just a little plowed land. . . ."

"Ooh!" Lependin clutched his head. "Oh, boy! What a pile of fruit we've got! We're up to our ears in cherries! There's plums there, sloes—the pigs can't eat 'em all. And our beds, our beds, boy, are all red with strawberries, and the strawberries—like that, the size of your fist! Got Victorias there, all kinds, early ripeners—ee-ee-ee! And as for those apples, we gorge 'em all winter; and soak 'em, and dry 'em—can't get rid of 'em nohow, there's so many! Our market in Semidol frightens you to look at it; how can a man use up so many apples?"

"And what an apple!" said his fellow-countryman excitedly. "There are apples and apples. *Our* apple—you bang it a bit and there's a tiny mark on it; put it on the ikon shelves—it'll keep all winter with that mark on it."

"It won't get rotten?" asked a goggle-eyed youngster.

"Not on your life, it won't get rotten!" joined in Lependin and rushed on: "It's real iron, it can stand anything. And then the sorts we've got! There's *tsarsky ship*, or *skvoznoye, borovinka, Oporto.*"

"D'you have bergamot?" asked the youngster.

"Our people don't eat bergamot. It's like a beet, they use it more in cattle-feed."

"They might've mixed in some bergamot for us here," laughed someone.

"That's the last thing they'd do here!" the youngster sighed sorrowfully.

"In our parts it's all steppe, hot, and it's always blazing."

"Heat, if there's not much, is also some good," responded the Semidol man.

"Never mind, my friend, don't be sad, come over to us, to the beds," said Lependin. "There's land aplenty now, take yourself as much as you can get. If you don't like it, clear out. If you like it, use if for what you like. Now, I've been left legless by the war. On the other hand, I'm good for gardening. The work's hard, even a woman couldn't do it. But what's it to me? My arm goes a foot into the ground without me bending my back. It's just the job!"

"A gay bird, eh!"

"And what's there to cry about? Ah, old man, we're going home, to freedom, to the peasant life!"

"You got swells in your party, or what?"

"Civilians."

"Gentlemen?"

"How'll I put it?" thought Lependin. "Educated, that's true. However, nothing . . ."

"They say we don't have any now."

"Not that we don't want them, but as long as they don't bother the peasants."

"That's so-o."

Lependin *had* brought good luck with him: by evening the troop-train had been made up and they had begun boarding.

A huge bearded man in a short sheepskin coat and cap settled down beside Andrei. He was ungainly in his unusual clothing among the shabby tunics and peaked caps. His hair and his mighty, blond beard curled in small spirals like pine shavings, his face was strangely small in this dense mass of hair and his transparent eyelids half obscured his shining black eyes. The muzhik was extremely tall and his shoulders rolled down in broad slopes, but he could stand only with difficulty and as soon as he entered the car he stretched out on a bench, putting his short coat under his head and hiding his cap beneath it.

"Sick, eh?" asked Lependin when they had taken their places and he was swaying through the car, inspecting his neighbors and striking up conversation.

The muzhik sighing, raised his flat chest; it creaked like torn skins and he pointed a finger at it.

"A-ah," said Lependin, "sick in the chest, I see. . . ."

"I'm spitting blood," said the muzhik in a tiny voice, which was entirely unexpected in view of his height, shoulders and wild *bogatyr's** beard.

"Ne-ver mind!" drawled Lependin carelessly. "That's the result of imprisonment. As soon as you get home it'll quickly pass. How did you get caught?"

"They took me to work, on rafts."

"Where did they capture you?"

"At home, near Minsk, my farm's there."

"Such monsters, God help us! On your farm?"

The muzhik coughed prudently without opening his mouth, then lowered his thin, chicken lids.

"He needs rest," said Andrei.

"He lo-o-oves rest!" sounded mockingly.

The muzhik restlessly adjusted his sheepskin and again coughed prudently.

Behind the backs of the soldiers who had collected around Lependin, Andrei made out a high-cheekboned face which looked as if hewn out of stone. A sharp straight line cut across its forehead.

"For the sake of rest he hired himself out to work for the Germans. But they didn't pay him his money and now he's suffering."

The muzhik said without opening his eyes:

"They ruined my farm, how could I get going again then?"

"You'd sell your soul to the devil for your farm."

Lependin pushed the soldiers aside.

"Let me take a look at him, you guys, and see who it

*A type of Russian folk hero renowned for his great size, strength and bravery.

is talking that way about a farm. . . . Ah, so that's who
you are. A tradesman obviously. How can you talk about
farming, for goodness sake?"

The high-cheekboned man screwed up his eyes at Lependin and rubbed his hands.

"And why shouldn't I?"

"Why not suffer over a farm? Can a muzhik live without
his farm?"

"Wait, don't get worked up, listen to what I'm saying. A
farm can be looked at several ways. In Russia the peasant
soon managed his farming: he worked all his life for his
masters, and then realized that if the work was his, it followed that the farm belonged to him and no one else. He
took it and cut up his master's lands into his own allotments
and the whole farm became the peasants'! Now that's a
worthwhile farm."

"That's right!" sounded somewhere at the back.

Around him everything grew quiet. The soldiers looked at
the high-cheekboned man suspiciously—he was obviously
out of place among them—sturdy, hewn out of stone, in a
coat and with a flat cap on the back of his head. No one
had noticed which party he had come with or when he had
joined the train. And the high-cheekboned man slid his
screwed-up eyes over the heads of the soldiers and the
sharp line across his forehead shortened and lengthened
like a measure.

"A worthwhile farm is one which brings good to all the
peasants. And there's no point in holding on to one which
does him harm. I feel sorry for this muzhik here as a fellow human being—he's ill, consumptive, in a word. However, he gets you. Of his own free will he hired himself to
the Germans in order to scrape some money together, to
put patches on his pants. While we in Russia are giving out
pants for free—there's enough for everyone! He would have
done better to move where people have started a new
way of life, but he went off to slavery to pick up a kopeck.
He doesn't believe that all our peasant property is now
being distributed free."

"Free!" doubted someone. "You're going a bit too fast!"

"And what's with you, didn't you hear him?"

"Oh, we heard about that all right; well, were you there, eh? You're a bit too free with your giving out!"

The high-cheekboned man winked and rubbed his hands.

"There or not, whose business is it? But I know a thing or two."

He was squeezed in by a solid ring of shoulders, chests and arms and dozens of eyes followed his alert glance. Suddenly he laughed.

"They call this muzhik Jelly, Uncle Jelly. I've felt him and he really is squashy!"

The sick man began to toss about and adjusted the sheepskin under his head.

One or two of the soldiers laughed.

"Your pity for him is a waste of time, boys. Pity won't help him, it's not the time for it now. You are also to be pitied—one is sick, another armless, another with no legs. We must have pity on ourselves."

The man from Semidol cut him short:

"Don't you spin us no fine yarns, kind sir, we know what's what. You tell us a bit about what you know about Russia."

"About Russia? We . . . okay."

The high-cheekboned man shook his head and said quietly:

"Let's go over there, there's more room there."

He plunged out of the ring of bodies crowded around him and—nimble, agile—darted into an empty corner of the car. The vacillating, maimed soldiers with pointed shoulders crowded after him, stumbling against benches and walls.

Lependin sat motionless in his basket.

Uncle Jelly half opened his lids, his shining eyes gleamed at Andrei, at Lependin, and he coughed.

"Well, are they telling the truth," he asked quietly, "has everyone got lots of money at home now?"

"Money's become cheap, I expect," said Andrei.

Uncle Jelly drew his thin fingers over the sheepskin and closed his eyes again.

Lependin suddenly banged his oarlocks on the floor, raised himself on his arms and said maliciously:

"They'll probably pay you a good thousand straight away for that coat of yours!"

He swung his trunk, landed, again banged the floor powerfully with his oarlocks and moved off toward the soldiers silent in the corner.

As far as the eye could see the field was scattered with people and bundles. A ponderous hubbub rose heavily over the siding. Trains made their way past by touch and dallied long on the points, testing the rails as people do a marshy road. Thin acrid smoke drifted overhead from camp fires.

The camps had been set up in a small pine grove. Behind wire torn from entanglements and wound around the tree trunks soldiers loafed in wooden clogs, clattering over the ground like small barrels.

In the settlement, small figures in clothes too small for them scurried about the Jewish hovels and shops like little balls of mercury, now scattering, now rolling together, head close to head, shoulder to shoulder.

"You going south? I wouldn't advise it."

"But why, why? I'm telling you, it's a gold mine, a gold mine."

"What's in demand?"

"Falberg's saccharin."

"I'll never believe it! Falberg's in demand in Moscow."

"But there's a man for you, there's a real live Kiev man for you. . . ."

"You can do your business in Moscow in two days, take my word for it! D'you believe me? D'you believe it?"

"The journey has to be taken into account!"

"Journey, journey, journey—they're always going on about the journey! Now it's the same everywhere, you can believe me. I've done twenty-five thousand miles."

"It will be risky."

"Everyone takes a risk in Moscow."

"Where are you going?"

"To Warsaw."

"What's the ost-mark like there?"

In old grass-grown trenches people were cooped up like gypsies—with children, with old women, with tin basins and broken crockery.

A woman in labor cried out from a dugout, a man with typhus lay delirious under a cart with three wheels, above him—in the straw—dirty-faced little two-year-old girls were playing.

A half-undressed woman with breasts like empty sacks was picking insects out of her rags. A legless soldier was baking potatoes in some ashes and driving away children with a many-branched switch.

People swarmed around the camp fires in pitiful broods; and on the ground, cut up by trenches, plowed up by exploding shells—the befouled, defiled ground—they were born, died, made love and exacted retribution from the new clean earth in hatred and despair.

Out of the misty dawns and twilights of the East the trains came feeling their way, crammed with prisoners, whose eyes were fixed both hopefully and despairingly on the West, where their homes lay. In neatly made Russian tunics, round-faced, seeming to smell still of Siberian kerzhak bread, the captured Germans made their way in a crowd to their quarantined huts.

Out of the West, from another kind of imprisonment, trailed crowds of emaciated Russian soldiers, with their eyes on the East, where *their* homes lay. They were also led into huts, on the other side of the sidings, behind a high fence.

But by-passing the wire, the fences and the enclosures, people came together face to face, and, like the ethereal camp-fire smoke, talk of the East, of the West, of grief, of deprivation and of hopes, drifted up.

When this human meadow unfolded before Andrei through the car window, someone nudged him. He turned round. Behind him stood the high-cheekboned fellow with the flat cap on the back of his head. His forehead was smooth, the line had disappeared, his eyes shone vividly and his mouth was twisted into a satisfied smile.

"This was cooked up by us!" he said, nodding at the ant-hill and rubbing his hands.

He radiated the freshness of a man who has slept soundly and he stretched himself elastically, cracking the joints of his awkward hands.

"We got a fine dough. Wow, how it's bubbling! I reckon," he said, moving his brows, "we could do with a few more boilers like this."

And again, vigorously rubbing his hands, he explained:

"The people are fraternizing."

Then Andrei saw him slip into a group of people in the field, twinkle there, plunge out, run to another group, then to a third. They turned to watch him go, sometimes laughing, sometimes in silence. He sowed some kind of unheard-of ideas in the crowd and resembled a speck of dust in a bottle of water which has been shaken: at one moment he was tossed swiftly forward, at another he stopped, then moved off again, as if from a blow.

When they had transferred to the camp, Uncle Jelly went among the people. Here he was deluged by contradictory rumors like stones from a hillside and he dashed over the field like a frightened beast.

"There's no such thing as a quiet life there, old fellow. These same Guards come along—give us your horse. The peasant on his own, you see, is helpless—he gives it."

"Our muzhiks are like bandits now: bombs are kept in every house, machine guns in the barn, a knife with 'em all the time. Without that you can't survive."

"Quit listening to those lies. My cattle died so I went away. But the life is pleasant, there's everything you could wish for."

"If life was at all possible, do you think we'd have faced such tortures? We've no more strength left."

"Every man is his own master. What he wants he takes. I'm telling you, go and don't doubt, you won't regret it."

The Germans in Russian tunics smiled enigmatically and said brokenly:

"Russia good, Germany good—everything good, when you have a head."

A little man in clothes too small for him screeched and waved his arms indignantly.

"How could you leave? You say that's hard, but I'm telling you—Russia is finished, all washed up, doesn't exist any more! Soon only the dogs'll stay in Russia to eat the bones. No business can be done there at all."

A handsome soldier from among the fighting men exhorted:

"The earth is God's gift to man. The Lord settled you on the Russian earth—she is your mother. Accept any insult from her, endure punishment. There is no greater sin than to abandon your mother in her tribulation. . . ."

At dusk Uncle Jelly returned to the camp, swaying as if from the wind. All night he fidgeted in the straw, tossed as in a fever. In the morning, as soon as the soldiers began to stir on their plank bunks, he went out into the middle of the hut and said tensely:

"Brothers, hey, brothers! Listen to me, brothers. I'm a sick man and here it's every man for himself. I ask your advice, where shall I go now, brothers?"

No one answered him.

He slowly bent down, put one knee on the floor, then the other.

"For the sake of Christ I ask you, brothers, where shall I go, give your advice."

Lependin coughed, looked around the bunks and said:

"Friend, I watched you while we were traveling. You haven't long to live, it's all the same where you die. And on the railroad you are taking up room, you lie down. At this time, when people need to go home—maybe they don't get on the train because of you. . . ."

Without getting off his knees Uncle Jelly asked:

"I guess it's easier to die in one's native land, brothers? To die, eh?"

Lependin again looked round the bunks. No one replied, as if they were all still asleep.

"Our advice to you is this," said Lependin. "Stay here, because there is nowhere a man can die well nowadays."

He adjusted the basket under him, tightened his belt and turned away.

Uncle Jelly remained on his knees, swaying and with his eyes closed. Then he got up, went to his bunk, took his short coat from its head, folded it and began to tie it carefully with rope. Having finished this he thought awhile.

They looked at him closely from their bunks, as if he were an outsider. He stood motionless, his head bent, his heard resting in a luxuriant billow on his chest, his hands stuck out as if he had dropped some work.

Lependin was suddenly struck by a fit of coughing.

Then Uncle Jelly rammed his cap down, hoisted his short coat on his back, took his bag and walked unsteadily to the exit, spreading his legs in the way of a muzhik.

For a minute or two after the door closed behind him it was quiet. Then, one after another, the prisoners climbed down out of their bunks and left the hut in single file, not looking at one another, then passed the camp gates and went out into the field.

Uncle Jelly was staggering over piles of bundles and baggage, over people stretched out like the thin smoke from the camp fires. The yellow sheepskin stuck out like a hump behind his back and he was bent beneath it as under a load too heavy for him.

He was walking back to captivity.

The high-cheekboned fellow slipped from somewhere into the group of soldiers accompanying Uncle Jelly with their eyes, and split the silence with words as solid as a wedge:

"That's how it is. I say that whoever wants to be solitary, on his own—such a man hasn't long to live in our time. The people have begun to live in peace now, by agreement, on equal terms. We don't need men like that."

And the man waved his hand in the direction where Uncle Jelly had disappeared.

Lependin responded in a low voice:

"That's what I told him: we don't need, I said, people like you, go and God bless you! . . ."

The road, the road!

Through mass graves full of quick-lime, through stumps of bodies crawling like amphibians, through wailing and moaning and groaning; over the earth sown with death— the road to life!

In the hospital car coupled to the tail of the train, digalen and morphine were being injected by needle-sharp syringes into the scrawny remnants of arms and legs, and solutions of salt were poured into veins swollen with ganglia. Pulses which had beaten out the requisite number of

strokes were filled once more with viscous blood, lips began
to move again and again emitted a whisper:

"Nu-urse, have we ar-rived? . . ."

"We'll arrive soon."

"In what . . . pro-vince are we? . . ."

"Smolensk."

"Is it far to Tan-bovsk?"

"Soon, soon."

The people filling the forward cars from top to bottom
were not injected with drugs. But they reeled like drunkards, as if having inhaled an intoxicating gas, hung onto
the windows and whooped incoherent songs at the head
wind smelling of spring corn. All of a sudden a deep-seated
goodness awoke in them and they opened themselves to
one another like spring windows—assisted in tying up sacks,
shared beets, gave benches to the ailing and sickly—with
good humor and clumsy simplicity.

The train stole along the tangle of rails, twisting its green
joints snake-like and crawling into the cracks between
wrecked cars. Its motion became ever slower; more and
more lifeless trains piled up on either side, and then it
stopped.

The high-cheekboned fellow leaned his shoulder against
Andrei and whispered distinctly:

"Look."

In an empty car standing on the next track a German
soldier, looking round on both sides, quickly took a pocket
knife from his pocket, cut off a window strap, rolled it up,
had it together with his knife in his pocket and dashed out
of the car.

"So-o-o," drawled the high-cheekboned man, "it's beginning."

He shook all over with crumbling inaudible laughter and
his eyes were woven with a mesh of fine spiderweb wrinkles. But suddenly he straightened up.

Somewhere a short way off a shot cracked like broken
glass.

The high-cheekboned man turned to the soldiers, took
off his cap and uttered distinctly:

"I congratulate you, dear comrades, on your safe return to your homeland."

As if as a result of these well spoken words, the train jolted forward and everyone in the car was gaily thrown backward.

Andrei grabbed hold of the high-cheekboned man's elbow and, in falling, looked at his face. It shone with boyish joy and on it there was not a shadow of the wrinkles.

"Stand up, stand up, Comrade," he said, pulling Andrei by the hands.

And then some kind of heat blazed upon Andrei and he sucked it in as a drowning man does the air and immediately breathed out with a wild howl.

And the whole car joined in the howl a hundredfold; from hundreds of breasts it rang forth like rolling iron, smashed into windows and doors, crushed, broke, strangled the din of the train and swept out across a heap of steel and stone onto the fields, into the open spaces.

And in the hospital car at the tail of the train a man returned to life by a capsule of digalen asked in a whisper:

"Is it far, nurse, to Tan-bovsk?"

"Soon, soon."

From here you could stretch out a hand to Tambovsk, it was close to Yaroslavsk and not far to Omsk. Here everything was attainable, simple, easy. This was home.

The soldiers sniffed at the elusive movements of the breeze and as if with a sixth sense divined the native scents of orchards, fields and ravines.

Gradually, hour by hour, the station emptied.

People patrolled chance trains, climbed into cars, under benches, onto sacks, settled themselves on steps and couplings and ran, ran into the open, into the fields, into Russia.

And when Fyodor Lependin sensed from where the Ruchi orchards were blowing—the *borovinka*, the *tsarsky ship*, the anise—and realized that now he was responsible for himself, he tightened the straps of his basket and jumped on his strong oaken hands toward the cars which the soldiers were taking by storm.

"Assist a cripple, Comrades," he yelled, knocking against

the soldiers' knees with his shoulders and elbowing his way toward the car. "Make way for an invalid, have mercy on a legless unfortunate, Comrades!"

Someone lifted him onto the step and he rolled over in the passageway like a sack of grain. Hard feet began to step over him.

Andrei looked at the prisoners dashing along the tracks and platform. He tried to catch someone's glance. But their eyes darted to either side, like the men along the lines—eyes pressed down under brows, concealed, incomprehensible. The spring windows flung wide open to one another at the first shout of joy suddenly had their shutters slammed and been locked with forged iron bolts.

Everything had been left behind. The mass graves filled with quick-lime, the hunger, the cries, the orders, the stuffiness of the huts, the rusty barbed wire and the window bars—everything that had united men into a submissive herd.

Men crossed the line, men made their way out into the open. And every one of them was healed by the hope of a new future for himself—in freedom, in his native land, in Russia.

Behind his back Andrei made out a doleful song interspersed with the wheezing of broken voices:

> Please oh Lord, our heavenly father,
> Take from a soldier his crown of thorns,
> Drive away, take away war, his troubles,
> Return his bread and work to the muzhik.

Three blind men were making their way slowly along the platform, their hands resting on one another's shoulders. A little girl was leading them, holding off soldiers from the other direction with a thin little arm.

The heads of the blind men were raised high and with every step they bobbed on thin necks with their chins forward. Their eyes were open and—milky-white—rolled incessantly within their dirty unblinking lids. It was possible to see these men's gaze. No brows hung over it. But it was empty.

Andrei recalled the Park of the Seven Ponds and the

blind Italians with eyes which reflected tree branches, he recalled Marie, separated from him by an avalanche of blind men.

And suddenly he clearly saw her leaning, as if bound to it, against a tree, saw her arms hanging weakly above the ground, her tightly shut eyes. He went over to the wall, leaned against it and his arms hung helplessly as Marie's had done then.

And now, as then, Andrei was separated from Marie by only a road.

NO BLACK OR WHITE

Of course everything here was strange.

Once, in far off Bavaria, a teacher of geography, swinging like a soft pendulum about the classroom, had told about this city:

"It astonishes with its savagery, which many travelers are inclined to consider beautiful. All the contradictions of Russian life, all the chaos of the Russian people's approach to life are revealed in the architecture of the gloomy and naïve Kremlin. The Italian of the Middle Ages has been mixed with late Byzantine and this mixture is not easy to recognize behind the Mongolian splendor of its decorations and superstructures. At the present time this memorial of barbarian life is surrounded by an Asian bazaar and European houses, built on German models by German engineers. Moscow is the Russian's native element but the civilized foreigner suffers in this city from the disharmony of its parts and the exasperating splendor of its buildings. Kurt Wahn, what can you say about the city of Moscow?"

Kurt Wahn jumped up and said:

"Moscow astonishes the civilized traveler with its savage beauty."

"I said: 'with its savagery, which many are inclined to consider beautiful.' "

Of course everything in this city was strange—from the

church cupolas, resembling beets, to the swan-like curves of the cabbies' droshkies.

In the evenings at sundown it was impossible not to wander over the deserted streets until exhausted.

The peeling pillars of the little houses, the good-natured half-lion-half-dogs by the dust-smothered doors, the long deserted basements, twined with figure-eight railings which looked kindly on the rearing warehouse boxes pierced with innumerable windows.

Every evening Kurt walked through the deserted side streets and every time they drew him into their hidden windings as a secret underground passage attracts one around its curves. And again and again he was halted by unexpected combinations of lines, repeated nowhere and by no one.

At this hour the side streets were inundated by the pealing of bells and the silence of the houses was deepened by it to the hush of an underwater bank.

And, as on a bank, everything began to seem deathly, stationary, like the gaze of a sheatfish, and the sunset-purpled churches seemed to have become a drowned kingdom.

Then Kurt made his way out of the side streets and headed to where the Kremlin towers were visible. They emerged, twilit, like some melodious crown of the city disappearing underground, and behind their enigmatic bearing he had a vision of the half-forgotten castle lying like an obelisk of the centuries over Nuremberg.

But Kurt knew another Moscow and for the kingdom sinking onto the bank he set aside only the hour of sunset.

Can there be found in all the world a city which would keep hundreds of thousands of tons of provisions in palaces, horse fodder in department stores, barrels of cement in manufacturers' apartments, iron ore on main street?

Everything that had managed to be collected in Russia for Moscow and had arrived on its stations was transferred to the center of the city and stowed with the greatest difficulty in restaurants, dance halls and merchants' homes. In the center of the city the loads were moved about, shaken

up and, split up into the tiniest portions—in drops, in grains
—were moved out to outlying warehouses and elevators
where there were more mice than goods and grain.

From morning on, freight trucks waddled elephant-like
over the dented and potholed cobbles of the tangled
streets and their step caused stone houses to tremble and
windowpanes to break.

Circling the Lubiansky Square, from the Myasnitsky
Gates and from Pokrovka, down the slope of Theater Way
and into the Tretyakov Gap the elephants piled into one another, snarling and jolting the loads on their backs—and
to look at them was as if some unknown burnt-out planet
were moving into Moscow.

And across Theater Square, along Mokhovaya and farther—along Volkhonka, along Ostozhenka—hastened the
elephant-frightened fire victims from the unknown planet—
with sacks on their backs, in an endless file—along that
part of the streets which the city had formerly yielded to
streetcars.

On Ostozhenka near the Crimean Bridge the file poured
into a white building and around the building lone figures
of fire victims pottered about before the windows and placard shields.

On the boulevard beside a booth trading in artificial
soap and essence of vinegar loomed a glass box with models
of human entrails, and tiny letters explained to everyone
the purpose of the kidneys and the spleen.

Jumping up a good six feet behind iron railings and facing the military store was a placard addressing the public
with columns of figures, and dozens of people were calcu-
lating how mighty and how accessible to all was science
in the new Russia.

New Russia!

That was she filing into the white building—where until
recently high-school uniforms had been properly stored—
indefatigable, capturing halls, stairways, attics, boxrooms.
And in the commotion, for whole days, the first point was
being written in the white house of a joint treaty between mighty sides—Science and Russia. This point was
endlessly long, so that a phalanx of typists worked in the

The man lowered the flag and squatted on the edge of the roof; something gleamed in his hand. A protracted, splintering rattle resounded in the hush of the street, as if a handful of peas had been thrown onto an iron roof and rolled down its slope into the gutter. The sound was repeated once, twice. The man stood up and began to run the rope quickly through his hands.

Then a narrow red strip separated itself from the tricolor panel lying in a ball on the roof and was jerked aloft up the flagstaff like a pennant.

The red flag had been raised on the flagpole of the German embassy.

The man picked up the black-white remnant of the flag, rushed it into a ball, stuffed it under his arm and, squatting on his haunches, disappeared behind the ridge of the roof.

In the courtyard an engine sprang forward as if breaking from a leash and at that moment was answered by another from around the nearest corner. The two automobiles almost collided at the gates. A gleaming polished limousine had been going out of the embassy yard—and a dusty battered torpedo, like a miner's trolley, had come flying down the street toward the embassy.

Andrei managed to approach the gates.

The dusty automobile's doors would not open, so the passengers jumped out of it over the sides of the body. The gray tunics of Germans and the reddish overcoats of Russians suddenly merged into a dense group and it was incomprehensible how all these people could have been contained in one automobile.

The door of the gleaming automobile slowly opened and a thin sleek man stepped onto the running board:

"What is it?" he asked and raised one eyebrow.

An undersized soldier cocked his faded peakless cap onto the back of his head and announced distinctly in German:

"A Soviet of Soldiers' Deputies of Germany has been organized among German prisoners in Moscow."

The sleek man lowered his eyebrow.

"What do I care what has been organized in Moscow. Please allow my car to pass."

office without a break and there was not a corner of the whole house which had not been invaded by the din of Underwoods, as if an iron roof were being repaired.

On the basement floor rotary presses rolled without respite and an artel of printers sweated over thousands, hundreds of thousands of sheets heralding the news of the unprecedented joint treaty.

In corridors and vestibules high spirits blazed with the din of Underwoods and the smell of rotary ink; and people ran about dazed by the figures which measured science, happiness, humanity, Russia.

In a hall with gilded furniture along the walls men and women were jumping about on canvases stretched over the parquet floor. On the canvases sprawled a blue-skinned man two stories high and behind him loomed the ruins of granite buildings. In order to examine the painting the artists climbed up step-ladders to the ceiling and rocked there, like electricians.

Kurt Wahn drew a line in the air with an arm bared to the elbow:

"I was saying! The blue cube must be removed. The green must be reduced to half its size. The shoulder has collapsed. We've got a cripple. Why?"

A small woman translated to the whole hall:

"Why have we got a cripple? . . . That is, we shouldn't have got a cripple, the blue cube must be destroyed and the green one reduced. Then the shoulder won't be . . . the shoulder will become . . . d'you understand?"

Men and women clamped cigarettes in their teeth and, tucking in their grubby smocks, descended the step-ladders to the floor.

Kurt dashed along the canvases with a brush in his hand and shouted:

"Comrade, how do you say in Russian: deepen the flatness of the frontal bone?"

The little woman translated:

"Comrade Wahn says that the forehead must be made energetic."

Then someone's brush stole up to the blue-skinned man and impressed a dab of cobalt on his forehead.

When darkness fell they wiped their hands on newspapers and went downstairs, and over plates of herring the interpreter laughingly told Kurt how they contrived to get two portions of soup on one coupon.

Kurt also laughed as he chewed his tough bread and said through his laughter:

"An extraordinary people! Amazing! That's funny about the soup. But in general. How could it dare to do all this?"

He cast his eyes over the faces buried in their plates and laughed again.

"Here even the soup smells of wax-paper and rotary presses. How much they write! An amazing people!"

He bent toward his neighbor and, lowering his voice, said mysteriously:

"Behind all this I see great sense. Very great common sense."

Once the tsar's weavers had been cooped up in the suburb of Kadashi—people just as patient as their foremen. They left the suburb only during fires, carrying out their belongings and cloth to the nearest vacant lots. After the fires they would rebuild their houses, repair their looms and sit down to weave. Carrion used to be scattered about the sites of the fires, no one removed it, and carrion crows circled above it, resting on exposed stove-pipes, on blackened pillars, on new, uncovered eaves. The weavers considered the fires, the carrion and the carrion crows to be their lot; from day to day, from dawn to dusk, they bent over tablecloths for the tsar's servants, burned, rebuilt and taught their children and grandchildren to weave.

Since then Kadashi suburb had grown over with stone, a city had grown up to the south of it and the memory of the weavers had been wiped away. But perhaps their great-great-grandchildren still went to midnight mass at the Church of the Resurrection in Kadashi. As they had done under that gentlest of tsars, Aleksei, they still made their way along the lanes, covering themselves with crosses when a flock of crows flew round a corner. And—as in forgotten times—after the fires, exposed stove-pipes peeped out here and there on the crossroads.

In Kadashi, by the Kanava, side by side with the ¡ perhaps the last descendants of the tsar's weavers, l carters—a daredevil difficult people. At midnight th their dead horses out along Ordynka and dumped t rion in a side street by the entrance to some forme chant's house. At dawn the carrion crows alighted roof of the house, on the iron umbrella of the croaked, descended upon the carrion and pecked horses' skulls with their strong beaks.

Of a morning the carters, their legs spread fork-li their carts, would dash to the stations. Through the c of wheels and horseshoes they would shout uproariou; the lines of people stretching along the streetcar track

"Watch out!"

"Pick 'em up, co-workers, pick 'em up!"

"Woo-oa!"

"Fel-low wor-kers! . . ."

That was how Andrei saw Moscow from the first da when he moved into Kadashi, and that was how it ap peared to him every morning.

He knew that somewhere in this city not far from i heart, at a junction of side streets over a low building, lik the wings of a vulture patrolling a herd, were waving t ends of a tricolor—

schwarz-weiss-rot—
black-white-red—

banner.

It had pursued Andrei inexorably, had hung over him ir the peaceful coolness of Rosenau, had burst into his Bisch ofsberg mansard and now had overtaken him again—im placable, rapacious—

schwarz-weiss-rot.

And then one fresh noon Andrei found himself in the street where this banner fluttered and he cast his eyes on the roof of the low building.

A man was standing beneath the flagstaff of the German embassy loosening the flag cord.

Andrei halted.

"The Soviet of Soldiers' Deputies of Germany in Moscow has resolved to take over all the affairs of the embassy of the former German Empire."

"I repeat, the resolutions of the Soviet you mention do not concern me."

The sleek man lightly raised his hand and ordered an armed embassy soldier:

"Clear the road for me and close the gates."

Instead of carrying out these instructions the soldier pointed to the roof with his gun.

The sleek man slowly raised his head.

Then one of the new arrivals shouted:

"Back!"

The sleek man was pushed through the door of the limousine, the door slammed, shoulders were pressed against the wings and radiator and the automobile was rolled back into the courtyard. The driver helped steer the car and over his weatherbeaten face there slid the trace of a crooked smile.

Andrei swayed toward the armed soldier.

"What happened?"

A cold stony look met Andrei and thin lips painstakingly uttered the broken words:

"Komrad doesn't know? Jermany organissed a ssofiet. Jermany Rossia togezzer."

Andrei did not hear out the soldier. He was looking into the courtyard where German tunics and Russian overcoats were crowded before the thin sleek man who had left his automobile.

One soldier thrust the crowd aside, went up to the sleek man and threw the black-white strip of flag at his feet. The sleek man did not move and the material lay before him a funeral pedestal.

Andrei looked at the soldier who had brought the flag pennant and thrown it down.

Kurt!" he cried and dashed through the gates.

The soldier stared at him as he ran through the courtyard, then took a step backward and asked quietly:

"Andrei?"

"Kurt! Kurt!"

Then the soldier darted to Andrei, pressed his head in his straight, even hands and said even more quietly:

"Andrei, dear friend . . ."

"If I had sat out this time somewhere in a workshop, perhaps the world would seem something whole to me, as it did before, as we said and understood before—humanity, the world—looking from above. But I sat below, under the floor, I saw how everything was arranged. In short it's a theater. Nothing is whole. Humanity is a fiction."

Kurt lit a slender, burned-out pipe, stretched out his legs and then continued fluently, evenly:

"Before, everything was complete, like a company on the march. Man was fitted to man like boards in a door. Now everything has disintegrated. There are cracks between the boards. Even a blind man can see that everything's fallen apart."

He laughed.

"Haven't you ever tried to write?"

"No, I haven't," said Andrei.

"Nor have I. But somehow I think that novels are written the way boxes are made. Every board must fit the other boards on all sides. That, at least, is how novels were written before the war. Now it's probably impossible even in a novel to bring more than two people together at a time. The glue is no good, it doesn't hold."

"The old glue?" asked Andrei.

"Of course, the old. It's something you can see clearly through the barbed wire of trenches, as through a magnifying glass. It makes you shudder to think of all that music —bombs, rifles, especially howitzers. But I think that if it weren't for all this din, we wouldn't have come to our senses for a long time yet. But now our head is clear and our heart refreshed."

Kurt lit a match, lifted it carefully to his pipe and lit up again.

"That's my story and those are my conclusions. Those boards which still hold must be separated, perhaps smashed, because they are artificially glued together and because people can't be glued together into humanity with that kind of glue. And in the last analysis that's our aim. Agreed?"

"Agreed," responded Andrei.

Kurt went up to him and took his arm.

"Well now. Good. And now, please tell me straight out that I was a swine . . . in Nuremberg, in the streetcar."

Andrei embraced him and laughed.

"No, no!" exclaimed Kurt, drawing away. "You must tell me what you thought then!"

"I was horrified. I almost cried when I remembered you . . . as you were then. . . ."

Kurt struck his head with his fist.

"A-a-ah! A-a-ah! What an idiot I am! Idi-io-ot!"

"That's not the point," Andrei stopped him. "You could think differently then."

"I thought like a swine."

"Now you think differently. But war didn't frighten you then, nor does it now. Has anything in you changed? I've remained the same: the very word war is repulsive to me."

"Wait," said Kurt, "wait, wait. I understand you. . . . But do you really suppose that I haven't thought about this? There are many kinds of war! And how will you annihilate war if not by war itself? If not by opposing war? Why, there's no other way, no, no, no!"

He stamped his foot and shouted:

"Blood, blood, that's what frightens you. And this eternal fear that evil gives birth to evil. And what can you offer me in exchange for evil? My veins are being drawn out of me, a thread at a time, endlessly, for the whole of my life. And it is suggested I build my life on good, because evil breeds evil. Where can I find good if there's evil all around me? Prove to me that it's impossible to attain good through evil."

"That I can't prove."

"Therefore, there's only one way?"

"Therefore, there is."

"Then what are you worried about?"

"About the fact that it's terrible and . . . degrading," said Andrei with such an effort as if he were being choked by tears.

Kurt pressed his hands.

"Dear, dear friend. You really haven't changed. I often used to remember you just like that—with that kind, embarrassed smile. I would even be sorry if you'd lost it. And listen, I'm your real friend, forever. Do you remember Nuremberg, from the hill? I experienced happiness then. You know, I've never lived with a woman, that is for any length of time, or well. What kind of feeling is it? If it's like it was then on the hill—and always like that, constantly—one probably needs to be born with a special gift to endure it. I'm talking of that rapture, remember? It must wear away. . . . You complement me. I feel good when I know that you are as you are, dear friend, with your perplexed smile. Now, here in Moscow, after everything that's happened, I want us to repeat our oath. And you are to forget what should be forgotten."

Andrei drew Kurt to him and encircled his broad back.

"I remember only one thing, Kurt: how we said to one another *forever*."

"Until death itself!" said Kurt, looking at Andrei with a kind of severe intensity.

Then he smiled and clumsily putting his words together, like a reader who has dropped his book, added:

"There is something schoolboyish or I don't know what in my feeling for you. Friendship is something mystical. But I don't feel like struggling with my tenderness for you. Although it's subconscious—funny."

He was silent a while. Then he straightened up and again started speaking, as if by the book.

"I believe that there must be no feelings inaccessible to the understanding. And, of course, all feelings should be subordinated to reason once and for all. Only then can you see sense beyond senselessness and joy beyond suffering.

"However, there's this," Kurt interrupted himself. "I've told you everything I went through, but I know nothing about you. Tell me. I'll keep quiet. Not another word. Why are you sad?"

Andrei nodded at the window.

In the yellowish dusk the crumbling Neskuchni Park loomed dark, the girders of the Crimean Bridge shook as if made of paper, the black Moscow River flowed on under it. And over the park, over the bridge, over the river—an impenetrable slab to the eye—circled a flock of carrion crows.

"Horrible. This phantom blots out everything. Hunger! In order to step over it one must be very brave. And what's beyond it?"

"Aah you, you revolutionary! Shame on you, Andrei."

"Me—a revolutionary? Up to now I've been ashamed to pass a beggar without giving him money."

"Nevertheless your hands trembled today when the soldiers at the embassy said what a hot time they'd give *dem oberen Zehntausend** in Germany."

"Ah, Kurt, Germany . . . How I'd like to find myself there now. . . ."

Kurt looked at Andrei guardedly and said drily:

"There's nothing for you to do there. You're either exhausted or can't understand that your place is here in Russia. An idea has just struck me. . . . Listen. I'm being sent into the wilds to evacuate prisoners, to form a soviet out of them. It's in Semidol—a deserted, neglected spot. Come with me. There's plenty of real work there for everyone. Will you come?"

"With you—yes," replied Andrei, not taking his eyes from a motionless dot somewhere in space through the window.

"Splendid, you're a good soul! You and I'll live magnificently. We'll move mountains! Quit watching the crows! A funny fellow! Stay the night, so that for once you won't hear that sinister croaking over your head. Crank! And tell me, tell me everything, from the very beginning, quickly!"

He pulled at Andrei's shoulders, dragged him away from the window and rushed to light the sooty oil stove, throwing to either side the rubbish which got under his feet. Kurt's

*The top ten thousand, i.e., the "cream" of society.

room here in Moscow, in the attic of a former high school, recalled his untidy Nuremberg mansard.

And that night when Kurt and Andrei lay down under overcoats on the narrow oil-cloth sofa, like the ones which stand in reception rooms—in the soundless Moscow night, Andrei told his friend about Marie in words which had come so simply in Nuremberg.

He told of their winter encounter on Lausche and of their meetings in the Park of the Seven Ponds and of how he had unlocked his door at the agreed hour and how Marie had stolen along the promenades during the hot nights.

He came to their last meeting, to the promise he had given Marie at the last minute.

Then Kurt touched Andrei on the chest and as quietly as Andrei had been speaking, almost in a whisper, said:

"I understand why you want to be there."

And since Andrei had fallen silent he asked after several minutes:

"That means the greatest thing in your life during these years was love?"

Andrei said:

"Yes."

And again waiting several minutes, in the cold night, in the darkness, he said:

"And in mine it was—hate."

FRUITS

To mislead the reader on account of the title of this chapter would not make sense. The chapters devoted to flowers have no particular connection with what is described below. Everyone, of course, is aware that the time for fruit comes after the flowers, and the very juxtaposition of these words might give birth to thoughts concerning the tendentiousness of the book.

But we are far from any kind of tendency and in order to dispel any doubts on that account we cite immediately the document which has prompted us to title this chapter so ambiguously and which is absolutely essential for objectives concealed from the superficial eye.

At the height of summer there appeared in the columns of the universally respected *Bischofsberg Morning News* the following appeal:

EVERYONE INTO THE WOODS FOR FRUIT! DO NOT LET OUR WEALTH PERISH!

German women! Let this word be heard by every sensible patriot. Everyone must aid the great work!

Our appeal is especially to housewives in small towns, and women's societies and unions. Set up permanent contact with villages and rural communities, induce the poor inhabitants there to gather the summer fruit!

Rural communities must make certain that, with the consent of the forestry authorities, the collection of fruit is carried out completely systematically. Do not under any circumstances entrust this work to children alone! Take care that the fruit is not brushed off the bushes, but is gathered by hand. Brushing off damages future crops and, for example, bilberry recovers from it only after several years. Strict observance of this advice will also save much labor in cleaning the fruit of leaves before it is preserved.

The system applied to the gathering of fruit in Fogtland seems to us to be the most expedient. Adult and experienced women who know the area direct groups of children. Having received permission from the forestry authorities to gather fruit, such groups get to work in open formation, carrying the gathered fruit to previously prepared baskets. The gathering begins early in the morning and ends by noon, before the heat sets in. The fruit is then sold by weight. The work is paid in accordance with the harvest. Wholesale dealing saves time which is usually wasted in weighing small batches. The women organizers are given money, if necessary, to be able to take the children on the railroad. This means a great deal—you can ride in a train for at least one way of a tiring journey.

Regulate supply and demand. But be careful of excessive

trouble. If the needs of private households, hospitals, etc., are soon covered, dispatch the fruit the shortest and most suitable way to neighboring large towns. The best of all is to sell the fruit to some wholesale merchant or jam factory, since only the appropriate special packaging will guarantee irreproachable transportation.

Remember that not a single fruit must perish in the forests of the fatherland! Fruit products are nutritious and cheap.

German patriots, it is up to you!

A cold piercing wind was blowing from Lausche; boisterous, dancing rings of leaves swept over stone and asphalt. It was November.

Its ninth day passed grimly and inexorably, like all the days before it—in scarcity and poverty. The streets ran their endless race, nothing disturbed the regulation working hours.

And only for one minute and in one spot—in the vicinity of the town hall in a cramped sloping side street—did life falter and come to a halt for a moment.

A battalion kitchen was located in that street and the soldiers who had received their rations, with bread and mess-kits in their hands, were running to their various sections billeted in neighboring houses.

One dawdling soldier, stepping heavily and swaying from side to side, looked gloomily into his mess-kit from which a grayish cloud of steam was wafted. He was being overtaken by hurrying, sprightly, younger men bandying shouts and whistles. The soldier was walking unhurriedly. Suddenly he stopped, raised the mess-kit to his face, thought a while, then waved his arms and hurled the vessel onto the road, crying loudly and abruptly:

"Ah!"

And immediately the whole street fell silent—the young soldiers and women with children in their arms. All looked at the mess-kit rocking on its curved side, at the yellow wash trickling between the stones, at the grayish steam being seized and dispersed by the wind. Then the glances shifted to the soldier and froze upon him.

He stepped into the road toward the empty mess-kit,

slowly bent down, lifted it and, still not hurrying, ponderously as before, went on his way.

No one uttered a sound during all this time and all went on their way silently, as if nothing had happened, and the side street resumed its former life, perhaps just a little bit slower.

That is how the ninth of November passed in Bischofsberg.

But on the following day the wind drastically changed its direction.

On the following day the widow of a bearer of the Iron Cross, Martha Birman from Teufelsmühle, came to her husband's grave. She picked out the dry leaves caught in the stonecrop planted on the burial mound, placed a heather wreath on it and knelt down. At first she prayed, then she began to look about her and read the plaques on the black crosses, arrayed in military fashion over the soldiers' graves. A single stone rose over these rows of crosses—a fraternal monument to the dead warriors. On the stone was carved:

SLEEP SOUNDLY, HEROES!
WE REMEMBER YOU WITH GRATITUDE!

Martha Birman read this inscription, repeated it aloud and the words echoed inside her like hollow blows:

"We remember you with gratitude."

"We remember you."

"We remember."

She left the cemetery and slowed her step at the gate to consider where she should go.

A cluster of women dressed in mourning were coming from town toward her down the wide, straight street. They were keeping close together in the middle of the road, walking urgently, and the wind swept them along, blowing up their skirts and tugging at their long black veils.

The women's harsh talk was soon wafted to Martha Birman, but she could not catch a single distinct phrase of what the wind brought her and she waited for the women to come closer.

The wind seized their voices, hurling them aloft, and

hands were raised like the wind over the heads of the
women, threatening someone and pointing forward with
outstretched fingers.

Snatches, fragments of speech whirled over Martha Birman.

"Everything's all right with them. . . ."

"And they have one answer, one answer to everything!"

". . . no end in sight."

"It's all the same!"

"Let them, let them!"

". . . concealed it all right . . ."

". . . calm. And what are we—corpses?"

"Under lock and key so that no one . . ."

"Cattle for slaughter."

"Concealed?"

". . . then we'll see. . . ."

Martha Birman expected the noisy procession to approach the gate of the cemetery. She stood straining forward as if on a leash, trying to make some sense out of
the broken phrases. But the women, quickening their steps
the whole time, moved past the cemetery in the direction of
Bismarck Avenue. Suddenly, distinct words flew out of the
chaos of voices:

"Hey, poor widow! Your man's lying in a safe place by
the look of it?"

Someone's hand pointed to the cemetery gate and again
the same distinct voice called:

"Come with us to resurrect the dead!"

And, as if they had cut the leash holding back Martha
Birman, she broke away and ran toward the crowd.

Someone asked her on the move:

"A war widow?"

"Yes," she replied, panting from the run and the unexpected agitation, "the widow of a bearer of the Iron Cross."

"Poor woman!" sounded a voice.

"Let 'em hang their crosses on dogs!" she heard.

"We're going to the hospital for the cripples!" they
shouted to her.

"Maybe our husbands are alive?"

"They're keeping the cripples locked up so we don't see them."

"Maybe they're keeping our husbands there?"

"So our nerves aren't ruined!"

"We've had no nerves for ages!"

"Not since they took our husbands away. . . ."

"It's time to end the war!"

Martha Birman darted ahead, ran round the dense crowd, stood facing the women and cried with a great effort:

"Stop, stop! I know what's in this hospital! Women, oh, unhappy women! My husband was also a soldier. They ripped off his arms and legs, he went blind and deaf, he didn't recognize me when I went to him in the hospital, just before he died. Now he lies over there. I know. The whole house is stuffed full with armless, legless men. Let them release them, let them show them!"

Piercing cries cut her short:

"To the homes of the wounded!"

"Bring the cripples out on the streets! Let everyone see!"

"We'll carry them around the parks and theaters!"

"Let them look!"

Martha Birman pointed to the cemetery:

"There's a whole city of men! My husband Albert is there. My husband. And there it's written: 'We remember you, we remember.' "

Suddenly her mouth twisted and her shriek rended all the cries:

"I remember you, Albert! Women, women!"

The wind jerked and caught up the wailing and groaning, jerked the long crepe veils, and the women in mourning broke into a run.

Behind the crowd in mourning, whirled into a funnel by the wind, swept other women, alone and in groups, who had flown down from no one knew where, like leaves at the height of fall.

The wind was blowing toward Bismarck Avenue.

And when the windows of the hospital sparkled like polyhedral crystal through the denuded rows of lindens pruned into coffee cups, the lone women and groups of women merged into a continuous lake of heads and the crepe veils washed over the lake in black combers.

"Women, wo-men!"

The satisfactory house gazed on the agitation of the women, listened to their shrieks and with unshakable pleasantness showed them its plastered walls beneath the brick-red tiles of its roof.

The women piled onto the porch and the heavy cathedral-like door opened wide and smoothly.

Some man or other in a dazzlingly white coat ran out to meet the crowd and cried desperately:

"Spare the wounded, the woun-ded, madmen!"

And in reply a hundred voices showered on him hysterically:

"We'll spare them!"

"We know!"

"Spare us!"

"We'll spare them!"

"We'll spare them!"

Where did the regulative inscriptions, paragraphs, sections and points disappear to? Who hid the neatly painted plaques with instructions, orders and extracts from the rules? Where did the men vanish, whose duty it was to observe the paragraphs, instructions and orders?

Into corridors permeated with the gleam of polished concrete, white ceilings and walls, burst the women in black. Together with them into the wards and halls flew the frenzy of the streets and before them, above them, multiplied ten-fold by the space of the corridors, swept the tearful wails of Martha Birman:

"I re-me-e-ember, Albert! I remember!"

And then:

"Look, here's where my husband lay, my husband, wom-en!"

And again:

"I re-member, Albert, I remember!"

Then men's full voices were mixed with the groans of the women:

"Carry us out into the street!"

"Show us to people!"

"Carry me in a chair—let them see what war is!"

"Take all who can be taken out of bed!"

And a solid mass of bandages yelled loudly through a black hole gaping in gauze where his mouth might have been:

"Show me, I can walk! Show me, I can walk!"

In open dressing gowns, in bandages, trusses, with plaster-of-Paris dressings, on crutches and sticks, the wounded men hobbled and pranced from ward to ward, calling:

"Whoever's able—to the square, to the city!"

"Whoever's able—get up!"

And this call was answered from the wards by incessant groans and curses.

And now the crowd of women raised an armchair overhead and moved toward the door, howling and shrieking. In the armchair a man half lay on a pillow with his back thickly bound in bandages. The bottom of the armchair was open and empty. The cripple's left arm hung tied to his neck. His right he weakly waved, sometimes pointing to his bandage-thickened trunk, at others threatening someone in space.

The procession wavered for a long while at the front of the hospital and grew into a crowd. Women rolled chairs and baby carriages out onto the street, sat the wounded men in them and the wounded men waved their crutches and cried out something in inaudible wheezes. A young soldier threw his uniform from one shoulder and lifted his arm, gleaming with nickel and varnish, and after him the wounded who were able to stand without the women's help bared their steel, cardboard and leather arms and the patent devices began to creak, to squeak and to whine with their springs and levers.

And then the crowd raised a frantic cacophonous howl and lifting the cripples upon its shoulders, with chairs, stretchers and artificial limbs in its hands, it moved along Bismarck Avenue and farther—along the street past the cemetery, and farther—into the city hall square.

And in front of the crowd, with her crepe veil soaring in the wind like a flag, proceeded the widow of a bearer of the Iron Cross, Martha Birman from Teufelsmühle.

That was a strange day.

The *Bischofsberg Morning News* unexpectedly lost its characteristic eloquence and with great difficulty, like a man with a bad stammer, muttered something about disturbances in the imperial capital. The editor spoke out brilliantly for the necessity of raising mail rates and the columnist described the heroic defense of the Cameroons by colonial troops. The whole remainder of that edition was filled with minor church news.

Frau Urbach, tired by her morning good works (in the mornings she tied tiny packages of cigars for the sick and wounded), sat by the window looking onto the square. Toward two o'clock people began to gather by the city hall and small boys climbed upon the building's ledges, upon lamp-posts and streetcar posts. Frau Urbach asked her housemaid what such excitement could mean. And since the housemaid did not know she decided:

"Probably some victory."

And remarked with annoyance:

"The same old story: the authorities are the last to learn of events. During the whole war the city hall hasn't once hung its flags out in time. . . ."

The square steadily filled with people pouring from all the streets, doors and gates. The crowd became dense and people turned to face the street which was invisible to Frau Urbach.

Everything that happened after that developed with surprising, almost inconceivable speed.

A flock of newsboys flew in from somewhere and scattered over the square and swift loud-voiced sellers scurried into the crowd. The people rocked. Tiny white sheets splashed overhead and ran from hand to hand. Waves of subdued murmuring rolled from end to end of the square.

Frau Urbach called her housemaid:

"Run down quickly and buy a *Dispatch*. Something unusual has happened!"

And when the door had slammed she said to herself, something very rare for her:

"Perhaps it's peace?"

At that time the crowd moved toward the street which was invisible to Frau Urbach, and, having gathered there, fell back under the pressure of a solid wall of human bodies. Above this wall swayed armchairs with incomprehensible lumps in them which were reminiscent of heads and hands. Suddenly everything became confused in a vortex of paper sheets, hats, sticks and umbrellas.

The maid ran into the room and fearfully handed Frau Urbach a crumpled sheet.

A word in black on white, not even black but bluish-black, was on the sheet:

r e v o l u t i o n

And not somewhere in Russia or China—which would have been nothing unusual, but in Germany, which was not only unusual, but even supernatural.

The sheet was put out as an "extra" by the Social Democratic newspaper.

In its right-hand column it announced the abdication and flight of the Emperor; in its left, the proclamation of a republic. Below, across both columns, stretched an inscription whose meaning was trivial in comparison with the flight of the Emperor and the proclamation of a republic.

But the words jumped before Frau Urbach's eyes and their meaning got mixed up. She connected fragments of one announcement with extracts from a second and exclamations from a third. The immediate result was a confusion which should have explained what had happened but did not explain it: abdication . . . elections . . . republic . . . assembly . . . end . . . establishment . . . flight. . . peace. . . .

Her eyes were accidentally arrested by some lines about elections to the Landtag or to some new Reichstag or to some constitutional assembly—was that really important? In this scattered collection of words, in this twaddle, she read the word—Urbach. And because, during all the time that the sheet had trembled in her hands, she had been thinking of herself alone, of her name, of her future, she began sud denly not only to see but also to understand. And she read sensibly:

> . . . our committee proposes, among others for candidature, party member Urbach from Lausche, who for twenty years has supported the Social Democratic Party not by word but by deed. We must not forget what party member Urbach from Lausche, never revealing himself publicly, did for . . .

Frau Urbach slumped to the back of her armchair and covered her eyes with her hands. The crumpled sheet slipped to the floor.

Here it was, retribution. . . . It was impossible to fore-stall it, impossible to avoid it; retribution knows its time.

Now, only now—toward the end of his life—did this man become comprehensible, with his mysterious projects hidden in drawers, his locked library, his inexplicable absences from home. All this had been done behind Frau Urbach's back, in *her* home with *her* money.

Now, only now, did her daughter become comprehen-sible—*his* daughter, Urbach's daughter—Marie, with her vulgar actions, her obstinacy and plebeian willfulness. Now you could believe those dark rumors which had coiled around Marie. Anything could be expected from that wench. Why, she was Urbach's daughter! She did not have a single drop of the von Freilebens' blood!

Now all was understandable. Retribution . . .

Oh, that disgraced name—von Freileben! How could she have dared soil with the name Urbach the honor and virtue of her first-born, the sole, the last one of her blood, her pride—Heinrich-Adolf?

Fly! Fly like the Emperor . . . renounce her home . . . Urbach. The end . . . retribution . . .

Frau Urbach got up to give instructions for her things to be packed for her departure. She had to hurry. She stood erect, like a rod of steel, adjusted her dress and picked up the cane with the rubber tip.

At that moment the housemaid came in, gave Frau Urbach a telegram and turned to leave.

"Wait, I'll need you in a minute," said Frau Urbach and, like a businessman, skillfully unsealed and unfolded the telegram. Its text was brief:

OBER-LIEUTENANT HEINRICH-ADOLF URBACH DIED A HERO'S DEATH ON NOVEMBER 1 IN THE BATTLE OF ANKOCHE.   REGIMENTAL ADJUTANT.

Frau Urbach ripped the telegram with her nails, bent slowly and sat down in the armchair. Then her whole body shook, as if she had been hit from below, and she thrust her bad leg in its shagreen shoe out in front of her.

The flashing disorder of the square was for a second reflected in her eyes, turned toward the window, and she remained motionless.

That was a crowd!

Demonstrations were organized by the unions and societies of Bischofsberg, demonstrations with lamps and bands lined up in ranks, companies, battalions; and children marched in toy regiments, and women—in close order, as if in a gymnasium. But that was a crowd.

Women and children, soldiers and burghers, cripples, beggars, garbage collectors, workmen, milliners running out of their workshops and laborers coming from the farms swept among the houses like a pack of cards let loose in the wind.

Not a single flag fluttered over them nor a single trumpet summoned them to march, but some invisible, joyful and terrible banner drew them through the squares, promenades and streets.

Peaceful people, thousands of whom knew one another by sight and hundreds of whom drank their morning mug of beer at the same table—suddenly turned into pariahs and for them doors were slammed, shops were shut, market trays, baskets and carts were hidden.

One burgher, still believing in the power of established

order as a father still believes in his authority, when his son for the first time fearlessly shows disobedience—one burgher locked his tobacconist shop and hung a card on the door with the announcement:

REVOLUTION IS FORBIDDEN HERE

Indeed, people waking on the morning of November 10 could not have gone out of their minds! And if they were dashing along the roads and sidewalks without any evident purpose, then, of course, it was only because neither on the road nor on the sidewalks was it written:

IT IS FORBIDDEN TO DISTURB THE NORMAL FLOW OF LIFE.

Because of such a lack of foresight on the municipality's part, movement through the streets proved so confused that it turned all pedestrians, regardless of where they were headed, in one direction and swept them, like fallen leaves, toward the citadel.

And then the grim crumbling citadel, like an old general, was revealed to the eyes of the crowd. Its graying roof scowled and the gates stood buttoned up on all bolts.

The crowd slowed its pace and almost halted.

But the crowd had been collected by women, and their voices were more piercing than a signal horn.

"Women! They shut German soldiers up here who don't want to go for mincemeat!"

The signal beat on the roof of the citadel and, reverberating, fell into the crowd.

It was swallowed by a rolling booming bass:

"Soldiers! Your friends are sitting here!"

Paul Hennig, his umbrella raised overhead, pointed it at the barred windows, burst from the crowd and ran across the square without lowering his umbrella. Then some young soldier, turning to the crowd, commanded gaily:

"Com-pany! Follow the captain! *Umbrellas fixed*, charge!"

At this command soldiers ran out of the crowd—the green youth of raw recruits, with faces dissolving into laughter.

They surrounded the commander in a buzzing swarm and hurled themselves toward the gates of the citadel, in the wake of majestic, triumphant Paul Hennig.

To run was enjoyable, as in recent childhood, when fodder had been weighed in the citadel which had looked kindly on the boyish pranks around its walls.

Running up to the entrance the soldiers began to beat their fists on the gates, with shouts, whistles and laughter. Paul Hennig's eyes flashed and his breast rose often and high. A head taller than the soldiers, he viewed them as if inspired and banged his umbrella steadily against the gates. He looked like a schoolteacher surrounded by mischievous pupils—in black clothing, hairy and irate among the gray tunics of the clean-shaven, cheerful soldiers.

Perhaps all the events at the citadel would have concluded with this schoolboyish uproar, if a minute later the wicket in the gates had not been flung wide open.

This was so unexpected that the soldiers started backward, as if from an explosion.

The wicket was blotted out by a massive monument of an officer.

His legs seemed to go down into the ground, as if something had struck him on the shoulders from above, and he fixed his white gaze into space over the peakless caps of the soldiers. His rectangular lower jaw suddenly descended, his taut stomach quivered and a siren-like howl hung suspended over the square:

"At-te-e-en-shun!"

But at that instant the advance wave of the crowd running toward the citadel rolled down upon the soldiers, swept them up and hurled them upon the officer. The monument proved to be not at all so strongly embedded in the ground: squeezed by the people he revolved heavily on his axis and was pushed to one side. In the crush he attempted to unbutton the holster of his revolver; something sharp struck his hand, he sagged, grew limp, and the crowd threw him under its feet like a sack.

Paul Hennig had bent his head to go through the wicket when a nimble young girl slipped past him. Under the pressure of the soldiers he tumbled in after her, through the wicket, and at once felt a slim hand grip his neck and draw it downward. Through the murmur of the crowd behind the gates he heard a spasmodic voice:

"Listen, Hennig! We must release Monsieur Percy!"

In the pale light which people alternately obscured then released through the wicket he caught the features of a familiar face:

"Fräulein Marie! You, are you here?"

"We must open the gates!" cried Marie.

Someone rattled the bolts, someone shouted, "The keys to the cells! Where are the keys to the cells?" Someone far off, running away into the darkness, tramped over the flagstones. And people poured through the wicket ceaselessly, like sailors into a ship's boat under gunfire—swift and identical.

And now the gates separated ponderously and together with the light a dense buzzing human flood poured into the citadel.

The soldiers who were the first to break into the citadel advanced haphazardly through the confused dark passages of the stone cauldron. Somewhere in the depths of this cauldron, seething with muffled voices, the clang of iron rose and fell, as if a huge bunch of keys were being torn apart. Then a bright light splashed on the crowd from a flung-open door and at once locks began to jingle one after the other. The cells were being opened by an experienced hand.

When a man came uncertainly out of the first opened cage a young, jarring voice cried:

"Hur-ra-ah!"

The crowd instantly took up the cry. And from that second, while the cells were being opened, a multivoiced roar rolled incessantly along the corridors and stairways:

"Hur-ra-ah!"

The crowd climbed higher and higher, the interlocking corridors of the citadel drew it ever deeper in, but the foremost group of people unbolting the doors was hidden by each new turn of the corridors: together with the liberated prisoners the people were hastening to the square.

Marie, Paul Hennig and three or four soldiers came to a narrow cul-de-sac up under the roof of the building.

The warder unlocked the door skillfully and with accustomed ease: the locks were everywhere of the same pattern, new, like everything in the citadel except the stone of the walls and floors.

"The last," said the warder.

"Now you can ask for a state pension," remarked Paul Hennig.

"Perhaps you'll look after me?" responded the warder.

Marie peered at the man standing in the middle of the cell.

"Come out, you're free!" shouted one of the soldiers.

"Hur-rah!" another supported him.

The semi-darkness of the cul-de-sac cut off this cry like a knife. Here it was quiet and the ceiling seemed to be descending slowly upon their heads. Everything fell silent.

"That's not him!" said Marie.

"I tell you," said the warder, "we have no record of a prisoner named Percy."

The soldiers led the man out of the cell by his arm.

"Percy?" he suddenly asked quietly.

"Yes, we're looking for a Belgian Percy who was imprisoned here three years ago," said Paul Hennig.

"But I'm telling you we had no such man! Who here ought to know?" said the warder, offended.

"That's not quite right," said the man from the cell just as quietly. "Monsieur Percy—the Belgian citizen. I knew him. He was kept here about two weeks, then disappeared. He was against the war."

"They killed him, Hennig!" exclaimed Marie.

"Very likely," said the man from the cell. "He was against the war and besides that a foreigner."

"Aah, damn it!" growled Paul Hennig.

"Has something happened? Has the war ended, maybe?"

Marie dashed toward the man from the cell:

"Are you Master Maier from Nuremberg?"

Hesitating a while, the man from the cell moved to one side. The dull light from the high window, ruled by the bars, lay on Marie's face and he looked at her somewhat askance:

"Quite correct. I am Master Maier from Nuremberg, an enemy of the people. I am against war."

"Master Maier . . ."

Marie's voice broke, she finished hardly audibly:

"Let's go," and softly took Maier's arm.

In the darkness, in the hushed stone labyrinths, Maier asked:

"What does this mean? I don't know you, Fräulein."

"Andrei Startsov told me about you."

"A Russian and a good lad," growled Paul Hennig into the back of Maier's head.

The light of the streets blinded Master Maier and—perhaps from the light, perhaps from the motley crowd of people—he clutched his head, closed his eyes and halted.

Paul Hennig cautiously separated Maier's hands.

Then he replied:

"Andrei Startsov, I remember. He was also against war?"

"Ach, he was . . . so . . . he was so . . ." began Marie, choking and pressing Maier's elbow, "he loved you so much, Master Maier!"

Tears appeared in Paul Hennig's eyes. He coughed, drowning out some singers who were working on an unfamiliar song.

"Andreas was a lad with a head, I always understood him," he said, moved.

Marie threw him the smile of a conspiratress:

"Andrei would have been with us now, Hennig."

Amid the scurrying, indefatigable people she stood serene, happy and as light as a sapling.

Paul Hennig looked her over with a proud encouraging look, blew his nose and coughed even louder.

"Where would you like to go, Master Maier?" asked Marie.

Master Maier looked around the square. Over the lake of swaying heads his old eyes made out a worn inscription:

*Bauernschenke**

He chewed with his lips as if clenching his pipe more comfortably, the grayish bristles of his beard moved and crept up over his cheeks. He bathed Marie and Paul Hennig with a warm smile and his words were equally warm and quiet:

"If I may express a wish, then I could do with a mug of dark. . . . Now, it seems, is just the time?"

And he touched the pocket of his knitted jacket, out of which a small chain had formerly run across his stomach.

The time has come to say our last good-by to the city of Bischofsberg. It will still be referred to, but our weary legs shall no more touch its washed cobbles, we shall not see its narrow, sparsely populated streets, shall not hear the sleepy chiming of the clock on the city hall:

> Zon-ne,
> Zon-ne,
> Zon-ne! . . .

We are filled with sorrow on leaving—on leaving this unique vision of a pink girl sinking into a brook in the morning.

We remember the tablecloths of gaslight spread out around the street lamps and the spring rustling of the Park of the Seven Ponds and the snowy summit of Lausche drowning in the frozen scent of pines. We remember even kindly Auntie Meier guarding the public rest rooms by the police station. Will she be knitting her invariable stocking much longer?

In Bischofsberg we take loving leave of Master Maier, who was against war. He was the last to whom Monsieur Percy granted his brief greeting: *bonjour, bonjour, bonjour!* In Bischofsberg, of course, the bass voice of the Treasurer of the Society of Friends of Choral Singing, Paul Hennig, still rumbles and roars. We do not know whether he has left the Social Democratic Party and therefore we

*Tavern (usually in the country).

speak about him cautiously, though we cherish him for his kind attentions to the heroes of our novel.

But we shall be honest.

We are deeply uninterested in the fate of the Secretary of Police and even in the fate of the police building, we are indifferent to the editor of the *Bischofsberg Morning News*, the barber's apprentice Erich, Senior Nurse Neumann, or Major Bidau, or His Majesty the King of Saxony. All these are small fry, who crawl into any novel like flies into sweet tea.

We are relieved that we have to make only one more mention of the secret socialist Urbach. We do not sympathize with him because he married a lame aristocrat with an illegitimate son in order to help a feckless political party.

Finally, only out of egotistical considerations concerning the composition of this novel shall we return to Frau Urbach, née von Freileben. She did not die, she was crushed by paralysis; and she was lying in her bedroom when the event that ends this chapter took place in the Urbach home.

Past these people ahead, ahead!

But the city!

Forgive us if a tactless word caused your pride to suffer. Forgive us!

You are worth singing about, like any other city made by man's hand and beloved of man's heart.

You are solid.

People live in you. You are faithful to them.

You rushed along with us to seek new paths.

And you have made no more mistakes than Rome made, or Athens or Paris.

You—modest, obscure Bischofsberg. Good-by . . .

On the evening of November tenth the proprietor of a tavern, who had contrived to do business all day without a break, stroked the fourteen hairs on his glossy, flattened skull with a most peaceful air. Like the tobacconist who had forbidden revolution around his shop, he believed in the durability of the existing order. In his restaurant there still hung, as before, an autograph of Prince Otto von Bismarck, with which the Iron Chancellor had thanked the *Münchnerbräuerei** for the gift of a cask of dark beer. In his restaurant, as before, the beer taps gurgled and there was perpetual noise. He did not pay much attention to this noise, he was used to it, he was chatting with an old habitué of his tavern.

"I said to him: What's changed, old boy? Here you've come out of the hospital on one leg, shook your crutch at the city hall, kicked up a racket in the citadel. And in the end went back to the hospital again to spend the night. He would have his way: You wait, it'll change! What, I said, will change? Why, you aren't going to grow another leg? . . ."

The round table in the middle of the tavern was plastered with soldiers. Sweating and red, they unbuttoned their collars and tunics. Ah, at last, at last they could unbutton their collars and tunics! Their voices were hoarse, but the soldiers quarreled without cease.

"What!" cried a freckled recruit threateningly. "The soldiers have nothing to do with it all of a sudden? The whole affair's in the hands of the parties?"

"They're awaiting instructions from the palace. . . ."

"There's no palace now!"

"Hurr-rra-ah!"

". . . a directive from the capital, others are in conference the whole day, still others . . ."

"To hell with parties!"

"Please, please," a Landsturmer in glasses banged on the table.

"We must assess the nature of the revolution. What is it? A popular revolt? A class revolution? The class struggle?"

"Abraham bore Isaac, Isaac bore Jacob . . ."

"A soldiers' mutiny!"

"The soldiers want peace."

Someone put in from the corner:

"As soon as a soldier wants peace he stops being a soldier. A soldier has to want war."

"Down with war!"

*Munich brewery.

"Do-o-own!"

The work's half done! The city hall is in our hands, the citadel also, our posts are set up everywhere. What's the question?"

The tavern suddenly grew quiet.

And in that second's quietness an unexpectedly high voice sounded:

"It's a question of authority to control your posts, the city hall, the city. It's a question of the soldiers' authority."

Heads were stretched toward the exit door where the voice had been heard:

"I seem to know that wench," said the owner of the *Bauernschenke*, stroking his bald head.

Marie was standing on a chair—slim, drawn taut as a bow-string. Her face was flung upward, her hair was scattered, her slightly raised hand was trembling.

In an English magazine, forbidden to be read in Miss Ronny's boarding school, there had once been a photograph of a suffragette giving a speech at a meeting in Hyde Park. The suffragette's face had been flung upward, her hair had been scattered, and she had been erect and slim like a bow-string.

But the Hyde Park orator's slightly raised hand certainly had not trembled and—really now, at this moment, was it possible to think about illustrated magazines?

"Right!" burst out from the freckled recruit.

"We understand that it's a question of authority. . . ." began the bespectacled Landsturmer, but immediately was choked off in a wave of uncontrollable groans:

"The soldiers' authority!"

"The soldiers' soviet!"

"The soviet, the soviet!"

And upon the abatement of the wave, scrambling desperately out of the noise, someone's voice croaked:

"But how, how, how?"

Then Marie, as if she had caught a word which had been slipping away from her all the time, raised her hand level with her shoulder and cried:

"Comrades! This is the third time I have come here and

heard you fooling around on the same spot. You must value every minute. You must come to an agreement. I propose we go to another place for that. Whoever wants the honor of founding a soldiers' soviet in Bischofsberg—follow me!"

She was practically hurled to the street by a battering ram of chests, shoulders and arms. And in a new wave of shouts which jarred the windows she distinguished only one refrain, long forgotten, disturbing and reckless:

"Ooh, they have fine girls in Saxony!"

Several soldiers went with her to her house.

She led them into Frau Urbach's drawing room. She moved a wide table into the center of the room, brought paper, ink and pens. She took from the wall an oaken board with the couplet:

Wir stehen in Ost und West
Wie Fels und Eiche Fest

On the reverse side of the board she wrote with a paper rolled into a tube and dipped in ink:

Provisional Soviet
of Soldiers' Deputies of the City
of Bischofsberg

She went downstairs and hung the board on the street entrance door.

And when the five soldiers seated about the table began to calculate how many deputies should be sent to the Soviet by the units stationed in Bischofsberg, Marie stood by the window in the corner of the drawing room—as inaudible as a shadow.

And with every minute running off into the future history of Bischofsberg, the soldiers' voices became firmer, and their words briefer and their meaning simpler.

At that moment the door slowly opened and, dressed in a black overcoat with a tightly rolled umbrella in his hand, a burgher came into the drawing room. He took off his derby, halted, looked at the walls, the cornices, the windows. Then, unbending, he approached the table but stopped not by it but a little way off, at a distance which could not damage his obvious respectability. Where he was looking it was impossible to say.

"Are you the soviet?" he asked through wooden lips.

"Yes," they answered him.

"Someone has set up soldiers' posts at the city hall. They demand soviet passes from those wishing to enter the building. No one in the city knows where this soviet is situated. I searched for it a whole hour. Hence I deduce that the soviet has no administrative ability."

"The soviet has only just been organized."

"You mean that at the time when passes from the soviet were being required at the city hall no soviet existed in the city?"

"The soldiers are displaying their revolutionary initiative."

"But are you the soviet?"

"Yes."

"Give me a pass to the town hall."

The soldiers looked at one another.

The burgher was motionless and his eyes looked no one knew where.

Then the inaudible shadow broke away from the window in the corner of the room.

"I know who this is," said Marie. "This is Herr Stadtrat. I think we can give him a pass if he tells us what he wants at the city hall."

The wooden lips said:

"Until the constitution is changed, authority in the city is retained by the municipality. If power has been seized by force, then responsibility for the city's economy still rests on the municipality. I have to be at the city hall: in the evenings I inspect the papers of the economic department."

"I'll write it," said one of the soldiers.

He tore off a sheet of paper and jotted down several words with a broad flourish. The pass went around the table, weighted with signatures. When the last had been put on, the writer of it declared:

"It would be good . . . some kind of stamp."

"Stamp?" exclaimed Marie and ran out of the drawing room.

Returning, she took the pass and banged a wooden stamp heavily on the paper to the left of the flourishes. On the pass were imprinted four violet words:

EX LIBRIS
MARIE URBACH

Herr Stadtrat took the pass to his office from Marie's hands, went stiffly to the door and put on his derby.

Marie ran after him, picking her feet up rapidly like a little girl. She wanted to watch how he would go down the stairs.

But in the anteroom, behind the door, she caught sight of her father. She stopped.

Herr Urbach looked at her as if he did not recognize her.

"What's the matter?" asked Marie.

"Don't you know, Marie? Your mother is seriously ill. She is paralyzed."

She was silent.

"And your brother was killed in action. . . ."

"Yes," replied Marie, "the housemaid told me about it."

She stood motionless for a second, then turned, entered the drawing room and closed the door tightly behind her.

THE NATIONALITY OF A FINNISH TRIBE

Here are some extracts from the notes of Ober-lieutenant von zur Mühlen-Schönau of the Saxon Army, which he made while a prisoner of the Russians. The separate notebook with these notes was found a long time after the events at Semidol. The bad, probably home-made, ink had run and the paper had been soaked. The preserved pages have managed to be restored and translated almost in their entirety.

February 19th
The willow-herb seeds obtained by artificial polli-

*nation have produced their first shoots. Frei is walking
about proud and happy.*

February 27th

A year today.

In all that time not a single letter from home. I wrote
to everyone I could remember.

Now, when Marie is so hopelessly far away, the
thought of her makes me shrink with longing. This did
not happen at the front. From there everything
seemed simple: the war finishes, I return to Schönau, I
marry.

I think of my family, of its fate and my own, and
marriage to Marie becomes a necessity to me. This astonishing creature made me feel that the salvation of
my family lies in her. We had five branches, all male.
Four of them came to an end during my lifetime, within
my memory. I am the last. Marriage must take place on
some special basis in order for the will to live to reap-
pear in the line. At the moment I have the will to survive. I do not see what I have to live for. Pictures? But
what else? Everything is inside me, in that segment of
life which is assigned to me. Everything ends with that.
I shall not be repeated, I do not live but survive, measuring out the ordained length. I must want centuries to
stretch out before me into the future—just as they lie
behind me in the past. I must want to be repeated.

Frei never stops talking about physiology. It is unpleasant to think of Marie when such terms are revolving in my mind. My forefathers loved at first according
to the droit de seigneur, then for money. It is unlikely
that any of them loved their wives. The wives were
apart, their responsibility was to continue the line. The
line sprang up apart from the essential life of my
forefathers. If they had loved within the family it
would have been strong, and I would live now hundreds of years and still not live out my span.

I am sure of this.

Frei talks of it in the same terms: one must love,

marry, produce children, and then everything will fall into place.

Marie carries within her the will to repeat, to continue. I close my eyes and see her as she was for the last time at Schönau. I am ready to scream—so much does it upset me.

April 30th

It has been announced in the camp that we may settle without hindrance in the villages and hire ourselves out to the peasants.

. . . some soldier came from town, an assembly has been organized. The soldier spoke of peace and of the fact that Russia seems . . .

June 16th

It is not the authorities, of course, who are keeping us here. There has been no authority for a long time. We are kept by impassable roads. Frei is gloomy. When we were moving into Picheur, the case with his herbarium rolled off the cart and landed under the wheel. More than a hundred leaves from the herbarium were crushed and broken. Frei beat the Mordvinian driver, there was nothing I could do to. . . .

. . . forty kilometers to Semidol. In comparison with the camp it is twenty-five kilometers nearer; but there is scant comfort in that. It is impossible to ride out of town, there are no trains. No one has heard anything about the exchange, and they don't know where to send the prisoners. They say that more than a thousand men have piled up there and are living on charity. I am also living on charity. Frei finds that we should take a closer look at the Mordvinians. They are our salvation. Salvation?

. . . haven't seen a single line of print. Frei has thrown up his morphology, is silent all the time.

A food detachment arrived in Picheur yesterday. A gathering has been called for tomorrow, corn will be collected for the towns. The Mordvinians are quite scared, they are hiding in their huts.

June 28th

The Mordvinians treat me with incomprehensible respect. Yesterday a Mordvinian wise woman came, brought some milk, invited me to prayers. Departing, she bowed low. Frei asked me to note down:

Karin-Paz—*god of the forests, protector of the lime tree and its bark for* lapty *(footwear).*

Kalma-azyr-ava—*protectress of graveyards, guarding the gates of cemeteries.*

Yurtava—*goddess of the hearth, a sorceress, sometimes a cat, sometimes a hare.*

"Perhaps it will come in handy," said Frei.

June 29th

At sunrise the Mordvinians led their families out of the village. The wise woman came to us. We set out on the road. We were two hours and ten minutes on the road. At first we went through fields, then woods, ravines. The ravines here are frightening. Not knowing the area it is easy to lose one's way. The people had gathered in a remote ravine, by a spring, which gushed half a yard in the air. The water in the spring was extraordinary—icy, and yellow with iron. The stones over which the brook flowed were covered with a brown coating like rust. The spring flows all winter. The people sat in families, each household forming a ring. In the depths of the ravine, behind the spring, burned four fires. In the middle of each ring of people stood sacks of groats, brought from Picheur. When they noticed us they became agitated and looked at one another. The wise woman ran around the circle whispering something. After that they calmed down and nodded their heads approvingly at us. Frei sat by the circle which consisted almost entirely of old men. I sat beside him. Soon it became quiet. The chief read a prayer in front of the spring. The elders in every circle repeated it. After that four rams were led out from the depths of the ravine. The elders went off to the fires where they began to sing incantations. Then they

slaughtered the rams, skinned them, sat around the
fires and began to roast the meat. The chief never
ceased praying. At that time a Russian priest arrived.
He was greeted with respect. He was obviously
pleased, undid his bundle without delay, put on luxuri-
ous golden vestments and commenced a Russian service just as soon as the Mordvinian chief told him that
the Mordvinian prayers were over. The differences in
ritual between the service and the prayers were insignificant. He was a curious type of missionary—a Russian priest getting along peacefully with paganism.

Frei told me that the priest, just like the Mordvinian
chief, prayed for rain and prosperity. Frei speaks Russian no better than the Mordvinians, he expresses himself oddly but they understand him perfectly. When
the rites were over the meat was divided among the
families. A purée was poured out into earthenware
saucers—a potent drink brewed from honey. The chief
drank first. After him it was offered for some reason
to me, then to the priest. The priest in drinking looked
at me and raised his saucer. The purée was very strong
—I felt intoxicated from the first swallows, perhaps
because I had drunk nothing for six months. The purée
was given only to the men. A part of the meat and
the sacks of groats were carried away by the women
into pens where the food was eaten. We returned in
the heat of the day. Frei walked with the old men. I
was alone, in front.

The prayers are called Baban Hasha.

. . . I am already accustomed to living in some
kind of seventh century. In the mornings we are
brought buttermilk and bread in an earthenware dish.
They take nothing from us. I wear a homespun shirt
embroidered with yellow crosses. They said it was
made by a Picheur beauty. I haven't seen her. In general, I have seen no beauties here. When you think of
them—you begin to pant, but as soon as you look
around you—everything passes.

Frei recounted that in the village a girl of twenty is

set behind a spinning wheel to spin an unbleached
thread as long as the circumference of the village. At
midnight she encircles Picheur with this thread in order
to guard it against infection. The spinner must definitely be chaste. While she is spinning only old women
are allowed access to her. Otherwise the thread will
have no power.

Typhus has been brought to us from the town.

After Frei's story I couldn't get to sleep all night.
Everything is moving? No. Everything stands still.
Oh, to burst out of this damned . . .

. . . you couldn't even get there swimming. In a
whole week we left our kennels only once. We went
to get acorns for ink. Frei is still relying on something,
says that since the Mordvinians are feeding us . . .

November 10th

I found Russia in revolution. I don't know her as being any other way. I think of the millions of kilometers
lying prostrate like Picheur. The seventh century. With
November, snow has started to fall. People hide in
their dens, sleep for six months. If that is revolution,
what came before it? Frei says we haven't seen Russia.
In my opinion it's the opposite. What we are seeing
really is Russia: snow, no roads, sleep. Here—ravines,
farther on—steppe, still farther—desert, at the other
end—forests, swamps, moss. Amid this primeval gran-
deur—settlements called towns and, here and there,
fields. These strata are suitable for colonization. A
colony has still to pass along the path of enlightened
tyranny. Then, perhaps, the future will open before it.
Here they need feudal lords, not socialists. (Are socialists needed anywhere at all?) Feudal lords will force
them to learn to work sensibly. There is no other
means of forcing them to plant corn where rye has
been scorched by the heat. In the towns civil war has
already begun . . . that revolution . . .

. . . snow, only snow. My God!

Last night I woke utterly exhausted. Marie again, living, warm. For the sake of seeing her . . .

December 20th

With the first opportunity to use sleds a rumor came from town alleging that Germany had signed an armistice and that His Highness the Kaiser had fled. What rubbish! And what worthless scoundrels the people must be who spread this slander! It's repulsive to think about.

Frei has become sullen and silent in the extreme. I counted up: today he said seven words—good morning, snow again, yes, good night. He always sleeps soundly, without dreaming. It is a week already since he plunged again into his morphology and sits over a magnifying glass. I am helping him raise swamp plants in plots. I tried drawing with charcoal. The Mordvinians produce magnificent charcoal. But there is no paper.

I pottered about outside two days, clearing snow away.

. . . from no one knows where. One of them is a Bavarian, the other a Czech. Frei persuaded the Bavarian to go to town to find out about everything. Promised to feed him all winter for this. Frei accompanied him out of the village. In the evening he suddenly warmed up and told me finally of his plan, which seemed fantastic to me. His premises, however, are correct. The Mordvinians want to interpret the whole of the so-called revolution as a national liberation. No such liberation, of course, can be expected. But the sympathies of the Mordvinians are on the side of the non-Russian nationalities. By carrying on war with the Russians we can most easily find a common language with the Mordvinians, even if it is Frei's Russian. We have a common enemy. Frei has managed to do a lot. They are certainly not feeding us for nothing and now I understand why they look upon me with reverence. Picheur is prepared. If Marie were told she

wouldn't believe it. It's out of A Thousand and One
Nights. Bravo, Frei!

                                St. Sylvester's Eve.

*Last year in the camp Frei was forecasting where
and how we would meet the new year 1919. Where—
we've almost guessed: we've gone twenty-four kilometers from the camp and, as before, are cut off from
the world by wastes of snow. But how could we
think that such disgrace awaited our country! Germany, our homeland! What powers were able to
break you?*

*This morning the Bavarian returned from Semidol.
It is true that His Highness the Kaiser has abandoned
the fatherland. Germany is a republic. A gang of
some parliamentarians or other is in power. The armistice is disgraceful. The army, navy, officer corps all
surrendered to the mercy of the enemy. His majesty
the Saxon king . . . No, I cannot! Frei, the iron unshakable Frei, sobbed. . . .*

*Death—that is all we speak of. We swore at New
Year—I, Frei, the Bavarian and the Czech—swore on
our weapons that we would not forgive the disgrace
to our homeland. So be it.*

*The Bavarian brought six revolvers from town. Frei
solemnly handed me the best of them. The Bavarian
is a brave intelligent soldier, he has three wounds,
bears the Iron Cross. I don't like the Czech much, but
Frei vouches for him. Besides weapons and newspapers the Bavarian brought the following news: in
Semidol there is a soviet of German Bolsheviks carrying on agitation among the prisoners it is supposed to
be evacuating home. The prisoners' camp is overflowing. Typhus is raging. Prisoners continue to arrive
and their dispatch is almost impossible since the roads
are out of action and civil war is in full swing. All this
is in our favor. The Czechs are penetrating Siberia in
order, by a roundabout way, on Japanese and American ships, to get to their own country. They always
were traitors and they'll always stay traitors.*

During the day the Mordvinians brought two dead wolves and laid them at my feet. The beasts were excellent. I accepted them and ordered them to be carried away and skinned. When the Mordvinians had left, Frei shook my hand.

"That's good that way," he said. "You must remember who you are to these people."

These people, to the present day, have not lost the instinct of warlike barbarians. Perhaps in their legends there still roams the ghost of the Ugrian sovereign who routed the Russian princelings? That instinct can be stirred up. In the last analysis, just the line of margraves von zur Mühlen-Schönau is worth the whole princely history of the Mordvinians!

Frei is right. It's all a question of time and the age.

CHAPTER THE SECOND
ON NINETEEN NINETEEN, PRECEDING THE FIRST

SATURDAY IN SEMIDOL

In Gattsuk's "Religious Calendar," before the word "Semidol" a liqueur-glass stood puffed out on its slender waist, and a coach horn hung above it.

And in truth, in the Semidol station buffet you could find even Nyezhin rowanberry brandy, and the mail and telegraph office retained nine officials and seven mailmen.

A great number of such Semidols was scattered throughout Russia's wide open spaces. They all resembled one another, like chickens, and their life passed chicken-like from dawn to dusk, from perch to perch.

The Semidolians roamed over the dusty, soft-as-featherbed streets and rotting footpaths, fed themselves, clucked, let out their chicks with a fearful look upward, whence descended all troubles, and ran without a backward look just as soon as they heard the warlike flapping of a cockbird's wing. The cocks, by prescription, trampled the Semidolians, guarded their morals and fought to the death for their parishes.

In order to distinguish new times coming to Semidol from the distant past it used to be necessary to live there not less than a human lifetime. In that case the observant eye would notice that a new lamp post had been placed in Monastery Street, that the fence opposite the district council offices had collapsed and that the fire-tower had been freshly painted.

But if the peaceful state of Semidol were invaded by any kind of event, then it spread with devastating speed.

Thus does the peace and plenty of a chicken run become converted into an absolute hell when its limits are invaded by a frantic dog.

It is difficult to resist the temptation to describe retrospectively the town in the days when it resembled a chicken run. What can be more affecting than the clucking of a broody hen, more touching than the cheep of yellow, feathered chicks or more inspiring than the crow of a cock? But we well remember that this idyllic hen-house has been the undoing of more than a few Russian novelists.

That is why we begin our narrative directly with that day when the first rumbles of alarm rolled over the chicken run, and when there soared on high, whence descend all troubles, a torn out tail feather. Soon such feathers swirled over Semidol in impenetrable clouds and in five days—in only five days—the air became clear again.

Comrade Golosov was a young man, and is it worth mentioning that at his age there was nothing to be ashamed of in appearing on the street hand in hand with a girl?

But Comrade Golosov was chairman of the executive committee and in Semidol was called the Mayor. Was it becoming to a mayor to chase after skirts? And then, how do you account for an executive committee chairman's appearance on the street with the priest's daughter Ritochka? True, Ritochka was secretary to the executive committee and so this was associated with her work. True, Ritochka was called Comrade Tveretskaya. But the Semidolians were a scrupulous people, prone and eager to gossip. Just try to din it into their heads that Semyon Ivanich Golosov—an orator and opponent of private property—was in certain respects not a bit different from any Semidolian who had reached the age of twenty-two.

But to hell with them!

One must walk about the town swiftly, printing one's soles on the trampled footpaths, twitching and pulling at one's upper lip, wrinkling a bump on one's forehead and looking at least half a mile ahead. And when passers-by bow, answer impetuously and briefly.

"Io, Comrade!"

And rush farther on, looking half a mile straight in front of one.

If one rides in a *tarantass** then it must be in no other way than with one's teeth firmly clenched, hands thrust into pockets and eyes fixed on the driver's back. Then it is clear to everyone that Comrade Golosov is hurrying upon some pressing business of national importance and does not use Soviet horses unnecessarily.

But who does one need to be upon seeing Comrade Golosov after work on Saturday, side by side in the executive committee's tarantass with the priest's daughter Tveretskaya, to think of business of national importance?

Of course, it was all a question of the irresponsibility of the Semidol bourgeoisie, who in the second year of the Revolution were still deeply convinced that spring was a contradiction of the *Communist Manifesto* and that love—most real, most fragrant, with rides in boats, brief embraces in bushes, salt kisses by gates—that such love had been abolished at some congress or other.

However, if the bourgeoisie had thought otherwise . . .

But to hell with them!

Comrade Golosov said as much, hiding a smile with his round little palm:

"But to hell with them! I'll go with Pokisen. . . ."

Andrei frowned.

"You seem to be trying on purpose to leave me alone. . . ."

"With Comrade Tveretskaya?" caught up Golosov. "Nonsense! But you can see that it won't work any other way?! And then . . ." Golosov pulled at his upper lip: "You should be somewhat kinder, Startsov. You really haven't noticed?"

"It's none of your business."

"It's in my interest to maintain the work capacity of the executive committee secretary. Comrade Tveretskaya has

*A small, springless carriage.

started mixing up the papers. I called her and began to question her, her eyes began to shift about, and in her eyes was Andrei Startsov."

"I understand," said Andrei with a smile, "at your age you feel embarrassed if you fall in love."

"Nonsense!"

"Not at all. You're laying your own fault at someone else's door. On Saturdays you're like a new man. That's from your anticipation of a date. Why, even today you're going to Starye Ruchi to . . ."

"Quit it! Who d'you take me for? I'm going to look out for a place for a children's home."

"What are you talking about? For a children's home? In the middle of winter?"

"Yes, yes, for a children's winter home," said Golosov, raising his voice, "and then I must try out a new Mauser."

"And for that go six miles?"

Comrade Golosov's face hardened, he was about to say something harsh, but suddenly his hand jerked up to his mouth and a jaunty smile flashed at Andrei before it was hidden in the palm:

"You'd go a hundred miles for that, I bet. . . ."

He turned abruptly and strode across the yard, straightening his shirt and crying through the open windows of a two-storied house:

"Nannie! Dinner!"

And as always Andrei went cold for a minute at the distinct shout—"Nannie!"

In the doorway Golosov turned.

"Then you'll come?"

"I'll come."

"Well, that's the spirit!"

That was Andrei's entire conversation with Golosov in the yard of the editorial office of the Semidol *News*.

The evening was calm and a rouged sky descended behind the monastery. A cart resembling an eggshell rolled crunchingly over a railroad crossing. Comrade Pokisen was sitting on some straw in the middle of the wooden body, stretching his legs and balancing a child's projector. Golosov had thrown one leg over the front of the cart and tucked the other under him like a real—oh, yes, a real!— veteran driver.

Before that they had sailed through the uneven streets in the crunching eggshell, unhurriedly squashing the dry lumps of mud and trailing behind them a lazy, yellowish-transparent doormat of dust.

Pokisen had severely regarded the little board houses through his gold spectacles and the half-rotten, queer little cupolas of the fat gateposts. At every jolt he had lifted the projector over his head, cautiously and carefully, as if he had been carrying a reliquary. Golosov clicked his tongue angrily and twirled the end of the rope reins in the air.

And for those who did not know chairmen by sight (and such people existed in Semidol): here go the land surveyors to the Sanshino *volost** to divide up the allotments. For those who did know: the executive committee must have thought up some new agitation for Bavaria, or—Heaven forbid!—for the complete leveling off of the soil of the Easter Week market, with the object of building some kind of playground for children under school age.

Thus the two chairmen sailed quietly and sedately past open, painted shutters, water hydrants and jammed-full grocery stores, and over frail plank bridges and streets as soft as a feather mattress.

Quietly and sedately—as far as the railroad crossing.

But after that comrade Golosov tucked his legs into the cart and looked around.

The round roofs of traveling workshops, like those in circuses peeped from behind the steep embankment of the railroad track. Behind them the cathedral cupola was stuck on the sky like a strong green patch. A sooty lodge stood up high beside the crossing and to the right of it, along the sandy foot of the embankment, like camp tents, there extended stacks of gray, latticed screens.

The closely cropped rectangles of fields lay alternately on either side of the road. Spindly sunflowers, still un-

*The name for a small rural district in Russia which includes several villages.

harvested, ran here and there into the naked strips like sporadic, blackened freckles.

In front could be seen the dark strips of Sanshino forest. "Shall we go, Pokisen?"

Golosov stood up, threw off his cap, scattering the straw, set one leg inside the cart and rested the other one on the front. Pokisen crushed a bunch of straw under him, aimed at Golosov through his spectacles and said, as if testing him:

"Let's go, Semyon. . . ."

Then Golosov pulled on the reins.

The dirt road to Ruchi wound from the railroad crossing to a bunch of Sanshino *volost* fruit orchards in a series of tight curves. In each curve there was a bend, in the bend— a loop, and the loop ran unevenly—twisting, thin and snakelike: one ought to have skirted every pothole, avoided bumps and gone around stones.

But Semyon Golosov was not the one to skirt, to avoid, to go around; Semyon Golosov had taught himself to walk straight and, walking or riding, to waste little time, because any journey, even the most perfect, even by air—any journey was a useless waste of time.

And doesn't it inflame your breath, doesn't it intoxicate, doesn't it burn, this head wind that whistles in your ears, ruffles and tears your hair, beats like a lash against your bared chest? The mare leaned tightly into the wet felt lining of her collar, her breechband plaited with brasses danced gaily on her foam-flecked back, her hooves faintly thudded against the front board like the butt-end of an ax, while Semyon lashed her skinny haunches time after time, quicker and quicker, harder and harder. Semyon's legs seemed to have their feet glued to the cart and he cushioned the jolts lightly with his knees. Semyon's shirt had come out of his belt and ballooned in red globes behind his back and his hair was plastered to the back of his head by the wind as smoothly as if by a fine comb.

Across grooves and ruts, through potholes and over mounds, now body-high in spindly sunflowers, now in a red cloud of dust, through holes, humps, oblivion—straight, al-

ways straight, against the wind, with a whistle, a roar and
a whoop:

"Semyon! Semyon, Semyon on! Hold it, you devil, hold
it!"

But the reins traveled over the cruppers and sides of the
skinny mare and now she flung up her muzzle, pulled on
the back of the yoke snorted and went into top speed.

"Semyon! Semyon! Devil!"

Not for nothing had the mare been broken in by the fire
warden. Not for nothing had it been frightening to watch
him when at night, wailing with terror in a voice not his
own, he had rushed about the town with a kerosene torch
on his back.

"Semyon, you d-de-evil!"

There was no stopping.

Then Comrade Pokisen sprawled out over the whole
cart, raised the projector over his head with both hands,
and suddenly, in a voice high and penetrating, like the
clang of a tin sheet, he began to sing a song. Its words
were simple but no one besides Pokisen knew them. And
its refrain was equally simple, and no one besides Pokisen
knew the refrain.

> *Eh, le-lele,*
> *Eh, le-lele,*
> *Eh, le,*
> *Eh, le,*
> *Eh, le-le.*

Golosov slackened the reins and squatted on his haunches. Turning his round, downy face to Pokisen he looked at
the sky. Thus they swept for about half a mile. The foaming mare contracted and expanded in her gallop like a
spring. The cart was being thrown from side to side and it
creaked like a sack full of scrap-iron.

Pokisen pierced the air with tinny sobs. And it was impossible to tell whether Golosov, swaying on his haunches,
was listening to the song or thinking of something else.

> *Eh, le-lele,*
> *Eh, le-lele,*

Eh, le,
Eh, le,
Eh, le-le.

And when they stopped at the entrance to the Ruchi orchards and began to straighten the wet, disordered harness, Golosov asked:

"Was that Finnish?"

Pokisen smiled like a baby.

Then Golosov also smiled.

"Well so, d'you know operas?"

Pokisen thought a while, then simply said:

"Fool."

The Ruchi orchards extended for hundreds of acres. They pressed their clay-smeared wattle fences closely together and across the fences offered each other hairy arms of cherry and plum trees. Every hut had its orchard and to every orchard there led a path wide enough for a cart to pass, scraping its axles on the canes sticking out of the wattle. When two carts met on the paths the peasants would deliberate as to who was nearest to the orchard gates, make their horse jib backward, bring their cart inside the gates and thus sort out the tangle. Only one road—a wide high road—cut through the orchards, and it led from the fields through Starye Ruchi to Sanshino.

People had lived here for ages: fathers' fathers and grandfathers' fathers had planted ebony here and *kitaika* apples, *tsarsky ship* and bergamot pears, and bitter blackthorn had bristled here in tangled thickets since time immemorial.

Only by mutual guarantee was it possible to give sufficient water to the hundreds of acres of apple trees, cherry trees and every other kind of plant, large and small. And the orchards lived as brothers. The narrow paths between the wattle fences were tiny bogs from spring days until the first frosts and nowhere could the grass-snakes and frogs live so freely as on these paths. Chutes stretched through the air from orchard to orchard, ditches crept along the ground, and in the evenings, when the bustle of work had

died down, the hasty dripping of water would ring out mer-
ry rounds as it pattered down from the chutes onto the
trees. Hundreds of acres-leafy, dense, flourishing-hun-
dreds of acres, tended by the hand of man, listened then
to the water.

Golosov and Pokisen entered Ruchi by the high road. But
in front of them ran a flock of sheep, raising an impenetrable column of dust, and it was necessary to turn into the
orchards in order to avoid suffocation.

Here the wheels vanished into ruts almost up to their
hubs. The horseshoes squelched in the thick, mashed, por-
ridge-like mud. The yoke parted the pliant tracery of the
cherry trees. Burdocks slapped their broad palms against
the axles. One chute ran along the road for about twenty
yards, and, while they were passing that stretch, a heavy
cold rain fell upon the horse's back and into the cart. The
horse threw up its muzzle, noisily puffed out its sides,
snorted and then walked quietly. Golosov wiped off the
drops of water on his face, looked at Pokisen, and, seeming confused, said:

"Good . . ."

"Does the committee chairman have the rights of a villa
owner?" asked Pokisen.

Then they were silent, listening to the murmur, the splash
and the ring of the flowing and dripping.

At the summer villa, Pokisen's eldest boy—a lanky lad
with pointed shoulders—crawled all around the projector,
touched and moved the screws and wheels and twirled the
handle. In the kitchen Pokisen's wife was breaking brush-
wood by the Russian stove and crooning a song in a language which no one in Starye Ruchi could understand or
had ever heard.

And in the same language Comrade Pokisen used to sing
to his three-month-old son of things which no one knew
about in Starye Ruchi; of the time soon, very soon, when the
social revolution would be won and the Party would say:

"Comrade Pokisen, you have served the revolution, you
are free to do as you like."—

And then he would take little Otti off to Lake Hepo-
Yarvi.

"Oh, Hepo-Yarvi! Otti, wee Otti, you haven't yet inhaled its bitter scent, haven't yet puckered your eyes against its keen wind. Otti, wee Otti, you haven't yet seen the wind of Hepo-Yarvi heel the pine masts northward, nor have your ears yet heard the whistle rising from the sand dunes.

"Oh, Hepo-Yarvi! Nowhere does the horse run so swiftly as over the ice of Hepo-Yarvi and nowhere do skis glide as they do down the slopes of its mountainous shores.

"And how silent can Hepo-Yarvi be! And how it cries, roars and whistles when a storm comes in off the skerries!"

"And what swings, Otti, what swings the brave people have set up on the shores of Hepo-Yarvi—swings so high that your heart is ready to jump out of your breast when they soar out over the water. And songs, what songs the people sing in these swings, at night, when the moon looks down on the bottom of Hepo-Yarvi! Otti, wee Otti, listen:

> *Eh, le-lele,*
> *Eh, le-lele,*
> *Eh, le,*
> *Eh, le,*
> *Eh, le-le."*

The high thin cries ran through the tops of the apple trees, burrowed into the thick of the orchard and were lost. Pokisen pressed the lace-wrapped Otti to his breast and fell silent.

To his wife, who came to feed the child, he whispered: "I was telling him about Hepo-Yarvi."

And she thanked him barely audibly:

"Oh, you!"

The air contracted with the cold of an early frost, such as falls in October after a peaceful sun-warmed day. Because of this cold and because it was nice to have that wintry feeling already—to sit in pungent intimacy around the fire—they had the villa windows shut tight.

The pilot Shchepov—thin, wearing a tight jersey, in narrow boots laced to the knees—walked past the table. The heroine of the Semidol theater was watching him from a corner with her big, penciled eyes. She was known to everyone by her first name and patronymic—Klavdia Vasilyevna

—and Shchepov was making fun of her: what popularity!

Rita had perched on the sofa and did not stir.

"You have an inflamed imagination," said Shchepov, cutting his words up with short steps. "And your feverishness comes from a fear that you are wrong. What the hell kind of revolution is there in Semidol? Four creameries and one windmill. The proletariat?"

"You don't understand a thing!" shouted Golosov, jumping onto a chair. "Our task . . ."

"Let me finish. Look at you—responsible Bolsheviks if ever there were any—you've left town on a Saturday. Do you know what's left there? Not counting the military commissar, Semidol remains in the inviolable chastity of the Middle Ages. The whole town's crept off to vespers, to the Feast of the Intercession of the Holy Virgin. In the executive committee the woman on guard is knitting mittens, the Red soldier in the Special Department has fallen asleep and the Chief of Public Education is cutting up cabbage in a trough for a pie. Granted that you print *The News* on dark green paper. It may be poor stuff but it lights fires. There's your revolution."

"It's our business to attract new cadres. . . ."

"To hell with such words! I'm telling you what kind of cadres you've got here."

"Excuse me," joined in Pokisen, "if I understand you rightly you are saying that Semidol is counter-revolutionary? Well, surely the struggle with the counter-revolution is the same. . . ."

"Yes and where the hell's the counter-revolution here? A bog full of frogs and no more. They croaked before and they're croaking now."

Shchepov paused and folded his arms. His gaze was shining from his cheerful outburst, his voice was keen and elastic.

"To look at you from the outside, you look like men of the Eighties. For a greater resemblance Semyon has even grown his hair long. They'd collect of an evening at a friend's, drink up the regulation drinks, the housewife would boast of her mushrooms and pickles. . . ."

"Oh, oh, oh!" exclaimed Pokisen's wife indignantly, her face stonier than usual.

"And then our Eighties men ended with a discussion of principles."

Golosov leaped up as if stung. His hands were jumping at his waist. He gathered the ends of his shirt into pleats behind his back, drawing it tight over his stomach and sides and a small tail was formed behind him which bounced at the slightest movement like a wagtail's.

"Nonsense!" he barked, stamping his foot. "It's people like you and like Startsov here, it's you who raise the chatter because you're feet-draggers, clods. For us everything is clear, we know what we want and in any bog we'll find something to do. Give us the sleepiest frogs there are and we'll make what we need of them. And if nothing can be done with them—we'll annihilate, we'll annihilate them. We don't need bogs! It's you—the Shchepovs, the Startsovs—who revolve eternally around principles, you who always want to reconcile the ideal with the real. We know that it's impossible to reconcile it, one can only subordinate it. And we can find the strength in ourselves to subordinate it! We don't look back, we're not afraid of what you'll say about us, and it's all the same to us how we strike the imagination of the Shchepovs. Men of the Eighties? I don't give a damn! We aren't afraid of eating pickles and visiting villas. But you've licked the jam and then immediately begun to debate: But does a revolutionary have the right to lick jam at a time when . . . and so on and so on and so on! That's where you get your feeling of superiority from! You laugh? I can see by your nose what you're thinking: 'But we can see the contradictions in which the Bolsheviks have dirtied themselves, and our snouts are clean,' We'd like to spit on your snouts! Think what you like! We can get by without the intelligentsia and its copyright on pure thinking. They're not the same as specialists, who have knowledge and who . . ."

Golosov stopped, scowled at everyone in turn and barked:

"Nonsense!" and sat down.

"A whole declaration," said Shchepov.

Pokisen adjusted his spectacles.

"You've still kept your sense of humor, Shchepov? Isn't that because Golosov left you a loophole? The superiority of an intellectual has been replaced on your face by the superiority of a specialist."

"Well, and you, what about you," suddenly cried Andrei who had been silent the whole time, "surely you are that same intelligentsia?"

"Those same half-educated students?" interjected Shchepov.

"And so on! One flesh and one blood! Drop it!" Golosov waved him away.

He jumped up again, frowned at Shchepov and asked gently:

"But are they right in saying a pilot can crash a plane so that the engine flies to God knows where while he stays in one piece?"

"What d'you mean?"

"No, no, answer my question straight!"

Shchepov spread his hands.

"Theoretically . . ."

"No, no, not theoretically!" pressed Golosov.

"Such incidents have been known with certain systems. When it falls on one wing the pilot is thrown out, sometimes twenty yards, the plane collapses onto its propeller, crushes it and sometimes crumples the other wing as well. In general . . . But it's ridiculous! To crash an aircraft on purpose!"

Shchepov drew himself up—tall and thin—pressing the fingers of his bony hands against the board ceiling.

"Risky?" asked Golosov, hiding an imperceptible chuckle in his palm.

"I get you," said Shchepov hollowly. "The risk, however, would be contained not so much in the deliberate fall as in the explanation it would demand. There has to be clarity in a smash-up."

He listened carefully to his last words—how they diagramed the air on a level with his head—and repeated:

"There has to be clarity in a smash-up."

"But you know that there's no one here for a hundred miles, besides you, who understands anything about airplanes—you can explain any crash however you like," said Golosov into his palm.

Shchepov stared heavily at him and kept silent. Everyone suddenly fell quiet, holding their breath and looking at some point between Golosov and the pilot.

"How boring!" sighed Klavdia Vasilyevna fearfully.

Then Shchepov's face quickly smoothed out and lightened.

"You're an entertaining man, Semyon. . . ."

Golosov stood up, the gathered tail of his shirt stuck out fussily and trembled, he shook his locks.

"You really are a terrible bore. I'm going to try out my Mauser. Who's coming? Rita, let's go!"

Comrade Tveretskaya quietly transferred her eyes to Andrei. He sat hunched up, alternately dispersing and gathering a wrinkle between his brows, as if trying to recall something which was dim and perpetually slipping away from him.

Golosov dashed to the door, forcing out in disgusted pain:

"Ah, well, drag your Startsov along!"

Rita asked:

"Do you want to, Startsov?"

He rose silently.

Probably it was all the same to him—whether to go or stay.

That happened to him often. Suddenly he seemed to go deaf and then to hear only what was going on inside him. The efforts he had to make not to cry out from terror at such moments had changed him beyond recognition. His face was warped like parchment in water, he repeated movements learned long ago, not noticing them, as happens to a man with concussion. He submitted to everything to which he was prompted from without, showing neither resistance nor assent, although his consciousness was as alive as before. He could not tear himself away from some single, tremendous, uncommunicable thought which had once astonished his brain.

He was walking beside little Rita, who pressed close to him. She had taken his arm and with his elbow he could feel the soft warmth of her breast and—behind it—the agitated beating of her heart.

Golosov was striding ahead, separating the branches he encountered with his hands. The night was pitch-dark, the thickets of blackthorn and cherry tree were dense and prickly, but Golosov obstinately struggled farther and farther into the thicket, into the cold darkness.

"Take it easy, Golosov!" said Rita. "Don't swing the branches like that, you've lashed me all over the face."

"But what are your hands for? Let go of Startsov and don't hang back, walk faster."

"There are two of us, the going's harder for us."

"Then to hell with you!" cried Golosov and, elastic, bent over, plunged away, broke and trampled the impassable thickets, then jumped over banks of bushes, muttering something angry and heated, like a fever.

Rita led Startsov out of a thicket of blackthorn into a thin row of apple trees and their legs felt for the loose holes around the short trunks. Andrei lingered, still obedient to Rita's suggestive movements. She was touching him with almost the whole of her body, he could feel her hip quivering and her firm knee bending.

"Are you cold?"

"Yes."

She leaned against him, shoulder to shoulder, shuddered frequently and slowed her step.

Andrei listened to Rita's scattered words and for a long time didn't understand them. They came to him from afar, like the ring and splash of the dripping water chutes, and, like the dripping, they enveloped him softly and insinuatingly.

"Have you experienced it?" he suddenly heard.

"Me?"

"Yes, have you?"

"What?"

"When both feel the same thing, exactly the same, so that there's no hesitation, nothing, but only one . . . Do you know it?"

"Yes."

"Does that happen once in a lifetime?"

"What?"

"What are you always thinking about?" he heard again. "Why does fate always push me where I'm not looking for anything? Golosov gives me no peace. Is it always like that, eh? I don't understand anything. I only know that life is a tiny fragment. Very tiny. It's pitiful if it passes by, just like that. . . ."

Rita stumbled, fell, and dragged Andrei down after her to the ground. He wanted to lift her but she resisted him. He sat beside her.

Here the thickets of blackthorn began again, and its astringent smell was strong and suffocatingly thick. On the ground the cold was still more piercing; on the ground it was harder and more burning; on the ground the body's warmth was stronger and sweeter.

"Once in a lifetime. That's all I want, Andrei. . . . My breast is scorched through with this, look here."

She took his hand and violently thrust his bent fingers into her breast.

"Cold, cold," muttered Rita.

Andrei heard her teeth chattering, heard her shudder all over from the cold, heard a feverish mutter escape from her chattering teeth:

"I'm not hesitating. . . . Why should you . . . why, Andrei. . . ."

Then hair, astringent like the smell of blackthorn, covered his ears, neck and cheeks, a tremor bound his movements, the cold became unbearable, and another inaudible whisper, like Rita's muttering, broke through his teeth:

"Who's hesitating? Can one really when . . . So cold . . . the ground . . . Rita . . ."

He tore himself from his single uncommunicable thought, thrust it away from him, again seeing what was before him, close to him, together with him. Yes, and had there been any thought? Had there not swum before his lips a moist, soft, burning ring that had slipped away from him for a whole year—more than a year!—each very moment when he was about to put his dry, inflamed mouth to it? Awake and asleep that moist, soft ring had swung somewhere in space like a tiny, red target and now—even now, in the impenetrable darkness of the night—Andrei could make out its hot redness.

"Cold . . . Marie . . . a whole year . . . Rita!"

The ring floated closer and closer to the dry, inflamed mouth, spread out over the lips, choked the breath in the throat and, through the choking, there slipped out barely audible, meaningless but human words:

"O-oh . . . oh! Ah, you . . . you, you!"

And at that moment, at the other end of the orchard in the thickets of astringent blackthorn, sheltered by the unattainable blackness of the sky, Comrade Golosov stood with his face pointing upward to the stars. The stars poured cold silver down upon the earth—distinctly round and large. Golosov looked at them intently, as if they were reflecting events which had to be watched.

Suddenly he shuddered, took the Mauser from his pocket, aimed its long barrel at the brightest and largest star, gritted through his teeth:

"Ah, you . . . you, you!"

And together with the last "you" pressed the trigger.

The shot ripped the silence apart and rolled over the orchard.

"Guk-a-a-a!"

Golosov unhurriedly emptied the whole magazine at the stars. The Mauser worked perfectly.

The muzhiks thronged through the darkness thickly and confidently. The places were well known, every little bush was recognizable by touch.

In front of all of them Lependin jumped along in his basket, moving his arms softly and swiftly. When the trees, illuminated by the lights of the summer house, showed up red he turned his head to the muzhiks and asked:

"Shall we knock at the window or the door?"

"We'll see there."

They approached the house quietly and stopped among the raspberry bushes, opposite the windows.

A round, black head approached the orange glass. The muzhiks waited silently without stirring.

"There's one skinny one. One with glasses is sitting with a lady," said the head.

"Is the chairman there?" asked a thin voice from the bushes.

"There are two of the comrades here. And two ladies as well."

"The chairman—a short guy with a long mane—is he there?"

"The chairman must be, too. Knock," said Lependin.

A hooked hand showed up on the glass, the window tinkled three times. They waited.

"They can't hear us," said the head and turned toward the bushes.

"Perhaps we should come in the morning?"

"Why in the morning, it's okay, knock louder!" shouted Lependin.

The hand rose again to the glass, the window tinkled more alarmingly and immediately both head and arm shied away into the darkness.

In the room a man came up to the window, his golden spectacles flashing, threw open the window and peered into the night.

"Semyon, is that you?" he asked.

The muzhiks kept quiet.

"Startsov?" asked the man again and after waiting a little turned his back to the darkness.

"Semyon's probably playing the fool."

Then a timid coughing came from the bushes.

The man in the spectacles rushed to the windowsill and shouted:

"Who's there?"

"M-ha, m-ha . . . we, Comrade, so tha-at . . ."

"Who's 'we'?"

"The comrade peasants from Ruchi, citizens generally."

"What's the matter, Comrades?"

Lependin swayed toward the light and loudly clearing his throat, announced:

"We want the comrade chairman, we wish to inform the comrade chairman of the result of our meeting."

"Pokisen is talking to you, Comrades, the chairman. . . ."

He was interrupted out of the darkness:

"We kno-ow tha-at! Only we wish to talk to Chairman Golosov."

"Golosov isn't here at the moment, he went out."

A hollow laugh rolled through the bushes.

"Now you're speaking falsely, Comrade. They're in there together with you now. When they were coming here we saw them very well."

"What fools!" exclaimed Pokisen. "What, d'you think I'm going to lie to you? Golosov's gone out to the orchard. How can I get him for you?"

"Have it your way, of course, but . . ."

"The meeting took the final decision to . . ."

"What's that?" said Pokisen, thrusting himself through the window. "Can't see a damned thing. Are there many of you here?"

"Ee-enough!" drawled someone with satisfaction to the side.

Shchepov came up to the window and flung sharply into the darkness:

"Well, what's the matter?"

The bushes shook:

"Let Fyodor say it. . . ."

"Fyodor!"

"Tell them without beating around the bush to . . ."

"Fire away like just now. . . ."

"Comrades!" shouted Pokisen distinctly, as if at a meeting, and leaned out with his fingers resting on the window-sill. "Comrades, if you wish to speak with the committee chairman then come tomorrow morning. He's just gone out. We are staying here until tomorrow evening. But you can inform me of the decision of the meeting you mention, I'll pass it on to Comrade Golosov. Only at the moment it's night, things are dark, I can't even see who's talking to me. You'll do better to come tomorrow."

"Things are da-ark, right enough!" drawled someone to the side again.

The bushes began to shake again.

"Fyodor, explain it, so he doesn't get mixed up. . . ."

From somewhere down below, seemingly from underground, a bold voice rang out:

"As you, Comrade, have addressed us, we desire to put to you the situation of the peasantry of our area. It's well known the new law has abolished the assessment and various requisitions made from the citizens of the worker-peasant class. It's just this law what the comrades don't know, what they conceal and hide from publicity. So that at a meeting of the Sanshino *volost,* poor men and other peasants, have resolved to demand from Chairman Golosov proclamation of the law and that he abolish the assessment and also order the food patrols removed. Meanwhile . . ."

"Stop, Comrade, or whoever's there!" cried Pokisen. "Your business is serious, I see; it can't be worked out right away. I can tell you one thing. The law on corn assessment hasn't been revoked and at the present time can't be. The Soviet Worker-Peasant Authorities . . ."

Out of the darkness the rumble of many voices fell upon the window, pierced by sharp cries:

"We've he-eard that!"

"He came by sled!"

"Quit hiding the chairman!"

Pokisen cried at the top of his lungs:

"Have you gone crazy? You're being told in Russian: Golosov went out. What the hell are we going to gab in the dark for, when . . ."

"Whoa, who-a, Comrade!" howled Lependin. "Everyone here's in his right mind and senses. With the *mir** you must talk serious, the mir's no 'xecutive committee. You listen to what's what. Our area's not for corn, it's market garden work, orchards, too. We've got more'n enough trouble in our farming; poverty, only carrots and potatoes. Corn we never see ourselves. And then they demand corn from us.

*Archaic form of peasant co-operative in Russia.

What'll we do now? The land, it turns out, is free for the peasants, but in the meantime the peasant   "

Shchepov pushed Pokisen away from the window, caught hold of the window frame and shouted:

"Come now, boys, let's put off our talk till tomorrow."

A loud hubbub greeted him. He wanted to slam the window, but thick, strong fingers fastened upon the frame from both sides.

"What's this?" he cried in his sharp chiseled voice. "Coercion?"

Pokisen spoke inaudibly to his wife. She responded in Russian:

"I've locked up."

"So that's how they want it," yelled someone out of the darkness.

And immediately the bushes which had melted into the night stirred, moved toward the windows, and dozens of motionless eyes shone forth in the dim light falling into the darkness from the windows.

"The meeting said to demand the new law, for it's not to be hidden and, therefore, for the food patrols to be removed."

Little Otti began to cry in the back room, Pokisen's wife rushed to him. Klavdia Vasilyevna seized Shchepov by the elbow and muttered:

"Aleksei, the muzhiks . . . they'll . . ."

"Stop!" Shchepov turned around and indicated the sofa with a nod of his head.

Pokisen was listening to the crying of the child, his face became hard, he stared with dulled eyes at the open window, then firmly stepped forward.

"Citizen peasants! I appeal to you for the last time. I propose that you quickly disperse to your homes and come here tomorrow to discuss your questions with Comrade Golosov."

Out of the hubbub which leaped with new force toward the windows a penetrating voice emerged:

"We won't go till you proclaim the law!"

"We wo-o-on't go-o!"

Shchepov darted to a dark corner of the room, seized

the projector leaning against the wall, lifted it up to the window and began to mount the apparatus with its beam pointing outward into the garden.

"Quiet," he whispered to Pokisen.

The hubbub began to subside. More eyes seemed to shine in the darkness, they all froze on Shchepov's hands running over the apparatus. The distinctly metallic clicking of the film spools became audible. Shchepov's movements were concentrated and skillful.

Someone asked timidly from the garden:

"What's this you're getting going, Comrade?"

Shchepov dallied with his reply.

"This, boys, is a wireless telegraph. Have you heard of it? That's it. For communicating with town just in case."

"What d'you need it for, Comrade?"

"How shall I put it. . . ." said Shchepov, humming and hawing. "Maybe we could do with . . . Request a few soldiers . . . or something . . ."

The silence was suddenly shattered by laughter—pealing, loud, and dozens of eyes were lowered to the ground. Lependin was laughing, banging his wooden oarlocks and slapping peasants on the thighs with them:

"You ma-ake me la-augh, make me laugh, Comrade! What sort of telegraph is that? Why at the front they showed us live people out of a machine like that!"

"Pictures, eh?"

"Yes, that's what it is—pictures. Huh, the fool!"

Someone laughed, someone boomed:

"They want to scare us. . . ."

"They reckon by taking us in . . ."

Then the voices grew dimmer, died away, and a stubborn threat ascended to the window:

"All the same we won't let you out."

Little Otti, as if hearing this threat, cried out and broke into tears.

"Break it up, I say, d'you hear?"

Then a shout in reply:

"Well, maybe we'll put a light to the house, eh?"

Klavdia Vasilyevna screamed and grasped her face with her hands.

"Aleksei!"

"Shut up!"

"A-a-ah, so?! You would! howled Pokisen, thrusting himself out into the darkness.

And suddenly a sharp stroke sounded in the distance and the frost-contracted night was torn asunder by a loud groan:

"Guk-a-a-a!"

And after a second, another:

"Guk-a-a-a!"

And again—three, four . . . another, another, as if somewhere in the rear riflemen were advancing from the town.

The barely illuminated bushes jiggled, something black fled on both sides from the window, then everything ceased.

"Guk-a-a-a!"

Pokisen listened to the quiet crying of little Otti, wiped his forehead and said:

"Good boy, Semyon, just in time!"

He adjusted his spectacles, aimed them at Shchepov and smiled.

"M-yes . . . Maybe we don't have a revolution yet. But, as they say here, there's a wee bit of a counter-revolution."

THE END OF LEPENDIN

They rode into the town at dead of night—like immigrants —with their household goods in carts, with a crying baby, tired by the jolting and the darkness. The house had been abandoned unlocked.

Golosov escorted the Pokisen family, rode to the fire station, handed over his horse and went home. In the hall, when Nanny let him in, he asked as always:

"Is there anything?"

"A telegram, I believe," mumbled the old woman.

In the large room furnished with merchant's furniture a lamp was always burning and its light timidly melted away into the corners as from an ikon-lamp.

Opening the telegram, Golosov slid his eyes over the address:

> SPECIAL SEMIDOL TO CHAIRMAN OF EXECUTIVE COMMITTEE COPY TO CHAIRMAN OF SPECIAL DEPARTMENT COPY TO MILITARY COMMISSAR.

He raised the pencil-covered blank to the light.

> UNVERIFIED INFORMATION FROM REGION OF VILLAGE PICHEUR SEMIDOL DISTRICT MOVING IN DIRECTION OF SEMIDOL BAND OF GERMAN CZECHOSLOVAK PRISONERS JOINED BY KULAK ELEMENT OF MORDVINIAN POPULATION ALSO ARMED DESERTERS PERIOD BAND IS LED BY GERMAN OFFICER AGITATING FOR MORDVINIANS TO LEAVE SOVIET FEDERATION PERIOD AGITATION MAY TAKE ROOT AMONG ELEMENTS WITH LITTLE CLASS CONSCIOUSNESS IN CONNECTION WITH KULAK DISCONTENT WITH ASSESSMENT PERIOD PRESCRIBE FIRST FORMATION OF REVOLUTIONARY COMMISSION OF THREE SECOND IMMEDIATE CLARIFICATION OF SITUATION ON SPOT THIRD ADOPTION OF REVOLUTIONARY MILITARY MEASURES FOR ESSENTIAL LIQUIDATION OF BAND FOURTH BEFORE ISSUING OF ORDERS COMMUNICATION OF COMMISSION'S ACTIONS BY TELEGRAPH EVERY TWO HOURS PERIOD POSSIBLE REBELLION MUST BE RADICALLY CRUSHED BY SEMIDOL FORCES UNDER PERSONAL RESPONSIBILITY OF MEMBERS OF COMMISSION PERIOD CHAIRMAN PROVINCIAL EXECUTIVE COMMITTEE.

Golosov stood motionless.

The room remained hushed, furnished in the old style by Nanny who had lived half her life in it. Here everything was discreet and the obstinacy with which the flower-pots, the furniture covers and the stucco cupids on the walls held on was extraordinary even for Semidol.

"So!" said Golosov and straightened his shirt.

He threw the telegram on the table, walked down the dark corridor with a heavier step, felt for the narrow door of the cubbyhole at the very end and asked:

"Nanny, are you asleep?"

"What d'you want?"

"Go get the compositor."

"And what else!"

"Well, to the printing works, for this, what's his name? . . ."

"Yes, I know him! What's got into your head at this time of night?"

"Go right away."

"There's no quiet in you, the Lord have mercy!"

Golosov threateningly mumbled something unintelligible and angry, but behind the threat Nanny detected the familiar, awkward, slightly shamefaced chuckle and asked, reconciled:

"Somebody'll lock the door after me?"

"Okay!"

Golosov lit the table lamp, moved the paper cut into strips closer to him, perched sideways at the table, lit a cigarette and began to write. Straight, clinging locks of hair hung down over his eyes like a maple leaf. His hand ran over the paper swiftly, creeping upward at the ends of the lines as if trying to string all the lines on the upper corner of the strip. He chewed the butt of his cigarette, spat wet scraps of paper upon the table and then knocked them from the table to the floor with jerks of his hands.

After quarter of an hour Pokisen and the military commissar came into the room.

Golosov darted a glance at them and his hand ran quicker still to the upper corner of the strip.

"Did you get it?" asked Pokisen.

"Yes. I'm finishing now."

"What's that?"

"For the peasants."

"Right," said the military commissar, puffing. He was ponderous and broad-backed and his red face was plastered with dark freckles, like raisins on an Easter cake.

Golosov threw down his pencil, moved the line-covered strips of paper away from him and said:

"Finished. Everything clear, Comrades?"

"Can't understand how the provincial committee found

out about this before we did. It's embarrassing!" said the military commissar.

"After what happened at the house today . . ." began Pokisen.

"I declare the meeting of the revolutionary commission open," interrupted Golosov in an odd tone and touched his upper lip. "I request Comrade Pokisen to act as secretary. I propose the following agenda: the reply to the provincial executive committee, the organization of reconnaissance and the question of the garrison's fighting fitness, the question of using the prisoners-of-war detained in the camp, then of party mobilization, or proclamations, then of everything that becomes clear during the resolution of these questions. Adopted?"

"Concerning the prisoners, that's a good idea of yours, only that's later, first the Party men," announced the military commissar.

"Agreed. Adopted? First question. I propose the following text: Revolutionary commission organized, will telegraph measures taken in an hour. Agreed?"

"I brought a messenger, he's out in the hall."

"What's that for?" asked Golosov.

"It's because a telegram won't fly through the air to the post office, and communication in general," replied the military commissar, and puffed so much that the papers on the table flew apart.

He went out and returned with the messenger.

"Next," said Golosov when he had handed the Red soldier the telegram. "I propose we outline a plan of military action for the next twenty-four hours and give our opinion on Semidol's military resources in general."

The military commissar was all puffed up, the dense redness of his face blended with his freckles in a solid dark patch and he was constricted by a wheeze as if he had gone up a nine-story staircase in one breath.

"Our resources are known, of course, Comrades. . . . A composite regiment . . . seven hundred men . . . a garrison company . . . The regiment can muster a hundred and fifty bayonets. . . . However . . . ammunition . . .

and boots . . . we don't have. . . . Ye-es . . . And furthermore training . . . training has only just begun. . . ."

"Concretely, Comrade, what can you put out today at seven a.m.?"

"You're asking me?"

"Yes, you."

"Who the hell are you to put on airs? At seven a.m. . . . At seven a.m. half the company from the garrison . . . ready to march . . . by midday a detachment from the composite . . . The other half-company is on duty in the town. . . . I propose generally that we declare . . . martial law. . . ."

"Is the military commissar's proposal adopted? Next . . ."

An hour later the room was closed, muffled voices sounded in the corridor, through the window horses' hooves beat the dusty mattress of the streets, while in the yard a pulley screeched and a loose gate slammed.

Nanny brought in a polished samovar and thick painted cups.

The members of the revolutionary commission were sitting at their former places around the table, heads close together.

The military commissar said noisily, panting:

"U-understand . . . Comrades. . . . The park . . . is not within the jurisdiction of the military commissar! The park . . . placed under . . ."

"Nonsense!" Golosov waved it away.

"Responsibility to the center," gasped the military commissar.

"You mustn't forget your other responsibility. Nonsense! Once it's expedient, then it's possible. I insist."

"But then the guarantees!"

"What guarantees? He doesn't have anything."

"Then hostages."

"Again twenty-five! I'm telling you Shchepov has nothing and no one. What can you take from him? We must risk it."

"Risk Shchepov. . . . Okay . . . but the . . . a . . . apparatus . . . how can we risk the a . . . apparatus?"

Pokisen declared firmly:

"I have confidence in Shchepov."

"Nonsense!" shouted Golosov. "I have confidence in none of the specialists. But we have the power and he's no fool."

Then the military commissar suddenly remembered something and, shuddering all over as he caught in some air, gasped:

"Let me . . . a-a that . . . a . . . actress . . . what's her . . . who's with Shchepov . . ."

"Well?"

"His mistress . . ."

Pokisen burst out laughing:

"Then . . . then, if we needed guarantees from Semyon we'd have to take Rita as his mistress—ha-ha! Rita Tveretskaya."

Golosov jumped up, his chair tumbled over with a bang, he fixed his inflamed eyes on Pokisen.

"Quit joking! We could take her if we needed guarantees from Andrei Startsov."

He lifted his chair, sat down and uttered distinctly in a cold obstinate voice:

"I accept the military commissar's proposal. Shchepov is a specialist. With regard to him it's a correct measure. Comrade Pokisen, write an order for the immediate arrest of Klavdia Vasilyevna. The military commissar is charged with setting the time for Shchepov's dispatch and defining the task of aerial reconnaissance. . . ."

And another hour later, when by now the gate in the yard never ceased to screech and the corridor was filled with ceaseless talking, the chairman of the German Soviet of Soldiers' Deputies in Semidol, Kurt Wahn, made a fourth sitting at the table in the room of the former merchant's house.

They listened to Kurt patiently, waiting long for him to select and pronounce the Russian words. Frowning, he translated in his mind from the German and a thick vein swelled up on his forehead.

"I don't hold . . . don't consider . . . rational . . . make intelligence . . . with German prisoner. . . . For

prisoner I cannot . . . be guaranteer . . . I hold possible
. . . recruit company volunteer . . . company volunteer,
if executive committee will supply weapons. . . . After organize today . . . meeting in camp . . . But talk meeting
I shall not. . . . Talk meeting will Andrei Startsov . . .
that . . . rational. . . ."

"Nonsense!" exclaimed Golosov. "Startsov's a foot-
dragger."

"What's a foot-dragger?"

"Well—a milksop, a nincompoop—an intellectual in general."

Kurt shook his head.

"You don't know what in camp . . . mood in camp.
. . . I find Russian must speak, not German. . . . Andrei
Startsov."

"Are you sure his speech will be of any use to us?"

"I am friend Andrei Startsov. I can . . . be guaranteer
for him. . . ."

Golosov extended his hand to Kurt:

"And so you give your word to help us?"

"I Bolshevik," replied Kurt and stood up.

The half-company from the garrison marched out of
Semidol at seven-thirty a.m. It was accompanied by a
dense sound of ringing bells, because it was Sunday and
Semidol—as in the Middle Ages—was beginning its festival
of prayer.

At seven-thirty a.m. the gaudily dressed women made
their way out of the Ruchi yards, between the wattle and
stake fences and up to the high road. One or two people
went to Mass with horses, cramming their children and
young wives with infants still at the breast into their carts.
Clouds of dust whirled over the highway, the spots of sara-
fans and shirts glowed with many colors. But half way to
Sanshino, when the turquoise cupola of the belfry appeared from behind a bare hill, the Ruchi pilgrims dawdled.
Toward them along the highway trotted a detachment of
armed horsemen. Rifles could be seen bouncing up and
down on their backs. The cart traveling in front of the Ruchi
people stopped, carefully crawled off the highway into a

field, then resolutely turned back. Within two or three minutes all the carts had gone back to Ruchi, rattling and raising clouds of dust. The peasants whipped their mares with all their might. Only the fearless women without responsibilities continued their journey toward the turquoise belfry cupola in a few flashily dressed groups. Someone among the cowardly muzhiks—perhaps in the first cart to come upon the detachment—let out a term not used since olden times:

"Avengers!"

And it spun round in the clouds of dust, accumulating anxiety, distress, terror.

It occurred to someone in Ruchi to ask:

"Where did avengers come from in Sanshino?"

But terror would not yield:

"Are they fools enough, d'you think, to come from Semidol? They went round."

"They went round!"

"They went round!"

"Avengers!"

Starye Ruchi went into hiding. The small boys were chased into the huts; doors and shutters were slammed shut.

The mounted detachment entered Ruchi at a walk and stopped on the highway in the middle of the village. The horsemen were in various dress—in what they had been able to find, and immediately reminded one of both muzhiks and soldiers, exactly like the Red soldiers of the composite regiment, whom the Ruchi people had seen in Semidol. Hastily they gathered around their commander, who looked like an officer but who was in an unprecedented, improvised uniform. He was a long time explaining something to them, pointing with his hand to paths going away from the high road into the orchards, then they again jumped on their horses, split up into pairs and were swallowed up by the luxuriant undergrowth of the orchards.

The commander moved at a walk along the highway toward Semidol, accompanied by a handful of soldiers.

And suddenly a shot cracked somewhere deep within the orchards.

Instantly it was answered by another and the sharp

rapid crackle of rifle fire scattered over the whole district, getting caught up in the undergrowth. The alarmed horses, unaccustomed to firing, carried their riders blindly on, trampling fences under foot and leaping over ditches. It was impossible to tell where the firing was coming from and the horsemen replied to it senselessly, into the air, into the thickets of blackthorn and cherry trees.

Gathering on the high road they fired several volleys into the orchards and dashed back to Sanshino in a straggling, disorderly cavalcade.

The half-company from the Semidol garrison, without replying to the volleys, went away from Starye Ruchi in the direction of the town and occupied a position on sloping hills facing the Ruchi orchards.

Starye Ruchi fell silent and lay without breathing until the sun had climbed to noon. By this time the sky had grown clear and the autumn day was asserting itself after a hard morning frost. And then into the quiet and clearness of noon there burst the wild drumming of hooves and mortal alarm swept through the village from hut to hut, from door to door and over the tangled tracks and paths.

Some frightened peasants ran up to the shrinking huts, hammered their fists on the doors and shutters, shouted some terrified words and ran farther on. Women raised piercing wails within the huts which were taken up by the supporting voices of the children; outside, sharp bustling unmarried women alternately appeared and disappeared. One by one, bending low to the ground, holding on to the wattle fences and bushes, the muzhiks made their way through the village.

The assembly gathered outside Ruchi on a sparsely covered place where isolated crabapple trees from abandoned orchards stuck up, and the iron-like strands of dried-up gooseberry bushes with wicked thorns crept through the hollows.

On a rise to one side of the Sanshino road, which was strewn with plantains, a group of people hurried along dressed in dun-colored Mordvinian caftans. Among the group a man in Mordvinian festive apparel sat on a fallen apple tree—not like a Mordvinian in appearance, with light eyes and clean shaven. Beside him swayed the gray faded tunic of a soldier. Saddled horses were being held by the bridle a short way off.

The assembly of Ruchi muzhiks surrounded and enclosed the horsemen in a ring not far from the rise where the man attired as a Mordvinian had settled himself. The horsemen were commanded by the officer in the unprecedented uniform.

"Who will speak for the assembly?" bellowed a mustachioed soldier, setting his arms akimbo and nudging his curved saber.

"Step forward, lively!"

An undersized, bearded peasant with small eyes hidden by their brows crept uncertainly out of the crowd of muzhiks clustering closely in a group. The soldier advanced upon him.

"Re-sist-ance?"

The bearded peasant shifted from one foot to another and blinked his small eyes.

"Re-sist-ance?"

The soldier half raised his saber, the chain to his sword belt clinked threateningly against the iron scabbard.

"With the Bol-she-viks?"

The bearded peasant swayed toward the soldier and joined in joyfully in a thin voice:

"Always, Comrade, with the Bolsheviks, invariably, with us that's . . ."

"E-eh, invariably?"

"Invariably, Comrade, as one man—the whole village is with the Bolshies. . . ."

Then the soldier raised his saber, shook it over the bearded peasant's head and howled:

"Give us the instigator! Who's the instigator? Are you the instigator? Talk—you!"

"Dear Comrade, let me say a word about how this business here . . ."

"E-eh, Com-rade?"

From the roadway, nimbly swinging his trunk forward on his swift, strong arms, Lependin came rolling toward the

assembly. He whisked between the legs of the horses surrounding the muzhiks and bounced up to the bearded
peasant.

The mustachioed soldier, going purple and stretching out
his neck, advanced on the crowd.

"Hide the instigator? Resistance?"

Suddenly the muzhiks became agitated, began to cough,
several hands waved in the direction of the soldier, one or
two men took off their caps and rammed them on again.

"Why are you dreaming? Have you gone dumb?"
shouted the soldier.

Then out of dozens of throats at once the clumsy word
tumbled over the soldier:

"Lependin . . ."

"Lependin all . . ."

"Fyodor, he'll explain, of course, how . . ."

"Lependin . . ."

The soldier grew quiet and asked:

"Which?"

Heads and hands pointed at Lependin. The latter's bulging eyes jumped from the soldier to the crowd. The muzhiks
would not look at him and their faces appeared the same
to him, like planed boards.

The soldier's lower jaw dropped and hung down, he
looked dumfoundedly at the human stump sticking up out
of the ground.

Greenish-yellow blotches came out on Lependin's cheeks
through his sunburn, his face turned spotty and his head
began to look more like a melon than ever.

"Ekh!" he groaned, looking despairingly at the muzhiks
a second time.

Then he shook his head and turned to the soldier:

"Well, Comrade, here's how it was. How could we— Take
a look for yourself. . . ."

But from his first word the soldier came to himself. He
pushed Lependin in the chest with his foot and the latter
tumbled over on the ground like a pail with a rounded bottom.

"Wait, said the officer in the unprecedented uniform who
had been quiet until then. He turned his horse and galloped

toward the rise where the man attired as a Mordvinian was sitting on a fallen apple tree. The man rose to meet him, went up to the horse, stood a while by the stirrup and returned to the fallen tree. The officer galloped up to the assembly.

"Bring him!" he said to the mustachioed soldier.

Lependin was still lying like an upturned pail. The soldier moved toward him and struck him with his saber. He rolled over from his back onto his stomach, bent his arms at the elbow, dug his oarlocks into the ground, raised himself and sat.

"Crawl, scum!" shouted the soldier.

Lependin bent down and spread his arms. But before swinging forward he again turned toward the muzhiks and again their faces appeared to him like planed boards.

"Get moving!"

On the rise Lependin sat down before the clean-shaven man with the light eyes, attired as a Mordvinian. He saw the man's slightly open mouth move restlessly, heard his smooth voice, but he could make out neither his words nor the words of some other men in dun-colored caftans, who were shouting at him and demanding answers. He only smiled guiltily and shifted his oarlocks about on the ground, trying to sit more comfortably.

The soldier in the gray faded tunic and the mustachioed man who had urged Lependin on while he made his way up to the hillock had quickly gone to one side. Lependin was still being shouted at, the din of voices was as before unintelligible and Lependin continued to smile agreeably and guiltily when the soldiers returned. The men in caftans made way for them and behind the men Lependin made out a rope hanging from the branch of a lone, crooked apple tree. The man attired as a Mordvinian rose hastily from the fallen tree, lifted his hand level with his shoulder, pointed to the apple tree with extended finger and shouted a word.

Then Lependin reeled and began to howl:

"Bro-thers! It's the Ge-ermans! Bro-the-ers!"

He fell on his side and rolled downhill toward the muzhiks.

But they stopped him with their feet and, seizing him by the arms, dragged him to the apple tree.

Then he began to strike with his oarlocks at the arms and knees of the men who were dragging him. They knocked the oarlocks away from him with their scabbards. He began to bite and, in despair, to scream. But the men dragged him without stopping, pulling him out of gooseberry bushes by force when the iron thorns stuck into his clothing and body.

"Bro-the-ers!"

The basket which had served as a strong convenient shoe for Lependin was torn off his short stumps and dragged along on its strap behind the trunk, leaving tatters of rags behind on the bushes.

"Brothe-e-ers!"

Lependin was hauled up to the apple tree, the rope was moved closer to the tree trunk so that the branch would not break with the weight and for a minute it was impossible to see what the men were doing bending over beneath the branch.

"Bro-the . . ."

Then the clumsy stump began to swing over their heads and the long arms stuck to it, after jerking once or twice to the side, suddenly straightened out alongside the trunk of the body and clenched into fists as if Lependin wanted to thrust his arms into the ground for the last time.

The man attired as a Mordvinian slowly threatened with his finger, first the hanged man and then the assembly, standing silently ringed by the mounted detachment at the bottom of the hillock.

Then someone in the crowd of muzhiks sighed barely audibly:

"May the Lord take him. . . . But all the same Fyodor was a cripple. . . ."

"Ekh, my boy! What a pile of fruit we have! Our cherries come in swarms! There are plums there, blackthorn—the pigs can't eat 'em all! And our beds, our beds, my boy, are all red with strawberries, and the strawberries—like that, the size of your fist! Victorias are there, early ripeners

—ee-ee-ee-ee! And these same apples we knock back all winter—and soak, and salt, and dry, can't get rid of 'em nohow, there's so many! Our market . . ."

Yes, yes, Lependin. To this day there is all that plenty in Starye Ruchi. . . .

The worst of all is to gaze at someone's face and see the eyes of a stranger. The worst of all is to feel suddenly that the crowd consists of a multitude of dissimilar men and that each man is an implacable enemy to strange ideas and hostile to strange words. Then—ignominy.

One must look over the heads, listen only to one's own words and not admire them, but throw them out fiercely so that they do not interfere with one's thought. Then—victory.

Just as now, alone, in a closed room—victory! Andrei had sought out all the words he needed to induce the exhausted soldiers to take up arms again. Andrei had constructed a speech. He had studied it. He had weighed the strength of every pause. He knew where and how to raise his hand, where to stop and where to give free reign to uncontrollable words. Andrei was ready.

But in the board hut of the camp there was not a crowd but a multitude of men. Each had his own eyes and over the eyes gloomily hung faded, bullet-holed, peakless caps. The eyes were suspicious, the eyes were tired and empty. What lurked behind this emptiness? The cold gloom of dugouts and the sweetish coal-gas of hospitals, white bones wrenched out of plowed flesh, blood dripping from the points of barbed wire and the musty stagnant dampness of the trenches. They had seen everything, they knew everything, they needed nothing; it was empty, it was infinitely empty for them, this world. The world of dugouts, trenches and hospitals had not yet invented words which could fill the emptiness of such eyes, and nothing in this world would remove the immobility from these faces, weather-beaten by a blood-stained wind.

They had gathered here in the low, boarded hut—hardened faces ground fine on the lathe of war. Hundreds of pipes of various styles were thrust into their clenched mouths and yellowish, gray, blue curls were breaking away from the faces and thickening the smoke screen above the peakless caps. The screen had been gathered from the scent of smoldering cherry leaves and it seemed as if the orchards were being set on fire somewhere nearby.

The prisoners puffed at their pipes and lazily stepped aside in front of Andrei. He was hurrying to get to the bench from which Kurt had announced to the hut that a Russian would speak.

A Russian will speak? Isn't it all the same? Let him. He'll chatter about the revolution for sure and about the brotherhood of peoples. The hell with brotherhood! They can't exterminate the typhus bugs and for six months they've been promising every day to send us home. However, let him. We can listen. Russians sometimes talk such nonsense that it's funny. And it's not often we get to laugh, we ought to appreciate it. Let him.

These words were on the mind of a one-eyed soldier standing directly opposite Andrei. His face was bronzed and the heavy lid of his good eye first dropped and then hastily flew up again, as if it wanted to wink and each time changed its mind.

If only one does not forget the beginning of one's speech, Andrei! If only one does not see the stranger's eye, which is about to wink to remind one of what is behind its emptiness—dugouts and hospitals, trenches and barbed wire. But what is behind this trembling fear in Andrei's eyes? He is going to summon to war? But has he seen even one dugout? Has he lain in a hospital cot with a smashed knee? Has he slept even a single night in a trench? Perhaps he cut barriers with scissors when lead was being poured over them? *He* will summon to war?

And now an encouraging voice carried through the quieting hut beneath the smoke screen smelling of burning leaves.

"Quiet, you poor devils! We can't hear what the Russian is saying."

It seems the soldiers are laughing? What's this? Someone pulls at Andrei's leg. Has he been up long on that bench? How did that well studied speech begin? Did the bronze-faced soldier seem to wink his empty eye? What's that he's chewing? A cookie or a pastry? An Austrian pastry.

"An Austrian pastry," said Andrei softly.

"Very tasty!" responded some soldier.

And again laughter. It's not often we get to laugh, we ought to appreciate it.

"An Austrian pastry," said Andrei more loudly.

Kurt said something briefly in a constrained voice. Andrei gulped in a chestful of smoke: the screen was floating level with his head; standing on the bench he propped it up as a mountain-top the clouds.

"Recently, Comrades, you were given packages which had accumulated at the soviet because it had been impossible to find the prisoners to whom they were sent. Most of such parcels came from Austria. I recalled this just now because one comrade here is chewing at an Austrian pastry. The Austrians are great masters at making pastries."

"I dare say we in Saxony . . ." remarked some soldier.

"Shut your mouth, you old coffee grounds!" another advised him.

"I have recalled the story of one Austrian pastry and I want to tell it to you. Several prisoners were working in the soviet here. During their break they made themselves some coffee. From the store they were handed a package addressed to some Schmidt or other. They shared it among themselves. And then one prisoner got so hard a pastry that he almost broke his teeth on it. The pastry crumbled but it was impossible for the soldier to bite through it. Then he soaked it in his coffee and discovered in the pastry a baked-in circle made of two pieces of tin, in the shape of a medallion. The soldier opened the medallion with a knife and in it he found a letter. I have preserved this letter. Here it is as it was in the tin medallion, which was slightly rusty. I'll read you the letter. Here.

"Dear Gustav,

"It's six months now since I had any news from you and Lizbeth says that it might be you are no longer alive. But I don't want to believe that. Gustav, you know that without you I have nothing to live for. Last

week Heinrich Meinert returned from being a prisoner, his arm was cut off at the shoulder and he said that it's not so bad in Siberia, that it's even very hot in summer and that there's still a lot of grain in Russia. He says it's good that you landed in Russia since being a prisoner will save you for us while it would have ended much worse for you at the front. I only pray to God for the war to end soon because it's gotten difficult. Dear Gustav. I think all the time how you'll find our village when you come back. The miller Thomas's eldest son has been killed, while the youngest came home blind, and he's stopped working so that we go to Lückendorff now to grind. Thank God we have to do that very rarely now, but then our Gray died just before Easter and now for every little thing we have to hire a horse. Because of Gray we didn't sow this spring and also because Father couldn't get up from his bed. Today is Whit Monday and yesterday at Whitsun Mass Auntie Anna lost her mind. Before that her picture was printed in the newspaper on account of her sixth son Hans also being killed at the front, like the other five, and she only had six, about which I wrote you twice, I don't know whether you received it. It happened just when the vicar was saying that Auntie Anna had given up on the altar of the fatherland everything that God had given her and the whole village was crying. Forgive me, dear Gustav, I was also crying for you and your dearly beloved brother August, who I wrote you about that he's wounded in the chest, and for father because he didn't live to see you come back. Lizbeth says . . ."

But at this point in the reading a jarring voice burst through the hut's dumbness to Andrei:

"That means they've buried father?"

Andrei fell silent.

"Maybe August's also dead?" jarred the voice sharper and higher.

Someone's hand with long unbent fingers reached out over the prisoners' heads toward Andrei.

"Give the letter here! Why, it's written by Elsa!"

"It's written by Elsa," said Andrei. "Look, here it's signed *Elsa.*"

Puffs of pipe smoke streamed up still thicker and faster from the caps to the screen under the roof. The prisoners pressed toward the bench, suddenly growing into a faceless, expectant crowd.

And then something cold blazed down Andrei's back—from head to foot—and he remembered his studied speech, remembered it in a new way, as it had never occurred to him before. And, not seeing the faces, nor the emptiness behind the countless eyes, nor the smoke screen, nor the barrack-room, but only bathing in the inexplicable cold blazing from somewhere, Andrei, with fierce hatred for the words interfering with his thought, shouted over the heads in bullet-holed caps, shouted about what had to be done to prevent mislaid letters from chasing vainly after the Schmidts mislaid about the world. . . .

Later Andrei and Kurt were standing in the yard of the barrack-room in the noiseless dusk, waiting for the prisoners' reply. And when it was quite dark the barrack-room door opened. A soldier came up to Andrei and puffed cherry leaf tobacco at him. The pipe illuminated his bronze-faced one-eyed head. He said shortly:

"You may inform your soviet the prisoners have decided to support the Bolsheviks."

FOR THE FIRST TIME IN LIFE

The samovar never left the table. Its chimney was thrust into the fireplace by means of a long joint, a basket of coal stood beside crockery, which was sticky and soiled by dirty fingers. The tea was being brewed alternately in two tavern teapots and they drank it thick and black as iodine. The second night without sleep or rest was coming to an end.

Golosov's eyelids were puffed up, his pupils had widened like a cat's, but they were dim and his glance was inattentive and sluggish. He was holding his head with his hands, his elbows stuck on the table, and he stared dully at Pokisen.

"I'll go!" he said hoarsely.

Pokisen was pale, the blue veins on his temples throbbed alarmingly, he was making an effort to speak calmly.

"You have the town and district round your neck. The military commissar understands nothing about this business. The newspaper is on you, everyone's on you. I'll go."

"No, me."

"I know you're a donkey. At ordinary times it's a good quality. Now we need calculation. I'll go."

"We'll see about that."

"We'll see!"

"I'll go."

"No, me."

A dull gaze moved close to the gold spectacles with the thick lens. Through the thick lens white eyes grew cold. The faces came together slowly and rigidly, the faces were obstinate and frowning, the faces were hard as stone.

"Me!"

"No, me!"

"What are you . . . like a couple of rams?" sniffed the military commissar, tumbling into the room.

As before, he was puffing, panting and shining with sweat, and he spoke in gasps, taking a long while to catch air with his mouth. He had grown tired once and for all in life and no new fatigue, nor work, nor sleepless nights could change his look.

"In an hour the detachment will be ready to march," he said, gulping down some tea. "The composite company is waiting for it in Starye Ruchi. Objective—to overcome San-shino by ten a.m."

He took a mouthful of tea and turned round.

Golosov and Pokisen were not moving. Their flushed foreheads were almost touching one another, their lips twitched soundlessly, the yellow spot of the lamp froze in their bulging eyes.

"H-huh, h-hell! What's the matter with you?" puffed the military commissar.

Then Golosov and Pokisen dashed toward him and howled, vying with one another:

"Din it into him, please, that my presence in town is quite unnecessary!"

"Rubbish, nonsense! To abandon the Special Department at a time like this . . ."

"Wait!"

"If it were a question of . . ."

"Stop! I'm saying that . . ."

The military commissar waved his hands.

"Enough! I understand, I understand!"

He went to one side, sat in an armchair and drew a cigarette case from his pocket.

"Before bothering myself with your squabbles," he said, sniffing and blowing through his cigarette, "I, Comrades, must pass on to you the resolution. After my report the committee nominated Comrade Pokisen as commissar of the detachment. . . ."

Golosov jumped away toward the window and stood with his back to the military commissar. Pokisen adjusted his spectacles.

"You say the detachment leaves in an hour?"

"To hell with you!" barked Golosov and jerked toward the exit. "I'll be in the printing room."

Banging his heels into the resonant floor he struck the door-handle with all his might and flung the door open. Then he stopped for a second, turned back abruptly and went up to Pokisen.

"Good luck, Pokisen," he said.

"Good-by, Semyon."

Twice they shook each other's hand briefly and Golosov flew out of the room.

In the hall he collided with Nanny. She was walking with a candle and its restless light fluttered over her dark wrinkled cheeks. She held Golosov by the sleeve and asked in a senile whisper:

"Is the samovar boiling?"

"Why?"

"I was thinking, will you return soon, shall I warm it up or isn't it necessary?"

"Okay!" Golosov waved it away.

Nanny hastily darted to his side and, like an old conspiratress admitted to all secrets, asked sternly:

"You're managing, I hope?"

Then a smile fluttered warmly over Golosov's face and he hid it behind his palm with his customary bashful movement.

"We'll get by, Nanny," he said and dashed out into the yard.

At dawn in the printing room, filled with smoke from the lamps, Golosov was reading the last of the galley proofs of the Revolutionary Commission's appeal "to the workers, peasants and all honest citizens of Semidol."

The hair hanging down from his forehead fell more and more often upon the paper. The pencil trembled on the crooked lines of thick kerosene-scented print. The last words of the appeal were set up as follows:

> Long live the victory of the workers
> and peasants in the whole world!

Golosov aimed his blunted pencil at the letter "v," but his long straight locks suddenly concealed the confused lines and his head fell on his arm. Golosov muttered something and drooped over the table.

The compositor carefully pulled the print from under the motionless, shaggy head of the executive committee chairman.

On the third day of the alarm, on a Monday, in the rainy dusk, pilot Shchepov returned to Semidol with his observer. They came on foot, wet and bedraggled.

"Where's the 'Newport'?" said the military commissar tensely as soon as they appeared in the editorial office.

Shchepov fell into a chair and began to unlace his boots.

"I told you it was no good undertaking a reconnaissance without a second test flight. That's an old heap. . . ."

"The 'Newport,' the 'Newport'!" gasped the military commissar. "Did you burn it?"

"Didn't think of it."

"You've gone out of your mind, the hell with . . ."

"Take a report."

"But tell me, what the hell . . ."

Then the observer, after adjusting a dirty bandage on his right arm, took from an inside pocket with his left a sketch of the area and laid it on the table. The military commissar, puffing and panting, leaned over the crumpled paper.

Reconnaissance indicated a concentration of the enemy in the region of the village of Sanshino in an area free of trees. The enemy's forces consisted of small foot detachments whose number did not exceed three to four companies. Advance posts in the shape of a broken chain of snipers were sent out along the high road to the Ruchi orchards. Reconnaissance was unable to establish the disposition of units in the region of Starye Ruchi. According to the conjectures of the observer the orchards were free of the enemy, since Sanshino lay on a rise commanding the area. The location of the enemy's transport had been established immediately behind this rise. The enemy had no communication with the far rear and no movements whatsoever were noted over a stretch of ten to twelve miles along the high road behind Sanshino or the country roads running into it. The enemy had no artillery at his disposal and the whole of his transport consisted of food carts. The enemy's flanks were not covered. Visibility for the flight was favorable, observation was carried out from a height of four hundred meters and referred to Sunday around two p.m.

"It has no value at all to us now," said Golosov.

The military commissar puffed.

"You, Comrade, are making all sorts of conjectures here about Ruchi. That's not your business. For the rest, the report does not contradict the facts received through other channels. Well, and what next?"

"The pilot will make his report to you."

"Is that all?" exclaimed Golosov.

"Well, not quite," said Shchepov, undoing his leather belt and tunic.

He dragged out from under his shirt some sheets of paper folded into four, threw them on the table but immediately clapped his hand over them.

"Stop, Comrades, a minute's patience. Having investigated the dispositions of the enemy, the observer signaled me to go to a height of eight hundred meters and keep a course along the high road. At approximately the twentieth kilometer there was an explosion in the engine. I switched off the gas and began to glide. After a minute I tried to switch on the gas and start up. Four explosions, one after another. I switched off the gas and began to come down, heading to the right of the high road. I glided down into a clearing hidden from the road by a grove of young oak trees. I put the engine into reverse, checking compression. In two cylinders the inlet valves were shot to hell. The trouble was that the test flight had established just . . ."

Golosov covered his face with his hands and burst into laughter. He was convulsed with laughter, as from attacks of unbearable pain, and his clinging, noodle-like locks shook and slapped against his hands.

Shchepov straightened up and shouted:

"What the hell, Semyon? I'm talking of a serious matter. . . ."

"Serious matter . . . ho-ho . . . of a serious matter which besides you no one for a hundred miles around has any idea about! There must be clarity in a smash-up? Eh? Ho-ho!"

"And the 'Newport,' what happened to the 'Newport'?" worried the military commissar again.

"With such an attitude, Comrade, I can't . . ."

"Now don't get angry, Shchepov," sighed the military commissar as if exhausted.

Shchepov muttered:

"A farce! God knows what he's thought up for Klavdia Vasilyevna, now. . . ."

"Ho-ho! Fool! Speak plainly!"

"In a word . . . well, in a word I couldn't really suck spare valves out of my finger! I took out of the engine . . .

well, hell, a part without which it isn't an engine. . . .
In a word we left the plane at our point of landing."

"So that the enemy would burn it?"

"Maybe he won't burn it since there's no enemy at all
there. And if we had burned it, then we . . ."

"Go on, go on!"

"We went by a roundabout way through the forest to
Lebezhaika. The band had spent Saturday night there,
requisitioned horses and gone on to Sanshino. The muzhiks
were hiding in their huts. The *volost* executive committee
was closed and on its doors was a signed paper. . . . Here
it is, look."

Shchepov unfolded the sheet of paper.

The proclamation was handwritten with bad, probably
home-made ink:

Russian peasants!

*The Mordvinian people, which has languished for
centuries under the oppression of tsarist satraps, has
risen for its independence and freedom. The Russian
Revolution which proclaimed the right of self-determi-
nation for oppressed peoples has proved to be a trap
for trustful, simple people. Since the Revolution, just
as before it, officials with the help of soldiers are holding all non-Russian tribes in slavish subordination.*

*From the Mordvinians they take away bread, gather
recruits by force, requisition cattle, taking no account
either of the people's will or of the impoverished situation of the Mordvinian villages.*

*Russian peasants! You all know what a peaceful
and industrious neighbor the Mordvinian people is. It
endured all the outrages of the tsarist henchmen un-
complainingly, realizing that the great Russian peasantry was suffering tsarist oppression together with it.
It realized that if it did not tear its freedom from the
hands of its oppressors by force, then its fate would
be horrible, and it rose.*

*The Mordvinian people sees that the great Russian
peasantry is deceived by the revolutionaries just like*

all the peoples who walked under the scepter of the bloody Russian tsar. The Mordvinian people would gladly help its brothers, the great Russian peasantry, but it is weak and is itself in need of help. It summons the Russian peasants to a joint uprising against oppression and believes that with a common effort it will not be difficult to throw off the Bolshevik yoke from the shoulders of the tiller of the soil and the toiler.

The Mordvinian people is struggling for the right freely to decide its own future. It does not interfere in the affairs of the great Russian people but demands by force of arms that the Bolshevik power recognize its right to land, religion, independence and equality with all other free peoples.

The liberation of the Mordvinian people is being assisted by disinterested friends who have organized a Mordvinian militia for the struggle with the Bolsheviks.

Russian peasants! In helping the Mordvinian militia you are helping yourselves, because it is struggling against your oppressors.

The Mordvinian people summons everyone to its banner, which brings peace to its friends and death to its enemies.

> *The friend of Mordvinian freedom,*
> *Commander of the Militia*
> *Margrave von zur Mühlen-Schönau*

"The crafty bastard!" sniffed the military commissar, fanning himself with a newspaper, as in a heat-wave.

Golosov tugged at his locks, then screwed up his eyes and hunched into a ball, as if preparing to spring.

"These papers are more valuable than any reconnaissance. Now we have something to sight with."

"From Lebezhaika we went . . ." Shchepov wanted to continue, but Golosov did not let him speak.

"Nonsense! Everything's clear. The rest are the adventures of a pilot in the civil war. You can tell us about them sometime over mushrooms and pickles. . . ."

He hid a smile in his hand, flashed an eye at Shchepov and unexpectedly, with anxious seriousness, he asked:

"Are you all right? Why are you trembling?"

Shchepov was pale and the upper lid of his left glassy eye strangely trembled.

"I caught a chill," he said. "I wanted to talk to you about . . ."

"I know!" broke in Golosov.

He grabbed a scrap of paper from the table and wrote several words on it in pencil.

"About this?" he asked, giving the paper to Shchepov.

Shchepov glanced at it, folded it neatly and put it in his pocket.

"Yes. Agree that it was stupid."

"Nonsense! Let's go, I'll get you warmed up," said Golosov.

A smile was about to twist his lips, he crushed it with an obstinate grimace, caught Shchepov and the observer by the sleeves and pulled them toward the door.

They had just come up to it when it opened. A mud-splashed messenger stepped in to meet them.

"What's the matter, Comrade?" asked Golosov, as if pouncing from a watch tower.

"The commissar of the composite company, Comrade Pokisen . . . in an attack . . . in the advance on San-shino . . ."

"Well?"

"Comrade Pokisen was killed."

Shchepov felt a dead weight hanging on the sleeve by which Golosov had been dragging him.

At this hour Comrade Pokisen's wife was sitting by the baby carriage over little Otti, who was buttoned into his bedclothes.

Otti would not sleep for a long time and looked at his mother with his enormous milky eyes.

Perhaps he understood what she was singing?

Her face was stony, frozen, her jaws and cheekbones were flat and only her long mouth twisted, showing her strong yellow teeth.

"Little Otti! You don't know yet what dances the girls do on the shores of Hepo-Yarvi. And you haven't fallen asleep

yet to their songs, and they haven't yet brought you fir
cones and you are still quite, quite wee Otti.

"Wee Otti! You won't see the girls from Lake Hepo-
Yarvi. And they won't sing songs over you or bring you fir
cones, and you won't swing with them in swings when you
are big, big Otto.

"Wee Otti! You don't know yet that your father's a Bolshevik and that it's better for Bolsheviks not to have wives
and not to have children, because then Hepo-Yarvi is far
away and—who knows whether their wives will see it, or
whether their children will get to it.

"Wee Otti! You don't know yet that your mother is unhappy because your father's at war, and because no end
to the war can be seen and no one knows whether your
father will come back.

"But, wee Otti, if your father doesn't come back from
the war and if your mother dies from grief and want and
no one sings to you any more of Hepo-Yarvi, promise me
from the cradle, promise, wee Otti, to revenge your father
and your mother.

"Because they loved you, wee Otti, because they loved
their Hepo-Yarvi.

"Promise to revenge."

She ceased singing and lowered her hard face to the
baby carriage, expecting an answer.

Little Otti had closed his eyes.

Little Otti slept.

From the basement where the heroine of the Semidol
theater languished there were two paths. One led to the
Semidol streets, to Semidol outbuildings, to samovars, ikon
cases and folding ikons, and, from the basement, Semidol
seemed an endless space, and hovels with ikon shelves, a
promised refuge.

The other path lay through the garden, and farther—
through the willow bushes in the marsh, past the creamery,
and farther—over pulverized, oil-caked wasteland into a
ravine—and more human feet walked toward the ravine
than came back from it.

At this hour Klavdia Vasilyevna was given a bag with

bread, butter and apples, with a piece of boiled pork and a dozen plums. The present had been collected by the actresses and they did not forget to put into the bag a pack of cigarettes and a box of matches.

Two eyes—gleaming and bright—lit up in the darkness of the basement and the bag scraped on the wooden bunk by Klavdia Vasilyevna's knees.

"With a package for you, Citizen. Let me have a cigarette."

She felt for the matches and struck one. A greenish track shone on the box, a blue flame hissed and twisted around the match.

"There are the cigarettes, on top," pointed brighteyes.

The flame turned yellow, grew, lit up the brown narrow face and then quickly went out.

"Thanks."

Closing the door behind him, brighteyes drawled soothingly:

"Don't worry, Citizen actress, there's not much time left. . . ."

Not much time?

And then?

Will her knees really begin to tremble, as on the stage when you take on a new role after only two rehearsals, and will she really lack the strength to smile in the darkness, as on the stage, so that they look at her face and not at her knees? However, Klavdia Vasilyevna will not be illuminated by footlights and no one will notice how uneven her steps are. The night will be black and she will go through the garden, and farther—through the willow bushes in the marsh, past the creamery, and farther—over the pulverized, oil-caked wasteland. Cold creeps out of the ravine under one's feet and Klavdia Vasilyevna will tremble on the edge of the ravine as she is doing now, in the basement—worse than now.

No, no.

Is there really not much time?

Not much time until the minute when they open the door, and another door, and still another, and, past the guard with the rifle, release her into the Semidol streets, into the

crooked wanton file of outbuildings and hovels. Klavdia
Vasilyevna will dash wherever her foot take her, perhaps
to her room—to the low-ceilinged little room with the ikon-
case, perhaps to the theater—to the actresses who did not
forget to send her cigarettes and matches, perhaps to
Shchepov. Shchepov will greet her with his tired smile and
sorrow will glint in his eyes. He will laugh at the fact that
Klavdia Vasilyevna trembled from the dampness and from
the thought that she would stand as a target on the edge
of the ravine. He will say for the tenth time that since the
Revolution began people have ceased to live a normal life,
that they are ready to die at every minute and that the
sole demand of the Revolution lies in this perpetual readi-
ness to die for the sake of victory. That there is no point
in meditating over the fate of the Revolution, one must only
not fear to die because the places of the dead will be
taken by the living, for whose sake the Revolution will con-
quer. He will talk of this, smiling wearily, and sorrow will
be in his eyes, and when Klavdia Vasilyevna calls in a
pleading voice:

"Shchepov!"

he will pat her on the back like a dog and will remain as
cold, grudging and sorrowful as before. But Klavdia Vasilyevna will think of the fact that she is the heroine of the
Semidol theater, that she is lonely, needed by no one, and
that her pleading voice and pencil-stained eyes have
grown boring to Shchepov, that all this is pitiful, degrading
and trivial and that it would be better to stand as a target
on the edge of the ravine.

Because all her life Klavidia Vasilyevna had suffered the
bitterness of an unloved, unwanted woman. Here she was
freezing for two days in the musty darkness and it had not
even occurred to the man who for her was master to glad-
den her with a pack of cigarettes and a box of matches.
It disgusted him to pity her—ludicrous, unwanted—and she
would never in her life see from him even the bitter sweetness of a sulphur match.

Bite off the brittle match heads, swallow them one after
another, hurrying more and more, quicker and quicker, in
order to swallow the whole box before the pains begin,

before the spicy saliva runs out from under her tongue and slips down her throat, before her mouth is cramped by nausea and before her dog-like pity for herself, for Shchepov, for the theater, for Semidol, for her dead mother, for Russia, for the whole world has passed away.

Let it be so. Quicker, quicker!

And when the empty box had fallen from her hands and the bitten matches had scattered over the floor, a sharp saw slashed where Klavdia Vasilyevna had not expected the pain—beneath her breasts, in her shoulders and shoulder-blades, as if poison had been poured through her lungs.

And in unbearable pity for herself alone and in some joyful malice toward the whole world, Klavdia Vasilyevna jerked toward the opening door wailing:

"Shchepov, I poi-soned myself!"

Shchepov seized her by the arms, lifted her and ran beneath the vaults of the basement in the quivering yellow lamplight.

The narrow-faced brown man holding the lamp moved his eyes brightly over a piece of paper with the signature:

Chairman of the Revolutionary Commission, Golosov.

Kurt was running from one corner to the other of his small room, at times tugging at his closely cropped head and at others undoing the collar of his tunic. His hands were not still for a minute, flashing before Andrei like boughs rocked by the wind.

"A-ah! Our friendship touched him? He is sensitive to brotherly affection? Well? What did he say when he let you go?"

"He asked whether I understood that he was violating his duty."

"He meant that he was making such a sacrifice for my sake?"

"It seemed to me that he really valued you."

"A-ah! Valued! Valued! Aren't you being indulgent with him? During the hour that you spent with him you didn't have time to discover that he was a hypocrite. Were you blinded by that degenerate's sentimental gesture?"

"Perhaps I owe him my life."

"What of that? You can owe your life to some branch or other, to which you clung when falling into an abyss. Surely you won't be praying to that branch for the rest of your days?"

"I'm not praying to him, Kurt. I'm telling you that he helped me because I was your friend. Probably you are dear to him for some reason."

"A-ah! You don't understand, Andrei! It's indispensable to him to feel himself a benefactor. He hides his brutality with good deeds. He justifies his existence to himself with trivial sops to virtue. Any favor from such hands should be loathesome to you! You must . . ."

"Listen, Kurt," interrupted Andrei. "It seems you suspect me of sympathy toward this man? I can't hate him with the same force as you do. To me, he doesn't exist as a person. An empty spot. And now, when he has proved so unexpectedly to be my enemy . . ."

"Well, what now?"

"You see he's lost his individuality even more for me now. He's an enemy, together with a hundred, a thousand, maybe millions of other enemies. A man whom I knew accidentally has become numbered among my enemies. Nothing more."

Kurt ceased walking and put his arms behind his back.

"That's complicated, Andrei."

"No, it's simple."

Kurt's face turned colder, his gaze sharper, he approached Andrei almost stealthily and lowered his voice:

"No, it's very complicated, Andrei. If this unsolicited champion of Mordvinian freedom, this estimable offshoot of a splendid margravian family, if he suddenly came into your hands . . ."

"Well?"

"Would you kill him?"

Andrei hunched his back, passed a hand over his forehead, encountered Kurt's gaze and lowered his eyes.

"I probably couldn't kill anyone. That is, just like that,

just a man of some kind. To know afterward that I had killed. What, exactly, am I? Just that sort of a man."

Kurt again waved his arms and broke into a run about the room.

"You're afraid of dread, Andrei, you are afraid of dread! That's terrible. You must overcome dread, go beyond it."

"I'm going with you to the front, Kurt."

"That's not the same."

"I'll be able to use a Mauser there as well as Golosov."

"Not the same, not the same, my friend!"

"Maybe at the time I'll even kill the margrave. But . . . only not to know it for certain. Not to see it."

"Not the same, my friend, not the same at all. How I hate that degenerate! Listen, Andrei. I felt myself—no, what was it?—I became an object in the hands of that benefactor. I went to sleep and awoke with the thought that he had bought me, that I didn't belong to myself. My every step was known to him, he spied on my projects, didn't let a single scrap of canvas out of my room. His agent bribed Master Maier to find out everything that was done by these hands here. Everything around me reminded me of my degradation just as everything reminds a consumptive of his consumption. Curses! What was it in aid of? A selfish, small boy had gotten the idea of giving luster to the faded and forgotten name of the margraves. He wanted to be talked about, remembered. A shabby little lieutenant, unknown beyond the regiment in which he serves, unexpectedly discovers a new artist. Ach, is that a margrave? Margrave, ha-ha! It's not a question of the artist but of his patron! Without the patron there'd be no artist! Hell! He followed his plan with the precision of a spider. A-a-ah! Offspring like that should be kept under lock and key! And you believed in his love for paintings? Believed it, ha-ha! Love for paintings, ha-ha-ha! Now this patron of the fine arts is not averse to adorning his restored title with new laurels. In his eyes, probably, things go dim: the margrave marches into Semidol, the margrave makes a triumphant entry into Moscow, the margrave restores the monarchy, Margrave von zur Mühlen-Schönau—friend of Mordvinian freedom, ha-ha-ha!"

Kurt rushed to the window, flung it wide open, leaned over the windowsill. Hollow voices sounded in the yard someone ran over the rain-softened ground, horses' hooves squelched in the mud, wheels rattled over the cracked floor of the coach-house.

"Ready, Franz?" shouted someone beneath the window. "Go and call them!"

Kurt straightened up and buttoned his tunic collar. His breathing had quieted down, his movements became precise and even.

"Time for us to go, Andrei."

Then Andrei shuddered, stood up quickly and strode to the table. Beside a pot-bellied field bag on the table lay a long-barreled blue-black Mauser. Andrei took it and handed it to Kurt.

"Show me how the magazine is filled, Kurt," he asked quietly.

In the town they were exchanging brief words with one another and one or two men stopped to straighten the bags on their backs or to pull their leggings tight. But when they had passed the railroad crossing silence fell and the ranks were no longer broken. The march was a heavy one. The drizzle falling since noon had soaked deep into the road. Boots became covered with soft slippers of mud and steps came to nought, as if they were on ice. But legs moved stubbornly and bodies swayed ponderously and regularly back and forth, like the clappers of bells.

Along the remote high road, lost in Russia, concealed by the autumn night, among miserable fields without end or limit, marched Essenites, Darmstadtians, Nurembergers to an unknown destination. Accustomed to marching, they easily heard its grim music and in a strange land under a strange unseeing sky they sang an unforgotten song:

I-ich hatte ein' Kamara-aden. . . .

In this land the sugary song became menacing and Andrei could not hear his voice in the choir of Darmstadtians, Essenites and Nurembergers.

But he was singing and his words were coinciding with

the words of the song, although their sense seemed different to him. And although the regular step of the march echoed in the ground heavier with every minute, to walk became easier. The past was going off into some kind of vacuum and the whole future was in that second step which came after the first. Imperceptibly there disappeared into the darkness indistinct visions of the margrave, Kurt, Rita, Moscow, Paul Hennig's huge room and Paul Hennig himself, thundering something about equality under socialism. Snatches of undisturbing words rose up and were extinguished in his memory, like the signal lights of a small station left in the distance.

In no way different from the soldiers, step for step, shoulder to shoulder, Andrei walked into the darkness and a foreign song poured lightly and painlessly from him:

> *In der Heimat, in der Heimat,**
> *Da gibt's ein Wiedersehen. . . .*

He was strong and calm, he was singing of Marie's homeland, he was singing of meeting her. He believed that Marie was the future, that she was the second step which he would make after the first.

He went to sleep on the ground when the detachment bivouacked in Ruchi. . . .

Dawn was late, the rain had not stopped, the orchards had been stripped by the windy night. In the dank morning fog Andrei discerned the soldiers for the first time. Their facial features were strangely alike as if they had all been cut on the same lathe and painted the same color. Their movements were sluggish and grudging and their mouths opened only in order to bite off some breath or to get a more comfortable grip on their pipes with their teeth.

When the order was given for departure to Sanshino the soldiers busied themselves with their pipes. Some knocked them out, some filled them anew, unhurriedly and diligently, as if this were the most important thing in carrying out the order. Then they took their rifles from the stacks, fell in in a column and left. At the end of the orchards they gave

*In the homeland, in the homeland
There waits a reunion. . . .

a command which Andrei did not understand. The column opened out into one long line and the line moved in a brittle chain over the hills covered with the melancholy, sparse remains of abandoned orchards.

"It smells of the enemy," growled Andrei's neighbor.

Andrei glanced at him. The soldier puffed some smoke out of his short-stemmed pipe and looked down at his feet. His toothbrush mustache was tinged on one side with gray.

"I've never been in the line," said Andrei, "I don't know what I have to do."

"Walk," replied the soldier.

"I'll keep beside you."

"It's all the same."

And they walked in silence, jumping over the creeping lashes of gooseberry and skirting the sickly trunks of wild apple trees.

Round a bend in the country road, on a steep rise, Andrei caught sight of a lone tree standing with a shapeless, reddish bundle hanging from a branch. He looked closer at this bundle. A stout, motionless carcass was hanging from a rope, looking from the distance like a slaughtered goose hung by the neck. Andrei did not notice that he had changed direction and, walking faster, got out of step. He walked straight toward the tree.

"What's that?" he said, extending his hand backward in order to grasp his neighbor. "A man?" he asked more quietly.

His elbow collided with someone's chest, he looked round. He was surrounded by a group of soldiers hurrying as he was toward the tree. The line was broken. Someone's voice wheezed questioningly:

"Did they cut his legs off?"

Andrei darted forward and ran to the top of the hill. The soldiers rushed after him.

The hanged man's head was bent to one side, heavily and helplessly like a dead bird's. His face had turned blue and one eye—huge and yellow—had slipped out of its socket as if knocked out. The cumbersome broad-shouldered trunk hung strangely on its long, stretched neck, level with a man's height. It seemed as if it would walk were legs to

be put under it. But in the place of legs there showed from
under torn rags the red wrinkled skin of thick stumps. The
hands dug their splayed fingers into the air as if the trunk
were being held up by the arms apart from the head secured to the rope. The soldiers surrounded the hanged man.

Andrei looked at the blue head with its eye slipping out.
He had seen this head somewhere—melon-like, spotted with
large freckles. It swayed back and forth on its thickset
stump by the waists of the soldiers crowding around it and,
baring its teeth gaily, whined some senseless words:

"Welcome, brother Comrades! We've waited long
enough, you might say, for peace, for home. . . ."

But Andrei couldn't recall when he had met that head
and it merged vaguely in his memory with another head,
just as blue, with dead lips which suddenly moved: *Adieu,
Frau Mama, adieu. . . .*

"We must take him down," sounded hollowly behind
Andrei.

He turned round. Andrei's neighbor in the line was speaking. The half of his face with the graying mustache was
dancing some sort of headlong quivering dance. He was
pale. Andrei threw a glance at the other soldiers. They
were strangely unlike one another, while a minute before
that they had all seemed alike.

One or two men stepped toward the human stump on
the tree and lifted him up a little. Their awkward trembling
hands jerked at the rope on the hanged man's stretched
neck.

But at that moment there fell on their heads from somewhere a dry brief crack, as if an old branch had broken.
Andrei raised his eyes to the apple tree. The soldiers ran
swiftly to the sides, scattered over the hill in a long line
and fell to the ground like cardboard figures blown by the
wind. The dry crack was repeated. And suddenly, uneven
bursts of short explosions chased one another over the hill
as if stout sacking were being torn to pieces somewhere.
And light, downy tufts flew up on the hill farthest from the
road, as from sackcloth.

Something jolted Andrei in the side. He flew away from
the tree and fell. Lying on his right elbow he used his left

hand to unbutton the wooden Mauser holster from his belt. Then he slowly fitted the handle of the revolver to the light butt of his holster, undid the safety catch, lay on his stomach and rested his chin on his fist.

The shabby, bare-headed sky quivered with puffs of blue-gray smoke. They thinned and melted, and in their place arose new ones which were sucked away to make room for others. Andrei looked long at them. Then he raised his head a little. About a hundred yards away his neighbor with the toothbrush mustache was lying on his stomach. Beside him lay his rifle. He was carefully and unhurriedly cleaning his pipe with a straw. Lower down the steep slope the chain of riflemen had lain down in odd groups. They were all motionless and quiet. Andrei glanced at the tree. Disturbed by the soldiers the hanged man was still swinging smoothly on the branch. Andrei turned away indifferently.

A strange calm spread through his body. For the first time in these years, perhaps for the first time in his whole life, he experienced the extraordinary levity of some kind of absence of thought. He had the feeling that he was not connected by anything to the world, which unexpectedly and surprisingly had opened out before him and accepted him. He was aware of only himself in the world and time suddenly ceased to flow, so that there disappeared both the future with the persistent thought of Marie and the present with its melancholy and its dread of the deformed, executed man.

Andrei was watching a huge red ant dragging a dried-up larva over the ground. The ant courageously overcame obstacles of withered pipe-shaped blades of grass, pebbles and tiny lumps of mud. Some kind of minute black ant in search of booty ran into the red one's field of vision and the latter, arching into a bow, hurled himself at the daredevil and put him to flight. Then he returned to the larva and crawled on his way.

Perhaps because the earth was close to his face, a trivial particle of it, worn down by the passage of worms and beetles, grew into a whole world and this world filled Andrei with an ever deepening unshakable calm.

A distant, inaudible command reached him. The bluish-gray puffs disappeared from the vault of the sky, the shots ceased. He looked at the slope of the hill. The soldiers, in a line as crooked as a folding ruler, with rifles in their hands, were running down into a hollow.

Andrei got up lightly, grasped his Mauser and ran down-hill. And with every tread of his feet on the sloping ground the feeling grew in him of a never before experienced strange lightness, as if all his clothing had gradually fallen off and he were running naked. When the slope of the hill had fallen away into the hollow and he had to gather speed in order to take the rise of the next hill, Andrei ceased to hear his breathing and the lightness was replaced by a feeling of some kind of incorporeality which carried him imperceptibly upward.

He came to his senses after he had gone beyond the rise over which the bluish-gray puffs had recently floated. He fell into some sparse oak saplings behind the rise, as a scrap of paper falls when the funnel of wind whirling it dies away under it.

The sound of a shot struck him in the head. Short staccato rifle shots echoed from all sides.

Then Andrei pressed the hollow butt of the Mauser to his shoulder and began to press the trigger, without counting or stopping, until the magazine was emptied. Then, without moving, he listened to the rumble raised by the fire rolling over the district. Through a thin tracery of oak branches he saw, to the right and left of him, smiling soldiers and only then realized that his Mauser was pointing up at the sky.

"Well, how is it?" asked someone, laughing heartily.

Andrei jerked the butt away from his shoulder and looked at the revolver. It was scorched with a bluish powder burn.

"Works perfectly," said Andrei and also laughed.

A MEETING

It was decided to meet at 10 a.m. at the camp to which they had been bringing the captured Mordvinian militiamen during the whole of the day before. The captured Germans and Austrians, among whom there was the prospect of identifying the "friend of Mordvinian freedom," were confined in a special hut.

Semidol had recovered from the alarm, and women with buckets on yokes were already gossiping by the water pumps. But the nearer Andrei came to the suburbs the more deserted it became around him and the little houses hid their little weak-sighted windows behind tattered shutters.

Suddenly, on the corner of a shabby side street, Andrei caught sight of a girl who seemed a stranger to him, out of place among the rain-blackened board shanties, fences and doors. He slowed his steps, looked closer, and, as if he had run into a rope stretched across the road, stopped.

The girl was standing on the other side of the street with her back to him and was looking at a rusty iron plaque on a gate-post. Then she walked slowly to the next house and set about finding the long-vanished traces of a number on it. After standing a little while, she moved on, uncertainly and quietly, like a person who doubts whether he is searching on the right road. Reading the faded or peeling plaques she pressed her right palm to her temple, as Marie used to do when she stared at something incomprehensible and foggy. Then she took her hand from her face but did not lower it immediately, carrying it for two or three seconds in front of her as if saluting. This tiniest of gestures, this immeasurably small fraction of a gesture belonged only to her—Marie. It could not, it should not belong to anyone in the world except her.

Oh, of course, it was Marie!

Her every movement—the way she raised her slim—perhaps a little too slim—leg in order to take a step, the way she moved her feet, hardly stirring her body and throwing her knees forward, as if her path lay always uphill—all these trivial characteristics of movement, known solely to him, Andrei, were Marie's alone.

Indeed, it was Marie.

She wore a dress which Andrei knew perfectly well—a heavy, brown, autumn dress with wide pleats around the belt and sleeves tightly buttoned at the wrists.

Now she raised her head to look at some small house. Her hair had escaped from beneath her traveling hat, the whitish sky was shining through it, and Andrei clearly saw its color—the color of Marie's hair.

There was no doubt, it was she.

But how had she come to be here, in this God-forsaken spot, in this suburb, at this hour?

My God, she had just come off the train, off the morning train. In her left hand was a small traveling bag. Perhaps Andrei would recall it, that traveling bag? Pale green leather, like a pistachio nut, almost square, secured around the middle by one strap. Surely he had seen more than a few such traveling bags in Bischofsberg? Surely she had had such a traveling bag?

Marie!

By superhuman efforts she had made her way to Russia, she had found out where Andrei lived, she had dug up unknown Semidol out of the ground, she had come and was here now, wandering around this God-forsaken hole, looking for him—Andrei.

Marie . . .

There are moments when the imagination conjures up incomparably more recollections, guesses, conclusions and scenes than those trivial snatches and scraps of thought which blinded Andrei while he was looking at the girl across the road. Probably there was no longer even a grain of doubt in him when he broke the invisible rope which had suddenly barred his way and dashed across the muddy street.

But he took only two steps. The girl, looking for something on the gates, turned toward Andrei. He caught sight of a strange and—it seemed to him—a repugnant, loathsome face.

He clasped his chest and turned back, almost knocking some man off his feet, and stopped. Distinct German words, pronounced very quietly, brought him to his senses.

"Strange . . . Strange . . ."

Before him stood a captured German soldier who, paying no attention to him, was looking at the girl across the street.

"What's strange?" asked Andrei.

The prisoner shuddered and quickly looked round. His puffy, badly washed face slowly changed under the touch of an enigmatic smile.

"Never mind," he said, "that fine Fräulein reminded me of an acquaintance. . . ."

"Yes? Strange . . . However that can happen. . . ."

"It can happen," agreed the German. "Are you bound for the camp?" he asked right away.

"Yes."

The prisoner dug his hands deeper in the pockets of his overcoat. The overcoat had been crumpled by marches and bad weather, light blue Austrian leggings which had been dried by the fire were warped about his legs and a peak-less cap from someone else's large head was slipping down over his eyes. The prisoner shuddered and hunched his shoulders from the cold.

"You don't happen to know if we'll be kept long in this garbage dump?" He nodded his head in the direction of the camp.

"Are you bound for Germany?"

"Yes."

"They're sending a few."

"To the other world?" grinned the prisoner and Andrei saw his mouth.

They recognized one another instantly—the German prisoner and Andrei Startsov. There escaped from them at one and the same time a strangled:

"You!"

They each fastened their eyes upon the other and froze in fright. But this lasted for one split second. The fright had shocked them like a cold shower and they stood prepared to fight. And perhaps because Andrei cast a quick, searching look somewhere the prisoner attacked first, swiftly and accurately.

"No, no," he said, almost going over to Andrei and taking a hand from his pocket, "you won't do that, you can't do that!"

"You're crazy!" exclaimed Andrei.

"You won't do that because the lives of a hundred innocent people depend upon one careless step on your part. Innocent people!"

"Listen. . . ."

"No, no. Don't be hasty so that you won't repent for the rest of your life. Don't be hasty, I beg you. Not for myself. For myself I don't care . . ."

"What do you mean? What people?"

"For God's sake. I ask you. Hear me out. If you give me up, if they catch me . . ."

"I know what I have to do!" shouted Andrei and looked around. Bands of hovels torn to tatters by the foul weather huddled wildly as before along the bumpy street. The deserted streets ran monotonously away into the fields. Not a soul.

"I know," shouted Andrei again, but his voice broke and fell silent.

Then the prisoner stepped to his side, confidently took his elbow with both hands and said:

"Okay. I can run away now, you will rush after me, raise a hue and cry, people will run out into the street, they'll catch me and capture me. Two soldiers are walking over there already. You're not alone. You can capture me. But I'm telling you: it will be paid for with the lives of twenty, thirty, fifty men, whose only fault was that they wanted to get home as soon as possible. I was captured together with my soldiers. They are all prisoners and I alone am to blame for the fact that they took to fighting. But they are honest, simple people and they got me out of trouble. They disguised me while we were still at Sanshino, before surrendering. I sat in the hut with them, over there, like a private. At dawn they helped me escape. I am speaking on their behalf. They won't be forgiven for helping me. Their fate is in your hands. Decide. I am ready. I am not afraid of death. I have lived under the same roof with death for five years. If you. . . ."

"That's all rubbish," Andrei waved him away and twitched his brows.

Too late, Andrei! You shouldn't have listened to this rubbish, shouldn't have allowed a single word, shouldn't have lost a single second. Then two soldiers would not have seen Comrade Startsov, whom all Semidol knew, standing on the road in the morning with a prisoner in a crumpled overcoat and Austrian leggings, and the prisoner warmly asking something of Comrade Startsov, holding him firmly by the elbow. Then a sleepy muzhik crawling out of his shack, beside which Andrei was talking to the prisoner, would not have noticed Comrade Startsov jerking away in confusion, as if he wanted to call aid, and then restraining himself immediately and listening to the hasty muttering of the prisoner:

"I am not asking for myself, believe me, I am indifferent. I am not even counting on you to remember how I once violated my duty in order to help you out, to save you, perhaps, from death. I see you remember that, you couldn't forget it, isn't that so? Your position was then slightly better than mine. Isn't that so? Do you remember?"

And then behind the trembling, sloping shoulder of the prisoner Andrei again saw Marie. Is such a resemblance really possible in the world? Unthinkable! Marie! She came through some gates, halted, put her hand to her temple, staring into the distance and then set off, lightly and decisively down the mountain, into the town. And the farther she moved away the more terrible grew the thought that she might go away forever, that he—Andrei—was doomed never to return to her, and suddenly this girl's face was not at all repulsive because this—this was Marie's face. Marie!

One second, another—and she was hidden by the crooked little shack on the corner.

And then a clear, strangely familiar word, pronounced in a strange abrupt voice, shut up the thoughts of Andrei.

"Bischofsberg . . ."

"Bischofsberg?" asked Andrei, astonished.

And the prisoner hastened to conclude something very important in a dry, hissing language:

"I swear I think of nothing else but returning to Bischofsberg. I am willing to repay you however you like. Oh, to return to Bischofsberg, to Lausche! Can't you really, in memory of what I once did for you . . ."

"You want to go back to Bischofsberg?" Andrei interrupted him.

"Oh, yes!"

Again not a soul around, the deserted spot was motionless and hidden from human eyes.

"It's crazy to talk about it!" exclaimed Andrei and suddenly, falling silent and bending toward the prisoner, he whispered quickly:

"Come to my place today, as soon as it gets dark, I live on the corner. . . ."

He gave his address concisely, shook the prisoner's outstretched hand, turned and heard the touched, restrained and faintly ironical exclamation:

"Oh, how noble you are!"

Then without looking back he dashed out of the deserted streets into the fields, past abandoned brick barns, across ravines, paths and hollows and almost ran to the camp.

Of course he would tell whom he had just met on the street, whom he had invited home that day when it got dark. He would rig up an ambush in his room, he would give up, betray the fugitive. Betray? No, he would fulfill his duty. Duty? But surely he had already violated his duty? Why, if a fugitive . . .

Andrei stopped suddenly, as if blinded by a cruel light, and again he dashed forward. . . .

Then he stood in a barrack-room between Kurt and Golosov and past him filed a line of Germans and Austrians captured at Sanshino. They stopped the prisoners and forced them to take off their caps and show their hands. Kurt was asking brief questions and shaking his head.

"Next."

Sweat was pouring from Andrei; he frequently wiped his

brow with a heavy soaked handkerchief and shook his head the way Kurt did.

"Tumorrow, Startsov, there's a meeting in the camp. You must thank the prisoners who fought on our side. They're being sent home on the first troop train. That's all we can do for them. We are deeply indebted to them."

Golosov hid a smile in his palm.

"And to you, of course . . ."

"Okay," replied Andrei, "next."

In the ribbon of people passing before him there remained only five, three, two. The last one came.

"A-a-ah, dammit!" said Kurt hoarsely.

"My God, my God!" responded Andrei.

"I knew it: got away, the devil. . . ."

And Andrei:

"Got away. Yes, yes, got away. My God . . ."

He turned his eyes away and it seemed to him that everything around him was curtained with heavy black smoke.

A DREAM

"If a month's stay in a besieged fortress counts for a year then a month's imprisonment ought to be counted as two. My life is essentially over. Imprisonment is a coffin. Its bottom and walls are snow, its roof the sky, stopped up with snow clouds. Buried alive. At times I fell on the floor in despair and banged my head. The snow was driving me crazy. The thought that snow would soon come again was driving me crazy. I can't bear to see it falling, falling, falling. My hair stands on end. . . . You want to know what I was guided by in starting this pitiful affair? Or is it all the same to you, as it is to me? But I feel the need to justify myself before you. My fate is in your hands and perhaps I don't deserve your indulgence."

"You are talking loudly again. Quiet!" whispered Andrei.

"Forgive me. I can hardly restrain myself from bursting into tears. I cannot look at you without tears. I can't hold this within me. How grandiose and absurd our life is. Not long ago, still enemies, we . . ."

"Speak quieter and faster. Speak faster."

"I'm so agitated I don't know what I must say. I had a single friend with whom I lived two and a half years in that coffin. He was called Frei. He was killed the day before yesterday, in the last skirmish which decided everything. He was a German officer and he was bayoneted by a German soldier. At his death I realized that he had started a stupid affair. It was his idea—to make the Mordvinians rise. He appointed me the friend of Mordvinian freedom and let loose a whole legend about me, I don't know what the sense of it was. He hated the Bolsheviks and despised Russians. I am curious about both. But I was bored. In the last analysis politics equals boredom. The mother-in-law always thinks her daughter-in-law a spendthrift, it always seems to the father that his sons are parasites, while the children languish under their parents' oppressions. But all this is in the family. Dull. I wasn't thinking of any politics. I simply admired Frei, admired the enthusiasm with which he wove the design which was to bring us home, to put an end to imprisonment. You, of course, know from your own experience what imprisonment means? You know what madnesses imprisonment can provoke a man to? Do you remember? . . ."

"Speak more quickly."

Andrei was wrapped in a wide coarse overcoat, as if a piercing stream of air were blowing through the closely curtained window against which he leaned. In the room it was quiet. The fearful wick of a wax candle on the table was not stirring, although the Ober-lieutenant's whispering lips were fluttering only an arm's length away:

"I hope, I almost believe . . . Everything depends on you, good friend. May I call you that?"

"How did you decide to come to me?"

"Oh, I didn't hesitate for a minute. You will understand me. I am so unhappy, I regret so much, I regret so bitterly. . . ."

"What are you hoping for? Tell me!"

The Ober-lieutenant leaned on the table and approached his face to the candle. It was immobile, emaciated, and only the mouth was filled with nervous life.

"I expect you to help me as I once helped you. Stop, stop! I understand that it goes against your conscience. But didn't I also go against my conscience in releasing you from Schönau? I can see what you want to say: you were harmless for Germany? But take a look at me. I came to you for charity, for mercy, and you are free to do what you like with me. Am I really a danger to your country?"

Andrei threw off his overcoat and stood up. An enormous shadow straightened its arms on the ceiling and rushed from corner to corner. Andrei laughed:

"For my country? For the country?"

The Ober-lieutenant echoed him with a quiet, thoughtful chuckle and muttered:

"Of course it's silly. For a great country, for the Great Russia . . . the friend of Mordvinian freedom! But even for Semidol, for you, for the work which you are carrying out. Am I really a danger? I am surrounded by emptiness, I am alone. My friend has been killed. I shall never forget how I spent two consecutive years collecting herbariums with him. Poor Frei. What is left to be done without him? Grant that I am free and am ruled by evil intentions. You've seen whose side the prisoners are on. I had a few odd men. I am harmless, helpless, worthless. If you help me to get out of here you will be doing no one any harm, nor will you do any good if you give me up. No, no. I can't permit such a thought. I mean that you may not possess those friendly feelings such as led me to help you then in Schönau. But I believe in your humaneness."

"You released me then as a friend of Kurt Wahn," whispered Andrei, bending over the table. "Do you know that as a friend of Kurt Wahn I ought to . . . give you up?"

The Ober-lieutenant jumped back in his chair, his eyes grew large, he had difficulty in holding his breath and he crushed his thin dry fingers into his palms.

"Why does Kurt Wahn hate me so much?" he muttered, barely audibly.

"Do you know?" Andrei continued to whisper. "Kurt

Wahn is here in Semidol. He is in charge of evacuating the prisoners—he is chairman of the Soviet of German Soldiers."

The Ober-lieutenant closed his eyes and seized his temples. Immobile, turning yellow, he remained silent, holding his head, and his parted mouth twitched convulsively.

"Fate," he said finally and raised his eyelids. His gaze was dim and lifeless.

"Fate . . . why does he hate me?" he repeated. "My hope is to do something through the soviet . . . my only hope. . . ."

Suddenly he jumped up, rushed around the table to Andrei and groaned:

"I beg humaneness, only hu-mane-ness!"

Then Andrei grasped him by his soft trembling hand, drew him down as if in a handshake, and spoke hoarsely into his face:

"Quiet, you! Humaneness? Humaneness? What about the legless cripple on the apple tree—humaneness? What about the blood of the unfortunate idiots who believed in your game—humaneness?"

"Oh, don't be cruel! Oh!"

"Cruel?"

"I implore you. Frei atoned for our sins by his death. I swear to you that for my whole life . . ."

Andrei released his hand and stepped away.

"I can't help you with anything more. You succeeded in flying. Well, fly farther. Go into hiding. I'm not hindering you. We're quits. We're quits, Ober-lieutenant!" cried Andrei suddenly and sharply.

"I understand you. You are passing by a man dying at the wayside. . . ."

"But what do you want from me? What can I do for you?"

The Ober-lieutenant hunched himself, rubbed his hands unexpectedly vigorously and whispered quickly:

"I need a name. Nothing more. A name . . ."

Andrei looked at him with a congealed, glassy gaze and his hands rose stiffly, as if something were moving them against his will.

"A name, even the worst sounding name, will take me to

Bischofsberg. I want nothing more: Bischofsberg, Lausche,
Schönau—these are my last desire in this world."

Andrei sank weakly upon the bed.

Bischofsberg—last desire in the world . . .

Silence welded the dusk of the room together, the candle
burned fearfully as before and the spicy, honeyed smell of
the melting wax slowly grew denser.

Andrei rose quietly and went up to the Ober-lieutenant.
He came level with him, touching his shoulder with his
chest, circled his back with his arm and approached his face
to his ear. He was trembling all over. He rocked the Ober-
lieutenant pressed to his chest with his quick labored breathing and his whisper was heavy and loud:

"If you get to Bischofsberg will you carry out one errand
for me?"

"It will be the aim of my life!"

"Listen, I have there . . . I have a fiancée, the only
woman whom . . . my fiancée . . ."

"Yes, yes, I understand, of course," whispered the Ober-
lieutenant and something childlike hovered over his parted
lips.

Then for the first time that evening a dark hue spread
warmly over Andrei's face and the yellow candle flame
multiplied and widened in his eyes:

"Find her out and tell her that I . . . that you saw me,
that I spoke of her. . . . I'll tell you later . . . give her
a letter . . . the first letter. . . . I parted from her a
year ago and she is expecting . . . I hate to think of it:
a whole year! And before us . . . But I'll write everything
in the letter. . . . Will you deliver it? She's easy to find.
Her name is Marie Urbach, Fräulein Marie Urbach. She
lives . . ."

Andrei staggered. The Ober-lieutenant's body had grown
heavy, broken and sagged in his arms like a sack. His head
was thrown backward and the sharp, bulging Adam's apple
slid like a canoe along his outstretched neck.

Andrei propped the Ober-lieutenant up against the wall.

"What's the matter with you? Are you ill?"

The Ober-lieutenant shuddered and straightened up.

"I have . . . you see," he muttered hollowly, pointing to his head.

From the right ear to the back of his head ran a wide scar, etched with wrinkles.

"In Champagne, in fifteen, this has happened since then. Pay no attention. . . . Fräulein Marie Urbach, you say? Ma-rie Ur-bach?"

The Ober-lieutenant frowned at Andrei.

But Andrei was not looking at him. He had craned his neck, listening to a rustling behind the window. Three distinct knocks clinked on the glass and broke the silence of the room.

"For me," whispered Andrei.

He left the room stealthily, noiselessly slipped through the dark room into the hall and clung to the outside door.

The Ober-lieutenant jumped away into a corner, pressed his back to the wall and drew from his pocket an officer's revolver. With his left hand he grasped the wrist of his right and aimed the revolver at the door. Thus he stood, inaudible and imperceptible, in the warm twilight of the watchful room.

Andrei listened to the uncertain, soft steps in the yard. They stopped on the porch and the half-rotten steps creaked complainingly, ready to break. Someone took hold of the iron ring on the door.

Andrei concealed himself. Then, relieved, he sighed noisily, unhooked and opened the door. From the glint of the round black eyes flashing before him in the dark night he knew that he had not been deceived, and he said quickly:

"Rita, my dear, I can't invite you in, I am busy. . . . I have a comrade. . . . I'll be free in a quarter of an hour. I'll come to your place, I promise."

Rita raised her arms, her wide shawl slipped heavily from her shoulders and she silently reached out to Andrei. He embraced her tenderly, as if delighted by her silence, and firmly kissed her soft, wet, cool lips.

"Andrei!"

"Yes, yes. In a quarter of an hour."

392 • KONSTANTIN FEDIN

"Do you know already?"

"What?"

She mumbled disconnectedly:

"The front . . . they've decided to send you to the front. . . . It's all Golosov, Golosov, I know. . . . He can't forgive me for . . . with you. . . . It's decided. . . . I know . . . in a few days, maybe tomorrow . . . they're mobilizing, Andrei . . . leaving now. . . ."

He embraced her tenderly again.

"Mobilizing? Well, so what? That's good. That's excellent! I'll be at your place in a quarter of an hour. Run along."

He picked up her shawl from the floor, wrapped it round her, turned her away from him and held her shoulders lightly while she descended the creaking steps of the porch.

Then he put the latch on and returned to the room. He didn't make out his guest right away. The Ober-lieutenant was standing, leaning against the wall and facing the door. He was silent, Andrei went up to him and touched the breast of his overcoat.

The Ober-lieutenant asked quietly:

"What did you say? Fräulein Marie Urbach?"

"By the way!" said Andrei. "You could have known her, Marie. Close by Schönau, the Villa Urbach, you remember?"

"I don't recall," mumbled the Ober-lieutenant and pointed absent-mindedly to his head:

"I have—you see . . ."

Then Andrei made haste:

"You must go. I'll try to do something for you. Stop. Tomorrow at eleven in the evening at the same place, where we met. . . . I'll be there. I'll prepare a letter. You'll deliver it? But remember the name and address, in case you don't manage to keep the letter: Am Markt, 18/II, Marie Urbach. . . . Now . . ."

He rushed to a shelf, seized a piece of bread and thrust it at the Ober-lieutenant, continuing to whisper:

"Am Markt, 18/II . . . Am Markt . . ."

The Ober-lieutenant tried to hide the bread in his breast, but the piece was large and angular, he broke it into two parts and thrust one part into his left overcoat pocket.

Then, pushed by Andrei, he passed through the room and the hall and approached the front door, noiselessly and waveringly, like a shadow.

There he grew suddenly firm, grasped Andrei's hand, pressed it and said carefully:

"I'll remember: Am Markt, 18/II, Fräulein Marie Urbach. I am eternally grateful to you. Until tomorrow."

He plunged into the darkness, ran confidently through the yard, opened the wicket gate wide and shot through the gap.

The harsh black night enfolded strange dead Semidol in its embrace. The hillsides with huts nestling on them rose up to the eyeless sky in barely perceptible humps. A melancholy hound howled in the empty depths of the town.

The Ober-lieutenant took out his revolver and held it in his palm, as if weighing it. Then he thrust the revolver back into his pocket and stepped decisively into the night, steadying with two fingers of his left hand the piece of bread bouncing up and down on his thigh, as once he had steadied his saber. . . .

At that moment, hunched over the table in the timid flicker of the candle, Andrei with a chipped pen was drawing repetitive, despairing, nonsensical words on a rough, torn sheet of paper:

My dear, my beloved little Marie. My every sigh, every beat of my heart, always and everywhere . . . You alone . . . My God . . .

Andrei came late in the evening, when Kurt was finishing work. He was unusually animated, talkative, even garrulous. He talked about the fact that the departure of the mobilized soldiers had been set for the next day, that he was busy mustering a detachment, that Golosov was a thousand times right to maintain that he, Andrei Startsov, could do with being warmed up at the front.

"I was completely reborn after Sanshino!" he exclaimed, rubbing his hands as if in a bracing fragrant frost. "Now I understand why until now I felt constantly depressed. A kind of darkness enveloped me, I was suffocating from it, I hadn't a moment's respite. Do you know what that was? It was a false call, pretending that I carry no responsibility for the horror being done in the world. Pretending that I wasn't to blame for that horror. But my conscience gave me no rest. Conscience—that's terrible, Kurt. Conscience . . . yes . . ."

Andrei hesitated for a minute, then continued more heatedly than before:

"A lie . . . you understand? A lie. I am to blame for the fact that men went to their deaths while I didn't go with them. Isn't it true? Everyone who didn't go to war, everyone who doesn't go to war—everyone's to blame in war. If death is necessary, if it is inevitable, one must oneself—you understand?—oneself must die, and not watch others dying. . . . At Sanshino, when I had to run after death together with everyone, I understood what conscience meant. . . . I understood that you have to take upon yourself the whole weight of the horror, and not run away from it, thinking the world is to blame for it, but not you. . . ."

Andrei jumped up, began to run about the room, sat down, again jumped up and, almost gasping for breath, spoke without stopping. His face was rumpled, as from a sleepless night, but his clouded eyes shone sharply and were brighter than usual.

"Oh, I am different now, quite different. I am going to the front with pleasure. I couldn't live any more now as I used to. I would simply die of longing. My breath comes short when I remember what I experienced at Sanshino. Do you know, Kurt? That was the only time in all my life, for a few minutes, that I ever ceased seeing myself from outside. Never before, even when as a youth I first knew a woman. . . ."

He stopped again, as if astounded by the unexpected thought, calmed down and stared at some invisible point somewhere on a level with his eyes. Then he shook his head and replied to his own thought:

"No. Even with Marie, when everything swam and swayed in her gaze, even then, Kurt, I didn't experience a

feeling like that. I always saw myself from the side. At Sanshino I ceased not only seeing myself but even feeling that
way. If that is death then death is wonderful. . . ."

Kurt followed Andrei with that growing and concealed
alarm with which one looks at a man who protests too
much that he is completely healthy. And when Andrei had
said his say and his voice fell like a bird which has battered itself in its cage, he said:

"You look very tired, Andrei."

"I seem no more tired than you," replied Andrei.

Kurt pointed to a sheaf of papers under the lamp.

"I've been busy since morning. We are sending an enormous party. These are all those who fought against the
margrave. . . . Perhaps you'd like some tea? I'll tell them
to get it ready."

"Oh, yes, I'll drink some tea. Tell them."

Kurt went out. The sound of his heels resounded in the
next room and died out in the corridor. A distant door was
heard to slam.

Andrei got up out of his armchair and stepped to the
table.

Blue files lay folded in an even pile. Bold letters showed
black on the cover of the top file:

P—S
Reichsdeutsche
Germans

Andrei unfolded a file in the middle. A thick, grayish
sheet of paper was ruled in half by a thick line. The right
side was filled by Russian print and tidy clerical handwriting. A cluster of legible words caught Andrei's eye:

MILITARY RANK: *Pfc.*
NAME: *Konrad*
SURNAME: *Stein*
TIME OF FIRST IMPRISONMENT: *February, 1917*

Andrei jerked the sheet out of the file and slid his eyes
over the reverse side. To the bottom of the sheet was stuck

the violet patch of a stamp, and a steep, bold signature was there:

K. Wahn

Andrei closed the file, folded the paper in two, thrust it adroitly into his pocket and turned his back to the table. In order to suppress the sobs which mingled with his breath, he strained all his muscles with such force that he swayed back, as on a spring, from the table on which he had perched. And together with this movement his stomach contracted and he hiccupped loudly. When steps sounded in the distance he dashed into the twilight of the next room and shouted several times in succession, each time more indistinctly:

"It doesn't matter, it doesn't matter! . . ."

He ran into Kurt in the darkness and seized his hands.

"It doesn't matter. I don't want it, I've changed my mind. . . ."

"What's up?"

"I don't want any tea, I can't, I haven't time. I've remembered that I still have to go . . . have to go on an important . . . I've been assigned. . . ."

"What's the matter with you?"

Kurt squeezed Andrei's hand hard and led him to the light. But he didn't calm down, he spoke over and over again about some unpostponable business, hiccupping, gasping for breath, now shouting, now whispering, and hastily, carelessly he drew on his clumsy overcoat.

"How could I forget? Good-by, Kurt, I can't possibly . . ."

Kurt seized him sharply by the shoulders.

"You're not quite in control of yourself, my friend. You've got a fever."

"Oh, yes! But it's a good fever, a good one. I'm so happy! Good-by."

Kurt pressed him to himself, embraced him and—tall, erect, unbending—stood there motionless.

"If you die, Andrei, then I shall have one consolation: you will die for a good cause. Well . . ."

He touched Andrei's cheek with his lips and then released

him. Andrei was seized by a terrible fit of trembling, as if from unexpected contact with cold iron. Restraining his hiccups he gritted out:

"Good-by," and ran out.

The streets were black and the wind rushed around corners in sudden gusts, furiously shaking the tattered branches of the trees.

Andrei ran without stopping for breath, repeatedly drawing the breast of his overcoat tight as if he had not thought to hook it shut. The hiccups were tormenting him, he was almost choking and the wind carried his loud, abrupt sobs into the darkness. But he did not stop.

He ran as far as the slopes on the outskirts of the town, passed his house and hurried up the hillside, along a road leading into the fields. Here he slowed his steps and began peering at the buildings. But the huts were trapped in the pitch-black night like flies in ink and it was impossible to distinguish one from the other.

Andrei stopped.

And at that very moment someone took his elbow from behind. He jumped back and quickly turned round; an attack of hiccups constricted his stomach and throat and he staggered from the pain.

"It's me," he heard through the howling of the wind.

He took a twisted sheet of paper from his pocket and held it out to the darkness. Cold fingers brushed against his hand. Jerkily and hollowly he said:

"Make your way alone . . . you can't go with the troop train . . . as far as Moscow . . ."

He broke away down the hillside but he was overtaken by a peremptory shout:

"The letter for Marie!"

Andrei tugged at the collar of his tunic, pulled a letter from his breast and thrust it into the cold, splayed fingers.

The wind blew along the road, the road plunged downward and Andrei's run was the flight of a stone hurled into an abyss.

He flew to the gate of his house, burst into the yard, onto the porch, and only here did he catch his breath. The door was opened to him, he went through the hall into the kitchen, felt for a pail of water on the bench, squatted on his haunches and, tipping the pail, began to drink from the rim. The water seemed to him boiling hot. He tore himself away, rested, then commenced again to drink in long, greedy gulps. He found a jug, filled it with water, opened the window, poked his head out and upturned the jug over it. Then he collapsed on the bench.

When he entered his room Andrei did not put on the light. He made up his bed by touch, slowly undressed and lay down, covering himself completely with a blanket.

Sleep came unexpectedly quickly, so that Andrei didn't once stir, and the stillness quivered less and less often from his hiccups.

And it seemed that as quickly as sleep came a vision:

An endless expanse filled with iridescent blueness. This blueness was everywhere—above, below, on all sides, only blueness—bottomless and streaming blueness. And in this blueness, somewhere within its depths—and at the same time somewhere very close—there stood before Andrei an empty, motionless chair. It had a high straight back, even legs and a smooth seat. It was absolutely motionless and no one was sitting on it. It was empty. No one was on it. But somehow it seemed to expect that someone would be placed on it. . . .

Andrei woke up. He was lying with his whole body hunched up and his face hard against the wall. His blanket, pillow and linen were wet with sweat. He jumped up, stood on the floor and kept silent. A pale weak dawn glimmered behind the window. But in front of Andrei, in the endless quivering blueness, there still stood an empty, motionless chair. No one was sitting on the chair. But it was expecting someone. That was obvious. . . .

Andrei heard his teeth chatter and, as if replying to this chatter, his naked heels began to beat a swift drum-roll on the floor.

That was the last day Andrei Startsov spent in Semidol. Everything he did that day rolled up into a tangled ball. Andrei could hardly remember the dusk covering the crowd when it saw the mobilized soldiers off: discordant voices, placards and banners rolled up for convenience, the crush on the narrow station platform. Andrei said something before the people seeing him off returned to the town and his creaking box swayed under his feet from the shouts. Then he bid farewell to his comrades, and their faces seemed timid, and their kisses—dutiful. Comrade Golosov slyly hid a fugitive smile in his palm and firmly shook Andrei's hand. The pilot Shchepov led Andrei to one side and gave him a letter for his father—Sergei Lvovich.

"Perhaps you'll be detained in Petersburg, so look . . . you can stay with my father. I wrote here . . . Yes, by the way, I wrote that I'm married and it seems I forgot to tell him my wife's name. . . . Tell him. You know, I suppose? I married Klavdia Vasilyevna. . . ."

Then—bustling about the black tangled tracks, between the blind cars; and the journey to the city where something had to be done—a long and lonely journey. All this was pushed aside by the relentless desire to experience again that feeling of complete freedom—that same feeling which had come to him in the fields near Sanshino: the feeling of disembodiment.

Perhaps Andrei was afraid to recall his dream? Perhaps he was hastening to atone for his guilt? But his will to offer himself to the best that he had known in life was relentless and blotted out everything else.

And this is what destroyed his constancy, hurled this whole day aside like a cannonball and made it a day of farewell:

The night was cold. The sky was unusually high and the stars in it were dead. The square before the station did not lie, as it usually did, like a vacant lot, but stretched away in a desert. The horse was moving its legs, the hired cab was lurching to right and left but there was no sensation of motion, no movement. All of a sudden a figure indistinguishable in the night jumped onto the step of the cab. The horse stopped.

"Rita!" cried Andrei.

"I didn't want anyone to see, didn't want Golosov to see," she said breathlessly. Then she fell on his neck, pressed her icy lips to his mouth, brushed against his face, his neck and his hands with her cold hair and, unexpectedly hotly amid the autumn cold of the night and the coldness of her lips and her hair, she scorched him:

"Farewell!"

He should have cried out, because a cry had risen in his throat, because Rita had burst away from the cab and fled into the night, because suddenly it seemed as if he were leaving his mother, leaving forever—he should, he ought to have cried out, but instead of crying out he prodded the cabby in the back and with a tremendous effort forced from his throat:

"Drive on!"

And again everything was pushed aside by his clear will to undergo, to experience, to feel again as soon as possible what had come to him in the fields at Sanshino.

"Drive on, drive on, drive on!"

Then Andrei huddled in the corner of a heated freight car and, raising his collar high, closed his eyes.

An hour later the train was dragging him on the way to Petersburg.

At that hour Kurt Wahn, composing a report to Moscow concerning the work of the Semidol Soviet of German Soldiers, was writing the last point in his notes:

I wish to report that a personal document in the name of Pfc. Konrad Stein of the Saxon Army has disappeared from the Semidol Soviet office. The bearer of this document should be detained. I shall provide the real Konrad Stein with a special certificate, in addition to a personal document. I am reporting this simultaneously to the Central Agency for Escaped Prisoners.

A CHAPTER ON
NINETEEN TWENTY

THE COVERS ARE REMOVED

A light, downy snow was falling slowly behind the windows. The mountains crowded together white and almost transparent, and their light filled the room with peace. The bluish flame of a spirit lamp fluttered on the table beneath a broad-bottomed coffee pot.

Ober-lieutenant von zur Mühlen-Schönau was carefully removing the canvas covers from his pictures. He threw a cover on the floor, leisurely descended a step ladder, went off several steps and looked at the picture. Then he climbed the steps again, exposed the next picture and looked at it too from afar. Sometimes he turned to the window, looked at the steady falling of the snow, adjusted the rolled-up sleeves of his still uncrumpled shirt and again set to work. He was helped by a silent servant who stored the covers in a corner and moved the step ladder.

The Ober-lieutenant drank two cups of coffee straight off, lit a pipe and ordered:

"Get a bath ready and saddle up."

The servant left, but returned in a minute and announced:

"Fräulein Urbach."

The Ober-lieutenant squeezed the arms of his chair, threw his body forward to jump up, but immediately gained control of himself, got up calmly and calmly replied:

"Ask her in."

Marie entered quickly and stopped in the middle of the room. She was still wrapped in the freshness of a light frost and the traces of melted snow flakes gleamed on her shoulders.

The Ober lieutenant bowed. She stood still. He stepped toward her and his right hand twitched barely perceptibly. He began:

"You came . . ."

Something prevented him from speaking; he looked around as if he had unexpectedly come into an unfamiliar room; he went over to the door and tried it to see if it were properly closed. Returning to the table he found it an effort to pass Marie: his steps slowed and he had to bend forward to prevent them from stopping.

"Have a seat," he said.

But Marie continued to stand, looking away. He looked at her and the fingers of his lowered hands were twitching, as if he wanted to take something or to make a movement and the entire time was changing his mind. His always slightly parted lips revealed the firm whiteness of his teeth and his face became simultaneously frightened and rapacious.

"Almost four years," he began to speak again. "I never thought that in this room I'd see you so—strange. In this room, Marie . . ."

Suddenly she interrupted him:

"Did you deceive me?"

"I?" exclaimed the Ober-lieutenant.

Their glances met for an instant, then Marie looked away and the Ober-lieutenant turned to the table. He pulled out a drawer, took a blotting-pad, opened it, removed a greasy, crumpled envelope, went up to Marie and silently gave it to her. She tore open the envelope, looked at the beginning of the letter, at its end—and the Ober-lieutenant saw the slow thick blood spread over her cheeks. She crumpled the letter and hid her hand in her overcoat pocket.

The Ober-lieutenant went over to the window and, frowning into the deep ripple of the snow, spaced out the distinct words:

"I never deceived you in anything. You deceived me."

Marie responded softly:

"I don't love you."

He did not reply. She hesitated, then suddenly she said hastily in a loud voice:

"I don't believe a single word in your letter. It's all lies that you wrote. . . ."

Then the Ober-lieutenant turned sharply toward her, folded his arms behind his back and burst out laughing. He laughed, swaying to and fro without taking his eyes from Marie and tapping the toes of his boots on the carpet. His laughter prevented him from uttering a word. At last he calmed down, raised an eyebrow and, shrugging his shoulders carelessly, advised:

"It occurs to me, dear Fräulein, that it would be best of all for you to take a drive to Petersburg to convince yourself of how far reality corresponds to everything which you care to call lies. . . ."

He frowned at her, tapped his foot on the carpet again, took up his pipe, but did not light it and threw it on the table. Pain and arrogance flitted across his lips and he asked:

"You hate me? . . . What can I do? I wrote you only the truth. . . ."

He noticed suddenly that Marie was pale and strangely swaying, without moving her legs. He moved toward her but she turned quickly and went out of the room.

He listened to her steps dying away, rushed toward the door but did not reach it, shouted something senseless, harsh and abusive, and stopped.

In the corner lay the tidily folded covers in a pile. Behind them rose a picture taken from the wall, "The Court of the German Museum in Nuremberg." He took a pen-knife from his pocket, opened it, stepped over the covers, landed the knife in the picture with a flourish and drew it from corner to corner.

It sounded as if someone had thrown a handful of peas upon an iron roof and they had rolled down the slope into the gutter.

THE NEW LAND

"Papa, you're being honorably asked to make room," said Shchepov-son.

"And when did you ever have any honor?" cried Shchepov-father.

"That's your personal opinion."

"My Lord God! One son robbed me to my last penny, sent an old man out into the world! Now the other comes and throws his father into the street, to die by the wayside."

"You're not being thrown out, but asked to use one little room less."

"I curse you with a father's curse for the rest of your life!"

"Papa, you're a bastard. . . ."

"I curse you, I curse you! Monster!"

Andrei heard senile, frenzied wails, the noise of chairs being moved about and the slamming of doors. Then everything became quiet and through the wall could be heard the voice of Shchepov-son:

"We can't turn Startsov out, Klavdia, when his wife's so far gone. . . ."

Wife?

Andrei straightened up, rose and went to the bed where Rita was sitting. He put his hand on her head, stroked her soft, straight hair and spoke so that only she could hear:

"My wife."

Rita pressed his hand to her cheek. He watched her smile —helpless, and it brought a strange radiance to her puffy, washed-out face. It was unattractive, unpleasant from some premature, strange flabbiness and he kissed it tenderly.

"I'll go," he said.

"Where?"

"I was promised . . . not far . . . a glass of milk. . . . I'll take a bottle with me. . . ."

"It won't be long now," she said.

"Yes, of course. The worst is over: winter . . . Today they're giving out bread, I'll call in . . ."

He smiled at her and left.

While he was looking for his cap in the anteroom the bell over the lintel of the front door trembled without a sound. Andrei opened the door just as there came a slightly more confident ring.

Leaning against the staircase banister opposite Andrei stood a girl. Her hair and white blouse and skirt were being ruffled by a warm draft which swept off the flight of stairs into the open apartment. She precipitately stretched out her thin arms, bare to the elbow, and drew toward him. He recognized her not by her arms and not by the look of her round, shining eyes, but by a certain curve of her body, emphasized by the clothing which the wind flattened against her leg. And as if defending himself, he jerked his hands up to his chest, palms outward, and retreated into the anteroom, into the semi-darkness, toward the dress hanging on the wall. The straight, slender arms stretched out to him through the door, closer and closer, and now it seemed to him that he made out a whisper:

"Andrei, don't you believe it, Andrei?"

Then he gasped out the wild, joyful word:

"You . . . y-you!"

"Marie!" he cried and his arms swept forward.

But just then he saw Marie looking away from him and her eyes lowered to half the height of a man. He turned his head.

Rita was standing beside him. Immediately he noticed her protruding stomach, already sagging and shockingly large, raising the hem of her skirt in front.

Marie leaned on the door, her arms fell, she seemed to be suspended in the air. Then she transferred her gaze from Rita's stomach to her face, her lips suddenly grew stiff, her eyes stopped moving.

Andrei wanted to move, he was hindered by the over-coats, topcoats and umbrellas that hung on the wall, and he himself went soft and limp like the overcoats. With his last remaining strength he thrust himself away from the wall,

stepped toward Marie and, before reaching her, stretched
out a hand to her.

"Marie . . ."

But he had hardly touched her elbow with his fingers
when she cried piercingly:

"A-a-a!"

Andrei jerked his hand away and, bending toward her
face, repeated barely audibly:

"Marie . . ."

And she again cried piercingly, on one note, neither lowering nor raising her voice:

"A-a-a!"

Then her cry was answered by a long drawn out dull
groan from Rita. Andrei looked round and saw Rita stooping to the floor, as if she had dropped something and was
rummaging for it in the dark corner, then she straightened
up and again bent down awkwardly and unexpectedly. He
moved toward her, but at that time Marie slipped through
the door and the tap of her heels rang out on the stone
steps of the staircase.

Andrei jumped out onto the landing, leaned over the
banisters and, without stopping for breath, shouted many
times while running down the flight of deep, deserted stairs:

"Marie, Marie, Mari-ie! . . ."

He saw her white dress flash once, twice, three times, her
hair flutter in one of the windows, heard the forcefully
slammed door shake in the entrance and the wail of a vio-
lent draft up the stairs. Then he dropped his head upon the
banister.

From the open apartment he heard Shchepov's ringing
voice:

"Klavdia . . . you must run for the midwife."

From behind a corner rolled a noisy crowd of children,
seething, foaming, with gaily colored cotton prints rippling
in the sunshine, and it flowed into the dense flood of human
bodies sailing ponderously down the avenue. The children
were flattened in this flood like fruit in a bag, but the

crowd of them seethed all the more, and their white teeth gleamed more and more often over the cotton prints, which resembled the curtains of country beds.

And then from who knows where a girl appeared in the crowd of children rolling around the corner. She looked around absent-mindedly, she wanted to cross the road in order to go on farther, it was necessary for her to continue her way farther—down the tall, endless rows of countless buildings. But the running children pushed her, pulled her, spun her around and, like a chip of wood in a waterfall, she revolved helplessly in the surging pack of gaily colored cotton prints. She was carried around the corner. The children squeezed her with their indefatigable, mobile little bodies which were flattened and almost crushed by the huge crush of people. A handful of funny, inquisitive little snouts were raised toward her, they shouted something to her in an incomprehensible language, white, flashing teeth were bared before her and dexterous little hands plucked at her blouse. She said something to them, laughter scattered over their heads in reply, she saw their tiny faces gaily covered with shallow wrinkles from the sun and their laughter and she again said something. Then the children raised a shout, endlessly repeating the same word and waving their hands at some place in the crowd. An old woman with a shaking head forced her way over to the girl, with a faded parasol over her shoulder. The children drew near to her, pointed their fingers at the girl and vied with each other in shouting something.

The old woman hissed at the children, tried to frighten them with a stern face, and they laughed all the more gaily, all the more uncontrollably. The old woman smilingly begged pardon for the persistent children and, shaking her gray, tangled locks, said in the girl's ear:

*"Probablement, vous n'êtes pas d'ici, mademoiselle?"**

"Oui, madame," replied the girl with her lips alone, stooping unexpectedly as if preparing to curtsey, *"je ne suis pas d'ici. . . ."*

*"I take it you're not from around here, mademoiselle?"
"Yes, madame . . . I'm not from around here. . . ."

*"Je vois bien que ce pays vous parait nouveau. Allez-vous quelque part?"**

"Non, en ce moment je ne vais nulle part. . . ."

"Voulez-vous, alors, nous faire compagnie?"

The girl looked around. Innumerable childish faces, swinging from side to side and craning upward, were sailing along behind her. She said distractedly:

"Oui, si vous voulez. . . ."

Then she asked loudly:

"Mais où est-ce-que vous allez avec ce tas d'enfants?"

"Nulle part, tout droit," and the old woman pointed with unsteady hand into the distance along the straight avenue which was propped against the sky.

Marie looked in that direction and she seemed to be on top of Lausche, and from beneath her feet an eternally new and eternally beckoning expanse ran away to the gently sloping sky. Banks of white clouds were flying overhead, the wind pounced in gusts, nailing the roar and tramp of the crowd to the houses as the noise of the forest on Lausche had been nailed to the mountain precipices. And, as on Lausche—when you climbed to the top and stopped for breath—her breast became enormous and she wished that the mountain might go higher and that the ascent might never end.

Marie glanced at the old woman. Her head was shaking so vigorously that her shoulders twitched, too. At times she seemed to whisper:

"Tout droit, tout droit . . ."

Straight, straight . . . A little girl offered Marie a fragment of a poplar twig. Marie took it, squeezed the little girl's sharp, bony shoulder and looked into her eyes. They were deep-set and gay, like little puddles played on by an autumn day. The crowd suddenly thinned, loosened up, the children chased after those who had gone ahead, two, three, four—perhaps more—little girls seized Marie by

---

* "I can see clearly that this country seems new to you. Are you headed for somewhere?"
"No, at the moment I'm going nowhere . . ."
"Then would you like to keep us company?"
"Yes, if you like . . ."
"But where are you going with this crowd of children?"
"No where, straight on."

the arms and laughingly dragged her after them. Marie laughed and ran. . . .

So this was what Andrei had brought her to!

"Tout droit, tout droit! . . ."

At that time Andrei was sitting by a bed on which Rita lay. He was holding her by the hand and looking into her face. It was gray and tears glistened on the bags under her eyes. Her pains had just begun, she bit her lower lip and turned her head to the wall. Andrei squeezed her hand in his sweaty palms and, as if fearing that she would groan, muttered:

"Now wait . . . wait . . ."

When the pain became unbearable, swift tears trickled behind Rita's ears and she blurted out in order to suppress a cry:

"Tell the truth . . . you . . . still love her? . . ."

WE ARE QUITS, COMRADE STARTSOV

Now we are finishing our tale of a man who waited wearily for life to accept him. We look back on the road he traversed, following cruelty and love, on a road of blood and flowers. He traveled it and not a single bloodstain spotted him, nor did he crush a single flower.

Oh, if only he had taken upon himself but one stain and had trampled but one flower! Perhaps our pity for him would then have grown into love and we would not have let him perish so painfully and so uselessly.

But up until the last minute he did not take a single step, but only waited for the wind to blow him to the shore he wanted to reach.

Glass is not smelted with iron. Of that there would be no need to speak, if the realization had not come at the end of the road that pity deserves more indulgence than cruelty. Is that not why we justify cruelty only when it is hallowed by sympathy?

But glass is not smelted with iron and it is beyond our powers to change anything in Andrei's fate.

Andrei received a letter. It had broken through frontier posts, through dozens of post offices and a hundred cases, and traces of their contact were all over it: colored pencils, colored postmarks, the fat imprints of fingers. It was strange, but the letter had by-passed the only cordon which would not have reacted indifferently to it.

Andrei locked himself in his room and sat with his back to the door. He opened his mouth wide in order to conceal the noise of his whistling breath, his hands shook and he slumped down on them, leaning his elbows on his knees. His face suddenly went white when he opened the envelope, as if he had been splashed with chalk.

Dear Mr. Startsov,

However, I don't know how I ought to address you. Perhaps—"Comrade" Startsov? I cannot deny myself the pleasure of informing you of circumstances which in all probability are not without interest to you. At our last meeting in Petersburg, when you did me the favor of which you are aware, you were so good as to inquire whether I considered myself quits with you, accepting from you the above mentioned favor. If you remember, I then announced that I would be indebted to you until such time as I had carried out the mission which I had accepted from you in Semidol. I am happy that I am now able to inform you that I carried out your mission to the letter and so we are completely quits. Yes, we are quits, Comrade Startsov! I sought out your fiancée in Bischofsberg with no difficulty and she called on me for your letter with great speed, bearing witness to the constancy of her feelings for Comrade Startsov. However, permit me to begin further back. I cannot deny you a correct instinct. In any case I was extremely embarrassed when you asked me in Petersburg whether I knew Fräulein Marie Urbach. You can well understand that to admit this to you then would have meant my being unable to fulfill the promise given to you in Semidol. Meanwhile I felt myself so indebted to you that I preferred to conceal the truth in order to obtain at such an extraordinary cost to myself the possibility of thanking you as you deserved. I shall not hide the fact that I was shaken by the force of your feeling for Fräulein Urbach. I understood perfectly that it was to precisely this feeling that I owed the degree of carelessness with which you ignored certain circumstances having decisive consequences for me at that moment. The whole affair for you came down to the problem of how to send a letter one way or another to Fräulein Urbach. I understood that better than you. And I guarded your letter as one guards only the dearest things in life. Why, I was so indebted to you, Comrade Startsov! When I learned from you that Fräulein Marie had been happy with you while I fought in Champagne and in the East—leaving your place that night by the gate, I decided with whom I had to square accounts in the future. I hesitated, because you were at hand, while between me and Fräulein Marie lay a distant and not undangerous journey. But the feeling of indebtedness to you prevailed and I decided to settle up with Marie. When consequently I met you in Petersburg again the thought of repaying you as you deserved again came upon me, and I had to make an effort while following in your footsteps not to lay your skull open. But fate was favorable to me. I was happy enough to be convinced a second time of your feelings for Fräulein Marie and to establish at the same time that the ardor of these feelings had not prevented you from deceiving your fiancée with a new mistress. Then I made my final decision as to what I should do. Note that not for a minute did I forget my word to give the letter, full of anguish and loving longing, to your fiancée. How could I descend to such baseness? Why, I owe my life to you, Comrade Startsov, and my life is valued by you at the cost of a letter in transit from Semidol to Bischofsberg. . . . Now I am again in my room and am surrounded by my favorite pictures. I would be completely at ease if it were not for the feeling of annoyance that I was once careless enough to release you from this room alive. By the way, concerning the pictures. If you still have occasion to communicate with Comrade (I believe that's correct?) Kurt Wahn, then inform him that I have burned all his canvases which were preserved in my collection. However, it is improbable that this will interest him, since politicians rarely occupy themselves with art, and then not properly. Has Comrade Wahn really not guessed yet who was responsible for the disappearance from his office of the deceased Konrad Stein's documents? I never thought him such a blockhead. . . . And so, returning to Schönau, I informed your fiancée of everything I had learned from your words and also what I had managed to learn of your feelings toward Fräulein Marie and of your new bride, etcetera. Naturally I described to your fiancée in detail the favors you showed to me and, I hope, to your socialist fatherland—to Russia. I did this all the more willingly since I had learned of your fiancée's feats in the field of the then still unstrangled socialist fatherland—Germany. In order not to make any unsupported statements in my dealings with your fiancée I promised to present her as evidence the letter in your own hand. I have already written that your fiancée did not wait long to pay me a visit. I had a meeting with her in the room which you know and in which once. . . . However, of this later. Your fiancée did not believe me; just as I had expected, incidentally. I advised her to go to you to convince herself of the crystal truth of my words. I put her under surveillance. Truly I took your fiancée's tender feelings for you so much to heart, Comrade Startsov! In order to reach you she decided on a step which was not so much heroic as it was unscrupulous: she married some Russian private or other among the prisoners in order to get the right to Russian citizenship and permission to enter Russia. This step convinced me of her passionate love for you and it is pleasant to think of how she *degraded herself to experience afterward an even greater degradation as a result of your deception and your worthlessness. I can imagine how you are taking this degradation, Comrade Startsov, and it decreases my annoyance that I didn't plant a bullet in your head when I heard that you considered Fräulein Marie Urbach your fiancée. Fiancée? I was not excessively insulted by the fact that Marie had deceived me with you, because women should be more careful to conceal their first lover from the second than vice-versa. As I didn't suspect my successor in you, so you didn't for a minute think that I had been your predecessor. The need to settle accounts with you I weighed not only against the fact that I was buying my life for the price of silence, but also against the recollections of the Weimar schoolgirl, Marie, who ran away from Miss Ronny's boarding school to me at Schönau, to that very room where my acquaintance with you began. We are quits, Comrade Startsov!*

With gratitude,
von zur Mühlen-Schönau

P.S. I hope that my name will not harm your safety. If it does harm it, then it will only be after your meeting with your fiancée, my mistress and the wife of an unknown Russian soldier—Fräulein Marie Urbach. In any case I am purposely dawdling with the dispatch of this letter in order not to forestall the meeting, the very idea of which puts me into an excellent frame of mind. Servus!

Andrei crumpled the letter and dashed out of the room. He was pursued by the thin sudden cry of a baby. He did not halt. A woman's voice called to him anxiously on the landing, someone called him by name at the gate, someone on the street shied away from him in alarm. He fled as if pursued.

Disheveled, crumpled, he slowed his desperate flight only at the outskirts of the city. Around him lay vacant lots, scattered with garbage and bricks. A fine rain was falling, thickening and chilling the evening twilight. The wind rocked in the stone skeleton of a ruined building like a beast in a cage.

Andrei turned back to the city, passed through some streets or other built up with low factory blocks, landed on the bank of the Neva, again went out to the factory streets and again found himself in a vacant lot.

The darkness became thick, night came down with unseasonal swiftness.

Andrei looked around, discerned through the fine sieve of rain the massifs of buildings crowded together in the darkness and again he moved toward the city.

He was swallowed up by the soundless masses of barns, elevators, towers and turrets. He penetrated deeper into the city of dead skyscrapers.

Suddenly something gray cut off his path and fell on the ground. His legs did not tremble, he walked like an animated doll—forward, forward. One behind the other, gray lumps slid across the road. Andrei walked on. Now something bumped into his boot and rolled off to one side. Now he stepped on something soft, like a rag, and a short squeal pierced his ears. He slowed his step because he had begun to bump into yielding obstacles scattered over the whole road. He stopped because the penetrating squeals which sounded with his every step had sharpened into a whistle.

He was standing in the middle of a street of barns which supported the black sky. He was standing up to the ankles in a kind of mass which rolled across the road in steep, hurrying waves and washed heavily against his legs. He looked at the dull-gray crests of these waves and they appeared to him to be the sloping backs of innumerable, smooth little animals.

And suddenly he heard an almost completely muffled voice:

"They're rats, rats Andrei! Step over them!"

Like a blind man he stretched forth his arms and called: "Kurt! Kurt!"

He was answered by an obedient echo.

He covered his face and went numb, like the barns surrounding him. Dull-gray waves rolled slowly over the road and one after another the rats crawled over Andrei's boots.

When he lowered his hands his face was a white spot in the darkness. The pavement was motionless and the rain beat out a tiny drum-rattle in the small puddles.

Andrei broke away and ran to the city. But the streets again led him to vacant lots. He descended a deep rut, fell, crawled out and rolled back into the pit. And while his legs and arms and all his body were crawling in the mud of the rut, a distant, muffled voice sounded in his ears:

"You are afraid of dread, Andrei. Step over it. Step over. . . ."

He leaped out of the pit with a howl and rushed into the night, crying:

"Help, he-e-elp! . . ."

And in the night, over the roadway, over the ruts, over the endless vacant lots he swept like a madman—a madman, perhaps, seeking his way. But around him lay vacant lots, above him hung the black sky and there was no human habitation and there were no ways.

Thus the vacant lots surrounded Andrei until the year which was fated to conclude our novel.

When that year came, Kurt did for Andrei all that should be done by a comrade, a friend and an artist.

REMBRANDT

by Gladys Schmitt

An outstanding biographer-novelist turns her pen to a larger-than-life portrait of Rembrandt Van Rijn—his artistic genius, huge zest for living, and tumultuous love for the beautiful heiress Saskia.

Here are rare insights into a supreme artist and into the city and country life of 17th-century Holland.

A nation-wide bestseller at $5.95.

Now complete and unabridged 95c

PB-37598
5-07